CW00552875

WINNER OF THE PASSIONATE PLUME

FINALIST FOR THE DAPHNE DU MAURIER AWARD &
ORWG'S HEART AWARD

"A very hot and perfectly paced page turner, all the way to happily ever after." -*NPR*

"An exciting rollercoaster of a love story! This book delivers on a variety of levels. A slow burn, friends to lovers story. The plot is intricate, intimate, and all consuming. The couple's passion burns through the pages." -*Jenna's Historical Romance Blog*

"This book has pretty much reduced me to describing it in one-word sentences. RAWR. YUM. YES!! SWEET. MORE... Livy and Ben together were ***swoon***. I really couldn't get enough of them. The writing, as always with Grace Callaway, was beautiful, heartfelt, and full of emotion. Every time I read something she writes, I can feel it completely. The storyline was fantastic, and I was captivated from beginning to end." -Candace, *BookBub*

"Olivia and Ben are so wonderful together. It is rare to find a match where the H & h share such a deep bond.... This book has it all—lead characters you truly love, fabulous side characters, murder, mystery, action, and a generous helping of steam and romance!" -Nazmin, *Goodreads*

"Ben and Olivia's friendship is detailed through the years, and you can't help falling in love with them and rooting for a happy ending. There's a mystery that finally helps bring Ben and Olivia together (I don't want give out any spoilers). There are some hot scenes between the two and lots of ups and downs in their relationship. If you love great character development, mystery, and a hot love story then this book is for you." -Rhonda, *Goodreads*

"This book was sexy, heartfelt, and exciting. Ben, the Duke of Hadleigh, may be Callaway's darkest hero yet... Livy has loved him since he saved her life when she was twelve years old. She's the one person who sees him as completely good and lovable. Grace did a great job of redeeming Ben. This book has Grace's signature sexiness and suspense that she's so great at writing." -Nancy, *Goodreads*

"This was another engaging and action-packed read that delivered likeable and interesting characters, mystery and intrigue, and steamy goodness galore!"-MG, *Goodreads*

"The platonic friendship between the two main characters was haunting and beautiful at the same time. The friendship defined both their lives. Watching the platonic love blossom into romantic love was breathtaking. Both characters had such an emotional journey." -Jenna, *Goodreads*

ADDITIONAL PRAISE FOR GRACE'S BOOKS

"Readers looking for a good historical mystery/romance or a historical with a little more kink will enjoy *The Duke Who Knew Too Much*." -Smart Bitches, Trashy Books

"Grace Callaway writes the way Loretta Chase would if she got kind of dark and VERY naughty." -Nicole, *Goodreads*

"We all have our top ten list of favorite romances. It has been forever since I have read something that enthralled me enough to add to my list. The book must be unique, something that resonates with me on an elemental level; it must have a beautiful storyline, intense passion, and unforgettable characters. *Pippa and the Prince of Secrets* checks all those boxes." -*Reading Rebel Reviews*

"Can a fairytale be sweet, funny, touching, action packed and super hot all at the same time? Yes. This series ender is all that and more. This book is like the fireworks display to end a spectacular series." -Joanne, *Goodreads*

"I have read hundreds and hundreds of different authors over the past five years but actually only have a handful of all time favorites. I have to say Grace Callaway is by far one of those favorites.... Her characters have so much depth and you just feel like you are a part of their story...You can never go wrong by picking up any of her books but be prepared...you will love them so much you will buy every book she has." -Pam, *Goodreads*

"I've now read each of Grace Callaway's books and loved them— which is exceptional. Gabriel and Thea from this book were two of the best characters I read this year. Both had their difficulties and it was charming to see how they overcame them together, even though it wasn't always easy for them. [*M is for Marquess*] is my favorite book of 2015." -*Romantic Historical Reviews*

"This writer to me is in the leagues of Johanna Lindsey, Lisa Kleypas, Julia Quinn and Amanda Quick." -Kathie, *Amazon Reviews*

"Callaway is a talented writer and as skilled at creating a vivid sense of the Regency period as she is at writing some of the best, most sensual love scenes I've read in a long while." -*Night Owl Reviews*

"Grace Callaway is becoming one of my all-time favorite authors. The Kents remind me so much of the Mallory-Anderson saga from Johanna Lindsay or the Spy series from Julie Garwood. I've read those books so many times and now I find myself rereading Grace's books." -Vivian, *Amazon Reviews*

*For my readers who asked for the next generation of the Kents: thank you for dreaming with me and hope you enjoy!*

*And for my besties: "sisters first" will see us through!*

# ALSO BY GRACE CALLAWAY

Her Husband's Harlot

Her Wanton Wager

Her Protector's Pleasure

Her Prodigal Passion

# Olivia
## AND THE
# MASKED DUKE

Lady Charlotte's
SOCIETY *of*
ANGELS

# GRACE CALLAWAY

*USA Today Bestselling Author*

**Olivia and the Masked Duke** © Grace Callaway, 2021.

ISBN: 978-1-939537-54-6

All rights reserved. Without limiting the rights under copyright reserved above, no part of this publication may be reproduced, stored in or introduced into a retrieval system, or transmitted, in any form, or by any means (electronic, mechanical, photocopying, recording, or otherwise) without the prior written permission of the copyright owner.

This is a work of fiction. Names, characters, places, brands, media, and incidents are either the product of the author's imagination or are used fictitiously.

**Cover Art:** EDH Graphics

**Cover Image Credit:** Period Images

**Typography Design:** KM Designs

Love consists in this, that two solitudes protect and touch and greet each other.

-Rainer Maria Rilke

# ONE

*1841, Strathmore Castle, Scotland, Estate of the Duke and Duchess of Strathaven*

B*y hook or by crook, I am going to win*, twelve-year-old Lady Olivia McLeod vowed as she left fresh tracks in the snowy field. *Then the boys will have to admit that girls are just as clever, or cleverer, than they are.*

It was the day before Hogmanay, the Scottish celebration of the New Year, and Livy's parents, the Duke and Duchess of Strathaven, were hosting a party at the country seat. Friends and family had gathered to join in the festivities, including all of Mama's siblings. Livy adored her aunts, uncles, and cousins from the Kent side of the family; when they were around, a rollicking good time was guaranteed to be had.

Indeed, Livy's older cousins had designed a "treasure hunt" to amuse the children. A trail of clues led to a prize: a tin crown painted gold and decorated with paste jewels. Whoever retrieved the crown would be declared the winner of the contest and king—or queen—for the day.

The prize was a worthy one. Especially since Livy had overheard her younger brother Christopher and some of his cronies betting on which one of them would be king.

*"Obviously, no girl is going to beat us,"* the boys had all agreed.

*Obviously?* The fire of competition had ignited in Livy's chest. Then and there, she'd resolved to make the boys eat their words, and there was one surefire way to do it: she would *win*.

Her goal would have been easier to accomplish had her bosom friends Glory and Fiona been there. Since the girls weren't scheduled to arrive until after the new year, however, Livy had to tackle the task on her own. When the first clue had been distributed at breakfast, she'd gone straight to work. She'd solved the riddle, which led to the stables. There, she'd found the second clue, which took her to the billiards room. Whilst everyone had partaken of luncheon, she had hunted down the next slip of paper hidden in the strings of the pianoforte:

Find me behind the page that never ages.

She'd wasted hours in the library, searching through books for the mysterious page. Her pulse had quickened when she heard two of her male cousins outside in the hallway; were they about to catch up to her? Luckily, she was saved by the tea bell. At the tinkling summons, the boys scampered off to fill their bellies, leaving Livy to contemplate the riddle in peace.

As she'd rifled through a book of medieval poetry, the realization had struck her. She'd dashed to the gallery, stopping in front of an oil painting. The portrait showed a knight in leather armor, his metal helmet carried by an adolescent boy—his *page*. The page's youth had been forever preserved in glowing paint.

Livy had slid her hand between the gilt frame and the wall, triumph surging as her fingers encountered a scrap of paper. Pulling it free, she'd unfolded it and read the scrawled words:

*Felicitations, intrepid explorer. You hold in your hands the final clue:*

Like Narcissus, I am captivated by my own glitter,
As I hang, suspended between earth and sky, where
the wind is bitter.

Livy had hurried to her chamber to don her forest-green mantle, shoving the matching hat with a white plume over her chestnut curls and slinging a leather satchel she'd purloined from her brother across her shoulder. Exiting through the kitchens to avoid being seen—she had no desire to tip off her competitors—she'd managed to snag a sandwich on her way out.

All the sleuthing had worked up her appetite.

Livy was brushing off crumbs when she arrived at her destination: a pond situated at the northern edge of the garden. In the summer, the water teemed with fish and playful ducks, but now the surface was iced over and dusted with drifts of snow. That opaque surface would have frustrated Narcissus who, Livy knew from Mama's stories, had been captivated by his own watery reflection. She scanned the icy perimeter, looking for a place between earth and sky...and then she saw it: a flash of gold in the branches of a Scots pine.

*I've done it,* she thought gleefully. *I have found the prize!*

She raced over to the base of the tree. Tilting her head back, she stared up into the thicket of blue-green needles: the crown was tied to the end of the lowest branch. After several futile jumps, she had to concede her vertical disadvantage. As Mama was fond of saying, however, there was more than one way to cook an egg.

Livy grabbed onto the bark, shivering at the chill that seeped through the smooth kid of her gloves. Nonetheless, she pulled herself up, finding the footholds, getting to the desired branch. Testing the ledge and finding it sturdy, she carefully maneuvered toward her glittering prize. She freed the crown from its rope and held it aloft.

"All hail the queen," she sang.

An ominous crack interrupted her tune. She watched in

horror as the branch she was sitting on snapped from the trunk. She plummeted, a shriek exploding from her lungs. Her back hit the snowy bank with a jarring thump. Dazed, she caught her breath and sat up. Looking around her, she couldn't find the crown.

"Botheration," she muttered.

Then she saw it: lying some twenty yards away on the pond. Rising, she dusted herself off and placed a foot cautiously onto the ice. Papa had issued countless warnings about walking on frozen surfaces, but the ice felt thick and solid beneath her boots. She would have her prize in a blink and be on her merry way.

She slipped and slid over to the golden circlet. Grabbing it, she shoved it into her bag and started back toward the bank...and froze. Had she imagined the movement beneath her? She took another step forward, and the ice groaned and swelled. A web of cracks shot through the surface.

Heart hammering, she raced toward the shore, but the ground vanished beneath her, her screams lost in an icy abyss. Freezing water burned her lungs as she fought to surface. Ice was everywhere, blocking her escape. Trapped, she pounded her fists against the thick translucent wall, a watery hand choking off her cries. As the world beyond grew blurrier and more distant, a terrifying conviction took hold of her.

*I am going to die. Here. Alone.*

She fought to survive with all of her strength, thrashing against the ice until the last of her breath bubbled from her. Until her limbs grew heavy, invisible chains dragging her downward. Numbness blanketed her as she sank deeper and deeper into oblivion...

Suddenly, she was reversing direction. Something dragged her upward, throwing off the darkness, exposing her to brightness, harsh and cold. She blinked up into a halo of light. Was she dead? The glowing ring seemed to be summoning her, and she felt herself floating toward it...but hands pushed her down. Pressed on her belly with painful force.

"Don't you let go," a deep voice commanded. "You *fight*."

Someone was telling her to fight. Which was strange, because people were usually telling her to be *less* tenacious. She tried to reply, but water gargled out instead. Exhaustion made her weightless, and she drifted up toward the heavens...

The voice anchored her to the earth. "Not you too. Bloody *hold on*, do you hear me?"

The mix of authority and anguish in those words halted her flight. Yet she couldn't make her lips or body move, as if she were trapped beneath ice still. Then a mouth sealed over hers, warm and firm, forcing air into her. Breaths billowed her lungs again and again until the halo above her vanished, and she surfaced with a gasp.

"Easy there, little one. Take a breath now. Slow and easy."

Blinking, she saw that she lay on the bank, a man kneeling beside her. Water dripped from the chiseled contours of his face, frost tipping his thick eyelashes and mink-brown hair. Stormy blue eyes bore into her.

"Are you all right, Olivia?" he gritted out.

He knew her name. As the haze lifted, she realized that she knew his too.

"I-I am fine, Your Grace," she said.

Her rescuer was Benedict Wodehouse, the Duke of Hadleigh, one of the party guests. Until that moment, she had thought of him the way children generally think of adults: as old and not terribly interesting. It didn't help that he had an air of detached boredom which grown-ups called *ennui* and which Livy did not understand. What was there to be bored about when there was an entire world to explore?

At present, however, he didn't seem indifferent. Emotion blazed from him, with an intensity that was painful to witness... like staring into the sun. He quickly turned away, but not before she glimpsed the sheen in his eyes. He shuddered, exhaling raggedly as he shoved his hands through his wet hair.

He muttered something to himself. It sounded like, *Thank Christ.*

Managing to sit up, she tugged on the sleeve of his coat. "Are you all right?"

He faced her again. She noticed the curious hollows beneath his eyes and cheekbones. Lines etched on his brow and around his mouth suggested a habit of frowning. Although he was tall and broad of shoulder, he lacked the brawn of, say, Livy's papa. This duke was as lanky as a scarecrow.

"You nearly drowned," he said grimly. "And you are asking *me* if I am all right?"

"You seem shaken," she returned.

His brows slanted together. "And you seem self-possessed for a chit of ten."

"I am twelve," she informed him. "As I said, I'm perfectly well."

"Let us not tempt Fate." He bundled her in his greatcoat, which he'd apparently shed before diving into the water because it was dry and warm, smelling of leather and woodsy spice. He rose, scooping her up with surprising strength.

"Why are you carrying me?" she asked. "I can walk."

"I can walk faster." His ground-eating strides proved he was no liar. "You're trembling, little one."

He was right. She hadn't noticed how chilled she was. Her teeth were chattering.

"A c-cup of tea will put me to rights," she said. "Mama says I have the c-constitution of an ox."

"Even so." He gave her a stern look. "What in the devil made you do such a foolish thing?"

His words jolted her...*the crown*. Her hands flew to the satchel which, miracle of miracles, was still strapped to her. She reached in and took out her prize.

"The crown survived the dunking," she said with a relieved sigh. "I will still be queen for the day."

"Bloody hell. You risked your neck for that trifle?"

At his scathing look, she clutched the crown to her chest. "It is *not* a trifle."

"It's a child's plaything. A piece of tin. You believe that it is worth dying over?"

His blunt words shoved her back beneath the water. To the suffocating darkness, the fear of perishing there alone, of never seeing her family or friends again. She looked at the shiny object in her hands: the gilt was already wearing off, showing the dull tin beneath.

All of a sudden, she felt foolish. Immature.

"No," she said in a small voice.

"Although I am a casual acquaintance of your family, even I can tell that they would be devastated if anything happened to you. Do you want to cause them pain?" he went on ruthlessly.

A lump formed in her throat as she realized how selfish she had been. Caught up in her single-minded pursuit, she'd thought of nothing but attaining her goal. How many times had Mama lectured her to consider the consequences before acting?

With deepening shame, Livy recognized that, in this instance, she was not the only one affected by her behavior. Her family would indeed be grieved if anything had happened to her...and she had also endangered the Duke of Hadleigh, who had braved the icy water to save her. Even though she was no watering pot, heat slid from her eyes.

"I'm sorry," she mumbled.

"There is no need to cry," he said gruffly. "Just don't do it again."

"But I c-could have hurt my family." Once the tears started, she couldn't seem to stop them. "And yours. You risked your l-life to save me. If you had died—"

"Don't worry about me." His mouth twisted. "I would not be mourned."

She tilted her head, certain that she'd misheard. "P-Pardon?"

The duke could not have said that he wouldn't be grieved. After all, he had a wife, whom Livy had been introduced to at the party. The Duchess of Hadleigh reminded Livy of a perfect porcelain doll with a painted-on smile that never faltered. The duke's sister, Mrs. Beatrice Murray, was a sister-in-law to one of Livy's aunts and in attendance as well. Livy adored Aunt Bea, as she called her, and was certain the lady would be heartbroken over the loss of her own brother.

"I know what it is like to make mistakes. Mistakes that one cannot come back from." The duke's gaze hardened. "Be wiser than me, little queen."

Livy didn't know what to make of his words. Of the curious contrast between his jaded expression and his aura of pain. Nevertheless, empathy expanded in her chest the way his breath had filled her lungs.

She tried to console him. "Mama says a mistake can be forgiven. As long as one makes proper amends."

The lightning flash of hope in his eyes made her twelve-year-old heart stutter.

"I hope you will always believe that. In fact, promise me that you will."

Although she was puzzled by his request, she did not hesitate to say, "I promise."

Being a McLeod and a Kent, she believed in loyalty and honor. She owed the Duke of Hadleigh her life. Although she knew she was too young to repay such a debt, she would endeavor to return the favor in whatever way she could.

"Good," he said softly.

"I also promise to fulfill my debt of honor to you," she said.

"A debt of honor?"

Now he seemed amused. The crinkles fanning from his eyes and the slow curve of his smile made him look younger, less like an aloof adult and more like a roguish boy. Livy wasn't certain of his exact age but knew that he was younger than Aunt Bea, whose twenty-seventh birthday celebration Livy had attended that summer. He was probably somewhere in his mid-twenties...old, but not quite ancient.

"You are a hero, Your Grace," she said solemnly. "I owe you my life, and from this day forth, I pledge you my allegiance."

"I am no hero," he said with rough certainty. "And you owe me nothing, little queen."

He was wrong. She owed him everything.

And one day, when she was old enough, she would repay him.

# Two

*Livy is 19; Ben is 31*

Livy was enjoying the ball her parents had given to mark her nineteenth birthday. After dancing most of the evening, she took a respite with her best friends, Lady Glory Cavendish and Miss Fiona Garrity. The trio was in a ballroom alcove shielded by a row of palms and a rosewood screen. Livy's parents were chatting with guests a few feet away on the other side...and Livy heard a deep, distinctive voice enter their conversation.

Although she couldn't make out the words, she would recognize that gravelly male voice anywhere. And if her mind knew who it was, then her body corroborated it: awareness tickled her nape like a feather. Her heart thumped as eagerly as the tail of a dog greeting its master. The warm tug at her center tightened every inch of her skin, its heady grip surpassing that of her corset. The tips of her breasts budded and throbbed against her bodice.

She sat up straighter, breathing, "He's here."

"Who is?" Glory asked absently.

The alcove was furnished with a settee, which Livy and Glory shared. Glory's russet curls were tilted to one side as she perused a newspaper she'd managed to filch from somewhere. Her pet ferret, Ferdinand II, was curled around her neck like a white fur scarf and appeared to be reading along with her.

Perched on an adjacent chair, Fiona rolled her azure eyes. "Who do you think?"

Her flame-red ringlets gleaming, Fiona sipped daintily at a flute of champagne. The youngest of the three at seventeen, Fi had made her debut this year. With her beauty and sparkling confidence, she'd taken Society by storm. It was widely rumored that she had broken the record for Most Proposals Received by a Lady in her Coming Out Year, and the betting book at White's was apparently overflowing with wagers over who would eventually win her hand.

One of Fiona's most endearing traits was that she didn't take things too seriously, including her own popularity. She was having too much fun for that.

"Who is the *one* person whose presence our dear Livy would care about?" Fi went on.

"*Shh*. Not so loud." Livy's gaze darted to the screen. "What if he hears you?"

"Are we talking about the Duke of Hadleigh?" Not sounding particularly enthused, Glory looked up from the paper. Ferdinand II did the same. "I thought His Grace sent his regrets?"

The same age as Livy, Glory was less interested in finding romance and more in locating the next adventure. Indeed, the three girls' mutual love of escapades had bonded them since they were children. If it hadn't been for her friends, Livy's adolescent years at Mrs. Southbridge's Finishing School for Young Ladies would have been dreadful. Being a girl who knew her own mind had often put her out of step with others. Luckily, Glory and Fi were cut from the same cloth and, what was more, shared the same sense of loyalty. A haughty classmate had dubbed them the "Will-flowers" as an insult, yet the trio had taken on the name with pride.

"He did, but he came after all," Livy whispered back.

The excitement bubbling through her was more potent than champagne. For months now, she had kept her passion for Hadleigh bottled up. The event that had triggered her realization of her romantic feelings had been impossible for her to bring up to him. The wicked memories of what she'd seen him doing in the stables sizzled through her, leaving her confused, alarmed, and...stimulated.

She didn't know how to tell Hadleigh what she wanted, especially when he persisted in treating her as if she were still a child and he an older brother or uncle. She cherished their friendship and feared ruining it and losing him altogether. When he'd wrestled her from Death's grip seven years ago, a bond had forever been forged between them. Her heart beat because of him...and, she had come to realize, *for* him. Yet for the first time in her life, she had been afraid to go after what she wanted because she had never wanted anything this much.

She feared that she wasn't beautiful and worldly enough for an urbane gentleman like Hadleigh. His deceased duchess and the ladies Livy had seen on his arm had all been sophisticated beauties. While Livy had passable looks, elegance and grace were not her forte. She also had a tendency to speak her mind which, apparently, wasn't conducive to flirtation.

Moreover, she feared that Hadleigh might only see her as a younger sister. He teased her in a brotherly fashion about her suitors, and while he seemed protective, he showed no signs of jealousy. The last time he had asked about her beaux, she had replied truthfully that she wasn't interested in any of them.

To which he had replied, *"Wise choice, little one. Marry in haste, repent in leisure, as they say. I, for one, shan't undertake matrimony again."*

His offhand remark had come as a blow. In truth, Livy ought

not to have been surprised. She knew that Hadleigh had fallen in love and married young. Three years ago, when his wife Arabella had passed away due to complications in her pregnancy, he had been devastated, withdrawing to his estate. Livy had written him letter after letter, despite his lack of a reply.

Then, a year ago, Hadleigh had returned to Society, and Livy had been relieved beyond measure to see him healthy and hale. He and she had picked up where they had left off, although she saw him less frequently. Nowadays he was a busy man; weeks could go by before he paid her a visit.

*The important thing is that he came tonight,* she told herself. *It must be a sign. You have to act.*

"Uh-oh," Fi said in a low voice. "Livy has that look."

"What...oh, *that* look." A knowing gleam lit Glory's hazel eyes.

Frowning, Livy said, "I have a look?"

"Pursed lips, furrow between the brows," Glory replied. "That expression has been a precursor to every adventure we have had."

"It is a hold-onto-one's-bonnet kind of look," Fiona agreed.

Livy drew a breath. "As it happens, I have decided that I am going to have a talk with Hadleigh."

At her announcement, Fi and Glory's gazes widened.

"*The* talk?" Glory said in a hushed voice.

Fi leaned closer. "You are going to tell him that you're in love with him?"

Livy nodded, busying her shaky hands by smoothing her blush-colored skirts.

"There is no better time," she said. "I am a lady of marriageable age. Hadleigh is an eligible widower in his prime. Now that I'm older, our age difference no longer matters."

"Not to you, perhaps," Glory said. "I thought the biggest obstacle to your romance was that Hadleigh treats you like a young relation?"

"The two of you certainly bicker like brother and sister," Fi said dryly.

"I shall simply have to make him see me in a different light. A more mature light." Livy rose, squaring her shoulders. "How do I look?"

She wore a gown specially made for the occasion. Indeed, her entire wardrobe had been refurbished as her figure had changed in a rather drastic fashion in the past few months. Resigned to her once boyish form, she'd been stunned when parts of her that had been as flat as the Scottish Lowlands suddenly turned as hilly as the Highlands. When the modiste revealed her new measurements, her jaw had slackened.

Mama had merely smiled. *"Didn't I tell you we Kent women are late bloomers, dear?"*

Livy hoped her new assets would nudge Hadleigh into seeing her as a grown-up. With that in mind, she had chosen her ensemble with care. The silk crepe was a shade between peach and pink, which she thought complemented her brunette coloring and light green eyes. The bodice bared her shoulders, crisscrossing to a point between her now discernable breasts, where she'd pinned a fragrant gardenia. The rest of the bodice molded to her corseted torso, elongating to a point. The full skirts draped over her petticoats, the overskirt looped up with peach ribbons to reveal her tiered underskirt.

"You look very pretty," Glory said.

"In a virginal debutante sort of way," Fiona said.

Livy furrowed her brow. "Is that a bad thing?"

"Not at all. But this is Hadleigh we are talking about," Fi said frankly. "You know his reputation. He is definitely not the sort of man who dallies with inexperienced misses."

Fi had a point. During his marriage, Hadleigh and his duchess had been rather scandalous, although Livy's adolescent ears hadn't been privy to all the gossip. She had once overheard two sticklers sniffing to one another that the Hadleighs were "not good *ton*" and wondering why Livy's parents had invited them to the affair. Livy knew the reason: ever since Hadleigh had saved her life, her parents had treated him as if he were a member of the family.

Neither a McLeod nor a Kent forgot a debt.

After his period of mourning, Hadleigh had emerged a different man. He looked healthier and stronger, emanating a male vitality that drew females to him like flies to honey. It also didn't hurt that he was a wealthy duke in his prime, with no heirs to boot.

Ladies and light-skirts alike swarmed him, and the scandal rags made fortunes off his supposed exploits. The only females he avoided were the marriage-minded misses. As far as Livy could tell, he was as unaffected by his new popularity as he was by his prior infamy. He was always the same with her, at any rate.

He laughed and bantered with her. Protected her.

And teased her mercilessly the way an older brother would.

*I will just have to change how Hadleigh sees me,* she thought determinedly. *To show him I am no longer a little girl.*

"Livy wants Hadleigh to offer for her, not dally with her," Glory pointed out.

Fiona arched her brows. "Doesn't one lead to the other? Plenty of debs have received proposals on the heels of being compromised."

"Livy does not want her reputation harmed." Frowning, Glory asked, "Do you, Livy?"

The rush of warmth in Livy's cheeks was accompanied by that in her lower belly. Although she shared most things with her friends, some details were meant to be kept private. She had not told the other girls about what she'd seen Hadleigh and Lady Cherise Foxton doing in the stables last year...

Longing, hot and confusing, knotted her insides.

She blurted, "What if I want both?"

Glory stared at her, but Fiona just laughed.

"It is your birthday, after all," the latter said. "If you want both, then both you shall have. We will simply have to make you look worldlier."

"You can accomplish that? With this?" Livy waved a hand at herself.

Fi arched her brows. "Do you doubt me, dearest?"

When it came to matters of fashion and flirtation, Fiona was the expert of the three.

"I am at your disposal, Fi," Livy said gratefully before turning to Glory. "I will also need a diversion for my parents so that I may speak to Hadleigh alone."

Glory's smile transformed her face into one of rare beauty. Setting her ferret back into its wicker basket, she said, "That you can leave to me."

Not for the first time, Livy counted her blessings that she had the Willflowers by her side. Glory went to set up the decoy. After Fi finished adjusting Livy's ensemble, the pair joined Livy's parents... only to find that Hadleigh was no longer with them.

Panic clutching her heart, Livy scanned the crowded ballroom. "Did Hadleigh already leave?"

"I doubt it, poppet," Papa said. "I am certain he would not depart without wishing you many happy returns."

Relief flooded Livy. "I should go find him."

"What happened to your corsage, dearest?" Her mama's acute brown gaze roved over her. "Your bodice looks rumpled, and your coiffure is coming down."

According to Fi, this look was known as *en déshabillé* and was irresistible to gentlemen.

Livy resisted chewing on her fingernail, a telltale sign of nerves. "I'll, um, go fix it."

"I will help you freshen up," Mama said.

Livy was saved by the strains of the orchestra.

"They are playing our waltz, pet." Papa smiled at Mama, his

fingertips flitting over the collar of diamonds at her neck. "You promised to dance with me."

"So I did." Mama's voice became breathless. "But our daughter needs attending to."

"Don't worry, Your Graces," Fiona cut in smoothly. "I will help Livy. And my parents will chaperone."

"Hear that, pet? Livy is in excellent hands."

Papa led Mama to the dance floor, his dark head bent close to hers. Even from a distance, Livy could see Mama blushing. Her parents disappeared into the colorful, whirling blur of dancers.

Glory ambled up to Livy and Fiona, a cat-got-in-the-cream smile tucked in her cheeks.

"This waltz does the trick every time," she said with satisfaction.

"How did you know to request this particular one?" Livy asked.

"Because *my* parents adore it." Glory nodded toward the dance floor just as her parents, the Duke and Duchess of Ranelagh and Somerville, floated by. "The older generation cannot resist this song, it seems."

"And there go my parents as well." Eyes twinkling, Fi added, "Perhaps this is not so much a tune for ancient folk as it is for those in love?"

"Speaking of love, let's help Livy find Hadleigh," Glory said. "The waltz shan't last forever."

The three hurried off to circle the perimeter of the ballroom. Livy had to stop now and again to accept the guests' well-wishes. Finally, she spotted Hadleigh: he was standing by the champagne fountain, his back to her...and he was conversing with the most beautiful woman Livy had ever laid eyes upon. The lady had golden hair the color of honey, her willowy figure draped in a stylish gown of claret taffeta. She was tall, only a few inches shorter than Hadleigh, and she looked around his age.

"Heavens." Even Fiona, the Incomparable, sounded awed. "Who is that glorious creature?"

"I do not know." Livy squared her shoulders. "But I am going to find out."

She marched over and cleared her throat.

Hadleigh turned around, and her heart gave a silly hiccup. Lord, he was handsome. His classic bone structure could have graced a statue, the strong slant of his cheekbones and chiseled jut of his jaw meant to be immortalized. Yet no marble could capture his eyes: they were bruised sapphires, pain and beauty moving through them like shadow and light.

To Livy, Hadleigh was the epitome of male virility, especially in formal evening wear. During his period of seclusion, he had gained at least three stone, all of it in muscle. His elegant midnight tailcoat clung lovingly to his broad shoulders and lean torso, his trousers skimming his narrow hips and muscular legs. Realizing that she was ogling him, Livy jerked her gaze back up to his face...and that didn't help her longing *at all*.

One thing that hadn't changed about Hadleigh was his preference for wearing his hair a trifle long. The thick brown waves gleamed beneath the chandelier and added a sensual touch to his hard-edged masculinity.

"If it is not the elusive birthday girl." The warmth in Hadleigh's eyes set off a flutter in Livy's chest. As he bowed, his gaze travelled beyond her, his mouth curving. "Accompanied by her intrepid companions, the Willflowers."

The fluttering stopped. He made her sound like a twelve-year-old with her troop of fellow tots, for heaven's sake.

"As I am nineteen, I am no longer a girl," Livy pointed out. "Nor am I difficult to find. That is, if one was actually bothering to look."

*Drat. Now I sound like a jealous nincompoop.*

"I stand corrected." Hadleigh's dark brows inched upward. "Are you young *women* acquainted with Lady Charlotte Fayne?"

Catching his sardonic emphasis, Livy flushed.

"I have not had the pleasure of meeting these lovely young ladies," Lady Fayne said.

The woman had a voice like mulled cider, earthy and warm. Her curtsy was a thing of art, and her graciousness made Livy feel smaller than an ant.

Hadleigh made the introductions.

"Your dress is beautiful, Lady Fayne," Fiona said. "The very height of fashion."

"Thank you, Miss Garrity. I must return the compliment two-fold."

Fiona preened. Livy bit back a scowl.

"His Grace was just telling me about the Willflowers," Lady Fayne went on. "What a delightful moniker."

"A classmate thought she could bully us with it, but we turned the tables on her." Glory lifted her chin. "We are proud to be Willflowers."

"And you ought to be." Lady Fayne's smile reached her grey eyes. "To be beautiful, bright, and bold is a rare combination indeed."

"Bold is one way to put it. Livy was voted the Most Stubborn Debutante at her finishing school," Hadleigh said.

Livy narrowed her gaze. "That was Most *Determined* Debutante, as well you know."

His reply was a bland smile.

"There *is* a difference," she insisted.

His smile turned even blander.

*Argh.*

"Livy, wasn't there something you needed His Grace's help with?" Fiona said pointedly.

*Right. Concentrate on the plan. On seducing Hadleigh...not strangling him.*

Inhaling, she mustered up her sweetest look. "That's right. I do need your help."

"With what?" he asked.

"I will show you when we get there."

"How mysterious," Lady Fayne murmured. "You mustn't make the lady wait, Your Grace."

"It is a matter of importance," Glory said.

"And great urgency," Fiona added.

"All right, all right." His expression beleaguered and eyes amused, Hadleigh offered Livy his arm. "Lead the way."

# THREE

"This thing you require my assistance with is in the garden?" Hadleigh asked.

Having led the way to a secluded stone bench surrounded by flowering hedges, Livy turned to face him. The scene was set for romance: music drifted from the ballroom, jasmine perfumed the night air, and the moon glowed like a beacon for lovers. The silvery light limned her hero's face, emphasizing the stern edges, the lines of experience enhancing his handsomeness. Above the crisp folds of his cravat, his mouth retained a faint curve as he regarded her.

*It's now or never. Do not be a wilting violet. Take your chance.*

She took a breath. "I wanted to talk to you. In private."

"Actually, I wanted the same thing."

His unexpected reply gave her thumping heart another jolt.

"You did?" she asked.

"Indeed." His smile curled her toes in her slippers. "We have not seen each other much of late, and I have missed your company, Livy."

Mesmerized by his tender expression, she felt light-headed with hope. Had Hadleigh realized that he was in love with her? Had he missed her as much as she had missed him?

"Then why haven't you called more often?" she blurted.

When her question snuffed out his tender expression, she wanted to kick herself. His long lashes briefly veiled his gaze before he spoke.

"I've had business to attend to," he said.

"What kind of business?"

"Nothing of import, little one."

"I am not little anymore," she retorted. "I am a grown woman."

"Right. How could I have forgotten?" Reaching over, he tweaked one of her artfully dislodged curls. "You are so ladylike these days. Not at all like the tree-climbing hoyden I once knew."

Gah. She would not let him evade her question, however.

"Do these 'matters' concern Lady Fayne?" she asked suspiciously.

"No, I only met the lady tonight." He drew his brows together. "Why would you bring her up?"

*Because I have a silly, envious heart?*

"No reason," Livy muttered to the pebbly path.

"Well, I do have a reason for wanting to have you to myself for a moment."

At the teasing note in his voice, she looked up and saw him take a box out of his pocket. Her brain did giddy measurements: was the box small enough to contain...a ring?

*Don't be a twit,* she chided herself. *That isn't just putting the cart before the horse; it is putting it in a different field entirely. Be grateful that he thought to bring you anything.*

"This is for me?" she asked breathlessly.

"No, it is for the other chit whose birthday ball I am currently attending." He aimed his gaze heavenward. "Go on, take it. Unlike you, I am not a spry young thing. My arm is getting tired."

"You are hardly in your dotage," she rejoined. "And what is the point of gaining all that muscle if you cannot even hold up a jeweler's box?"

"Vanity, of course," he drawled.

She snorted. "You are the least vain person I know. You don't care what others think."

He gave her a true gift then: his rare, slow smile. As a girl, eliciting that smile had always made her feel as if she'd won a precious prize. Now her chest squeezed with longing.

"I care what *you* think, Miss Argumentative," he said. "Will you just open your gift?"

"I am not argumentative..." Scowling at his grin, she snatched the box from him. "Fine."

"Ladylike *and* gracious."

She resisted the urge to pummel him in the arm and instead opened the box. Nestled in a bed of white satin was a golden charm. She lifted it out: the miniature crown swung gently from its fine chain, the *pavé* diamonds on its arches sparkling in the moonlight.

"Zounds. How lovely." Reverence hushed her tones. "You had this made for me?"

"A little crown for my little queen," he murmured.

Her heart thumping, she tipped her head back to meet his gaze. She felt their connection: the unbreakable bond that had been forged in the icy waters of Scotland, that had grown stronger in the intervening years, and that now pulsed like a magnetic force between them. His unique wood-and-spice scent curled in her nostrils. Setting her gift on the bench, she took a step closer to him.

"Thank you, Hadleigh," she said.

His eyes were as deep as the night. "It is just a trifle, but I am glad you like it."

"Not just for the necklace, but for saving my life. If it were not for you, I would not be having a birthday," she said tremulously. "You have given me far more than I can ever repay."

"There is no need—"

"Even so, there is one more thing I would ask of you."

"Anything."

His immediate reply thrilled her heart.

"If it is within my power to give it to you, it's yours," he said solemnly.

Since it was easier to demonstrate what she wanted, she gathered her courage and rose onto her toes, pressing her lips to his. This being her first kiss, she wasn't sure how to go about it. She just slid her gloved fingers into his thick hair and smooshed her lips against his.

For so long, she'd dreamed of kissing him, and the reality was even better than her fantasies. Everything about him felt *right*. Familiar yet new and exciting. The texture of his lips, hard yet velvety, made her feel swoony. She had a hint of his taste: darkly male and tantalizing. Oh, she wanted more. Overcome by giddy desire, she instinctively licked the seam of his mouth. He made a muffled sound, his arms closing around her like iron bands.

Their kiss caught fire, the new sensations incinerating her capacity for thought. All she could do was *experience*: the heat melding their mouths, the powerful sweep of his tongue, the intoxicating flavor of him saturating her senses. Squished against his hard chest, her breasts felt full and sensitive, the stiff tips chafing against her corset, setting off tingles of delight. Molten need gathered inside her. Mad with wanting, she moaned, rubbing herself against him, trying to get closer...

In the next instant, she was thrust aside. Her head spinning at the abrupt motion, she stared dizzily at Hadleigh's stark features. His eyes blazed in the moonlight.

"What the devil was that?" he ground out.

She blinked, trying to clear away the haze of passion. He was...angry?

"You...you said I could have what I wanted," she stammered.

"Bloody hell, Livy." He dragged a hand through his hair,

glaring at her. "Is this some sort of game to you, kissing unsuspecting men in the dark?"

"Of course not. I haven't kissed anyone before. You are the first...the only one I want to kiss," she said in a small voice. "I love you, Hadleigh. I've loved you for years. I want...I want to be yours."

She realized then that she hadn't truly seen Hadleigh surprised before. His gaze widened, and his jaw slackened in a way that would have been comical if her future happiness hadn't been hanging in the balance. His chest heaved as he took a deep breath, then another.

Finally, he spoke. "You do not mean that."

"Yes, I do—"

"No, you do not," he said firmly. "You drank too much champagne, and it went to your head, that is all. We will forget this happened."

"I only had half a glass of champagne. And I will *never* forget our kiss," she vowed passionately. "It was everything I dreamed of...and you do not seem, um, unaffected."

Although her cheeks burned, she directed her gaze to the front of his trousers, the crisp tailoring ruined by a rather large and interesting bulge. A virgin she might be, but she was not without knowledge of essential facts. Having spent time on her Aunt Violet and Uncle Richard's stud farm, she understood the mechanics of mating and how offspring were produced.

Unfortunately, Hadleigh did not seem impressed by her worldly knowledge. He bit out an oath and tried to pull his coat over his protruding part...which he could not, since he was wearing a tailcoat. Swearing under his breath, he turned his back to her. His hands braced on his hips, he appeared to be staring out into the distance.

She wondered what he was thinking.

She didn't have long to wonder. A few moments later, he turned to face her, and it was clear that he had regained control.

"Livy, listen to me." His voice was stern. "What happened tonight was a mistake. I understand what it is like to be young and impetuous, and while you may think you know what you want, you do not. You are a young lady, with your future ahead of you. One day, you will find a gentleman who is deserving of you and who will give you what you want—but that gentleman is not me."

Her throat constricted. "Why can't it be you?"

"I am too old for you, to start with. I have done and seen too much to believe in the kind of love you seek." He exhaled. "Keep your dreams for the man who will cherish them, who will cherish *you*."

Her pain was a physical thing, a rough tearing in her chest.

"But I don't want anyone but you," she whispered. "You are the only man I could ever love. If I can't have you, then I won't marry at all."

He closed his eyes briefly. When his eyelids lifted, Livy found herself staring into sapphires bleeding with darkness.

"That shows how innocent you are," he said quietly. "You think you know me, but you do not. If you did, you would not want to waste yourself on a man like me."

"I *do* know you, and I'm not innocent." Prodded by desperation, she blurted, "I saw you with Lady Foxton."

He froze, his stillness that of a cornered beast of prey.

*In for a penny.*

"It was last year at Aunt Bea and Uncle Wick's house party," she confessed. "I was looking for you to see if you wanted to play a game. I ended up at the stables."

A muscle stood out in his jaw, but he said nothing.

"I heard strange noises coming from one of the stalls," she continued in a rush. "I went over to investigate, and there was a hole in the stall door, so I looked through it and saw you. With Lady Foxton. You had her bent over a bale of hay, her dress lifted up, and you were...spanking her."

A harsh breath broke from him, and his gaze was grimmer than she'd ever seen it.

"I wasn't hurting her," he said roughly. "Not in the way you think."

"Oh, I know you weren't," she reassured him. "Why else would she have been, um, begging you for more?"

His expression was pained. "Goddammit, Livy—"

"Eventually, she pleaded for you to...to do something else to her."

Livy swallowed. As bold as she was, she couldn't force herself to say the words that had cemented themselves in her deepest, darkest fantasies. *Fuck me, Hadleigh. Put that huge cock of yours inside me. Master me like the splendid beast you are.*

"I knew then what I wanted from you," Livy said, her voice trembling. "I wanted you to touch me, kiss me. To be with me the way you were with her."

"You do *not* want that," he snapped. "Lady Foxton meant nothing to me, nor I to her."

"And I do mean something to you?" Livy said hopefully.

"Ah, Livy." He drew a ragged breath. "You know you do."

Rejoicing, she said, "Oh, Hadleigh, I knew—"

"You are the sweet little sister I never had. That is how I think of you."

Each soft word struck her heart like a hammer.

"And that will not change."

She stared at him. His face was carved from granite, his body rigid. Her hopes dashed against his implacability like a bird against a glass pane.

*His little sister. That is how he sees me...how he'll always see me.*

"But I love you," she said brokenly. "I will always love you."

"You think that because you are young and innocent. When you see more of the world, you will find a better man. One who will give you everything you deserve...or he will have to answer to me, hmm?"

Hadleigh's gentleness somehow hurt more than his firmness, a feather-tipped arrow that struck into her tenderest core. She had always known that she had his protection and care. If she could only have his love and desire as well, then she would have had...everything.

*But you don't.* Despair seeped through her. *You never will.*

"Come, dry your eyes, silly chit," he murmured. "Then I had best escort you back inside."

She realized that he had pressed his handkerchief into her hand and wetness was trickling down her cheeks. His concern was more than she could bear.

"I can see myself back in," she said stiffly. "Good-bye, Hadleigh."

"Livy..."

She dashed toward the house without looking back.

# Four

*You hurt Livy, you bastard. She is like your sister, for Christ's sake. The only good, pure thing in your life, and you've ruined everything—again.*

The sound of the gong cut through the maelstrom of Ben Wodehouse's thoughts.

He opened his eyes, returning to the Spartan room. Dimly lit by candles, the walls were bare and the floor covered in mats of woven bamboo, from which his fellow attendees of the nightly contemplation session were rising. The crowd was a mix of Chinese, Lascar, and Spanish sailors, as well as a few Englishmen who had found their way to Master Chen's clinic in Whitechapel.

Chen was a Chinese healer who specialized in the treatment of opium habits. The drug's tentacles reached all strata of society and could pull you into the depths of oblivion, no matter where you came from or the color of your skin. Even a title and wealth were no protection; Ben had found this out the hard way.

Two years ago, after a visit to an opium den in Whitechapel, he had been ripe pickings for a gang of cutthroats. They hadn't been satisfied with taking his money; they'd wanted to punish him, a well-dressed nob, for daring to tread through the streets they considered their own. Lying half-conscious in that filthy alleyway, agony radiating from broken bones and torn flesh, Ben had been certain he was going to die, slowly and painfully.

A part of him had felt he deserved it: a miserable end to a miserable life.

As he had awaited the final blow that would deliver him from his pathetic existence, a masked figure had emerged out of nowhere. It had moved like a figment of feverish imagination. Through swollen eyes, Ben had made out the bodies of his attackers hurling through the air, thumping with a groan against the alley walls. He had heard curses and retreating footsteps before blackness claimed him.

When he had awakened, it had been in this clinic. His injuries had been treated, and he had met his rescuer, the man who approached him now. Chen, whom many of the men respectfully addressed as *shifu*, or "master," was the founder of this center. The practitioner of Chinese healing arts had made Ben see his opium use clearly for the first time.

*"It is not a mere habit if you cannot stop, Your Grace,"* Chen had said. *"Opium rules you, not the other way around."*

Chen's treatment of Ben's noxious cravings had involved cleansing the body and the mind. With the master's help, Ben had wrestled free of opium's grip. He had purged his demons—the ones involving opium, at any rate—and come out stronger. Yet he never forgot how close he had come to succumbing to that abyss. The sensual and inexorable gravity of that despair. Nor did he forget the debt he owed to the man who had pulled him from those abominable depths.

"Gor, guv, that were the longest 'our o' my life." While the others had filed from the room, a lanky, ginger-haired lad remained. He approached Ben, cracking his neck and grimacing. "Watching grass grow would be a sight more interesting."

Peter Watkins, also known as Pete the Pinch, was a relative newcomer to the clinic. At sixteen, the barest hint of fuzz upon his chin, the lad was an accomplished pickpocket whose budding career had been compromised by his opium use. The drug had hampered Pete's reflexes while inflating his sense of invincibility, and he'd been beaten half to death by a brute he'd tried to rob. After Chen had nursed the boy back to health, Ben had taken Pete under his wing.

Privilege had buffered the impact of Ben's need for opium. He could afford to use the drug until it killed him, and being titled and rich, his use would always be viewed as "recreation." Pete's drug use, however, was seen as a vice and evidence of moral failure amongst the lower orders, even though Ben knew that he and the lad had more in common than many would think. Class differences aside, he, too, had been a brash youth, a neck-or-nothing whose impulses had led him to trouble time and again. He wanted to steer Pete in a better direction than he himself had gone.

"Contemplation gets easier," Ben said.

Pete shook his head. "Not for me, guv. Makes me right twitchy, it does. Where I come from, you don't stay still 'less you're crippled or dead."

It was the harsh reality of Pete's life as an orphan of the slums. While Ben's own background had been far more privileged, he understood the feeling of restlessness. He had been a hotheaded rakehell at Pete's age.

"Have you thought about my offer?" Ben asked.

"Right kind o' you to give me a job in one o' your mansions, guv, but that life ain't for me." Pete shrugged his shoulders, his grin cocky. "My skill be in pinching silver, not polishing it."

"You could try to learn a reputable trade," Ben began.

"I'll think on it. For now, the theatres are closing, which means pigeons are returning 'ome to roost. No be'er time to pluck some fine feathers." Pete winked. "Good evening, guv."

"Pete—" Ben found himself looking at the lad's retreating back.

"Some horses were not meant to be tamed."

Turning at the calm words, Ben bowed. "Master Chen."

Chen returned the bow. A few inches shorter than Ben, the healer embodied strength and balanced power. This evening, his wiry form was clad in a plain grey tunic with matching trousers, but he often walked the streets dressed like an Englishman. His precisely clipped layers of black hair surrounded a noble face with piercing eyes.

Chen was probably not much older than Ben's own age of one-and-thirty, yet the master possessed an air of sagacity that made him seem beyond the reach of time and place. His accent had the polish of elocution lessons. Although Ben had heard whispers in the clinic about Master Chen's origins—rumors circulated that Chen was everything from a retired sailor, exiled royalty, to a former monk—the *shifu*'s past remained shrouded in mystery.

"The English have a saying about leading a horse to water," Chen said.

Ben bit back his frustration. "Yes, but Pete could do much better for himself."

"It is not your choice to make, Your Grace. I noticed your practice was disturbed this evening."

As usual, the master missed nothing.

"Yes, *shifu*," Ben admitted.

"We will discuss over tea."

Chen led the way to his study, a room as simply furnished as the rest of the clinic. There was a desk, a pair of vertical calligraphy scrolls on the wall behind it, and a round rosewood table where tea awaited. The men took their seats on the round stools, and Ben picked up his cup, a lidded porcelain vessel with no handles. When he lifted the lid, a faint jasmine scent escaped, bringing back the moonlit garden and the yearning in Livy's eyes.

*You are the only man I could ever love. If I can't have you, then I won't marry at all.*

His chest clenched. She was so young and innocent. He supposed it was normal for a girl her age to form a *tendre,* but she deserved far better than him. She needed a younger man and one who didn't have a veritable army of skeletons rattling in the closet. As a man of experience twelve years her senior, Ben should have anticipated their kiss and prevented it.

He *definitely* should not have responded to it.

With twisting guilt, he recalled the crazed instant when he'd lost his mind. When she'd pressed herself against him, giving and soft, her sweetness flooding his senses. When he'd pulled her closer instead of pushing her away...

*I deserve to be drawn and quartered.*

His sins were already too many: he was a murderer, a recovering opium addict, and an all-around bastard. He would not add seducer of an innocent to the list.

Furthermore, he would not betray his friendship with Livy's father, the Duke of Strathaven. For years, Ben had kept company with selfish scoundrels like himself. Ben's destructive tendencies had led to his estrangement from his remaining family member, his sister Beatrice. While he'd worked to make amends, she remained wary of him, and he did not blame her.

Some sins were unforgivable.

Strathaven was the rare male friend Ben had who he actually respected. The duke and, indeed, the whole Strathaven family, had offered Ben steadfast support. The thought of dishonoring their kindness churned Ben's insides with self-loathing.

And hurting Livy? His tenacious little queen who had reminded him how to smile, to laugh, to see the promise of life rather than its worst?

*I would rather tear my heart out than harm a single hair on her head,* he thought starkly.

"Your mind is a restless ocean this eve," Chen said.

Ben dragged his attention to Chen, who was drinking tea and watching him.

"I cannot seem to control my thoughts," Ben admitted.

"The harder one tries, the less control one has." Chen set his cup down on the table without making a sound. "The goal, therefore, is not to try."

This sort of paradoxical saying was typical fare for the *shifu*. At first, Ben had thought Chen's principles were nonsensical and wholly un-English. Over time, however, he had begun to see the wisdom and usefulness of the other's philosophy.

Unlike the quacks Ben had previously consulted for his opium problem, Chen had not prescribed the taking of waters, bedrest, or bloodletting. He'd introduced Ben to a new set of skills. Ben had learned to sit and contemplate the workings of his mind, a surprisingly daunting task (who knew that being still could be so damned difficult?). He'd built his stamina and strength through physical and mental exercises. He'd even temporarily removed meat from his diet...which had led him to consider terminating the treatment.

Yet his instincts had urged him to continue. Had known this was his last hope. Having hit despair's rocky bottom, he'd had nothing left to lose. He had been a wreck, his drinking and opium use raging beyond his control. His entire existence had been focused not on chasing the pleasure of the drug but on avoiding its consuming anguish.

More and more and more. For less, less, less.

The more he took, the less of a man he became. Less of a human. Less of a soul.

He had dabbled with opium for years. Arabella had introduced it to him...the way she had introduced many damaging things into their marriage. The familiar tide of regret and remorse rose.

"Tossed on the waves once more." Chen raised his brows. "What is this storm that has taken hold of your mind?"

Ben set his cup down with a clink. By nature, he was a private man, disinclined to trust. Yet Chen had been present with him as he had sweated, hallucinated, raged, and wept through his withdrawal. Chen had also helped Ben to recognize that the demon of craving would always have a corner of his mind. It was ready to pounce at any opportunity. And nothing gave it more power than anger, shame, and secrets...things Ben possessed in spades.

Expelling a breath, he said, "It is a girl."

"Ah," Chen said.

Ben heard a hint of disapproval in the other's tone. During the recovery period, Chen recommended abstinence from what he called "vices" (and what Ben had thought of as a good time). On the list were activities such as sexual congress, drinking, and gambling. It was rumored that Chen, himself, was celibate from all three.

Ben had managed to give up alcohol and gambling which, he had come to realize, had fueled his temper and recklessness. Without them, he was clearer of mind and more in control of himself and his actions. Giving up fucking, however? That was a different story.

To his credit, he had abstained for several months. During that time, he had recognized how destructive his marital relations had been. His relationship with Arabella had brought out the worst in both of them.

When he'd started bedding women again, he did it on his own terms. His rules were simple: no games (other than those mutually agreed upon), no manipulation, and no emotional attachments. He was always in control of his sexual encounters, and the women he tupped had matching needs. Cherise Foxton, for example, craved the feel of a man's firm hand on her backside as much as Ben liked the feeling of dominance.

His partners were, without exception, ladies of experience, and he made sure they got what they wanted out of the negotiated transaction: pleasure, money, or both. He thought he had found a way to appease his hot-blooded nature without anyone getting hurt...or hurt in a bad way, at any rate.

Livy had destroyed his complacency.

*I knew then what I wanted from you.* Her words tore through him like a bullet. *I wanted you to touch me, kiss me. To be with me the way you were with her.*

He did not know which was worse: the fact that he had inadvertently exposed Livy to his degenerate behavior or that she had been *intrigued* by it. Recalling her wide-eyed interest sent a hot, unsavory thrill up his spine.

*Stop it, you bastard. You will not fantasize about debauching Livy. Ever.*

"Your lady must be quite fascinating." Chen's tone was dry. "She appears to hold your thoughts captive."

"She is not my lady," Ben said curtly. "She is the daughter of a friend. I've mentioned her before. The girl I rescued from the pond."

As part of his healing, he had shared his history with the master. Not all the gruesome details, but the essential facts. He had told Chen that he'd caused the death of two people. Four, if one counted the fact that Arabella and his unborn child had died due to complications in her pregnancy. Yes, Chen knew about the damage Ben had done. He also knew about Livy, the one good thing in Ben's life.

"Ah, yes," Chen said. "Her name is Olivia?"

Ben rotated his cup in its saucer. "Yes."

"And why does she create ripples in your contemplation?"

The master oft compared the still mind to a smooth, glass-like pond upon which all reflections could be seen. Ben did not know if he was capable of achieving such a state.

"If you knew Livy, you would know the chit doesn't create mere ripples," he said with dark humor. "She throws herself into the pond wholeheartedly and splashes water everywhere."

Chen raised his brows. "Why is she splashing in your pond?"

Ben expelled a breath. "She kissed me."

"The little girl?"

"She is not little now. She is nineteen—still young," Ben said hastily. "Far too young for me. Not that I would ever think of her in that fashion. She is like a sister to me."

"She is like a sister...or she is a sister to you?"

At the mild inquiry, heat crawled up the back of Ben's neck. Of course he thought of Livy as a sister; if he didn't, he was a damned pervert. A lecher. He had known her since she was a child, for God's sake. Through the years, she had turned to him as a trusted adult, and God knew she'd been the only one to do so. He had tried his best to guide her through painful formative experiences and to cheer her on during her triumphs.

In return, she had been his stalwart little friend. The one person in his life who always thought the best of him. Who gave him hope that even a bastard like him had something worthy left to give.

He told himself that the kiss had happened because he'd been taken off guard. By Livy's new buxom figure and his own neglected needs. He hadn't tupped a woman in weeks.

"I would never hurt Livy," he said flatly. "She is not for me."

"You rejected her advances?"

"Of course I did. What kind of man do you take me for? No—don't answer." Ben dragged a hand through his hair. "You know me too well for your reply to be flattering."

"I am not in the business of flattering. I seek the truth." Chen sipped his tea. "As should you."

"The truth is that kiss should have never happened. It was my fault that it did. Now I've hurt Livy and that..." *Infuriates me. Makes me want to punch a wall—better yet, myself. Why am I cursed to hurt anyone who comes near me?* "That is unacceptable."

"What do you intend to do about it?"

What could he do? "I'll stay away from her, I suppose."

The idea of avoiding Livy did not sit well with Ben. In the past few months, he had embarked on a secret mission with Chen. The worthwhile cause had taken much of his time, and he'd seen less of his plucky little queen. He'd missed her. Missed bantering with her, listening to her amusing anecdotes, or even just sitting with her in companionable silence. She was the dancing flame in the gloom of his existence.

"It is for the best," Chen said. "You have other matters that require your concentration."

The master's somber tone indicated a shift in the conversation, one that Ben welcomed.

"Do you have news?" Ben asked. "Concerning the body we found in the alleyway?"

Months ago, Chen had spearheaded an ambitious project to keep the streets around the clinic free of opium. He'd done so to reduce temptation to his recovering patients. As the drug was readily available from druggists, tobacconists, and the like, the task had not been easy. Nevertheless, Chen had convinced local merchants that it was in the interest of neighborhood safety to limit sales of the drug.

This victory, unfortunately, had brought other problems. With his efforts to limit opium's damaging effects, Chen had made no friends in the dark underbelly of the trade. Men who profited from the drug—including opium den owners, moneylenders, thieves, and other cutthroats—viewed Chen as a threat. The healer's clinic had been vandalized on several occasions, the front step littered with slaughtered rats.

Authorities showed no interest in what they considered fighting among underclass factions. Nor did they take the concerns of a "Chinaman" seriously. Consequently, Chen had taken matters into his own hands. For he was a master of both healing and fighting; the physical exercises he taught his students could be used as powerful tools for defending oneself and defeating opponents.

Chen had set up a night watch composed of volunteers. The initial aim of protecting the clinic and its patients had expanded to include the neighborhood at large. Ben had joined the group, wanting to give back. For the past few months, he'd spent three to four evenings a week keeping watch over the streets; like the other guards, he wore a mask to safeguard his identity.

The work had given him an unexpected sense of purpose. For the first time in his life, he was channeling his energy toward something good. While redemption was too much to hope for, at least he was atoning for some of his sins. He and his fellow guards had protected their territory with success...with two notable exceptions.

A month ago, Ben had come upon Baron Winford, an acquaintance. Since many gentlemen ventured into Whitechapel to sample its sordid pleasures, encountering the young rake had not been surprising. What had shocked Ben had been Winford's state: the man had been viciously out of control. Winford had seized an innocent bystander, a hapless chestnut hawker, strangling the man half to death. When Ben had intervened, Winford had turned on *him* with eyes crazed and blinded by animal rage.

It had taken Ben and another guard to subdue Winford. Suddenly, the baron had begun to convulse, falling to the ground. His eyes had rolled back in their sockets, saliva frothing, twin trails of blood dripping from his nostrils. Chen had been unable to save Winford, concluding that the man must have been afflicted with some rare illness.

Then, five days ago, another toff had died in the same fashion.

Ben had found this second man attacking a prostitute, the dilated pupils and raging expression eerily familiar. He'd just hauled the man off the woman when the bastard's knees buckled, his body shaking with paroxysms as he hit the ground.

This time, Chen had managed to revive the man. Searching through the fellow's pockets, Ben had found a small snuffbox. Made of glazed crimson ceramic, the distinctive round container was trimmed and hinged with bronze. The letters "D" and "B" were painted in gilt on the lid...and it was identical to the one Ben had found on Winford. Inside the box were the same white powdery dregs.

"Is this what made you ill?" Ben had demanded.

The man had stared up at him with glassy eyes. "I had a wager with the Devil..."

"Where did you get this drug?" Chen had asked.

"All gone. But the Devil will be at London's fanciest masquerade—"

The man's singsong voice had dissolved into a choking fit. Convulsions seized him, blood leaking from his nose. Despite Chen's best efforts, the fellow had soon lain lifeless in the dirt.

"His name was John Hagan," Chen said now. "We located his family. His father is a well-to-do merchant and had no inkling of his son's drug use."

"Have you spoken to Hagan's friends?" Ben asked. "Perhaps they know more about his habits."

"Not yet. I have been focused on identifying the substance in the snuffboxes. The chemist I consulted thought it might be some highly potent derivative of opium. Something neither he nor I have seen before." Grooves bracketed the healer's mouth. "I've also been inquiring at shops to see if anyone has information on the snuffboxes themselves. No luck thus far.

"This drug is dangerous, killing two men—that we know of— in a month alone. We must find the source, the Devil Hagan spoke of, and put a stop to the spread of this poison."

"I have an idea where to look," Ben said.

Chen lifted his brows.

"Hagan mentioned that the Devil will be at London's fanciest masquerade. The Earl and Countess of Edgecombe are holding a costume ball in ten days, touted as the *fête* of the Season."

"How does one secure an invitation to such an exalted event?" Chen asked.

"As it happens," Ben said resolutely, "I already have one."

# FIVE

*1843, LONDON*

*Livy is 14; Ben is 26*

"Are you in here, little queen?"

Hearing Hadleigh's deep voice, Livy quickly dashed away her tears.

"In the nook," she called back.

The nook was a lush alcove in the orangery and her private hideaway. It was shielded by a wall of potted citrus on one side with a glass-framed view of the gardens on the other. Usually, she enjoyed the tranquility of the space, yet today she found no comfort in the solitude. She felt separated and cut off, a barrier between her and the outside world.

A fresh wave of heat rose behind her eyes. Befuddled, she didn't know what was wrong with her. She prided herself on being a level-headed girl. Since she had turned fourteen and started Mrs. Southbridge's Finishing School for Young Ladies, however, her emotions had been as bumpy as a country road. Up and down, up and down they went, like a runaway carriage she could not control.

She hated feeling powerless. Hated acting like a ninny.

In fact, she felt so unlike herself today that she was even avoiding Hadleigh, one of her favorite people. In the two years since he'd saved her life, he had been a frequent visitor to the house. He and Papa had become friends and partners in various business ventures, and Mama invited him to all the family celebrations. He often came alone as his wife apparently kept a busy social calendar and was in much demand.

Livy did not mind. The few times she had interacted with the Duchess of Hadleigh, she had run out of things to say. In the glamorous lady's company, she felt gauche and as dull as ditchwater.

Seeing Hadleigh's lanky form round the lush green wall, Livy composed herself.

"I thought I would find you here." He strode over in his easy, long-limbed stride. He sat beside her on the wooden bench with the familiarity of an old friend. Studying her with dark sapphire eyes, he said, "Did you not know that I came to call?"

She considered lying, but she was no good at social niceties. That was part of her problem.

"I knew," she said.

"But you didn't come to see me?" A furrow appeared between his dark brows. "Have I done something to annoy you, little one?"

He was the only adult she knew who would ask such a question. It was one of the reasons she liked him. He cared what she thought and treated her as his equal.

"Of course not." She expelled a breath. "I just wasn't in the mood for company."

"Come to think of it, neither am I." He smiled faintly. "Do you mind if we are alone together for a while?"

She shook her head. Quiet settled, each of them lost in their own brooding thoughts. Of late, Livy had discovered that silence had many forms. The awkward kind when one had nothing to add to conversations about frippery and eligible matches. The cruel kind when one's classmates stopped talking when one approached, their backs forming a wall.

The present silence was comforting, like a trusty and time-worn blanket. It made Livy feel safe. Safe enough to let the truth out.

"They hate me," she blurted.

Hadleigh angled his head at her. "Who does?"

"Everyone. All the girls at Southbridge's," she said morosely.

"Why?"

This was another reason Livy liked Hadleigh. Whenever she had brought up this topic with her parents, they tried to fix the problem for her. Papa had even threatened to have a "discussion" with the headmistress and parents of the other girls, which Livy knew would make matters worse.

Hadleigh, on the other hand, actually *listened* to her.

"Because I'm not like the other girls," she admitted. "I don't care about gowns and gossip, and I detest needlepoint. They think I'm peculiar. And it didn't help that last week one of the girls tried to squish a spider with her slipper, and I stopped her."

Hadleigh nodded in understanding; he knew about Livy's fascination with spiders. Ever since Papa had told her the story about how a spider's perseverance had inspired Robert the Bruce, the great Scottish king, to win a battle, she had become an ardent admirer of the arachnid. How many creatures showed such tenacity and fortitude? Could weave something as lovely, fragile, and lethal as a spider's web?

"Since spiders seldom harm humans and rid us of household pests, there is no good reason to kill them," he said gravely.

"Precisely." She jerked her chin in emphatic agreement. "But my interest in spiders isn't the only problem. The girls are calling me a troublemaker."

Hadleigh quirked a brow. "Are you?"

"No—I mean, not on purpose. But if someone does something unjust to someone else, one cannot stand by and do nothing, can one?"

"Depends on who 'one' is. If we are talking about you, then, no, probably not."

"The most popular girl at the school, Sally, Lord Sackville's daughter, broke an expensive vase," Livy said furiously. "I saw her, and so did a roomful of our peers. But Sally blamed it on Tilda, one of the maids. Tilda got sacked. And all the girls are saying how clever Sally is and how Tilda deserved it because they never liked her manner. As if that is sufficient justification to cause that poor woman to lose her position and livelihood!"

"You told the headmistress the truth, I gather?"

"Of course I did!" Livy clenched her skirts in frustration. "But it did not make an iota of difference. She said that there was no evidence that Sally broke the vase, and if one wishes to get on in society, it is best not to gossip about one's peers. I was *not* gossiping; I was providing eyewitness testimony!"

Hadleigh's lips gave a faint twitch. "If the headmistress didn't do anything, how did the other girls figure out that you talked to her?"

"Because I went to Sally and demanded that she write out a confession," Livy said grimly.

He coughed in his fist. "How did that, er, go over?"

"She laughed in my face. Then she told all the girls I am a tattletale. And that is why," she finished darkly, "they all hate me."

"I see." He paused. "It seems to me you have to decide how to move forward."

She crossed her arms over her chest. "I am *not* apologizing to Sally."

"I would not expect you to. But you do have to decide: what matters more, being popular or being true to yourself?"

"Being true to myself. Without question."

"Then let that guide what you do next." His eyes were the

warm indigo blue of a summer night. "Listen to your heart, Livy. It will not guide you wrong."

She canted her head, considering the advice. "Do you listen to your heart, Hadleigh?"

Storm clouds darkened his gaze. "My heart is not good and pure like yours. I do not trust it to make good decisions."

"Your heart *is* good." Shocked that he would think otherwise, she said staunchly, "You are one of the most honorable men I know."

"I am flattered that you think so. Now about these chits at Southbridge's—"

"I *know* so." She wasn't about to let him divert the topic. "You risked your life to save mine."

"I did as anyone would have done." His tone was dismissive. "It was nothing."

"It's not *nothing* to me," she protested. "I like being alive, thank you very much."

He gave her one of his rare smiles that involved his lips *and* his eyes. Reaching over, he tugged gently on one of her ringlets. When her brother Christopher pulled her hair, Livy found it annoying, but she didn't mind when Hadleigh did it. He brooded too much, and it was nice when he acted more carefree.

"I am glad you are alive too, little one," he said softly.

Glad that he was back in good spirits, she said, "What were you going to say about the girls at school?"

"Find a friend amongst them," he said. "I would wager not everyone agrees with what Sally did. Unlike you, they are probably just too scared to stand up to a bully."

"I will try." She sighed. "I cannot wait until next year when Glory and Fiona join me at the school. Then I will have true friends by my side."

"The three of you together?" Amusement lit Hadleigh's eyes. "Sally Sackville—nay, the world—had better watch out."

## PRESENT DAY

"Drat." Beneath his floppy chestnut curls, Will's little face was disgruntled as he looked at the board. "Livy wins again."

Livy gave her youngest brother an affectionate look. At eight years old, he was as competitive as she was. It was lucky that Christopher, their middle brother, possessed an easy-going temperament, or their games would devolve into bloodshed.

At present, she and Chris were sitting with Will on his bed. Will had delicate lungs, a fact that frustrated the poor dear to no end. In particular, the London air brought upon a shortness of breath that prevented him from romping around as he liked. To cheer him up, Livy and Chris had brought in a game of anagrams.

The game was also a good distraction from Livy's own despair. Since Hadleigh's rejection three nights ago, she had shed countless tears in private, crying herself to sleep. Even though Fi and Glory had visited, giving her encouragement, she'd been despondent. Could there be anything more devastating than the man you loved telling you that he only thought of you as a younger sister?

"You could let Will win for once," Chris said under his breath.

Livy was glad to have her mawkish thoughts interrupted. At sixteen, Chris was tall and lanky, with their papa's handsomeness and dark coloring. He was the charming peacemaker of the siblings.

"How would that help our brother become a better player?" Livy pointed out. "I am teaching him what it takes to win."

"I don't want Livy to go easy on me," Will said adamantly. "I am going to beat her all on my own. It is like that story Papa tells about the spider and Robert the Bruce: *if at first you don't succeed, try and try again.*"

"All right, little king," Chris said good-naturedly. "You can go first this round."

As they took turns drawing letters from the pile and using them to form words, Livy found it difficult to keep her mind on the game. The tale of Robert the Bruce and the spider, one of her childhood favorites, whirled in her head.

As the story went, after losing six wars to the invading English, the Scottish King had taken refuge from the enemy in a cave, where he saw a spider try to weave a web from wall to wall. Six times the spider tried to throw the thread to the opposite wall; six times she failed. Yet on the seventh try, she succeeded.

According to folklore, this inspired Robert the Bruce to persevere, which led to his trouncing of the English army in his seventh battle. Scotland's independence was recognized...all because the brave warrior—and the spider—refused to give up.

A sudden recognition flared in Livy. *If they didn't give up...why am I doing so?*

Love was a battlefield, and fortune favored the bold. Hadleigh might think of her as a sister now, but surely she could change that. After all, her own feelings for him had been transformed in a single, scorching moment. Livy felt a hot flutter as she recalled seeing Hadleigh with Lady Foxton. Until the moment she had peeped into the stable, she had thought of him as a friend. Yet as she'd watched Hadleigh spank his voluptuous lover over a bale of hay, wanton longing had spread through her.

A part of her had known that she ought to be shocked. Disgusted by such a display of depravity. What she had *actually* felt was fascination...and need.

When Lady Foxton had begged Hadleigh to give her release, an electrifying sensation had swept through Livy. The peaks of her breasts had stiffened, a pulsing urgency at her core. As Hadleigh had rutted Lady Foxton, his lean hips slamming against the other's jiggling bottom, his hands holding her hair like reins as she mewled in delight, Livy had shivered with a strange and undeniable recognition.

She wanted to be where Lady Foxton was. To be Hadleigh's lover. To be the only one to feel his masterful touch, to moan beneath his potent caresses...and to hold his heart. The truth had cascaded through every cell and fiber of her being: *I am in love with him.* In that instant, her girlish adoration had been transformed into a woman's awareness and determination.

She wanted to spend the rest of her life with Ben Wodehouse.

And she would not let one measly failure dissuade her from her goal.

"It's your turn." Will's impatient voice cut through her flash of insight.

Chris gave her a quizzical look. "Is something amiss? You never wool-gather during a game."

Her cheeks warmed. "Everything's fine." *Now that I've sorted things out.*

Her mind back on task, she trounced her brothers readily.

Amidst Will's groans, Mama entered the room in a rustle of rose silk.

"Heavens," she said with an exasperated smile. "Are the three of you still at it?"

"Livy keeps winning, and Will keeps demanding rematches," Chris explained. "I am stuck in the middle."

"William, you need your rest. Chris, consider yourself unstuck," Mama said. "And Livy, why have you not changed for Mrs. Hunt's charity symposium?"

Livy had forgotten about the event. Hosted by Mama's friend, Persephone Hunt, the symposium aimed to match young ladies with charities that interested them. Mama was taking Livy and the Willflowers.

"Sorry, Mama." Livy jumped up. "I'll get ready now."

"I will help you," Mama said with a sigh.

As they headed to her bedchamber, Livy considered confiding

in her mother about Hadleigh. As much as she loved her parents, she doubted that they would approve of a match with him. They would say he was too old for her, despite their own gap in age. And how many times had she overheard them discussing his rakish tendencies? Just yesterday, she'd eavesdropped on their conversation from outside the breakfast room.

*"Fine fellow,"* Papa had said. *"But he is his own worst enemy when it comes to females. He is too old to carry on in this fashion and ought to settle down."*

*"Like you did?"* Mama had teased.

*"I've found domestic bliss. No reason Hadleigh cannot do the same."*

*"Hadleigh isn't you, darling. I'm afraid he might not be capable of being reformed..."*

The last thing Livy needed was additional barriers to her romance. Mama, in particular, had a tendency to be managing. As a girl who was inclined to follow her own counsel, Livy had learned early on that it was best not to solicit parental opinions, particularly if she knew they would be opposing.

*Sin first and ask for forgiveness later* summed up Livy's lifelong philosophy.

Which reminded her that she needed to put her campaign to win Hadleigh's heart into action. Time was running out. With the Season coming to an end in a few weeks, she and her family would be leaving for Scotland. She might not see Hadleigh again for months.

After her mother and her lady's maid helped her change into a lavender promenade dress and sat her in front of the dressing table, Livy pounced.

"Mama," she said. "How are the plans for the supper party this Saturday coming along?"

"Fine, dear." Mama fussed with a braided loop of Livy's hair.

Livy tried to sound nonchalant. "Did Hadleigh send a reply?"

"Come to think of it, I do not believe he has."

*Botheration. How am I going to win his heart if he makes himself scarce?*

Her frustration must have shown because Mama dismissed the maid and said, "What is the matter with you, Livy?"

She tried not to squirm beneath her mother's tea-colored gaze. Mama was uncommonly, and at times *annoyingly*, acute. Before marrying Papa, Mama had apprenticed with her brother, Livy's Uncle Ambrose, in his private enquiry business. During Livy's childhood, Mama had continued to take on a few cases...nothing too dangerous, of course. Papa would not allow that. Being an overprotective sort, he'd insisted on escorting Mama on all her investigations.

In recent years, Mama had taken a hiatus from her enquiry work. She had not lost her powers of observation, however. And she used them frequently on her children.

"Something has been amiss since the ball," Mama stated. "I wish to know what it is."

"Everything is fine," Livy said.

In the looking glass, Mama's gaze veered heavenward. "You take after your papa, no doubt about it. But I am your mother, Livy, and I can tell you have not been yourself."

Knowing her mama could be like a mongrel with a bone, Livy searched for an excuse. "I am sad that the Season is coming to an end, that is all. I shall miss my friends when we return to Scotland."

"I do not blame you, dearest. Strathmore is not the liveliest place for a young woman, is it?" Mama sighed. "If it weren't for William's condition, we could stay here longer, but the London air is so trying for his lungs."

At her mother's torn expression, Livy was struck with guilt.

"I do not mind," she said quickly. "Will's health must come first."

Mama studied her, then gave a brisk nod. "Now about the supper party. I am working on the seating arrangement and wondered who you preferred to be placed next to, Lord Sheffield or Lord Kinley?"

*Neither. I'd like to sit with Hadleigh.*

Suppressing a sigh, she said, "Either would be fine."

"Lord Sheffield has been paying you marked attention these past months, and Lord Kinley has all but stated his intentions to your papa. Do you have a preference for either of them, Livy? I would like to know where your inclinations, if any, lie."

*With Hadleigh. Always and forever with him.*

"I have no preference between Lords Sheffield and Kinley," she said honestly.

"Well, there's no rush, is there?" Mama adjusted a ribbon in Livy's hair. "You are young, and you have the Kent blood running in your veins. It is a proven fact that we Kents marry for love, so when the time comes, your heart will guide you true."

*Listen to your heart.* Hadleigh had given her the same advice once.

Hearing Mama reinforce this message lifted Livy's spirits. The Kent side of the family was legendary amongst the *ton* for making love matches; surely that would hold true for Livy as well? All she had to do was convince Hadleigh that their love was meant to be.

*I will wage a battle to win Hadleigh's heart,* she thought fiercely. *I'll try and try again until I succeed.*

# Six

The charity symposium was held at the Hunt Academy, located on the fringes of Covent Garden. Mr. and Mrs. Hunt, who were close friends of Livy's parents, had purchased the former spice warehouse, transforming it into a bright, cheery school for foundlings. The academy's purpose was to provide its students with food, shelter, and the tools to earn a living once they graduated. The curriculum included reading and writing, as well as instruction in a variety of trades.

As Mama led Livy and her friends into the packed auditorium, they were greeted by Persephone Hunt, a pretty blonde whose slender form was clad in a flounced frock that matched her vivid blue eyes.

Mama exchanged air kisses with her friend. "Percy, my dear, you have outdone yourself. Your symposium is an absolute crush. Half the *ton* must be here."

"The response has been even better than I had hoped." Mrs. Hunt beamed. "There are over two dozen charities represented today. With such a selection, I hope the ladies will find a cause worthy of their time and energy." Addressing Livy, Fiona, and Glory, she said with a smile, "Go on and browse the tables, my dears. And be sure to stop by the Hunt Academy booth. Pippa is manning the table—or *womaning* it, as she would say—and would love to see you."

Pippa, Mrs. Hunt's daughter, was a few years older than Livy. She was vivacious and fun, and Livy looked up to her like an older sister. Since Pippa's marriage last year, Livy hadn't seen as much of the other.

"Thank you, Mrs. Hunt," Livy said. "We cannot wait to catch up with Pippa."

Livy, Fi, and Glory wandered into the perfumed throng. Booths lined the perimeter, and ladies were perusing the charities like they would shops on Bond Street. Glancing at the tables, Livy saw groups dedicated to sewing garments for those in need and reading the Good Book to women in prison. Although these were commendable causes, she could not work up much interest: needlework was her nemesis, and her reading taste ran toward sensation novels.

"I daresay I've never seen so many do-gooders gathered in one place," Fiona murmured.

"Don't you want to do good?" Livy queried.

"Yes, but I want to have fun while I'm doing it."

Livy agreed, her eyes widening as she took in the taxidermied animals parading along the next table. All the creatures had gory wounds and looks of agony upon their furry faces. The banner hanging from the table read, *Society for the Protection of Animals Subject to Cruelty and Untold Abuses.* The two representatives of the organization were wearing white blouses and skirts speckled with what was, Livy hoped, artificial blood.

As Glory walked by, one of the ladies let out a huff of outrage.

"Have you no shame, young miss?"

Blinking, Glory looked around her. "Pardon. Are you speaking to me?"

"Indeed I am. That fur scarf you are wearing is an offense to decency," the second lady decried. "To think how that poor ermine must have suffered for the sake of vanity and fashion."

"Oh, this isn't an ermine. Or a scarf." Glory looked relieved. "This is Ferdinand the Second, and he's a ferret."

At that moment, Ferdinand II, who'd been napping in his favorite position draped around Glory's shoulders, raised his head. He hissed at the ladies, who shrieked. One fainted; the other called for smelling salts.

The Willflowers forged on. They fared no better at a neighboring booth, where Glory got into a heated debate. The charity's purpose was to protest the existence of opium dens; to illustrate the threat, a poster was on display. The caricature depicted a Chinese man with slitted eyes and a cunning smile, holding out a pipe to an unsuspecting Englishman. In the background lay cadaverous bodies draped with the British flag.

"You do realize you have it the wrong way around?" Glory was saying. "We are the ones importing opium to China. Not to mention the harm the East India Company is doing to the Indian economy and culture with the opium trade."

The charity lady's lips pinched together. "What do you know of such things, young lady?"

"My papa gave speeches on the topic in the House of Lords," Glory replied.

"It is best not to repeat things one does not understand," the lady said in patronizing tones.

Seeing the fire in Glory's eyes, Livy and Fi dragged her away before more damage could be done. They found a quieter spot at the back of the room.

"Perhaps charities aren't for us after all," Fiona said. "How are you faring, Livy dear?"

"Much better. I've decided to redouble my efforts with Hadleigh," Livy announced.

Glory looked at Fi and muttered, "I owe you an ice at Gunter's."

"Glory and I had a wager going," Fi explained. "She said it would take a week for you to start campaigning for Hadleigh's affections again. I said three days."

"It is nice to know one's bosom friends are invested in one's welfare," Livy said dryly. "Now, do you want to hear my plan?"

"We're all ears…" Fi trailed off. "Is that Lady Fayne?"

Livy saw that it was Charlotte Fayne standing at the next table. She felt a prickle of antipathy, which she knew was motivated by sheer envy. Lady Fayne had looked so perfect standing next to Hadleigh, and the widow was everything Livy was not: glamorous, mature, *and* tall. She was the sort of woman Hadleigh would find appealing.

*If Lady Fayne had kissed Hadleigh in the garden, he probably wouldn't have rejected her.*

Livy was ashamed by her peevish thought. Especially when Lady Fayne greeted them with a smile of genuine pleasure.

"If it isn't the Willflowers," Lady Fayne said as they made their curtsies. "How lovely to see you all again."

"It is a pleasure to see you, Lady Fayne," Fi said. "Your ensemble is ravishing."

Livy had to admit that Lady Fayne looked faultless in a carriage dress of pale bronze, paired with a redingote lined with blue satin. Her honey-gold hair was arranged in a fashion similar to Livy's own: parted in the middle, with braided loops over the ears. Compared to the worldly widow, however, Livy felt like a gawky miss fresh out of the schoolroom.

"If it is not too bold, may I ask that you call me Charlie?" the lady said. "All my friends do, and it is my fondest wish to become better acquainted with the three of you."

Fi dimpled. "It would be an honor, Charlie. You must return the favor and call me Fi."

Not wanting to be churlish, Livy said, "There is no need to stand on formality with us."

"Ladies who share my own sensibilities. How delightful," Charlie said warmly. "How are you finding the symposium?"

Glory crossed her arms. "Problematical."

As Glory relayed their misadventures, Livy studied Charlie's booth. The lady had no leaflets or paraphernalia to indicate the purpose of her charity. There was not even a sign with the group's name. In fact, only two objects sat upon the table: a piece of paper and a blue satin reticule.

Curiosity prompted Livy to ask, "What is the nature of your charity?"

Charlie turned to her. "It is a bit of a secret, actually. One that I am only revealing to those who can correctly solve a riddle. Would you care to try?"

*Curiouser and curiouser.*

Despite herself, Livy was intrigued. "All right."

Charlie picked the paper up from the table, handing it to Livy. Glory and Fi huddled in.

Livy read the single sentence aloud. "What is seen in the middle of March and April, that cannot be seen at the beginning or end of either month?"

"Hmm," Fi said. "That is tricky."

"A seasonal pattern, perhaps?" Glory guessed. "The weather or maybe animal migrations?"

"Neither are universal. They depend upon where you are, and this riddle sounds absolute." Fi tapped her chin. "What else happens in the middle of March and April? Celebrations of some sort?"

"Would those not also depend upon where you live?" Glory said. "Different countries have different festivals, after all."

"The answer is not a celebration," Livy said definitively. "Nor is it weather or animal related."

"What is the answer then?" Fi asked.

"The letter *R*." Livy pointed to the letter in both words. "It is in the middle of both 'March' and 'April' but not at the beginning or end."

"Very good," Charlie said with warm admiration.

Tamping down the urge to preen, Livy gave a shrug. "It was not that difficult."

"Not for an agile and inquisitive mind. But those are rarer than one would think." Charlie leaned closer. "Can the three of you keep a secret?"

"Of course," Fiona said promptly. "Would you like to pinky swear upon it?"

"Your word of honor will suffice."

The lady retrieved a card from her reticule, handing it to Livy. Printed on thick ivory stock, the calling card had elegant lettering that spelled out three words, with an exclusive Mayfair address beneath.

"*Society of Angels?*" Livy canted her head. "Is that the name of your charity?"

"If you are interested in learning more about a group whose aim is to give intelligent and independent young ladies a worthy purpose, then come for luncheon on Monday." Charlie tucked her reticule onto her wrist and donned her gloves. "It would be best if you arrange to come unchaperoned. Good day, Willflowers."

With a graceful nod, Charlie glided off, disappearing into the crowd.

Fi stared after her. "When I grow up, I want to be just like her."

"Shall we go to her luncheon?" Glory asked.

Although Livy hated to admit it, her curiosity was piqued. She loved a good adventure. Nonetheless, she forced herself to logically consider Charlie's proposition.

"Why the mystery and lack of chaperonage?" she wondered aloud. "What is the agenda of the Society of Angels? We should discuss this before making any decisions—"

"There you are, girls!"

Pippa, nee Hunt and now the Countess of Longmere, approached in a swish of butter-yellow skirts. Pippa had inherited her mama's sunny coloring and disposition. When she entered a room, everything seemed to light up.

"I've been looking all over for you." Pippa hugged Livy and the girls in turn. "How are my favorite Willflowers?"

"We are well." Livy beamed at her. "And you, Pippa? How is married life?"

To Livy's surprise, a shadow passed over Pippa's lovely countenance, the way a cloud obscures the sun. It was gone the next instant, and Livy wondered if she had imagined it.

"It is splendid." Pippa's smile seemed a bit forced.

With a prickle of concern, Livy asked, "Is everything all right, Pippa?"

"All is well." Before Livy could decide whether she believed the assertion, Pippa gave her a teasing look. "Still the inquisitive poppet, I see."

"I am not a poppet." If Livy was going to win Hadleigh's heart, she would have to learn to project a more mature image. "Why does everyone think I am a child?"

"I apologize. It is just a habit." Pippa's eyes twinkled. "After all, I have known you since you were in leading strings."

"Can we not talk about me in leading strings?" Livy requested.

"As you wish." Pippa tilted her head. "By the by, who was that striking lady you were conversing with before I arrived?"

"Lady Charlotte Fayne," Fiona volunteered. "She is here representing a charity today."

Pippa's brow furrowed. "That is curious, since her name is not on the list."

Livy exchanged glances with the other Willflowers. "Curious indeed."

"What is the mission of her charity?" Pippa asked.

"Something about giving ladies a noble purpose," Fi said in an offhand manner, then smoothly changed the topic. "Any luck recruiting for the Hunt Academy?"

"We have had some interested volunteers," Pippa replied. "But we could always use more help, particularly in tutoring the students in reading and writing."

"I would be glad to assist," Glory said earnestly. "In addition to English, I am fluent in French, Chinese, and German. My Italian is not quite up to scratch, but I am working on it."

Glory was the linguist of the group. As she was a quarter Chinese from her papa's side, she had a special interest in China's culture and language.

"Thank you, Glory." Pippa looked over at her booth where potential candidates were lining up. "Duty calls, I'm afraid. Hopefully I shall see you all soon?"

"I almost forgot," Livy said. "Will you and the earl be attending our supper party this Saturday?"

"Oh dear, I forgot to reply, didn't I? How rude of me." Pippa bit her lip. "I shall have to consult Longmere. He has been, um, in demand of late."

This time, Livy knew she wasn't imagining the strain tautening Pippa's pretty features.

Not wanting to add to the other's distress, she said, "If your schedule permits, I do hope you both come."

"Thank you, Livy. It was lovely seeing you girls." With a flustered smile, Pippa headed off.

"Pippa doesn't quite seem herself, does she?" Fi murmured.

"She does not," Livy said with a frisson of worry. "What do you suppose is the matter?"

"According to the *on-dit*, Pippa's papa has no particular liking for his son-in-law." Fi was the expert on *ton* gossip. "That could cause tension."

Since Livy had overheard her mama and Mrs. Hunt discussing the matter, she knew that Mr. Hunt did not approve of Lord Edwin Longmere, who fancied himself a painter and ran with a fast crowd. At the same time, Mr. Hunt loved his daughter and supported her, despite their differences of opinion concerning her husband.

"Perhaps we should pay Pippa a visit and talk to her in private," Livy said. "She is the sweetest of ladies, and it pains me to see her unhappy."

The others nodded in agreement.

"Now, what were you saying before Pippa arrived?" Fi asked. "About Hadleigh?"

The mention of Hadleigh brought Livy back to her own problems.

"I am going to send him a personal note asking that he attend our supper party. Once he is there, I will endeavor to get him alone again. To convince him that we are meant to be together," Livy declared. "As Robert the Bruce once said, '*If at first you don't succeed, try and try again.*'"

"That is a splendid battle plan." Fiona winked at her. "It's not for nothing that you were voted Most Stubborn Debutante."

"Most *Determined*," Livy corrected.

And she was determined to win Hadleigh's heart. No matter what.

# SEVEN

Saturday evening, Ben found himself at the Strathavens' supper party, seated in the place of honor next to the host. As both Strathaven and the lady to Ben's right were engaged with others, Ben had time to mull over his decision to attend. In the end, he was here because of Livy's note:

*Please come. It would mean the world to me. It may be months until we meet again.*

Simple words, yet he'd been powerless to resist them. Written in Livy's bold and feminine hand, the message reminded him of all the letters she'd sent him during the dark period after Arabella's death. When he had been at his lowest, Livy had been there for him; he owed her for her sweet and steadfast loyalty. He could not bear the thought of them parting as anything but friends.

Not that he'd had a chance to converse with her. She was seated on the opposite side of the table, two chairs down. An epergne sat in his line of vision, yielding peek-a-boo views of her through the silver branches piled with fruit and fragrant blooms. He caught the dazzling smile she bestowed upon her supper partner, Lord Ian Sheffield.

Ben clenched his jaw. He had a clear view of Sheffield, and he

did not like the way the young blond Adonis was looking at Livy...
as if she were the next course of the delectable supper. Sheffield had
been sneaking glances at her bosom all night, and Ben was tempted
to tear the bounder's well-coiffed head off. Luckily, a liveried
footman arrived with the next course, interrupting Ben's
murderous fantasy.

As Ben slashed into the tender veal roulade, exposing its
innards of asparagus and lobster, he brooded over his reaction to
Sheffield. He told himself that he was *not* jealous. Knowing the
dangers of that green-eyed beast, he'd vowed to keep it locked
away.

Arabella had adored his possessiveness, poking and whipping
his bestial nature into a frenzy. She had been delighted every time
he fought a duel over her. Every time he lost a friendship. Every
time he stupidly and shamefully hurt another in the name of her
honor. Whenever he'd come home bloodied and damaged, she had
always wanted to fuck like mad.

Chen had helped Ben to realize how destructive his jealousy
had been. His temper had controlled him, rather than the other
way around. Now he took pains to separate his emotions from
tupping. He would never let himself be manipulated by a woman
again.

But Livy was different. Ben was protective of her...in a brotherly way. He wanted to keep her safe from cads like Sheffield who
might take advantage of her youth, innocence, and beauty.

And, hell's teeth, she *was* beautiful, he thought in bemused
wonder. He caught another glimpse of her through the center-
piece. His little queen had always been a pretty thing, but when
had she blossomed into an irresistible woman?

Seemingly overnight, Livy had unfurled with sensual perfection, every detail of her designed by nature to stir the male imagination. Her glossy coronet looked almost too heavy for the
tender stem of her neck, begging for a man's hand to take down
those thick tresses. Although her mouth was a bit wide for

conventional beauty, her lips formed an alluring pink pout. Her pale blue gown exposed her creamy shoulders, the rounded swell of her breasts...

*Bloody hell, this is* Livy. Ben's mind whirled in confusion. *Why are you thinking about her lips and breasts?*

At that instant, Livy's glance collided with his. His breath caught oddly when her eyes, the clear green of a mountain spring, lit up in a way that they hadn't for Sheffield. As he watched, she brought her hand to her *décolletage*, and he had to swallow as those fingertips trailed over the upper swell of her breasts. Christ, what was she doing...?

Then he realized that her fingertips had landed on a glittering object in the hollow of her throat: the tiny golden crown he had given her. She was showing him that she was wearing his gift. Then she smiled at him.

Beneath the table, he went instantly and ignominiously hard.

"Do you prefer it young and tender, Hadleigh?"

At the commanding voice, Ben swung his gaze to his host. Seated at the head of the table, the Duke of Strathaven was looking at him, raven brows arched over eyes too much like Livy's. Guilt seared Ben's insides, his neck heating beneath his cravat.

Devil and damn, had his host gleaned his salacious thoughts? While Strathaven was a famously devoted husband, he had been a rake in his younger days, and Ben did not doubt the man was familiar with the less than civilized workings of the male mind. And he was even more certain that Strathaven would not take kindly to Ben lusting over his daughter.

"I beg your pardon?" Ben cleared his throat. "To what are you referring?"

"The use of veal instead of beef in the roulade. Her Grace insisted it would make a difference." A crease formed between the duke's brows. "What else would I be talking about?"

"Nothing, Your Grace." Ben felt like a fool as well as the lowliest form of life. "I misheard you. The roulade is superb."

"I suppose that means my better half is right again," Strathaven said with a mock sigh. "I hope it doesn't go to her head."

"I heard that," Her Grace said clearly from the other end of the long table.

Strathaven raised his glass. "To my lady, whose hearing is as impeccable as her judgement."

The guests laughed and joined in the toast to the Duchess of Strathaven, who blushed and rolled her eyes. Livy, Ben noticed, was smiling at the affectionate banter between her parents. He wondered what it would have been like to grow up with the security of a loving family. His own had maintained the appearance of harmony until the incident that had led to his sister Beatrice's scarring. Then the familial façade of contentment had come tumbling down, and Ben's pursuit of vengeance against the man who'd injured Bea had resulted in more tragedy and pain.

Ben knew better than to trust happiness. He was neither equipped for nor deserving of it. These days, his goals were to maintain his hard-won self-mastery and, if possible, to atone for some of his past sins. If he could achieve those two things, he would count himself content.

"What do you think of Sheffield?"

At Strathaven's low-pitched query, Ben felt as if he'd suddenly been dropped into a jungle full of tar pits. He ventured forth warily. "In what sense?"

"In the sense of having him join my family."

*He is not good enough for Livy* was Ben's immediate thought. *No one is.*

He forced himself to say casually, "He is rather young, don't you think?"

Strathaven shrugged, the gesture belied by the shrewd gaze he had trained upon the fellow in question. "Sheffield is four years older than Livy. His fortune is large, and he will inherit a marquessate."

"But will he be a good husband to her?" Ben questioned in an undertone. "She is a rare sort of female, not cast from the usual mold."

Strathaven gave him a wry look. "If by *rare,* you mean that she is as headstrong as they come, then I cannot disagree. She gets it from her mama."

"Livy is a spirited girl who knows her own mind," Ben replied. "Any fellow lucky enough to marry her should appreciate those fine qualities."

*He had better treat her like the queen that she is,* he thought. *Or he will answer to me.*

Lines deepened on his host's forehead. "You do not think Sheffield appreciates her?"

Seeing Sheffield sneak another peek at Livy's bosom, Ben gritted his teeth.

"Sheffield is conventional," he said flatly.

"Given Livy's unorthodox ways, perhaps she would benefit from a strait-laced sort of husband. One who will keep her wilder impulses in check." Strathaven sighed. "These are the concerns that keep a man awake at night. Take it from me, my friend: daughters are the antidote to sleep."

If Strathaven knew of Ben's improper thoughts about Livy, he might never sleep again.

Ben's throat constricted. Bloody hell, he was behaving like a scoundrel. Strathaven and his lady had been good to Ben, welcoming him into their circle. Ben would not betray their friendship by sniffing after their daughter.

Most importantly, he could not hurt Livy. Even if he wasn't twelve years her senior and didn't have a past filthier than London's streets, he had appetites that made him an unsuitable husband for any well-bred virgin.

"That is why I do not plan to have a family, Your Grace," he said firmly. "I value my peace of mind."

"Would you believe I once said the same thing?" Strathaven looked down the table at his wife, then at Livy and his sons, his smile rueful. "Yet I have learned that one's sanity is a small price to pay for happiness."

Entering the orangery, Ben told himself he was doing the right thing. What needed to be done to salvage his friendship with Livy. After supper, the ladies had departed to the drawing room, leaving the gentlemen to their brandy and cigars. During the feminine migration, Livy had furtively slipped him a note.

*Meet me at our spot as soon as you are able.*

He had waited a few minutes then made the usual excuse to leave the male group. He went to the conservatory at the back of the house. As he opened the door, the scent of blossoming citrus enveloped him, bringing back memories of the cozy hours he had spent here. The Strathavens entertained family and close friends in the elegant glass-walled room, and Ben counted himself fortunate to be included amongst them.

The conservatory had been an oasis and shelter from the turbulence of his life. A place where he did not have to explain himself or worry about the outside world. Here in the airy room lush with life, he had enjoyed simple pleasures like playing cards and anagrams with an adolescent Livy, their bantering as much fun as the game. Sometimes they did not speak at all. It was one of Livy's many fine qualities that she was not prone to unnecessary chatter; their shared silence was as companionable as everything else they did together.

At present, the orangery no longer possessed that nostalgic innocence. Moonlight streamed through the glass, bathing all in a seductive, silvery glow. The foliage formed a fragrant maze, and as Ben followed the winding path, he felt as if he were venturing into the heart of man's first garden.

*Stick to your plan*, he told himself. *Mend fences with Livy. Then get the hell out of here.*

He found her standing in an alcove formed by potted palms and lemon trees. With a glass wall framing the outdoor garden behind her, she looked like a princess lost in the woods. Her hair was a shining crown, her skin pearl-like in its luminosity, her figure petite and curvy perfection in her gown of light blue crepe. In the past, he never had trouble reading her, yet now, cloaked in starlight, she seemed as mysterious as womanhood itself.

"I am glad you came," she said. "I wasn't sure you would."

The uncharacteristic tremor in her voice tightened his chest. He never wanted her to doubt his regard for her. The truth was he would do everything in his power to protect her...especially from himself.

He forced himself to say, "We should not be alone."

"What utter claptrap." Her voice regained its usual resolve, and she gave an impatient shake of her head. "We've been alone countless times in the past."

"That was before..." He caught himself; referencing their kiss was a bad idea. "Things are different now. Back then, you were a child—"

"So you *do* agree that I am grown up," she said doggedly.

"Devil take it." He expelled a frustrated breath. "That is not the point."

"It is entirely the point and why I needed to speak with you. We do not have long," she said in a rush. "But Hadleigh, I did not want there to be any awkwardness or animosity between us. I...I have missed you."

He had steeled himself to deal with her willful nature: the sweet yet stubborn essence of who Livy was. Yet he was wholly defenseless against the honest hurt glimmering in her eyes. He couldn't stem the tenderness that welled inside him. The longing that he, too, felt for the easy closeness of their past.

"I have missed you too," he said gruffly.

Hope lit her thickly lashed eyes. "You have?"

"You are my dear little friend." Out of habit, he reached out and chucked her beneath the chin. It was the gesture of an older brother...or had been, at any rate. Now the silky glide of her skin against his finger caused a hot quickening in his blood, and there was nothing sister-like in her shiver of response.

He jerked his hand away. Fought for control.

Her gaze searched his. "Why can't I be your friend *and* your *petite amie*?"

Her voice had a sweetly pleading quality that tested his self-discipline. Feminine entreaty never failed to set off a dominant drumbeat in his blood. Coming from Livy, a spirited and willful creature, it was doubly alluring.

And doubly forbidden.

*Are you mad? This is Livy,* he berated himself. *Get your mind out of the gutter.*

"Last time, you said that I am too young and impetuous to know what I want," she went on. "While I cannot deny our age difference, you *know* me. You cannot deny that I have always known my own mind."

"Even clever misses can be fooled by an infatuation." He strove for a brotherly tone. "Let it go, Livy. For the sake of our friendship."

"It is *not* an infatuation. I love you," she insisted.

Her words elicited a tingle of pleasure...which he quickly quelled.

"At your age, a lady changes her mind as frequently as she does her gloves," he said.

She narrowed her eyes. "Do *not* dismiss my feelings."

"I am trying to spare your feelings, little one. To protect you." He willed her to understand. "Livy, you deserve a better man than me. One whose honor is untarnished, whose life is not tainted by filth and darkness."

His sins were too many to count, his hands stained with the blood of the people he'd destroyed. Redemption was beyond his reach, but through his work with Chen's night watch, at least he was doing something good. The only area where he allowed his base nature to surface was tupping, and he always chose sophisticated partners whose carnal needs matched his own.

Livy knew nothing of this: the brutality of his past, the covert activities of his present, the depravity of his sexual tastes. She was pure and bright, and he wanted her to stay that way. To be the North Star that lit up his universe, whose shining beauty his darkness could never obscure.

"What if I do not wish to be protected?"

She tilted her chin up, and God help him, her defiance yanked at his dominant urges. That part of him that reveled in taming a lady...

"What if I want the same things that you do?" she persisted.

"You do not know what you want—"

"Dash it all! *You* do not get to tell me what *I* want." She poked him in the chest with her index finger, her eyes flashing with challenge. "And if you will not give it to me, then I will find it elsewhere."

"Elsewhere? What the bloody hell does that mean?"

Her lashes veiled her gaze an instant before she looked him straight in the eye. "Lord Sheffield finds me quite appealing."

Did she think she could *manipulate* him? Goad him into jealousy?

Icy rage flooded Ben. For years, Arabella, an *actual* expert, had played him like a puppet. The idea that *Livy* thought she could pull on his strings with her transparent ploy made him want to laugh or snarl...he didn't know which. Seeing that she was about to punctuate her childish threat with another poke to his chest, he captured her wrist in his hand. He backed her into the glass wall, caging her. Her awareness quivered in the sliver of air between them.

"Do not play games with me," he said.

Arabella would have backed down at the quiet menace of his tone.

Livy, however? Her gaze sparkled with defiance.

"I am not afraid of you," she retorted.

"You should be."

"*You* are the one who is afraid."

"And what, precisely, am I afraid of?"

"Of...of wanting me." She wetted her lips, a provocative swipe. "As much as I want you."

The chit wanted to play, did she?

He raised his free hand, trailing a fingertip down her throat, feeling her nervous swallow. He brushed the tiny crown before moving lower. Beneath his touch, her skin rose and fell in a silken wave. He stopped at the neckline of her gown, resting the tip of his finger on the fabric just above the crevice of her breasts.

Her eyes were glazed, her lips parting on uncontrolled breaths. Her fresh, girlish scent of peach blossoms was ripened with a woman's sensual musk. He knew she was aroused. Knew that beneath her bodice her nipples would be stiff and aching, and in the secret cove between her thighs, she would be wet with virginal dew.

Aye, Lady Olivia McLeod had grown into a vixen who tested his restraint. She had transformed from his trusted little friend to a young woman whose innocence and boldness was an arrow headed straight for his Achilles' heel.

She was temptation, and she was forbidden.

The recognition raged through him, yet he remained in control. As much as he craved dark games, he would never, ever allow himself to despoil his little queen. No matter how much he craved it.

"I do not play with little girls," he said softly. "Nor do I tolerate manipulation. Try it again, Livy, and our friendship will come to an end."

He released her. Saw the shock in her eyes and did not wait to see the pain.

Turning on his heel, he walked out.

# EIGHT

E ntering Lady Charlie's Mayfair townhouse with her friends, Livy was unsurprised to find the antechamber as elegant and fashionable as its owner. The marble floors and rosewood paneling gleamed, the scent of lemon polish mingling with the perfume of roses. The man who had opened the door introduced himself as Hawker, and Livy assumed he was the butler, although his strapping build, eye patch, and rough-hewn features gave him a distinct resemblance to a pirate.

As the girls trailed Hawker to the drawing room, Fiona whispered, "Charlie has a rather unusual butler, doesn't she?"

Livy thought everything about Charlie was uncommon, which was why the Willflowers were intrigued by her. Fiona was obsessed with the lady's style, Glory with the promise of adventure, and Livy...

She stifled a sigh. *I came because I need a distraction.*

Two nights ago, Hadleigh had rejected her...again. She was stubborn, but she wasn't stupid. He had made it abundantly clear that he was not interested in her—as a woman, at any rate. Perhaps he could only ever see her as a younger sister, she thought, the ache in her chest billowing. The wise course of action would be to cut her losses; if she persisted in trying to win his affections, she might end up losing him altogether. Where would she be then?

*You have to move on,* she told herself. *If you love Hadleigh, then you must not destroy your friendship. You owe him your loyalty... even if he doesn't want your heart.*

She'd shed tears on the sympathetic shoulders of her friends. Fi had suggested taking a break from Hadleigh. Since it was the rare instance in Livy's life when she did not know what else to do, she'd agreed. Allowing her mind to spin like the wheels of a stuck carriage was miring her deeper and deeper into despair. If she could not have her heart's true desire, then she would focus on her second love: adventure.

The butler deposited the girls in the drawing room, a chamber papered in blue silk and furnished with warm woods and goldenrod velvet. Small niches throughout the room displayed alabaster statues of Greek goddesses. It was an ideal setting for their hostess, who glided over to meet them.

"Welcome, Willflowers." Charlie greeted each girl warmly in turn. "I am delighted that you decided to join me today."

"But not surprised," Livy said.

Charlie smiled. "No, not surprised."

Livy had the impression that her hostess was rarely caught off guard. Although Charlie looked every inch the society lady in her ivory walking dress embroidered with a pattern of flowering vines along the hem, pearl pins studding her honey-gold hair, there was a shrewdness to her grey gaze that hinted at experience beyond tea parties and balls.

"I hope you do not mind an informal luncheon." Charlie waved toward the sideboard, where a petite woman dressed in a bombazine gown was arranging platters of meat, cheese, and fruit. "This is Mrs. Peabody. She keeps my house—and my life—running smoothly."

The housekeeper dipped her knees in a curtsy. She had shiny

brown hair wound in a thick coil at her nape and appeared to be of mixed race, perhaps with Asian ancestry.

"Pleased to make your acquaintance." Livy noted that Mrs. Peabody's bun was anchored in place by two silver hair sticks. "What lovely and unusual hair ornaments."

"Thank you, my lady." The housekeeper's golden gaze gleamed. "I find them quite handy."

"That will be all for now, Mrs. Peabody," Charlie said pleasantly. "I shall ring if we require anything else."

Inclining her head, the housekeeper departed.

Livy cleared her throat. "We can only evade our chaperones for a limited time. As such, we would like to know the purpose of this visit. Specifically, what the Society of Angels is all about."

"A woman who speaks her mind. I admire that." Charlie gave a brisk nod. "Why don't we sit and discuss my proposition?"

They arranged themselves around the coffee table, Charlie taking the wing chair in front of the tea service. While gracefully pouring the brew into *Sèvres* cups, she said, "My organization is an exclusive one. I am looking to expand it, and I believe the three of you fit the bill."

"Why would you think that?" Glory asked. "You barely know us."

Smiling, Charlie doctored the cups with sugar and cream before distributing them, and Livy felt her eyebrows rise. How did Charlie know the exact drink preference of each of the Willflowers? She had added a splash of cream to Fi's cup and two lumps of sugar to Glory's. When Livy sampled her own cup, the concoction was precisely how she liked it: deliciously creamy, with a sprinkle of sugar.

"I have gone to the liberty of doing some research." Charlie sipped her tea. "I know that the three of you have been friends for years. You attended Mrs. Southbridge's School for Young Ladies together, where you were first dubbed the 'Willflowers' by Lady

Sally Sackville after an incident involving her and Miss Rachel Tomlinson."

Livy blinked. The incident had happened years ago, and she didn't think the gossip had travelled that far. How did Charlie know all this?

"Sally Sackville was picking on Rachel just because Rachel's papa is in trade," Glory said, her hands balling in her lap. "She and her friends made a cruel game of reducing Rachel to tears. When we asked Sally to stop, she told us to mind our own business."

"And the headmistress refused to step in because Sally's papa possesses one of the most ancient titles in the land." Fiona's lips curled in contempt. "It was not the first time Sally used her position to torment others, either. Livy started Southbridge's the year before Glory and I did, and during that time Sally tried to bully *her*. All because Livy stood up for a maid who was blamed for something that Sally did."

"Which is why you arranged for Lady Sally to be, ahem, deluged with rubbish?" Charlie asked in neutral tones.

"To be fair, we did not deluge her with anything," Livy said. "She and her cronies had a habit of leaving malicious notes in Rachel's storage cupboard at school. We simply stuffed Rachel's cupboard full of refuse, and when Sally opened the cupboard..."

Livy lifted her shoulders. No one had *forced* Sally to open Rachel's cupboard, after all.

"Sally stopped harassing Rachel after that," Fiona said. "After all, what is worse: reeking of trade...or reeking of garbage?"

"Indeed." Charlie looked contemplative. "If I may ask, what prompted the three of you to act on Rachel's behalf?"

"Isn't it obvious? What Sally was doing was *wrong*," Livy said with a frown. "She picked on Rachel because she knew Rachel could not fight back."

"And Rachel is a sweet, shy girl whose so-called 'fault' was coming from a middle-class background." Fi's beautiful face was grim. "If that is a crime, then I, too, am guilty. The only reason

Sally and her band of simpering simpletons did not target me is because my papa is wealthier than Rachel's."

As Fi's papa was richer than Croesus and a powerful industrialist, few dared to cross him.

"While Livy's papa and mine have titles, both our mamas came from the working class." Glory held her slim shoulders proudly back. "In point of fact, before Mama married Papa, I helped her to collect fossils to sell at our fossils shop."

Having witnessed Glory's athletic feats, from fence climbing to horse riding, Livy could imagine the other girl scaling cliffs and committing other derring-do.

"And did you not fear repercussions for your actions?" Charlie inquired.

Fiona's look was that of an angel. "They would have to prove we did it."

Clearly fighting a smile, Charlie asked, "What about Sally? Surely she had to know."

"She retaliated by labeling us the 'Willflowers.'" Glory shrugged. "She meant the moniker to be derisive, but we could not have come up with a better name for ourselves."

"Besides, we had to see justice done," Livy said. "It was the principle of the thing."

"How splendid." Charlie beamed at them as if they were her star pupils. "You Willflowers are everything I had hoped you would be and more."

"You seem to know a lot about us." Livy narrowed her gaze. "And yet we know little about you or your charity."

Fiona, the Society expert, had managed to dig up a few facts about Charlie from Debrett's, scandal rags, and general gossip. Charlie had been born and raised abroad by her father, a gentleman scholar. Little was known about her until her marriage to the Marquess of Fayne. Even then, the Faynes had lived a private life abroad; after Fayne's death, his title had gone to a distant relative, and Charlie had apparently travelled extensively before settling in London.

She was rich, her reputation spotless. Men vied for her hand, but she showed no interest in marriage or dalliances. She appeared to be as she presented herself: an independent widow in her prime, with the power and propensity to live life on her own terms.

"For the right ladies, the Society of Angels will offer adventure, purpose, and the opportunity to develop their strengths to the fullest," Charlie said. "All while serving the greater good and seeing justice done. I, myself, will take on the role of mentor and guide, training my charges in a range of exciting and unusual skills." She looked at Livy, a twinkle in her eyes. "I can promise no needlework will be involved."

*How does she know that I hate needlework?* Livy wondered. *What precisely is Charlie's background to qualify her to be our mentor? And, more importantly...did she say exciting and unusual skills?*

"That sounds capital to me," Glory declared. "When can we enlist?"

"As to that, there is a final test," Charlie replied.

Glory's brow pleated. "There's a test?"

"I think we've already been tested," Livy said. "Twice, if I'm not mistaken."

Nodding slowly, Glory said, "The riddle at the Hunt Academy. What was the other one?"

Livy looked at Charlie. "Getting here unchaperoned, I presume?"

"Very good," Charlie said appreciatively. "From the moment we met, I had an intuition that the three of you would be a perfect fit with the Society of Angels. I do hope I am right."

"If evading chaperonage is the bar you set, then our success is guaranteed," Fi said airily.

"I'm afraid the last trial is not quite that simple." Picking up her tea, Charlie took a sip.

"You are planning to attend the Edgecombes' masquerade?"

The Earl and Countess of Edgecombe's masquerade was one of the biggest events left in the Season, the coveted invitations issued only to the *crème de la crème*. The Willflowers were going and had even coordinated their costumes.

"Yes." Livy canted her head. "Will the last test take place there?"

Charlie's lips curved above the rim of her cup. "Indeed."

# NINE

That Friday evening, Livy stood by a row of potted palms with Glory and Fi, taking in the glittering masquerade. Guests wore elaborate costumes in every hue, their jewels and ornaments sparkling beneath three enormous chandeliers. The mirrored walls amplified the sea of bodies and the whirl of the dancers over the parqueted floor. The strains of the orchestra could scarcely be heard above the gaiety of the crowd.

Livy's heart thumped with anticipation, but not because of the ball.

Because of the mission.

"Is it time?" she said under her breath.

"Be patient," Glory whispered back. "When their favorite waltz plays, Mama and Papa will dance, leaving us under the watch of Aunt Hypatia." She slid a look at their three chaperones, who were nearby chatting with guests. "Fi and I will keep Aunt Patty distracted, and *that* is when you make your move."

Through a bit of maneuvering, the Willflowers had managed to whittle their chaperonage down to one set of parents and an aunt. Glory had mentioned to her mama that the other girls' parents were tired from social demands. This was based in truth:

Livy had overheard Papa say to Mama that he would enjoy a quiet evening at home. Ever the sympathetic soul, Glory's mother had volunteered to take all the girls to the masquerade, and Livy and Fi's parents had accepted, offering to return the favor in the future.

The fewer chaperones the better when it came to Charlie's final challenge: to retrieve a diary from the Earl of Edgecombe's study. According to Charlie, Edgecombe had stolen the diary from a young governess named Marie Jardine and was using its contents to blackmail her into having an affair with him.

*The despicable blackguard*, Livy thought indignantly.

It had taken all of her willpower to be civil to Edgecombe at the receiving line. On the surface, he was a handsome man with auburn hair and patrician features, yet his predatory behavior made Livy's skin crawl. When he'd run a smirking gaze over her, calling her a "pretty chit," she'd wanted to growl at him. It had fueled her resolve to recover Miss Jardine's diary.

A smooth male voice cut into Livy's thoughts. "Ah, if it is not The Three Graces."

She turned to see Lord Ian Sheffield making an elegant leg to her and the Willflowers. He was dressed as a courtier from another century, his guinea-bright hair hidden beneath a powdered wig, his fit figure garbed in blue velvet, lace cascading at his collar and cuffs. After exchanging niceties with Glory's parents, Sheffield turned to Livy.

"Allow me to guess," he said with a charming smile. "You are Aglaea, the Grace of Beauty?"

*Botheration, did all my costume planning go to waste?*

Livy and her friends were wearing matching gold demi-masks, white sleeveless robes that fell in a straight column, and tasseled gold cords knotted at their waists. Dark wigs fashioned *à la Grecque* covered their hair. The only difference between their costumes lay in the large, gilded charms suspended from leather thongs around their necks: Fiona's was in the shape of a spindle, Glory's a measuring rod, and Livy's a pair of scissors.

Livy had thought the theme of their costumes was rather obvious. However, since arriving at the ball, everyone had mistaken them for The Three Graces.

Livy heaved a sigh. "I am not Aglaea."

"Pardon. Then you must be Euphrosyne, the Grace of Pleasure." Sheffield waggled his brows. "For in your presence, we mortals can feel naught but joy."

"Guess again," Livy said impatiently.

"Allow me to give you a clue, my lord." Fiona held up her golden spindle. "While I spin the thread of life, my second sister measures the length."

She gestured at Glory, who cheerfully waved her measuring stick.

Turning to Livy, Fi said, "My third sister here determines the span."

Livy lifted her golden shears, opening and closing them in a *snip snip* motion.

"Ah...you are The Three Fates. How clever." Sheffield's smile faltered for only an instant. "As you have the power to determine destiny, Lady Olivia, will it be mine to secure a spot on your dance card?"

As it would be ungracious to refuse the gallant request, Livy held out the card that was secured to her wrist by a ribbon. Sheffield signed it with a flourish before departing.

"I should have stuck to my original plan and dressed like a crone," Livy said in disgruntled tones. "No one is going to guess that I am Atropos in my current attire."

Livy had volunteered to be Atropos, the deadliest, and thus the most interesting, Fate. She had wanted to dress up the way the character was often portrayed: as an aged hag with missing teeth and an arresting stare. Fiona, however, had put her foot down.

"As your bosom chum, I could not allow you to don a scraggly grey wig and apply blacking to your teeth," Fi said with a shudder.

"We may be on a mission, but we cannot overlook the eligible *parti* here tonight."

*I can overlook them,* Livy thought.

The only gentleman she wanted was not here, and she did not give a farthing about attracting anyone else. She hadn't seen Hadleigh since their encounter in the orangery. When she'd fished for information from Papa, he had mentioned that Hadleigh had been absent from their mutual club and the usual places.

Was Hadleigh now intent upon avoiding her and her family? Thinking back, she regretted that she'd angered him with the mention of Sheffield. The attempt to make him jealous had been a stupid and childish thing to do. When she had the opportunity, she would apologize to Hadleigh and patch things up somehow. She told herself that the current break from him was probably for the best...and tried to believe it.

"More importantly, we needed matching costumes," Glory was saying in a hushed voice. "If we look interchangeable, at least from afar, it will be harder for Mama, Papa, and Aunt Patty to keep track of us."

For the next hour, Livy did the pretty and danced with various partners, including Sheffield. It was difficult to make polite chitchat when her mind was on the important task ahead of her. Finally, the favorite waltz of the Duke and Duchess of Ranelagh and Somerville played. As Glory's parents headed toward the dance floor, Glory cleared her throat.

"Aunt Patty, I wanted to ask you about a painting on the other side of the ballroom," she said. "I believe it is an allegorical representation of one of the Greek goddesses, and I am trying to figure out which one."

"How fascinating." A proud bluestocking, Hypatia Newton was dressed as an owl in a feathered brown frock, her eyes bright behind her spectacles. "Let us take a closer look, girls."

Hypatia steered a path through the crowd, Fi and Glory flanking her and keeping her occupied with questions.

Looking back at Livy, Glory mouthed, "*Go.*"

With a nod, Livy headed in the opposite direction. As she reached one of the arched entryways, a familiar awareness tingled over her nape. She spun around and surveyed the ballroom.

When she did not see Hadleigh, she expelled a breath.

*You just imagined the feeling, Livy.*

Straightening her shoulders, she hurried toward Edgecombe's study.

Ben arrived at the end of the hallway in time to see Livy disappear into Edgecombe's study.

*What the devil is she up to?* he thought grimly.

When he'd spied her furtive exit from the ballroom, he'd known that she was up to something. What in blazes could she want in Edgecombe's study? The fact that he, himself, was here to find the source of a deadly drug was a coincidence that filled him with unease.

In his younger days, Ben had run in the same pack as Edge-combe. Indeed, the two of them plus Viscount Bollinger and the Honorable Simon Thorne had been dubbed the Four Horsemen for their destructive rakehell ways. Their wealth and family connections had insulated them from repercussions, their noto-riety even gaining them admiration among the fast set. Yet Ben knew his fellow Horsemen for what they were: jaded sensation seekers who cared only for their own pleasures.

He was not proud of the fact that he'd once been one of them. When he had tried to get his marriage back on track five years ago, his first act had been to sever ties with the Horsemen, who'd been a bad influence on him and his duchess. Now to see Livy venturing into Edgecombe's lair...

A sense of foreboding clenched Ben's gut. Since the exchange in the orangery, he had avoided Livy. Losing her had been hard;

hurting her would be a far worse consequence. One he could not live with. Yet now his concern for her safety propelled him down the hallway. Casting a quick glance around to ensure that he was not seen, he twisted the knob and entered the study. He closed the door, muffling the sounds of the masquerade.

He scanned the luxurious male retreat dominated by heavy wood furnishings and studded leather upholstery. A fire crackled in the stone hearth by the seating area, and a large desk sat next to floor-to-ceiling windows framed by voluminous red drapes. No sign of Livy.

He crossed the room, the thick Aubusson muting his steps. Striding behind the desk, he crouched and said sardonically, "Good evening."

Livy stared up at him from her hiding place beneath the desk. She was wearing a sleeveless white robe, her bare arms hugging her raised knees, her eyes huge in the holes of her golden mask. She looked like a naughty nymph caught in the act of mischief.

"Hadleigh?" she breathed.

He held out a hand, hauling her from the cove. "Expecting someone else?"

"Um, no. Not really." She averted her gaze as she straightened her costume.

He noticed the golden shears suspended around her neck and, amidst his roiling concern, wry humor twinged. It figured that she would choose not only to be one of The Three Fates but the most lethal.

"I suppose there is an excellent reason for you to be here," he said. "Other than testing the limits of your own life span, Atropos?"

She beamed at him as if he'd paid her the greatest compliment. "You know who I am."

"I would know you no matter your disguise," he said sternly. "What I wish to know is what you are up to in our host's study."

"There's, um, a perfectly reasonable explanation..."

She trailed off as voices sounded just outside the study.

*Devil take it.* Ben scanned the room, identifying the best place of concealment. He dragged Livy over to the curtains and behind the roomy folds. Pressing himself against the wall, he held her securely against him, her back to his chest.

"Don't move," he whispered in her ear.

He felt her shiver as the door to the study opened.

# Ten

As male voices entered the study, Livy felt a tremor travel from head to toe. Partly the tremor had to do with the fear of discovery: she'd found the diary, now hidden in the concealed pocket of her petticoat. Mostly, though, the shivery feeling had to do with the fact that her backside was nestled against Hadleigh's front. His arm circled her waist, holding her snugly against his muscular form.

*"Don't move,"* he'd whispered in her ear.

*As if I would ever* want *to,* she thought dreamily.

The perils of the situation faded in Hadleigh's presence; he made her feel safe. He always had. Even if they were caught, he would protect her. She knew this to the core of her soul, and her fear dissipated. In its place, a wicked excitement sparked.

Conversation filtered through the thick layers of velvet. Thankfully, the men didn't sound too close to their hiding spot. The voices seemed to be coming from the seating area at the other end of the room.

"I say, Edgecombe," a nasal voice said. "This is a damned fine cigar. French?"

"Undoubtedly, Stamford," another man replied. "Edgecombe

h-here is a true connoisseur, and thus likes his cigars the way he likes his t-tarts."

As the men guffawed, Livy's cheeks heated. *I don't think they're talking about pastry...*

"Thorne has the right of it," Edgecombe drawled. "A good French light-skirt is the antidote to domestic drudgery."

"An eager bit o' muslin is a fine way to lift a man's spirits," a fourth man agreed.

"More than just his spirits, I daresay," Stamford said with a snicker.

The men laughed again, and Livy shuddered with disgust. She would call these men swine, but that would be an insult to pigs. Hadleigh's arm tightened around her.

"It will be over soon," he murmured into her ear.

Livy realized that the moment *would* end soon...and she didn't want it to. She wanted to prolong this closeness with Hadleigh. In their velvet cocoon, the tension of their recent interactions had vanished. He was holding her, whispering to her, just like she had dreamed he would.

What if she didn't have another chance to be like this with him? She had to make the most of the opportunity. She would live up to her costume and decide her own destiny.

She relaxed further into Hadleigh's embrace. Since her costume was cut in a classical Grecian style, she had dispensed with her usual voluminous layers. Beneath her white tunic, she wore only a chemise, single petticoat, and short stays, and she could feel every part of Hadleigh pressed up against her. Goodness, he was like a wall of muscle...with a distinctly protruding edge.

Her eyes widened. *Zounds. Is that his male member?*

The night she'd kissed him at her birthday ball, she'd glimpsed the bulge in his trousers. It had appeared sizable from afar. Poking into her spine, it felt like a huge fire iron. Intrigued, she wriggled against him.

"Stop that."

His whisper smoldered with warning...and something else. That husky edge had been present in his voice when he'd issued carnal commands to Cherise Foxton in the stable. It had made Lady Foxton mewl in desperate delight and beg for more—and Livy squirm with jealousy and longing.

Because she had wanted Hadleigh to speak to *her* that way.

In that deliciously dictatorial tone that said, *You will listen to me because you belong to me and me alone.*

An impulse took hold of Livy. She could not afford to move much; to do so would disturb the curtains and give them away. Instead, she gently rocked back against Hadleigh, and his response was instantaneous: his harsh breath scalded her ear, his arm cinching tighter around her waist. His member became a thick, insistent pole lodged against her spine. The sensation of being surrounded by all the male virility that was Hadleigh made her feel light-headed.

The more she rocked against him, the more sensitive she felt. The air trapped by the curtains was a humid caress over her throat and décolletage. Her breasts ached, the tips taut and tingling against her stays. When she squeezed her thighs together, dampness trickled from her core.

The world faded away. There was only the desire raging through her like a fever.

And the cure was Hadleigh.

Ben gritted his teeth. Given her determined nature, Livy excelled at anything she put her mind to. At the moment, she seemed intent upon driving him out of his godforsaken mind. And he could not stop her without giving away their presence to the bastards on the other side of the curtain.

His former Horsemen cronies Edgecombe, Thorne, and Bollinger were scoundrels who'd think nothing of ruining a lady's reputation or using it as leverage to get what they wanted. Stamford, who appeared to be the group's newest recruit, had a reputation for being equally ruthless.

Thus, Ben had no choice but to hold still as Livy rubbed against him like a needy kitten. The rounded curves of her derriere rocked against his groin, testing the limits of his self-control. To his eternal damnation, he was hard. Her blend of innocence and sensual intuition made her a better tease than the most experienced of courtesans. She somehow managed to wedge his erection into the crevice of her arse, caressing his turgid length between her pert curves.

*Bloody fuck.* He bit back a groan as her movements wrung a drop of seed from his tip.

He reminded himself of all the reasons this was wrong. This was Livy: she was too young and innocent. She meant too much to him and was the daughter of his closest friend.

His arguments were countered by the naughty persuasion of Livy's bottom. He tried to hold her still, tightening his arm around her waist and putting his other hand on her hip. That only made matters worse, for then she was tucked up even closer, and he felt the lushness of the curve beneath his palm as well. Christ, she had perfect hips, the kind a man could hold onto as he plowed her from behind...

*No.* He clenched his jaw, fighting to master himself. *Do not go there.*

But Livy would not hold still. She started a new circular motion that dotted his brow with sweat. He began to recite the Kings of England in his head. When that didn't work, he tried the breathing techniques he'd learned from Chen. When that failed to override the sublime cradle of Livy's arse, he resorted to praying.

*Please, God, don't let me do this. Don't let me ruin the one good thing in my life...*

"Well, gentlemen, back to business, eh?" Edgecombe drawled. "We've rounds to make."

The men left the study—about bloody time.

Hearing the door close, Ben shoved his way out of the curtains. He dragged in breaths, fighting his raging arousal. The tap on his shoulder nearly made him jump. He swiveled to see Livy standing there, her eyes glowing jade jewels in her mask, her cheeks flushed beneath the rim of gold.

"I want you, Hadleigh," she whispered. "Please won't you make love to me?"

Her entreaty nearly undid him. Christ, how could he have not known that his little friend would mature into the stuff of his deepest, darkest fantasies? She was the very blend of spirit and submissiveness that never failed to arouse him. Combined with her wanton innocence, she was a Siren's song to his lustful nature.

God, *God,* how he wanted her...

He curled his hands. *You cannot have her. You are not good enough for Livy, and you cannot hurt her...the way you've hurt so many others.*

He opened the cages of his past, forcing himself to confront another pair of eyes, these ones staring up at him in the darkness. *Hold on,* he heard himself shout. His soul rumbled with the force of the oncoming train as she smiled and let go, choosing death over his attempt to right a wrong...

Arabella surfaced from the swamp of memory, rising in a blood-soaked chemise. She walked toward him, her raven hair tangled and wild, her eyes unblinking. *"You wanted this pregnancy. Now it has killed me and our babe, and it is all your fault..."*

A man's voice cut in. *"I beg of you, Hadleigh, have mercy. Don't destroy me, I didn't mean to hurt your sister..."*

With will borne of practice, Ben shut his demons back into their cages. They had served their purpose. He was in control once more and aware of what needed to be done.

*I'm destined to hell, but I will not take Livy with me.*

"I will never make love to you, Olivia. There is no future for us," he said with cold ruthlessness. "You cannot give me what I need. I want a real woman, not some silly little girl."

She blinked, the sheen in her eyes slamming into him like a fist. Yet Livy, being Livy, didn't give up.

"I know I shouldn't have tried to make you jealous...with Sheffield, I mean," she said, her voice hitching. "That *was* childish, and I'm sorry. But if you'll only give me a chance—"

"How many times must I reject you in order for you to understand?" he said harshly. "I'm telling you once and for all: give up your juvenile fantasies and stay the bloody hell away from me."

He saw the moment he broke her. The pain in her eyes reminded him of how he'd felt, beaten and bloodied, in the alleyway. Yet that suffering had been a necessary step in his healing, and it would be for her too.

Hell, he was her goddamned opium, even if she didn't know it. But he did. Unlike that unfeeling drug, however, he refused to destroy her. His little queen...who meant too much to him.

"You want me to stay away?" Livy choked out. "Fine, I'll go. And you'll never have to see me again."

She ran from him.

Hands fisted by his side, he let her go.

# ELEVEN

*1844, STRATHAVEN ESTATE, SCOTLAND*

*Livy is 15; Ben is 27*

Livy wandered down the holly-festooned halls of Strathmore Castle. It was Christmas Eve, and the sounds of merriment spilled from the drawing room. Her parents were hosting a week-long holiday party with over three dozen guests in attendance. After supper, the furnishings had been pushed aside for an impromptu dance party, with Aunt Thea playing the pianoforte and Aunt Rosie singing along. Everyone was having a wonderful time, and no one observed Livy leaving. She had noticed that someone was missing.

Hadleigh. She hadn't seen him since supper.

Livy wove in and out of the public rooms, looking for him. Perhaps he had gone up to bed, but it was early yet, and she was concerned about him. She hadn't seen him for a few months, and when he and his duchess had arrived yesterday, he'd looked wearier than she'd remembered. His eyes seemed permanently bloodshot, and he'd dropped a stone, his tall frame approaching gauntness.

*Is he ill?* she fretted.

She'd tried to ask him about it, but he'd ruffled her hair and told her not to worry. But she *was* worried. Something was wrong with Hadleigh. She'd tried to ask her parents, but they were also keeping mum about it.

*"Perhaps we should send for the physician?"* she'd persisted.

Papa had sighed. *"Hadleigh isn't ill. You are too young to understand, poppet, but suffice it to say, the nature of his problem requires that he address it himself. No doctor—and no one—can fix it for him. Trust me, it is best to leave him be."*

Livy did not believe in letting things be. Especially when her friend's well-being was at stake. Thus, she continued searching for Hadleigh, and her tenacity was rewarded when she found him in the upstairs gallery. He was on the floor, slumped against a wall, his long legs splayed in front of him. His eyes were closed. He'd lost his jacket and cravat somewhere, his shirt open at the throat and his waistcoat splotched with wine stains.

Hadleigh was always impeccably dressed. At the moment, however, he was a frightful mess. Anxiety percolated through her: she'd never seen him this way before.

"Hadleigh?" she said loudly to wake him. "What is the matter with you?"

His long lashes flicked open. He stared at her with eyes that were red-rimmed and more black than blue. This was a stranger's gaze, and it chilled her nape.

"Livy?" His gaze focused, his voice emerging thick and slurred. "What're you doing here?"

"The better question is what are *you* doing." She peered at him. "Are you in your cups?"

"I'm foxed, all right." He gave a strange, hoarse laugh. "Wish it were just that, little love."

Not understanding, she frowned. "What else have you overindulged in?"

He looked at her with those dark, lost eyes. "Life, Livy. I've had too much of life."

"Don't say that," she protested. "Life is a gift, and you should be glad you've many more years ahead of you."

"I'm tired," he whispered.

"Of what?"

"Of running from ghosts. So many of them…" Although his gaze was aimed at her, it was as if he was looking beyond her into some spectral world that only he could see. "One day they will catch up to me and wreak their vengeance." His lips twisted. "Perhaps they already have. That is why my life is hell…just like I deserve."

"Why would anyone seek vengeance upon you?" She forced herself to ask the question. "What have you done?"

"What *haven't* I done?" Anguish slashed deep lines around his mouth. "I've committed every sin, little queen. Everything I've done commits me to perdition."

Unable to bear his pain, she sat down on the floor next to him. She didn't know what he had done. She only knew that he had saved her life and, in the three years since, been a true and steadfast friend.

"Not everything." She nudged her shoulder gently against his. "You saved my life, remember?"

"You are my one good deed." His laugh was mirthless. "And as sweet and pure as you are, even you cannot outweigh my sins."

As he rubbed a fist over his eyes, she noticed he was clutching something.

"What have you got there?" she asked.

He slowly opened his palm, and Livy recognized what lay within. She had helped her mama tie together the bunches of leaves and bright red berries, hanging them in rooms throughout the house in the spirit of Yuletide cheer.

She tilted her head. "Why do you have a sprig of mistletoe?"

"Wanted a kiss from Arabella. But she wouldn't kiss me...even with this."

His misery tore at Livy's heart. She couldn't fathom why his wife would refuse a kiss. Her own parents kissed *all* the time. In fact, her brother Chris had taken to groaning, *"Not in front of the children, please."*

"Perhaps she refused because you're inebriated?" Livy suggested tentatively.

"No, it's because I'm me. A wreck of a man. Not worth a kiss... not worth anything." His eyelashes lowered, settling against his cheeks.

Within seconds, he was asleep again.

Livy bit her lip. He looked more relaxed, but she couldn't leave him here when he was in such a state. Anyone could stumble upon him, and she was certain he wouldn't want to be found this way.

She pushed his shoulder. "Hadleigh?"

"Hmm?" He didn't open his eyes.

She spoke directly into his ear. "We need to get you back to your chamber."

He winced, opening one bloodshot eye. "Too tired."

"You cannot sleep here, and you are too heavy for me to carry. Get up, and I will support you."

Grumbling, he managed to get onto his feet, swaying, and she ducked beneath his arm.

"Easy, there," she said. "I have you. Just lean on me."

She navigated their way to his guest chamber, which was luckily on the same floor. By the time she got him inside, she was perspiring from her exertions. He might look skinny, but he was all lean muscle, all of it leaning heavily upon her. Somehow, she got him to his bed, and he flopped onto the mattress with a moan.

"Don't know why you're complaining," she muttered. "I did all the work."

He snored in reply.

Rolling her eyes, she wrestled off his shoes and pulled the counterpane over him. She paused to look at his face, which even in slumber was not peaceful. His muscles twitched, grooves deepening here and there against his sculpted bones. He moved restlessly, dislodging the blanket, and that was when she noticed that he still had the mistletoe clutched in his hand.

*I'm me. A wreck of a man. Not worth a kiss...not worth anything.*

Sorrow squeezed her heart. How could Hadleigh think such a thing? She did not know his past, and it did not matter. Because she knew *him*. Knew that he was honorable and good, worthy of the best life had to offer.

Impulsively, she leaned down and kissed his lean cheek.

"Merry Christmas, Hadleigh," she whispered. "You are deserving of all good things. May your dreams be sweet."

He mumbled something, his features relaxing.

She doused the lamps and closed the door softly behind her.

## PRESENT DAY

The afternoon after the masquerade, Livy and her friends entered Charlie's drawing room. Charlie rose from the chaise longue in a sweep of cerulean moire silk.

Smiling, she said, "Welcome, Willflowers. Do you have something for me?"

Opening her reticule, Livy removed the small leather-bound journal and brought it over to Charlie. "Miss Jardine's diary."

Taking it, Charlie waved them to the seats around the coffee table. She sat as well, flipping through the journal before putting it aside.

"Splendid work," Charlie said warmly. "I shall return this to its rightful owner, who I know will be most grateful. You have saved her from Edgecombe and his nasty plan and allowed her to move onto her future. She is in love, you see, and could not in good conscience accept her gentleman's offer until she was free of the blackmailer."

The thought of love and marriage was more than Livy could bear. After Hadleigh had smashed her heart into smithereens last eve, she wanted nothing to do with either. She was done with Hadleigh. Done with chasing after him. Done with him patronizing her and treating her like an infantile idiot. If he did not want her, then she had better things to do with her time.

Helping others seemed like a good place to start.

On either side of her, Fi and Glory watched her with concern. Her bosom chums knew her state of affairs: they had comforted her in the retiring room at the masquerade while she'd wept over the shards of her dreams. They had suggested canceling their appointment with Charlie until Livy was in better spirits, but Livy had insisted on coming today.

She shoved aside thoughts of her ill-fated love and addressed Charlie.

"It was our pleasure and duty to help," she said resolutely. "Now that we have done our part, we wish to learn more about membership in the Society of Angels."

A smile touched Charlie's lips before she spoke.

"The Society of Angels is an agency that offers investigative services to female clientele," Charlie said in business-like tones. "It is an organization run by women for women, the first of its kind in London."

Livy tilted her head, absorbing this new information. Given that sleuthing was a profession that ran in her family, she did not find Charlie's proposition as outlandish as other young ladies might. In truth, the notion of investigating sounded intriguing... and like the perfect remedy for a broken heart.

"I started this organization because the needs of women are not well served by agencies run by men," Charlie continued. "The concerns of female clients are often not taken seriously, the clients themselves labelled as 'silly' or 'hysterical.' And if the cause of a woman's travails happens to be a man in power? Well, you can guess the outcome."

Charlie's words had a razor-sharp edge.

"Do you speak from personal experience?" Livy asked.

Charlie acknowledged her question with a nod. "I was once a young woman in need of assistance. I had the resources to afford the very best. Time after time, I was let down—if not swindled outright—by the male investigators I hired. Some even tried to take advantage in other ways until I dissuaded them."

Livy's nape tingled at the flinty look in Charlie's eyes. The lady reminded her of a bumblebee: golden elegance that housed a deadly stinger.

"In the end, I took matters into my own hands. I acquired the necessary skills to conduct my own inquiries and decided to use those skills to benefit other women in need. I have assisted ladies who had lost all hope of finding answers, helping them when no one else would."

"Jolly good!" Approval shone in Glory's hazel gaze.

"The Society generates a handsome profit, but no woman is turned away because of financial hardship. I ask my clients to pay what they can afford," Charlie said. "For instance, I assisted a dowager duchess by uncovering her nephew's plot to lock her in an asylum and steal her wealth. She expressed her gratitude through a donation that covers the costs for women like Marie Jardine.

"The demand has become such that it exceeds what I am able to do alone. I have agents—genteel spinsters, widows, and working-class women—who assist me, but I realized that I have another goal: to pass on my knowledge and legacy to a new generation of young ladies."

"Like a finishing school for female investigators," Livy breathed.

"Exactly. I want to teach exceptional young women to become

the best that they can be, mentally and physically." Charlie leaned forward. "Society uses the label of the 'weaker sex' to keep us from recognizing our true strength. I was once like you: a sheltered miss who was taught from birth how to be a lady. My worth was measured by my ability to make a good match. When it came to courtship, my looks and fortune were seen as my main merits. My spirit was deemed an inconvenience, my intelligence an even bigger flaw."

"But you did make a good match." Fiona tipped her head, her red curls swinging to one side. "You married the Marquess of Fayne."

"Which is how I learned that entrusting one's happiness to anyone but oneself is a mistake." Charlie's words were matter-of-fact. "Learn from me: independence, not love, is the key to happiness. Never give up who you are. For anyone or anything. And that is my ultimate goal for my Angels: to give them the ability to choose their own destiny."

For Livy, the words resonated like a church bell. After all, she had invested her dreams in another, and what did she have to show for it? Nothing but tears and a broken heart. Perhaps Charlie was right. Perhaps true fulfillment came from self-reliance and the power to determine one's future.

"Where do we sign up?" Glory asked.

"There is one more thing. An inviolable condition," Charlie said. "If you decide to become an Angel, you must take a vow of secrecy. You are to tell no one about the group—not your family, your friends, or even lovers—without my express permission. This is to protect the safety of all involved in my organization. Do you want time to consider my proposition?"

Livy looked at her friends and saw her answer in their eager faces.

"We do not need more time. We accept." She drew a breath. "There is, however, a problem."

"Problems are merely solutions waiting to happen." Charlie took a sip of tea. "Go on."

"My parents are taking me back to Scotland in a fortnight, and I will not be back in Town for several months," Livy said glumly. "If you wish to start training us immediately, Fiona and Glory will be available, but I will not."

"We don't want to start without you," Glory protested.

"We'll wait for you," Fi said simultaneously.

Gratitude filled Livy. She had the *best* of friends...and she would not hold them back.

"You mustn't refuse the opportunity on my account," she said firmly. "Perhaps I can join when I get back from Scotland—"

"Would you like to stay in London and train to be an Angel?" Charlie asked.

Livy's nod was fervent. "More than anything."

Charlie smiled. "Then, my dear, leave it to me."

# TWELVE

The moon's silvery glow limned the outline of the figure lying face-down in the alley behind the butcher shop. A chill snaked through Ben as he saw the unmistakable reddish gleam of hair. He'd hoped against hope that the urgent summons Chen had received had been a mistake.

"Found 'im when I was tossing out the rubbish, Master Chen." The somber tones came from the butcher, a man with a stained apron tied over his bulging midsection. "Thought you'd want to know. Poor sod were one o' your students, weren't 'e?"

"He was," Chen said quietly. "Thank you, sir. I will take care of things from here."

The butcher nodded, making the sign of the cross before heading back into his shop.

Crouching next to the body, Ben inhaled before rolling it over. Pete stared up into the heavens, his gaze a still pond that reflected the white crescent moon. Twin rivulets of blood were crusted beneath his nostrils and over his lips.

Ben's eyes grew hot and gritty. He didn't know why he was so affected. He hadn't known Pete long and yet...

*He was just a lad. It's such a damned waste. If only I'd convinced him to leave the streets...*

Kneeling on the other side, Chen closed the boy's eyes.

"You were always running," the healer murmured. "Now may you finally be at rest."

Grief swelled, and Ben fought it off by searching for clues to Pete's death. He didn't have far to look: clutched in the lad's still-warm fingers was the familiar red box with the entwined "D" and "B." Opening the box, Ben saw it was empty, and a sudden fury rose in him.

"How did Pete get his hands on this poison?" he bit out.

"Probably the way he attained most things," Chen replied.

The healer was going through Pete's coat with methodical precision. He removed a golden disc from Pete's inner pocket. A fob watch—an expensive one, Ben reckoned, by the exquisite filigree work on the cover.

Chen opened it. "There is an inscription: *To my husband and our everlasting love. P.*"

"Do you think Pete filched the drug and the watch from the same cove?" Ben asked grimly.

"It is possible." Chen's features were stark. "The watch is a lead, and we must try to find its owner."

With swirling misgivings, Ben mounted the steps to the Strathaven residence a week later.

*What does Strathaven want? Did he find out about Livy and me? Coming here is a mistake.*

When he'd received the duke's summons, Ben had debated putting the other off. However, he could not think of an adequate excuse, especially since his friend would soon be leaving for Scotland. If Strathaven merely wanted to say good-bye, then Ben's refusal would not only be ill-mannered but would perhaps raise suspicion.

Guilt mangled Ben's insides as the butler greeted him and led him toward his host's study. He felt as nervous as a damned schoolboy as he looked for Livy. He both dreaded and hoped that she would come dashing toward him the way she had in her younger days, her green eyes bright with welcome. Her presence had a way of banishing shadows, and given the darkness of the last week, he found himself craving her light.

Today, however, Livy was nowhere to be seen, and her absence tightened the knot of longing, frustration, and confusion in his gut. Pete's death had been a tragic reminder of how fleeting life could be...and how it should not be wasted. If Ben were to die tomorrow, he knew that his biggest regret would be not making things right with Livy.

Yet how could he restore their special friendship when Livy insisted that she wanted to become his lover?

Just thinking about Livy and the word "lover" in the same sentence sent him spiraling down a forbidden path. For an instant, he felt her curvy bottom rocking against his cock, tasted the sweetness of her lips pressed so innocently against his. Her whispered words emerged from his darkest fantasies: *I wanted you to touch me, kiss me. To be with me the way you were with her...*

Simultaneously, memories of their friendship flashed through his head. Twelve-year-old Livy, wet and bedraggled, pledging her allegiance to him. Adolescent Livy, playing games and sharing her schoolmiss adventures with him. Searching him out at parties and making sure he was never alone. And Livy of just a year or two ago, keeping him company through her letters, easing his solitude in a way that only she could...

His throat cinched. She was so damned precious to him.

How could he lust after her when he should think of her as a sister? How could he even contemplate corrupting the one person who'd been determined to see the best in him? How could he wake up in the middle of the night, with his cock hard as a pike and his mind filled with torrid fantasies of claiming Livy?

The answer to all of that was simple. He could *not*.

*It is good that Livy is leaving for Scotland,* he told himself. *The absence will help us both. If I am invited to visit, I will make excuses. Surely the months apart will help us both regain our bearings. By then, she will have moved on from her silly tendre and perhaps found a proper suitor. And I...*

*I will be alone.* His chest tightened. *As I deserve to be.*

Arriving at the study, Ben was ushered in by Strathaven.

"Good afternoon, old boy." The older man was dressed in a Prussian blue frock coat, his striped silk cravat fashionably knotted. His manner was amiable, with no sign of animosity in his pale-green eyes...thank God. "I have been waiting for you."

Ben followed the other to the wing chairs by the fire. As he settled into the soft leather, he recalled all the other times they'd reposed here, discussing business and other mutual interests. They shared a similar temperament, being reserved gentlemen who respected the need for privacy.

Strathaven gestured to a cart of refreshments. "Will you take tea or coffee?"

Ben's illicit thoughts about Livy, coupled with the fact that he was now in her papa's presence, made him long for something significantly stronger. Strathaven stocked the best whisky, sourced from an ancient distillery in Scotland, but Ben had sworn off drink since his hard-won recovery. Now was not the time to pick up his old bad habits.

"Coffee, please." Accepting the cup, Ben took a drink of the brew.

"Haven't seen you of late at the club," Strathaven said in conversational tones.

"I have been busy."

Working with Chen to trace the origins of the lethal drug had been a welcome distraction. Ben had spent the last week visiting countless watchmakers, trying to discover the owner of the watch found on Pete's body, who might also be the source of the drug. Thus far, he'd had no luck.

Chen had fared better with the snuffbox, tracing it to a jeweler on Pall Mall. The jeweler had recognized the box, minus the initials which had been painted on after he'd sold them. Apparently, he'd received a large shipment of the boxes from China several months ago; soon after he'd placed one in the shop window, a manservant had come by and purchased the lot. Unfortunately, the jeweler had no further information about the servant or his employer.

The dead end did not deter Ben. He was determined to forge on in the investigation. To ensure that Pete's death would not go unanswered for.

Strathaven lifted his dark brows. "Anything of note?"

"Just business." Ben switched the subject. "How are the trip preparations for Scotland coming along?"

"You know my duchess. She has everything well in hand." Strathaven's eyes held a glint of amusement. "My job is to stay out of her way."

"Is that why you are hiding in the study?"

"Not hiding, my friend. Enjoying one of the many perquisites of marriage," the duke said a bit smugly. "Emma excels at domestic management, and I am happy to let her have at it. In fact, she baked my favorite cake...probably to distract me and keep me out of her hair, but I have no complaints. Care for a slice?"

Having sampled the lady's culinary skills—which were highly unusual for a duchess—Ben did not turn down the offer. The cake was delicious, light and fluffy, layered with a citrus curd and whipped cream. Not for the first time, he felt a pang of envy. He wondered what it would be like to have a wife who cared about one's preferences and made one's life easier, not more difficult. A wife who was loving and devoted and who demanded the same in return from her husband.

"Surely you did not invite me over merely to boast?" he asked mildly.

Strathaven's lips twitched. "Not to boast, no. Perhaps to lead by example."

"You forget that I've been married." Hearing the bitterness seep through, Ben lightened his tone. "Marriage is an institution which I have no desire to be locked into again."

"Not all marriages are like Bedlam. But I take your point that it is not a decision to be made lightly." Strathaven's expression turned somber. "And that brings me to the reason I asked you here today: I would like for you to keep an eye on Livy."

Ben stilled. "What do you mean? She'll be in Scotland with you, won't she?"

"There has been a change of plans." Strathaven drummed his fingers on the arm of his chair. "Livy has set her heart on joining some charity headed by Lady Fayne. Apparently, this group aims to help females in unfortunate circumstances, and Livy has decided she must start straight away. She asked to remain in London while our family sojourns in Scotland."

"Surely you are not going to allow it?" Ben asked in disbelief. "A girl her age, alone in Town unsupervised?"

"Of course I would not allow her to be unsupervised." Strathaven frowned. "She will be staying with Lady Fayne, who has offered to be her chaperone. And Fiona Garrity and Glory Cavendish will be part of this group as well."

Unease prickled through Ben. Since when had Livy been interested in genteel charities? She was not the pamphlet-writing, handkerchief-sewing type.

Suspicion brewed in him. "And you trust this Lady Fayne?"

"My wife has entertained Lady Fayne several times and is quite taken with her. Says the lady is a 'modern woman'...whatever that means." Strathaven crossed his long legs. "I, myself, have made discreet inquiries into Lady Fayne's background. Although she has not been in London long, the sticklers sing her praises. Even the

Dowager Duchess of Moncrief vouches that Lady Fayne is a woman of great virtue, and that old harridan does not like anyone. Lady Fayne appears to be what everyone says she is: a wealthy, independent widow with a penchant for doing good."

Ben set his jaw. "Regardless, I do not trust her with Livy."

"You sound like me." Strathaven's smile was wry. "Her Grace informs me that I have a tendency to be overprotective and overbearing...and that is just as a husband. She says when it comes to being a papa, I am even worse."

"Your caution is justified." Leaning forward, Ben chose his words with care. "Livy is not an ordinary sort of female. While she is undoubtedly clever and capable, she needs someone to look after her. To make sure she is acting in her own best interests."

"I wish you had been there during my argument with Her Grace. I could have used the support." Strathaven dragged a hand through his dark silver-threaded hair. "The truth is it wasn't just Emma who convinced me, it was Livy herself. You know my daughter, Hadleigh. All her life, she has been a spirited girl full of purpose and zeal. She has always treated life as an adventure."

Nostalgia warmed Ben's chest. He had always loved Livy's natural exuberance. She explored life the way a child looks for seashells upon a shore: with tireless delight. No one—not even a jaded bastard like him—could be bored in her presence.

"Of late, however, my daughter has lost her shine," Strathaven said in concerned tones. "According to my wife, Livy hasn't been herself since her birthday ball, and I have noticed it too. Perhaps it is a normal part of the maturation process, of coming into womanhood. But I do not wish for Livy's spark to be dimmed...by anything. When she asked permission to join this Society of Angels, she had that gleam of excitement in her eyes again. And I could not say no."

Ben understood the difficulty of saying no to Livy. Yet he also understood the necessity, at times, of doing so. Perhaps more than her own parents did.

"When she is not volunteering, what of her free time?" he pointed out. "Do you trust Lady Fayne to keep a close eye on Livy, especially with Sheffield and other suitors milling about?"

"Not entirely. Which is where you come in."

Ben stilled, his heart lurching. "Me?"

Strathaven sat forward in his chair, his expression intent. "You were there when Livy needed you most, my friend, and I am asking you to look after her once again. There is no one I trust more with my daughter. She listens to you, insofar as she listens to anyone, and I know with you she is in good hands."

Ben flashed back to the last time he'd had his hands on Livy. The plump curve of her hip beneath his palm, the torturous bliss of her bottom rubbing against him...

"This is a lot to ask, I know." Apparently mistaking Ben's silence for refusal, Strathaven said earnestly, "It would be for a few weeks only, at which time I will return to fetch her. I would consider it a personal favor and would be in your debt—"

"There will be no talk of debt." Ben gathered himself. "I would be happy to keep an eye on Livy in your absence."

*You will keep your eyes on her,* he lectured himself. *And your bloody hands off.*

Relief softened Strathaven's features. "You have my gratitude. She looks to you like an older brother, and despite her desire for independence, I am certain she will find your presence a comfort. In fact, it is strange that she has not burst in on us the way she has always done."

*You want me to stay away?* Livy's voice rang in Ben's head. *You'll never have to see me again.*

Livy could hold a grudge as well as anyone...which was why Ben had used cruel words to drive her away. Knowing that he'd done the right thing did not quell the hollowness in his chest. Although he lived a life of privilege, he possessed few things of true value. And now he had lost something dear...something that could never be replaced.

"She is probably otherwise occupied," he said gruffly.

"The Society of Angels certainly keeps her engaged. I wonder what they do all day; how many pamphlets can a lady write, after all?" Strathaven's look turned wistful. "It seems like just yesterday when Livy would come dashing in here, arms akimbo and plaits flying. And now she is a young lady, with a life of her own. Where does the time go?"

"I do not know." It was the truth. Ben had no idea how Livy had transformed from his little friend who made him smile into a tempting minx who twisted him into knots.

Strathaven's smile was rueful. "I confess, my friend, I am not quite ready to let her go."

Ben wasn't ready to let that little girl go either. As he promised her father, he would protect Livy—from afar. He would never let anyone hurt her, least of all himself.

# THIRTEEN

Blinking, Livy lay on the mat and waited for the stars to fade. When her vision cleared, she saw Mrs. Peabody hovering overhead. As it turned out, the half-Chinese, half-English woman was not only Charlie's housekeeper but an expert combatant. For the past two and a half weeks, Mrs. Peabody had been training the Willflowers in a unique fighting style adapted to women's strengths. The techniques relied on speed and accuracy rather than brute force and focused on maneuvers that quickly disabled an attacker.

"Do you need to rest?" Mrs. Peabody asked.

"No, I'm fine." Livy rose, dusting off her loose linen tunic and trousers, the uniform for sparring practice. "I am ready for another round."

"Good," Mrs. Peabody said approvingly.

Despite Mrs. Peabody's diminutive frame, she could take down a man in seconds...and had demonstrated this with Hawker, the mountain of a butler. At first, Hawker had held back; despite his rough-and-tumble appearance, he'd clearly been afraid of hurting his colleague. Mrs. Peabody had not shared his qualms. Time and again, she'd sent the brawny man flying onto the mats, the last time pinning him in an inescapable hold that had Hawker grunting in annoyance.

*"Train your instincts to anticipate your opponent's moves,"* Mrs. Peabody had instructed. *"Then strike, using his strength against him."*

Livy and her instructor circled one another, the other Will-flowers watching on. The hours of drills helped Livy to notice when Mrs. Peabody shifted her weight to the left. Livy instinctively parried the oncoming right punch, then the left punch that followed. She issued her own offensive, aiming a sidekick to her opponent's front leg, throwing the other off-balance. She took that opening to strike the other's chest, sending Mrs. Peabody sprawling onto the mats.

Livy leaped on top, stopping her punch a hairsbreadth from the other's head. Mrs. Peabody looked at the fist above her, and her golden eyes gleamed with respect.

At the sound of applause, Livy looked up.

Charlie had entered the sparring chamber and was standing next to Glory and Fi.

"Well done," Charlie said. "You are making excellent progress, Livy."

"Thanks to Mrs. Peabody's instruction." Rising, Livy offered her hand to her teacher, who rose with the grace of a ballerina and the efficiency of an assassin.

Mrs. Peabody inclined her head. "You are a quick study, Lady Olivia. Much like Lady Fayne."

"Hopefully you will emerge from Mrs. Peabody's training with fewer bruises than I did," Charlie said with a rueful smile. "But the important thing is that you will know how to fend for yourself if danger arises."

Charlie had emphasized the importance of safety throughout. While Mrs. Peabody had concentrated on physical combat and conditioning, Hawker had trained the girls in the use of weaponry.

He also showed them useful skills such as lock-picking and employing "sticky fingers."

Charlie, herself, was in charge of developing the girls' mentation skills. She taught them that the core of investigation lay in the ability to observe through the senses. She showed them how to note even the most minute details and then applied her lessons in real-life settings.

One afternoon, she took them to Burlington Arcade, an exclusive shopping area off Piccadilly, and assigned each of the girls a passerby. The task was to glean as much information about the target as possible without being noticed. Livy had surprised herself with the number of tidbits she'd collected, including her target's name, address, banking institution, birthdate, and favorite tea blend.

The Willflowers also honed their problem-solving abilities. Charlie summed up the main strategies as falling under one of three categories: finesse, flee, or fight. In acting out various scenarios, it became clear that the girls had different strengths. Fiona was the best at finessing, Glory at making a quick getaway, and Livy... well, she'd developed a fondness for Mrs. Peabody's techniques.

"What lesson do we have next?" Livy asked with an eagerness that she'd never felt in all the years at Southbridge's.

Unlike the finishing school, Charlie imparted knowledge that was of interest to Livy. Yesterday, they'd spent half a day practicing different accents, from Cockney to Scottish (Livy had a leg up on the latter). The day before, they'd paid a visit to a shop owned by Mrs. Quinton, a talented African modiste and friend of Charlie's. The Angels had been ushered into a backroom, where Mrs. Q, as she was known to intimates, outfitted them with her innovative designs, which included parasols with hidden blades, dresses with detachable skirts and trousers beneath, and reticules with secret compartments.

Livy couldn't wait to see what was next.

"It's time for luncheon, actually," Charlie said.

"Capital." Glory grinned. "I'm starved."

Changing back into their usual attire, the girls followed Charlie out of the training chamber, which was located in the building behind the main house. They stopped at the next room to exchange cheery hellos with the "Janes." The three women, all named Jane, were expertly embroidering handkerchiefs and writing pamphlets.

Someone had to do the work of the "charity," after all; Livy was grateful it wasn't her.

Livy and the others crossed the cobblestone courtyard to access the main house, her home for the next month. Her family had departed for Scotland yesterday, and while she'd been teary-eyed bidding adieu to her parents and brothers, she was also brimming with excitement at her newfound freedom and the adventures ahead.

It was almost enough to distract her from thoughts of Hadleigh. *Almost.*

Pushing aside the maudlin thoughts, Livy entered the dining room, a high-ceilinged space with pristine plaster moldings and sumptuous forest-green curtains fringed with gold. The table had been cozily set for four: Charlie and Livy took the head and end seats respectively, and Fi and Glory the ones in between. After the rigorous exercise, Livy was famished, and silence reigned as the women tucked into the delicious repast of consommé, sliced meats, pickled vegetables, cold puddings, and freshly baked rolls.

"I hope you do not mind if we discuss some business," Charlie said.

"I don't mind." Livy bit into a buttered roll, nearly swooning at its crusty goodness.

"Me neither." Fiona helped herself to a slice of ham. "Mama is coming to fetch me at two o'clock for a fitting at the dressmaker's, and I don't want to miss anything important."

Although Fi and Glory managed to stop by Charlie's almost every day, they still had to carry on with their regular activities. As did Livy. She found it the oddest thing, training to be an investigator while living a debutante's life. In between sparring and target practice, she'd gone to luncheons and balls. When Lord Sheffield had come to call unexpectedly one afternoon, she'd had to hurriedly change out of a disguise she'd been perfecting. Luckily, before Livy rushed off to meet Sheffield, Charlie had plucked off the fake mustache still glued to Livy's upper lip.

Livy felt like she was leading a double life, and it was exhilarating.

"I believe you are ready for your first case," Charlie said.

"By Juno, we have a case?" Glory's hazel eyes sparkled; perched on her shoulder, Ferdinand II twitched with excitement. "Who is the client?"

"The Countess of Longmere."

Shock rammed into Livy. "*Pippa* is hiring us?"

"She believes she is hiring an investigator I know," Charlie corrected, "and I am merely the go-between. She does not know of your involvement. For your protection and hers, you must keep it that way. Secrecy is paramount; without it, the Society of Angels will not survive. You recall the vow you took when you joined?"

Nodding, Livy chanted in unison with Glory and Fi:

> No matter what danger may await
> An Angel is loyal, brave, and true.
> We will not betray our society's aim,
> "Sisters first" will see us through.

Charlie smiled. "Very good, Angels."

"But why would Pippa need to hire an investigator?" Livy persisted.

"For the same reason most women do: a man," Charlie replied. "In this case, her husband, Lord Edwin Longmere."

Livy remembered Pippa's ill-hidden distress at the symposium. With creeping dread, she asked, "What has the earl done?"

"Nothing yet, Pippa claims. But his behavior has been unusual enough to cause her concern." Charlie took a meditative sip of tea. "She describes his mood as irritable and erratic and says he hardly sleeps at all. In the past few months, he has been spending more and more time in his painting studio. Whenever she has tried to bring up the change in his behavior, he dismisses her or gets angry. She fears he might be in some sort of trouble...or that he might be having an affair."

"Oh no," Livy whispered.

She knew from personal experience that rejection was painful. To be betrayed by the husband one adored? She did not even want to imagine it.

"How could anyone do that to lovely Pippa?" Fi said indignantly.

"It is the way of the world." Charlie's tone was flat. "Only the truth will help her now."

Glory's brow furrowed. "Do Pippa's parents know of her troubles? I am certain her papa would not stand for her to be mistreated. I know mine would not."

"Neither would mine," Fiona said wryly. "Which is why I would not tell Papa...at least, not if I wanted my husband to *live*."

Fi had a point. Both her and Pippa's fathers were powerful men with roots in London's underworld, and they would not hesitate to protect their own by any means necessary. In truth, Livy's own father was no different. A Scotsman to the core, he would bring his wrath down upon anyone who dared to harm a single hair on her head.

"Pippa was adamant that she does not want her parents to know," Charlie replied. "For the reason you suggested, Fiona, and also because she is not yet certain what is going on with Longmere. If he is embroiled in some sort of trouble, she wishes to help him. She wants to handle the situation herself and enlisting her father, who apparently has never approved of Longmere, will only complicate matters."

Livy understood Pippa's desire to take charge of her own destiny. She would feel the same way. And she was fiercely glad that the Angels could take Pippa's back.

"Tell us how we can help Pippa," Livy said.

"We will follow Longmere and see what he is up to," Charlie said matter-of-factly. "According to Pippa, he and a group of cronies enjoy gallivanting in the less savory parts of London. Every Friday night they convene at the Black Lion Inn in Whitechapel. That will be a good place for us to begin our reconnaissance."

Looking crestfallen, Glory said, "I am promised to a soiree on Friday."

"I have an event as well," Fi said glumly.

"Do not fret, my dears. There will be other chances to observe the subject." Charlie's eyes met Livy's across the table. "Are you ready to accompany me on your first mission, Livy?"

Purpose gave Livy an invigorating charge. For the first time since Hadleigh's rejection, she felt some of the heaviness leave her heart, like sandbags dropping from a hot air balloon. While true love might evade her, she still had a destiny to fulfill, and being of service to a friend was an excellent place to start.

Pulling back her shoulders, she said, "I am ready."

# Fourteen

"Don't turn around right away, but they've arrived," Charlie murmured as she passed by, a tray of empty tankards clinking in her hands.

It required all of Livy's self-discipline not to spin around on her rickety stool at the bar. Instead, she pretended to drink from the glass the barkeep had earlier slammed onto the sticky counter in front of her. It was Friday night, and she and Charlie were at the Black Lion Inn, a packed East End public house that catered to the laboring class.

Charlie had managed to get hired on as a barmaid for the eve. A brunette wig, face paint, and padding beneath her low-cut dress transformed her; with her bold manner and Cockney accent, she masterfully blended in with the boisterous crowd. Livy watched and learned from her mentor. She, herself, was disguised as a light-skirt with brassy blonde ringlets and heavily sooted lashes, but she had to work at roughening her accent and substituting her finishing school posture for one far saucier.

After counting to ten, she casually directed her gaze toward the entrance. Through the smoky haze and throng of bodies, she spotted Lord Edwin Longmere. Tall and slim, the earl had wavy hair that gleamed like a raven's wing beneath his hat. He was handsome, with a brooding Bohemian quality that drew females to him like flies to honey. For Pippa's sake, Livy was relieved when he shook his head dismissively at a bold wench who approached him.

When his gaze collided with Livy's, her breath snagged in her throat. Would he recognize her? They'd mingled at a few social events. After an instant, he looked away and spoke to a member of his group. Exhaling, Livy noted that he was accompanied by Edgecombe and three other dapper gentlemen.

Charlie emerged on the other side of the bar. "Another pint for ye, luv?"

"Be obliged to ye." Lowering her voice, Livy said, "I recognize Edgecombe but not the others in Longmere's party."

Charlie swiped a dirty rag over the counter, murmuring, "The blond is the Honorable Simon Thorne, the brown-haired fellow Viscount Bollinger, and the one with the balding pate Baron Stamford. Once they are seated, try to get closer."

The barkeep shouted for Charlie to quit gabbing and serve customers.

"'Old your bloomin' 'orses, can't ye see I'm wif a payin' customer?" she retorted.

With a wink at Livy, she sashayed off to do her employer's bidding.

Longmere and his group settled in a private booth at the back of the tavern. Evading groping hands and salacious offers, Livy made her way to an adjacent booth. The etched glass partition between the tables gave her fleeting views of the men as their conversation drifted through.

"The Black Lion is a breath of fresh air," Edgecombe drawled as he loosened his cravat. In the dim light, his pomaded auburn hair had the slickness of an icy road. "Mayfair can be so stifling at times."

"Mayfair or m-marriage?"

This came from the man Charlie had identified as Mr. Simon Thorne. Livy recognized his slight stammer from the time she'd eavesdropped in Edgecombe's study. With his ice-blond hair and sculpted features, Thorne had the look of an angel...if one overlooked the sly gleam in his blue eyes.

"Nothing is as oppressive as the parson's mousetrap. Especially when one's papa-in-law holds the purse strings. The bastard pays for my wife's every whim, from masquerades to jewels. When it comes to my expenses, however, he's a bloody cheeseparer," Edgecombe muttered. "You bachelors should enjoy your freedom for as long as you can."

"I m-might not be able to avoid the shackles of matrimony much longer," Thorne said mournfully.

"Alas, I am in the same predicament." Bollinger sighed.

The viscount had curling brown hair and long-lashed brown eyes that gave him a boyish appeal. He downed a tankard with astonishing ease, which probably accounted for the softness of his jaw and waistline.

"All is not lost, fellows." Stamford's distinctive nasal tone gave him away. With a narrow face, close-set eyes, and hair gone thin at the top, he lacked the physical graces of his friends. "We still have our enterprise. The last shipment alone netted a thousand pounds apiece."

"The cargo is the only thing keeping me afloat." Thorne lowered his voice. "I received confirmation of another d-delivery. Two evenings from now, at Cremorne Gardens."

"We'll make a night of it," Edgecombe said. "Perhaps we'll finally meet our elusive Chinese friend—"

"Shh," Bollinger said in a panicked whisper. "You know we're not supposed to speak of him. He has eyes and ears everywhere."

When Bollinger scanned the room, Livy hastily averted her gaze. She saw Charlie serving a rowdy table nearby. Although

Charlie gave the appearance of flirting with the patrons, playfully slapping a bricklayer's dusty hand off her derriere, Livy knew her mentor was eavesdropping on the same conversation that she was.

"Very well. Mum's the word," Edgecombe said. "We cannot afford to offend our mighty benefactor."

"I cannot do this anymore." Longmere suddenly spoke up. "Count me out."

*Out of what?* Livy thought. *What are you and your cronies up to? What business do you have with this mysterious Chinese friend?*

"Don't be a fool." Although Edgecombe's words were low and calm, they had a warning edge. "You need this as much as we do."

"I don't give a damn," Longmere said.

A sudden tingling awareness distracted Livy. Goose pimples prickled her skin. She swung her gaze to the entrance...and her heart stumbled into her ribs.

*Zounds, it's Hadleigh. What is he doing here?*

He stood head and shoulders above the crowd, his dark-brown hair gleaming like a pelt beneath his hat. His cravat had a stylish knot, his frock coat and trousers fitting his muscular form like a glove. His lordly, commanding presence caused the longing she'd locked away to break free. Oh, how she'd missed him. With a swoony feeling, she watched the play of light and shadow over his chiseled features as he scanned the crowded tavern. His sapphire gaze narrowed on Longmere's party...then shifted to her.

*Drat.* She came to her senses, swiftly turning away. *Did he recognize me?*

Pulling the coarse blonde curls of her wig over her cheek, she tried to think over her thudding panic. Most people would never recognize her while she was in disguise and all the way across a dimly lit tavern, but this wasn't most people. This was Hadleigh, and he had a way of seeing right through her.

"Anything I can get you, luv?" Charlie arrived, positioning her body to shield Livy from Hadleigh's view.

"Hadleigh's here," Livy whispered. "I think he spotted me."

"Take the back exit," Charlie said under her breath. "Hawker's parked two blocks away."

With a slight nod, Livy rose and headed to the closest door. She walked as quickly as she could without looking suspicious. She felt Hadleigh's presence behind her, but she didn't dare to glance back. All of a sudden, she heard loud clattering, the sound of coins hitting the floor.

"Oh, dearie me. I've dropped me tips."

Charlie's dramatic moan was lost in the roar of patrons diving for the money. Livy risked a backward glance and saw the sea of bodies now blocking the path between her and Hadleigh. Reaching the back door, she ducked outside and found herself in an alley bordered by decrepit buildings. She navigated through the fog-cloaked night, rank smells assailing her nose and scurrying sounds making her pulse skitter.

*Ew, rats. Never mind, keep going...*

"Oof."

The sound left her as she ran into something. Steadying herself, she looked up...into the face of a brute. Another man emerged behind the first, holding a lamp that illuminated the menacing leers on their faces.

"What 'ave we 'ere, eh?" the first said. "A lost dove?"

Dodging the man's hand, Livy sized up the threat the way Mrs. Peabody had taught her to.

*Two men, big but slow. Three sheets to the wind, by their stench. Overconfident.*

"Let me pass, and I won't hurt you," she said.

The first brute gave a bark of laughter. "Feisty wench, eh? I like me sport lively."

He made a grab for her, looking surprised when she parried his move. She did it again, staying out of his reach. Then he lunged at her, and this time she engaged, sidestepping and shoving at his back with both palms, using his forward momentum to send him flying into the side of a building. Before she could enjoy the satisfying crack of his skull against stone, the other fiend grabbed her from behind, one burly arm around her waist, the other hand clamping over her mouth.

"I've got you now," he bragged.

*By my waist. But you left my hands free, you moron.*

She reached into her skirt pocket, her fingers closing around her pistol. Before she could yank it out, the arms around her loosened.

"What the bleeding 'ell—"

She spun around to see Hadleigh plow a fist into her captor's face. The man staggered but regrouped. A blade flashed in his beefy hand, and Livy's heart shot into her throat as he charged at Hadleigh, weapon raised. Hadleigh took him head on, grabbing the other's wrist. The two of them grappled for control of the knife. As Livy was trying to see if she could get a clear shot, Hadleigh gained the upper hand. He twisted his foe's arm, and the blade dropped, skidding into the darkness.

A moan from the cobblestones momentarily distracted her. The other bastard was coming to. As he began to sit up, she crouched, aiming a jab at his nose. Groaning, he fell back once more.

She rose and saw Charlie materialize at the end of the alleyway, behind Ben and the brute he was pummeling, neither of whom noticed her. Livy lifted her chin to let her mentor know she had everything in hand, and Charlie melted back into the fog. Hadleigh finished the job with powerful punches that made his opponent howl in pain and Livy's blood rush hotly in her veins.

Her heart sighed. Hadleigh was *such* a hero...even if she didn't need one.

Her pulse hiccupped as he stepped over the foe he'd vanquished and strode up to her. Fresh from the fight, his hair falling over his brow, he'd never looked more dashing and virile. Or more dangerous.

"Hello, Hadleigh," she said breathlessly. "There is a perfectly good explanation."

*And I had better think of it quickly.*

"Is there indeed?" His tone was calm, his gaze stormy. "I cannot wait to hear it."

# FIFTEEN

Depositing Livy into his carriage, Ben instructed his groom to take them to Lady Fayne's. He drew the curtains and tried to calm his simmering rage as the conveyance rolled off. Livy was seated on the opposite bench, and studying her in the light of the carriage lamp did not improve his mood. She'd transformed herself from a demure debutante into a tantalizing trollop.

Devil and damn, her breasts were nearly spilling out from her poor excuse for a bodice, the firm rounded tops jiggling with the carriage's movements. Her scarlet sateen dress clung to her waist, so narrow he could span it with his hands. The hem ended above her trim ankles, which were scandalously displayed in black silk stockings. She'd darkened her lashes, the smoky fringe highlighting the brilliant clarity of her eyes. The innocent pink of her lips was covered by a smear of glistening red paint.

Gone was the little girl he'd known. In her place was a sultry, seductive tart. And the change unleashed his bestial appetites, hot hunger clawing at his gut.

*Fucking hell.*

His anger and lust seemed to feed on each other. Reining them both in, he bit out, "I am waiting for your explanation as to why you were at the Black Lion."

Being a quick-witted female, Livy knew how to dodge the truth. But she'd never been able to evade him. He could always tell when she was lying, and from the brief lowering of her lashes, he knew he was about to be treated to one hell of a tale.

A deviant part of him wanted her to lie. Wanted to punish her for being a naughty, reckless girl who had endangered her own life. Equally strong was the instinct to protect her, to keep her swaddled in cotton so that nothing and no one could ever harm her.

"I was there for the same reason you were," she said.

Her calm reply shot up the pressure in his veins. He'd been at the Black Lion because, earlier that day, he'd located the maker of the gold watch he'd found on Pete. Eager to see the piece returned to its owner, the watchmaker had identified his client as the Countess of Longmere, who'd commissioned the watch as a wedding present for her husband.

Ben had tracked Longmere down to the Black Lion, spotting the man with the group of bastards he was all too familiar with. The years he'd kept company with the Horsemen told him it was no coincidence that the trail had led to them. The question was not whether they were involved with the deadly drug, but in what fashion.

Yet at the sight of Livy, Ben had abandoned his quarry. What in blazes was she doing by herself, dressed like a whore, in a disreputable Whitechapel tavern? Having blown his night's mission for her sake, he wasn't about to do further damage by telling her about his covert quest.

"I was in pursuit of a diversion," he said shortly. "A gentleman's prerogative."

She narrowed her eyes at him, but not before he caught the hurt that flashed through those peerless celadon orbs. A moment later, the hurt was replaced by a mutinous gleam.

She tilted her chin up. "Not only a gentleman's. I was there for the same reason."

While Livy was undoubtedly bold, she wasn't a hussy. From what he'd observed over the years, she was not much of a flirt, nor did she actively encourage male attention. If he were honest, the only man she'd shown any interest in...was him.

And, damn his eyes, he couldn't deny that he liked it that way. As wrong and forbidden as it was. As undeserving as he was of her adulation. Regardless, her assertion that she was out chasing carnal thrills tonight was preposterous and maddening.

"The devil you were." He clenched his jaw. "Don't lie to me."

"If you can go gallivanting, then why can't I?" she shot back.

"You know full well why not. Because you're a damned virgin and a lady."

"Dash it all. That isn't fair!"

"Too bloody bad. I do not make the rules. Now stop trying to evade the question: what in blazes were you doing at the Black Lion dressed like a light-skirt?"

She took a breath. Exhaled slowly. Buying time, no doubt.

"Because I wanted to know what it was like to be a real woman...the kind you would be interested in."

Her words, wholly unexpected, stunned him into silence.

"You called me a *silly little girl*," she burst out. "Said you only wanted a real woman. Well, I wanted to know what it was like to be such a female."

"And you thought parading like a trollop in a tavern was the way to gain that experience?" he said incredulously. "Are you mad?"

"I am perfectly sane, as you know. And I can take care of myself." She gave him an annoyed look. "Why do you care what I do, anyway? You've rejected me three times and told me to stay away from you. As I've been minding my own affairs, I expect you to extend me the same courtesy. I am no concern of yours."

*Stay calm. Stay in control.*

He drew in a breath through his nose. "You know that is not true, Livy. I do care about you. I just...I just cannot be the man you want me to be."

"I only want you to be you."

God help him. Mesmerized by her sincerity and unwavering gaze, he felt his control slip a notch. She was so damned beautiful, inside and out. The promise of a life he'd once longed for and which he knew could never be his. She was everything good... everything he was not.

"You don't know me," he said hoarsely.

Confidence shone in her eyes. "I do so."

She crossed over to his side of the carriage, and he automatically reached out to steady her, his hand engulfing hers. She sat beside him, lacing her fingers with his and, bastard that he was, he couldn't make himself let go. Bloody hell, he'd missed her. The connection between them had always felt right. Even as it was shifting, changing in ways that left him confused and torn, he could not deny himself the simple, exquisite pleasure of holding her hand.

"Is that why you've pushed me away?" she asked with her usual acuity. "Because you think you are not right for me?"

"I *know* I am not," he said darkly. "I am not a good man, Livy. My sins are such that they can never be erased. You deserve someone far better."

"Let me be the judge of that. I am perfectly capable of deciding what I want. And I can tell you this: regardless of what you have done, you will always be a hero in my eyes."

He gave a humorless laugh at her *naïveté*. She was so sweet... and so damned *young*.

*You want to do the right thing?* his inner voice challenged. *Tell her the truth. Let her know the kind of man you truly are, and she will want nothing to do with you.*

He let go of her hand. Said the words that would set her free.

"I killed a man."

Livy had suspected that Hadleigh's past was dark. He'd alluded to it more than once, and even as a girl, she'd sensed that he had his demons. Why else would he drink and brood so much and at times seem so lost? Nonetheless, his admission took her aback.

"Why?" The word popped out of her mouth.

She knew Hadleigh: if he had committed such a sin, there had to be a reason.

His expression stark, he said, "Do you know how my sister Beatrice was scarred?"

Livy drew her brows together. "My parents said Aunt Bea had a riding accident."

"That is true, but there is more to it. She was riding in the park when she came upon a man named Griggs beating a street urchin. She interfered, and Griggs retaliated by whipping her horse. She was thrown and nearly trampled. In truth, she was lucky to escape with only the scar."

"How *brave* of Aunt Bea to stand up for that boy." Livy's voice trembled with emotion. "And *shame* on that blighter for hurting a lady who was only doing the right thing."

"At the time my sister was hurt, I was sixteen," Hadleigh said tonelessly, "and I swore to avenge her honor. Not just hers, but that of my family. Before Beatrice's injury, she was feted by all of Society, poised to make a match with a duke. We Wodehouses were the envy of the *ton* for our happiness. Then Griggs came along and destroyed everything.

"My beautiful sister was shunned because of her scar and became an object of ridicule. Our mama was beside herself with despair and locked herself in her bedchamber. Livid at everything that had befallen the family, our formerly doting papa spent more and more time away from us, the source of his unhappiness. When he died two years later, it was in his mistress's bed. My mama followed him to the grave soon thereafter. She died, I think, of a broken heart."

"Oh, Hadleigh," Livy whispered, hurting for him. "How dreadful it must have been to witness your family in such pain."

He gave a terse nod. "When I inherited the title at eighteen, I was consumed with the need to avenge my family's honor. Looking back, it seems absurd now: how could revenge possibly give me back everything that I had lost? But I was a reckless, arrogant fool. I made it my life's mission to destroy Griggs. He was a rising middle-class industrialist, and I used my influence to crush him. Rumors in the ears of the right men in the right clubs was all it took to blacken his reputation, to get his loans denied and investors to flee. His business crumbled. He came to me, begged me for mercy...and I turned him away."

Swallowing, Livy asked, "What happened next?"

"Beatrice begged me to stop, told me this was not what she wanted, but I was obsessed with righting the wrong done to her. I had Griggs in the corner, and I wasn't about to stop until he had lost everything. Several weeks later, I had my wish: Griggs was found dead in his flat. He had hung himself, but I was the one who put the noose around his neck."

Hadleigh's dark confession sent ripples of shock through Livy. Yet she also knew *him*...and no matter how hot-headed and arrogant he might have been as a youth, she knew that he had not meant for this fellow Griggs to die. Even now, anguish was written over his features, shadows of remorse swallowing up the blue of his irises. He stared off into space, statue-still save for the shallow heaves of his chest. It was as if he were trapped in that time, cursed to relive his actions over and again.

Livy reached for one of his hands again. Surprised to find how cold he was, she chafed his large palm between both of hers.

"What you did was wrong," she said. "But you did not mean to kill Griggs, did you?"

"No." Hadleigh's reply was hoarse, his gaze sheened with moisture. "I was hell-bent on destroying his happiness the way he had destroyed that of Bea and my family, but I didn't think that he would..." He jerked his hand from hers, clenching it into a fist. "It seems impossible now that I did not consider the consequences of cornering Griggs the way I did. Of forcing a man into a situation so desperate that he would see only one means of escape."

"You were young and rash," she said quietly, "and Griggs had hurt your sister and your family. While that does not excuse your actions, I can understand your anger."

"I cannot tell you how many times I've asked myself, *Why didn't you see what was coming? How could you push this man into taking his own life? What the bloody hell were you thinking?*" Hadleigh's voice was as choppy as a tempest-tossed sea. "And I have no answers, nor will I ever."

Livy said nothing. There was nothing she *could* say. All she could do was sit by Hadleigh's side and share his burden the best she could.

"There is more," he said. "Griggs had children, a legitimate son with his wife and a bastard daughter with his mistress. I sent money to support the boy, anonymously of course, but I lost track of the daughter. She emerged several years ago and was behind a nefarious plan to hurt Beatrice. To destroy my sister, the way I had her father. She nearly succeeded, too."

Livy's heart wrenched at the guilt in Hadleigh's eyes.

"How horrible," she whispered.

"If anything had happened to Beatrice..." He shoved both hands through his hair, his elbows planting on his knees. He stared at the carriage floor. "During the fight to save my sister, Griggs's daughter fell off a high platform, and I grabbed onto her. I was the one responsible for this cycle of revenge, and I wanted to save her, to stop the violence I'd started. I told her to hold on, but she looked up at me and smiled and...and then she let go."

Livy shuddered at the harrowing image. The words he'd said to her that fateful day at the pond surfaced.

*Not you too. Bloody hold on, do you hear me?*

Had he been thinking of Griggs's daughter, the woman who had chosen violence and death over his help? Whose choice had destroyed his attempt at atonement?

Overwhelmed by the tragedy of the story, Livy sat bogged in heavy silence. Her throat thickened at the thought of all that suffering. Suffering that, she realized, had never really ended for Hadleigh. All the years she had known him, he had held this inside. Had been hurting in ways she could not have begun to fathom as a child.

*I wish I could have grown up faster.* Her eyes heated. *Then I could have taken better care of you, my dearest friend and love.*

"In truth, I killed not one person, but two." Hadleigh's face was taut with self-loathing. "That is the kind of man I am. A bloody murderer. Now do you wish to be with me?"

"Yes." Her voice quivered, not because of uncertainty but the opposite.

"Devil take it, Livy! Just once, don't be so goddamned stubborn." Rage and anguish smoldered in his eyes. "You should want nothing to do with me."

"That will never happen," she said firmly. "You made a mistake—a grievous error that led to tragic consequences. But you were younger than I am now when this all started, and it is obvious that you repent your actions. You take responsibility for what you did. You have tried, to the best of your ability, to make amends. What more can you do?"

"Nothing." The word dripped with frustration and pain. "I can never change what I did."

"Exactly. The only thing you *can* do is learn from your mistakes," she said earnestly. "According to my mama, a mistake can be forgiven if one makes proper amends."

A ghost of a smile flitted over his mouth. "You told me that the day I rescued you."

"Because it is true. And regardless of what you have done, you will always be my hero." She touched his arm, his muscles bulging at the contact. "Because I know who you are, Hadleigh. The true you. That is why I love you and why I will always be here by your side."

The longing that rippled over his handsome features hugged her heart. She recognized that she'd always felt the desire to take care of him. To look out for him, the way he looked out for her. As a girl, she'd cheered him up and eased his solitude. As a woman, she could do so much more...if he would only let her.

"My little queen." His voice jagged, he framed her face between his palms. "Ah, God. How can I resist you?"

He bent his head, his mouth claiming hers.

His kiss was gentle yet masterful, a far cry from her first clumsy attempt. There was no smooshing of lips, just soft pressure and brushes that sent wisps of heat over her skin. He slid his fingers beneath her wig, anchoring her as he courted her mouth with slow, drugging kisses. Caresses so sweet they stirred her very soul. Utterly awash, she surrendered to him. Their mouths clung as if they had nothing to hold onto but each other.

When his tongue swept against the seam of her mouth, it felt natural to open to him. To receive the wet, tender thrust that sent a wave of awareness through her body. The tips of her breasts throbbed, molten warmth gathering at her center. She felt dizzy, overcome by sensation yet wanting more. More of his kisses, more of him. He delved deeper, sliding his tongue against hers, and she moaned with desperate need.

He broke the kiss, resting his forehead briefly against hers.

"You're so bloody sweet," he said raggedly.

"Oh, Hadleigh." She had to catch her breath. "Does this mean you do like me as more than a friend?"

He stared at her...then let out a guffaw. His laughter was infectious, and she joined in, enjoying the lighthearted moment, the burst of sunshine after the rain. When they both calmed, he took her hand and kissed the knuckles before tucking it against his thigh.

"I *am* attracted to you," he admitted. "That is the problem."

"Why is it a problem? You told me about your past, and it doesn't matter to me."

"I haven't told you everything. And, no," he said, cutting off her argument, "there's not enough time to do so tonight. We're back at Lady Fayne's."

Livy hadn't even noticed that the carriage had stopped.

"Beyond that, I am too old for you," he went on. "Your parents are bound to disapprove and rightly so. And while you and I are attracted to one another, we may not be compatible. There are things I want that are not suitable for a young virgin."

"As Papa is older than Mama by a dozen years, they would be hypocrites for disapproving of our age difference. And clearly age has no bearing on marital bliss: look how happy my parents are," she argued. "As for the other matter, how will we know unless we, um, try?"

He gave her a stern look; for some reason, it added to her tingling arousal.

"There is no way in hell I would dishonor you in that fashion," he said. "If we decide to pursue something beyond friendship, then that path can only lead to marriage. Our physical relationship is not like a hat to be tried on and returned if the fit isn't right."

"But isn't that the point of courtship?" she persisted. "As long as we don't do anything, um, irrevocable, I see no problem with us spending time together to see if we are a match."

He inhaled deeply. "Let me think upon it."

"How long will you—"

"I will call upon you tomorrow. *If* you stop pestering me about it."

Despite his exasperated expression, she saw the amusement in his eyes and knew she was getting her way.

"All right," she said happily.

"I must also ask you to be discreet about our relationship. Until things are settled, I don't want your reputation to be compromised in any way."

Livy wasn't sure she could keep things a secret from Charlie. Her mentor was perceptive...and undoubtedly going to interrogate her the minute she walked through the door.

"May I at least tell Fiona and Glory?" she asked. "They can be trusted."

"I would not presume to stand between the Willflowers," Hadleigh said wryly. "Now we had better get you back inside. How did you manage to slip out earlier?"

"I, um, climbed out my bedchamber window. There is a tree right outside of it," she improvised. If she had had to leave undetected, that would have been her chosen route. "But I can go in through the front door. I have a key, and no one is awake at this hour."

He descended from the carriage first, scanning the dark and quiet street before handing her down. "Until tomorrow," he murmured.

"May your dreams be sweet," she whispered.

She rose up on tiptoe, brushing her lips against his jaw. Feeling his surprise, the tightening of his grip on her waist before he let her go, she smiled to herself. Then she dashed toward the house, floating on clouds the entire way.

# Sixteen

*Livy is 16; Ben is 28*

Hadleigh was in his study, where Livy thought he would be. Peering through the crack in the doorway, she saw that he wasn't alone. Papa was with him, the two men standing by the window, looking out into the rain-drenched garden. She was struck by their similarity, their height and broadness of shoulder emphasized by the dark garb they wore to honor the somber occasion.

The men were silent and, at age sixteen, Livy was old enough to understand why. Things happened that defied the comfort of language. There was no cure for grief, only time and the support of loved ones to make it more bearable. She didn't think Hadleigh had many people who loved him...and now he had lost the one person who was supposed to love him most.

She was fiercely glad that Papa was there to offer his friendship.

And she would do what she could to help ease Hadleigh's pain. Clearing her throat, she pushed open the door.

Both men turned in her direction. Hadleigh's expression was as bleak as the rainy day. He had lost even more weight during the preceding months he'd spent secluded with his wife at their country estate, his skin stretched drum-taut over the sharp frame of his bones. His eyes were bleary, rimmed with red, and he looked as if he hadn't slept for months.

"Livy." Papa appeared relieved to see her. "I was about to find your mama. Why don't you keep Hadleigh company until I return?"

Livy nodded, and as her father walked by her, he gave her a meaningful look.

"Be a comfort and not a bother, poppet," he murmured. "Poor chap's been through a lot today."

Did he honestly think she would bicker with Hadleigh on the day of his wife's funeral? Resisting the urge to roll her eyes, she dipped her chin in acknowledgement. Papa squeezed her shoulder then exited, and she went to stand next to Hadleigh, who'd resumed his brooding watch over the grey and misty landscape.

"You needn't stay with me, you know," he said. "Regardless of what your papa thinks, I am too old to need a nanny."

"I am not here to mind you." Knowing Hadleigh would despise even the slightest sign of pity, she said lightly, "I am here to get away from the crowd."

This wasn't untrue. The house was packed with so-called "mourners" who'd obviously come for the spectacle and gossip rather than any sense of caring. To Livy's disgust, she'd overheard people whispering horrid things about the deceased. The rumors of the Duchess of Hadleigh's infidelity were not new; they'd even reached Livy's young ears before. Nonetheless, Livy was shocked that people would show such blatant disrespect, not just toward the dead, but the living.

"I do not blame you." Hadleigh looked at her then, the agony in his eyes piercing her heart. "Most of the people are here out of curiosity, if not downright spite. Arabella did not have many friends. Yet she always liked an elaborate affair, and I wanted to give her a procession fit for a duchess."

"The arrangements you made are very grand," Livy said softly. "I am sure Her Grace would have approved."

"It doesn't really matter, does it? Arabella is gone." He exhaled. "Because of me."

"You mustn't say that," Livy protested.

"Why not? It is the truth," he said harshly. "She died due to complications in her pregnancy—a pregnancy she did not want in the first place. I was the one who insisted. The one who thought that a child would make things better between us..." His throat bobbed above his dark cravat. "Instead, I killed her."

"No, you did not." Livy placed a hand on his quivering bicep, over the black mourning band. "I do not know why these things happen, but they do. A part of God's mysterious plan. But whatever the reason, you are not the cause of Arabella's death."

"I loved her, you know. Despite everything that...that went on in my marriage." His voice broke. "I loved my wife."

How Livy wished she could shoulder some of his pain. "I know you did."

And because he looked like he needed it, she gave him a hug, the way she might comfort her brothers when they had a bad day. Since he was much taller, she wrapped her arms around his waist, tucking her head against his spice-and-Hadleigh-scented waistcoat. After a heartbeat, his arms circled her, nearly crushing her with the force of his grief.

That was the thing most people did not understand about Hadleigh: his jaded insouciance hid a man of intense feeling. Over the years, Livy had come to realize how harshly he judged himself. She could not let him take on one more sin.

"I am sorry you must go through this," she whispered. "But know that you are not at fault. And that you are not alone."

A tremor travelled through his lean frame. "What would I do without you?"

"You'll never have to find out," she promised.

"But maybe I should."

Before she could puzzle out his gruff words, he let her go.

Jamming his hands into his coat pockets, he said, "I need to get away, Livy. I am not...I'm not doing well."

"You do look a bit worse for the wear," she said candidly. "Why don't you come to stay at Strathmore Castle? Mama says Scottish air is medicine, and it has done wonders for Will's constitution—"

"No. I have to be alone."

"Your country seat, then. It is not too far. Papa and I can come to visit and—"

"I won't be seeing visitors."

She paused at his stark look. "Not...not even me?"

"Not even you, little one."

"But why not?" she asked in bewilderment. "I wouldn't be a bother. You and I are good at being alone together, remember?"

"I am not right, Livy."

"You're not ill, are you?" she asked with sudden anxiety.

"Not in the way you mean." He shoved a hand through his hair, dark without the burnished kiss of the sun. "It is a grown-up matter, something I must take care of on my own. But I promise you that when I am well, you will be the first person I seek."

"How long will your recovery take?" she asked, her bottom lip trembling.

"I do not know."

"Days? Or weeks? Not *months*—"

"Livy." He cut her off with a look. "I truly do not know, and you hounding me isn't going to change that."

Panic beat inside her chest at the thought of losing him. "But what will I do without you? Soon I will be introduced into Society, and it is bound to be a disaster. I will need your advice." An even worse thought slammed into her. "What if you forget all about me?"

He laughed, and for a moment, the shadows receded from his thin face.

"How could I forget my little queen, whom I fished from a pond, hmm?" He chucked her beneath the chin. "If anything, it will be *you* who forgets me. You'll be too busy taking Society by storm to pay your old chum any mind."

"I could never forget you," she vowed fiercely. "And I will always be here for you."

"We shall see." His smile faded into something exquisitely sad. "Nothing lasts forever."

He was wrong. The love and loyalty of a McLeod *did* last forever. Yet from his expression, she could see that words were not enough; she would have to prove it to him.

"May I at least write to you?" she asked.

"Yes."

She narrowed her eyes at him. "And will you write me back?"

"I will do my best," he said gruffly.

"All right, then." She sighed because there was naught else to do. "Hadleigh?"

"Yes?"

"Don't take too long getting better," she told him. "I don't wish to grow up without you."

## PRESENT DAY

Ben had Livy where he wanted her: on her hands and knees, naked on the bed. Standing, he ran his palms up the backs of her thighs, loving the way she shivered at his touch like a mount recognizing its master. She was a filly not yet broken, and he burned to train her in the ways of desire.

Palming her arse, he spread her dark thatch with his thumbs, finding her as soft and juicy as a peach. His mouth watered with the need to taste her. To discover the flavor of his little queen's surrender.

He leaned down, swiping the flat of his tongue up her pouting pink seam. Her sweet and salty essence drenched his senses, her breathless moans tugging on his turgid cock like a fist. He parted her secret folds, delving deep, groaning when her virgin passage clenched around his tongue.

Christ, she was irresistible. Innocence and sensuality wrapped up in one.

Possessiveness roared through him. *And she's all mine.*

"There's my good girl," he growled. "Grind yourself against my tongue."

She gasped, and he wondered if she was blushing even as she obeyed his command with wanton enthusiasm. She pushed her pussy against his ravenous mouth, presenting him with a veritable feast. He ate her until she screamed out her climax, anointing his tongue with her dew.

Swiping his hand across his mouth, he straightened. "Did you enjoy being licked, Livy?"

She tossed her dark tresses over her shoulder and turned her head. Shock punched him in the gut when he saw it wasn't Livy looking at him...but his dead duchess.

"I loved it," Arabella purred.

He stumbled backward. "You...you're dead."

"You killed me." Her green eyes glowed with preternatural spite. "But I could never forget you, Hadleigh. I will always be here..."

Ben jerked awake. Heart thudding, he swung a panicked gaze around his surroundings...and saw that he was in his bedchamber, in his own bed, the sweat-soaked sheets clinging to his bare skin. Dawn's watery light was just beginning to seep through the crack in the drapes.

Sitting up, he took a deep breath, trying to disentangle himself from the phantom web of the dream. Simultaneously, he felt an insistent throbbing in his groin. Glancing down, he saw his cock-stand tenting the sheet.

Planting his elbows against his raised knees, he raked his hands through his damp hair.

*Devil take it.* Lust and guilt pounded in his veins. *What am I doing?*

Last night, Livy's sweet acceptance of his past had torn down his walls, and he hadn't been able to resist her. Even now, the memory of their soul-stirring kiss sent a hot sizzle up his spine. Yet he was also assailed by second thoughts. Was he taking advantage of her innocence? Was he being fair to her? Was he acting in her best interests?

His chest tautened. She deserved a better man, one who wasn't damaged goods. Some fine young chap who would court her with poesies and an untainted heart. Instead, she would have Ben: an older man with a filthy past and even filthier desires.

If his dream was any indication, the kiss and conversation with Livy had obliterated his denial. He could no longer ignore the desire she ignited in him—could not fool himself into believing that his feelings for her were in any way brotherly. The truth confronted him: he wanted to do dark, depraved things to her... and he wanted her to love it.

His gut twisted; his cock throbbed. *Christ, I am a bastard.*

*I am perfectly capable of deciding what I want,* her voice reminded him.

Wry humor punctured his grim mood as he realized that, even in his head, his little queen bantered with him. Yet she did have a point: she should be the one to decide her future. She might be young, but if any woman knew her own mind, it was Olivia McLeod. She was not short on opinions, nor shy about sharing them. He trusted her to tell him if she found him unacceptable, a fact he found oddly relieving.

His job was to present her with the facts. When he called upon her today, he would tell her the other sordid details of his past: the catastrophe of his marriage and his opium habit. His neck tightened, and he rubbed at the corded muscles, wondering starkly if she would decide that he wasn't worth the trouble.

*"I could never forget you,"* Livy had once vowed. *"I will always be here for you."*

He'd been promised forever before. On his wedding day...and look at how that had ended. Before that, during the halcyon period of his childhood, he'd believed that he would have the love and support of his parents and sister for all his life.

He had ruined that too.

As much as he wanted to believe that Livy was different, he had to be realistic. She might be too young and innocent to give him what he craved, the fantasies reality had pulverized. Yet the ashes of his dreams were still there, hope buried in the Pandora's box of his life, taunting and tantalizing him in equal measure. A part of him feared those needs, for they made him vulnerable...weak.

Arabella had used them to play him like a puppet. And though Livy was as different from his dead wife as he could imagine, the two women did have one thing in common: they were both headstrong by nature. His failure to do his husbandly duty and guide Arabella had destroyed their marriage.

He could not ignore that Livy was equally willful...hell, he'd found her dressed like a whore at a tavern last night. Even though he believed that her gambit had mostly been innocent, there was no telling what she could get up to if he didn't keep a close eye on her.

It had been one thing to find her Willflower antics amusing when she'd been his little friend. Now that his feelings for her had taken a decidedly different turn, his instinct to protect her was amplified by possessiveness. If he married her, he would not make the same mistake that he'd made with Arabella. He would have to guide Livy and maintain a firm upper hand. It would be his duty to keep her safe from her own worst instincts.

*Am I up to the task? Or am I going to fail...again?*

Pushing aside his self-doubt, he got out of bed, ignoring the heavy sway of his cock. He could, obviously, take matters into his own hands...but he didn't want to. He hadn't had a sexual release with others or by himself since the first time Livy had kissed him at her birthday ball. It was the second longest period of celibacy in his adult life.

*Master Chen would be proud*, he thought wryly.

Yet Ben wasn't withholding pleasure from himself for any moral reason. The simple fact was that he only wanted gratification with Livy. She made him long for things he hadn't felt in years...maybe ever. He'd never been friends with a lover before. Never felt this protective over any woman. Never wanted to cherish her rare self even as he fantasized about debauching her and laying claim to her in every filthy way imaginable.

Filled with restless energy, he rang for his valet to help him dress. He would go for a ride before calling upon Livy. Then he would tell her the remaining facts about his past and his expectations for marriage, and she would make her choice to accept him...or not.

# SEVENTEEN

Livy cocked her head, halting in front of the fire. "Is that Hadleigh?"

Posted by the drawing room window, Glory reported, "No. Just a passing carriage."

"He said he would call." Livy recommenced her pacing. "Where is he?"

"It is only five minutes past two," Fiona said from the settee. She was dealing cards onto the coffee table, polishing some of the tricks Hawker had taught them. When she turned over a royal flush, she smiled with satisfaction. "Perhaps Hadleigh is being fashionably late."

"I wish he would show up," Livy grumbled.

"For heaven's sake." Seated at the escritoire, Charlie peered over her wire-rimmed reading spectacles like a disapproving schoolmistress. "All this fuss over a man."

"Not just any man," Livy protested. "This is Hadleigh we're talking about."

*The man I love.*

As Livy had predicted, upon arriving home, she'd been met by a worried Charlie. That had led to Livy giving an abbreviated account of the evening's activities. Since Livy hadn't been able to hide her giddiness, Charlie had guessed the state of affairs between Livy and Hadleigh...and hadn't seemed too pleased about it. Unlike Glory and Fi, who'd cheered when Livy told them her dreams were finally coming true.

"Livy has been in love with the duke for ages," Fi said blithely. "She is going to marry him."

"Not too soon, I hope."

Charlie's testy tone was jarring because, up until now, her attitude had been warm and obliging. The coolness in the lady's grey eyes sent an uncertain slither up Livy's spine. Livy crossed over to the escritoire, her peach silk skirts swishing.

"Do you have a problem with Hadleigh?" Livy asked.

Charlie's lips formed a tight line. "He has a reputation for being a rake."

"That was in the past, and I do not care," Livy said bluntly. "I've known him since I was twelve, when he risked his life to save mine. I know his true character, and I love him."

"You are young, Livy. Too young to give up your dreams for a man."

Livy frowned. "Who says I am going to give up my dreams?"

Charlie rose, neatening the piles on her desk. "Do you truly think that Hadleigh will allow you to carry on your work with the Society of Angels if you are wed?"

The truth was Livy hadn't thought that far ahead. She'd been focused on getting him over the hump of admitting his attraction to her.

"I don't see why he would stop me from doing something I wanted to do," she said uneasily.

"Because he is a man," Charlie said brusquely. "He will see you as nothing but an extension of himself, and the law gives him that right. As a *femme couvert*, you will cease to exist as a person after marriage. Your very being will be subsumed under the identity of your husband. Is that what you want?"

Every fiber of Livy's being rebelled at the idea. But surely not every man wanted a woman to be subservient. Surely Hadleigh wouldn't.

Aloud, she said, "My mama is married, and she is very much her own person."

"An exception does not the case make." Sighing, Charlie said, "You have so much potential and have come so far, Livy. Look how well you did last night until Hadleigh came along."

Pride sparked in Livy as she thought of her successful disguise, the way she'd handled the brute in the alleyway. Moreover, she and Charlie had discovered new clues. They now knew that Longmere was neck-deep in intrigue with Edgecombe, Stamford, Bollinger, and Thorne...and some mysterious Chinese partner whose name could not be spoken.

What were the men up to? Why did Longmere want to stop participating in whatever they were doing? For Pippa's sake, Livy was determined to find out the answers when she, Charlie, and the Willflowers surveilled Longmere at the pleasure gardens tomorrow evening.

"You have many accomplishments ahead of you," Charlie pressed on. "Many women you could help. Don't sell yourself, or our clients, short over a fleeting passion."

"Hadleigh is *more* than a temporary passion. I love him," she declared.

"And that makes him even more dangerous," Charlie said. "Nothing is more deceptive, more capable of betrayal, than love."

Livy cocked her head. "Were you hurt by someone you love?"

Charlie's composure cracked, and the anguish that bled through stunned Livy into silence. She looked to Fi and Glory for help, but they only looked back at her, wide-eyed. This was the first time any of them had witnessed their leader as anything but utterly self-possessed.

In the next heartbeat, Charlie's poise returned. "I have been hurt, yes, which is why I don't want you to make the same mistake. Be wiser than I was, Livy."

"I am sorry for your pain," Livy said softly. "But I know I love Hadleigh."

"And if he forces you to choose between him and the important work you are doing now?"

Livy squared her shoulders. "He will not make me choose."

Inside, she wasn't quite as confident. She was forced to admit that while she knew Hadleigh as a friend, she did not know him as a lover or husband. What were his expectations for marriage? Her disquiet grew as she recalled the rumors of his possessiveness over his duchess and the duels he'd fought over her.

Then Livy's thoughts bounced to his dominant behavior in the stables with Lady Foxton. At the time, his mastery over his lover had stirred a deep and primal response in Livy, but she hadn't considered the possibility that he might be domineering in other spheres of life. It was one thing to play wicked games of passion, which she was all for; it was another if he expected her to be obedient in everyday life.

*This could be a problem.*

She chewed on her lip, not liking her uncertainty. The possibility that her two great passions might be pitted against one another. She wanted everything: the man she loved and the freedom to do what she wanted.

"You are as headstrong as I was, Livy. And just as blinded." Shaking her head, Charlie said, "Whatever you decide, I will remind you of the vow of secrecy you gave when you joined the Angels. You kept the truth about our society from Hadleigh last night, and you must continue to do so. For the protection of our clients and all involved in our group. I want your word, Livy."

Livy hated lying to Hadleigh. Yet she could not go back on her word to her mentor, who had given her so much...the keys to a dazzling new world of adventure.

Livy released a breath. "You have my word."

*Solving problems is my specialty,* she reassured herself. *I'll find a solution. First, I need to ascertain what Hadleigh's expectations are for marriage. Then maybe I can find a way to convince Charlie that he can be trusted...*

"The duke is here!" Glory exclaimed.

Livy's heart thumped with eagerness...and a hint of trepidation for the ruse that was to follow.

"Take your positions, Angels." Charlie's tone was brisk. "You know what to do."

As Ben bowed to the ladies, he had a feeling that something was not quite right.

He tried to pinpoint the cause of his assessment. Lady Fayne was politeness itself, the quintessential hostess in her drawing room graced by white marble goddesses. Against the elegant backdrop, Livy glowed with a dewy freshness that heated his loins, her chestnut hair radiant against the blue walls. She was seated on a buttercup-yellow settee, the other Willflowers on adjacent chairs. All three ladies had embroidery hoops on their laps.

Everything was proper and perfect.

*And therein lies the problem.*

"Your Grace, how lovely to see you again." Lady Fayne's gracious tones drew him out of his thoughts. "To what do we owe the honor?"

He shook off his odd intuition. Told himself he was imagining things. Who was he to question why Livy was doing needlework? He ought to be grateful that Lady Fayne managed to keep the minx occupied with genteel activities...during the daytime, at least. His eyes met Livy's, and the playful warmth in those celadon orbs hit him straight in the chest and lower.

*Hell's teeth, I am* not *going to get hard in this bloody drawing room.*

Clearing his throat, he said, "Before he departed, the Duke of Strathaven asked me to keep an eye on Lady Olivia, and I fear I have been remiss in my duties."

"How kind of you to stop by." The impish curve of Livy's mouth begged to be kissed. "I've been thinking about you since our last visit. It has been far too long."

Damnit, if the chit didn't stop flirting with him, he was going to pounce on her and give them away to her chaperone.

"Why don't you have a seat, Your Grace? I shall pour tea," Lady Fayne said.

Joining Livy on the settee, Ben could smell her fruity, feminine scent, and it made his mouth water. She looked fetching in a gown the shade of peaches...which immediately reminded him of his dream. Of tasting and licking her juiciest part. Devil and damn, this was going to be a torturous visit. To distract himself, he studied the embroidery hoop in her lap.

Using pink silk thread, she'd stitched a pair of wings, surrounding a monogram of "SOA," on a fine linen handkerchief. The stitches were neat and precise. He noticed with further surprise that there was a stack of handkerchiefs on the coffee table in front of her, all embroidered in the same impeccable manner.

He lifted his brows. "Your needlework has improved."

"Has it?" She gave him an innocent look. "Perhaps I never applied myself before."

"And you are motivated to do so now?"

"It is for a good cause," she said demurely.

"The proceeds of the handkerchiefs go toward helping women in need." Lady Fayne handed him a cup, settling on the other side of the coffee table. "Perhaps you would care to purchase a few, Your Grace, to help our cause?"

"I'll take the lot." He sampled the beverage. Oddly enough, the tea was exactly how he preferred it.

"How kind of you," Lady Fayne murmured.

"It is my pleasure to support your charitable efforts. I confess, I am awestruck that you have managed to corral Livy into needle-work." He suppressed a grin when Livy wrinkled her nose. "Is that what you ladies do all day?"

"We do a little of this, a little of that. We also, for instance, write pamphlets that build on the foundation of Wollstonecraft's superb treatise, *A Vindication of the Rights of Women.*" Lady Fayne gestured at a stack of papers on a nearby escritoire. "Perhaps you would care to take one?"

"Thank you," he said politely.

Due to Livy keeping him tied up in knots, he'd suffered a few sleepless nights. Some soporific reading material might be just the ticket.

"I hope you find the pamphlet edifying," Lady Fayne said. "Lord Sheffield professed to find our views on the plight of women quite enlightening."

Ben frowned. "Sheffield has read it?"

"Indeed, he was one of the first to do so." Lady Fayne smiled complacently. "He has been a regular visitor here since Livy came to stay."

"Has he?" Ben swung a glance at Livy, who looked back at him with wide eyes.

Why the devil hadn't she mentioned anything about seeing Sheffield? Was she dallying with the bastard...while keeping Ben dancing on her string? Jealousy scalded his chest. He'd been played in that fashion before. Had sworn to never let another woman make a puppet of him.

"Surely you do not disapprove, Your Grace?" Lady Fayne said with arched brows. "Sheffield is excellent *ton*, and the Duchess of Strathaven told me that she quite prefers him."

"Livy's papa, the duke," he said through his clenched teeth, "has a different view."

"A mother knows what is best for a daughter, don't you think?"

"I do not," Ben snapped.

"Charlie," Livy cut in. "Could Hadleigh and I have a moment alone?"

"Without chaperonage? My dear, would that be proper?"

"Hadleigh is a trusted family friend," Livy insisted. "We will leave the door open."

"Fine. You may have fifteen minutes and not one more." Lady Fayne rose, her smile pleasant and fixed in place. "Come, girls, there are women in need of our assistance."

After the others departed, Ben leaned toward Livy. He planted his hands on the back of the settee, caging her.

"What the devil is going on with Sheffield?" he demanded.

"Nothing." She blinked at him. "You're not jealous, are you?"

"What if I am? Is that what you want?"

Looking into her beautiful face, he suddenly saw Arabella's green eyes looking back. The gloating glow in them as she whispered, *"Prove to me that you're a man, Hadleigh. Prove that you're the only one deserving of me."*

"Of course not." Livy's bewildered voice dispelled the memory. The eyes that stared back at him were once again guileless, with the clarity of a mountain spring. "That is precisely why I didn't mention Sheffield. Not that there is anything to mention. He has visited a few times, yes, but you know he likes to pay attendance upon me. It isn't anything serious, and I could hardly turn him away."

Her rational explanation dumped sand upon the flames of Ben's jealousy. He felt like a fool. And the veriest cad. Jerking away, he dragged a hand through his hair.

"I apologize," he muttered. "I did not mean to alarm you."

"I am not alarmed," she said. "And I will accept your apology —*if* you explain why you acted like a madman."

He owed her an explanation; there was no getting around it.

He forced the words out. "I thought you were trying to goad me into jealousy."

"Why in heaven's name would I do that?"

"Because Arabella did."

He'd never spoken much about his marriage to Livy, due to her young age back then and also his loyalty to, if not his wife, then the vows he'd made. Yet the rumors about the state of his marital affairs had been plentiful, and Livy had always been a little pitcher with big ears. Since Arabella's death, he hadn't hidden the fact that he had no desire to wed again.

His clever queen had probably put two and two together. Thus, he wasn't surprised at the understanding that filled her pretty eyes. Or her next question.

"Why did she wish to make you jealous?" Livy asked quietly.

"It made her feel loved, she said." His lips twisted as he stared at the coffee table. "I was foolish, had married her when I was eighteen and far too young. And I took her at her word that she lied and kept secrets because she wanted my attention. It took me years to understand that what she really enjoyed was having power over me."

"I'm sorry." Livy placed her hand on his jaw, turning his gaze to hers. "I'm sorry she did that to you. But I am not Arabella. And I would never play with your feelings in so shabby a fashion. Love is not a game."

"Livy." His throat constricted; he couldn't look away from her bright sincerity. "Hearing you say that...I cannot tell you what it means to me. Because that is the one thing I would insist upon in marriage: total and complete honesty. I will not tolerate lies from any future duchess of mine."

Livy wetted her lips, looking...anxious? He did not blame her. When it came to romance, he was no idealistic young buck like Sheffield. What he had to offer wasn't poetry and ardent promises but hard truths and a closet full of skeletons.

"Other than, um, honesty, do you have other expectations for marriage?" she asked.

He glanced at the open door, which offered a partial view of the empty hallway. The situation was far from ideal for this conversation, but he had to lay his cards on the table and see her reaction. Had to know whether it was pointless for him to hope.

"They all have to do with the failures of my first union," he said bluntly. "In short, I failed in my duty as a husband and will not make that mistake again. If I marry, I will be the master of my own house. I will expect my wife's honesty and obedience, particularly when it comes to her well-being and safety."

"O-Obedience?" Livy stammered.

His chest tautened. *This is why it is important to have this discussion now.*

"I admire your spirit and always have. But I will treat you differently if we are more than friends," he said with ruthless candor. "From experience, I know that I am a possessive lover. I will want you to belong to me as completely as I will belong to you."

Seeing her pleated brow and obvious confusion, he felt a sinking sensation. Never was he more aware of the differences between them, not just in age but experience. Unlike him, she had never felt a lover's jealousy. She'd never experimented with infidelity and suffered the painful consequences. She'd never questioned whether she was enough to keep her lover interested.

"I do want us to belong to each other," she said slowly. "But I would also want to pursue my own interests."

He thought of Arabella's interests, the intrigues and peccadilloes. The nights she'd come home smelling of other men. The nights she hadn't come home at all. While Livy was loyal, she was also headstrong, indulged by her parents and used to getting her way. And, Christ, she was young and curious, last night's adventures at the tavern being a case in point. What if he couldn't protect her from her wilder instincts? What if he failed as a husband...again?

Jaw clenching, he said, "I would expect to have the final say on whether such interests are acceptable."

Livy's eyes widened just as Lady Fayne's voice sounded in the distance.

"Take time to think upon this," he said firmly. "To consider whether you truly want me to court you. If we halt things now, we can still turn back. Be the friends we've always been."

He didn't know if that was true. If he could ever look at Livy and not think of how sweet she tasted, how right she felt in his arms. Yet it was better to cut their losses now, before they reached the point of no return.

Livy swallowed. "I don't need time. I love you, Hadleigh, and want to be with you."

"Take a day to contemplate," he insisted. "Can you get away tomorrow night? We can discuss the matter then."

She hesitated. "I, um, unfortunately have plans."

"What event are you attending? I will meet you there."

"It is not an event per se. I...I am having a quiet evening at home with Charlie."

He frowned. "Afterward, then. I will pick you up, no matter the hour."

"Charlie will want to drink wine and chat, stay up late. I'm afraid I will be too tired."

He narrowed his eyes. "If I didn't know better, I would think you're making excuses."

"I do want to see you." As Lady Fayne's voice came from just outside the room, Livy whispered, "How about the night after next, around ten o'clock?"

"Done." He wanted to kiss her but satisfied himself with giving her hand a brief squeeze. "Until then, my little queen."

# EIGHTEEN

"Cremorne Gardens seems different tonight," Glory said. "Like a whole different world."

"I know," Livy replied. "It feels strange, doesn't it?"

While she and her friends had been here before with their parents to watch one of the famous hot air balloon ascents, the ambiance tonight felt different. The fog from the nearby Thames hung thick and heavy in the air, diffusing the light of the colored lanterns overhead. Tall, shadowy trees surrounded the sumptuous buildings and stages. All strata of society were represented in the boisterous crowd. Some folk were in fine evening wear, some in masked costumes, and some wearing very little at all.

"Perhaps being sans chaperones and dressed like circus performers might have something to do with it?" Fiona suggested.

"You have a point," Livy said.

The three girls were dressed like the many acrobats giving performances throughout the gardens. Their short dresses, wigs, and face paint concealed their identities. Blending in with the crowd, they sought out their target. They passed an ornate pagoda where a full orchestra played a polka to the delight of the dancers stomping across the stage that circled it.

"I don't see Longmere or his cronies," Glory murmured.

"Me neither. I wonder if Charlie and Mrs. Peabody are having better luck," Fi replied.

Disguised as gentlemen, the other ladies were somewhere in the crowd. They had split up from the Angels to surveil the gardens' main area. The two groups were to reconvene by the banqueting hall in an hour.

"Do you smell that? Roasted chestnuts." Glory sighed. "My favorite."

"You ate supper just before we came. How you manage to maintain your figure while—*oof*." Fi's reply was cut off when a gangling adolescent bumped into her.

"Pardon, miss. Weren't watching where I was going on account o' being distracted by your beauty." He winked, tipped his cap, and continued along.

Livy caught him by the arm. Remembering to disguise her accent, she demanded, "Give my friend back 'er coin purse."

"My coin bag?" Fiona searched her reticule, her gaze thinning at the pickpocket. "Why, you thievin' rotter. Give it back!"

Livy twisted her captive's wrist.

"Ouch!" he protested. "Bleedin' 'ell, no need to break a man's arm o'er a few coins."

"I'll break more than your arm if you don't return my friend's blunt *now*," Livy stated.

Grumbling, the thief gave the purse back to Fiona.

Livy released him with a shove. "Get on wif you."

"Feisty filly, ain't ye?" He grinned cheekily at her. "'Ow would ye like to kick yer 'eels wif me on the dance floor?"

She scowled, and he scampered off.

"Jolly well done," Glory said admiringly. "Your Cockney accent is improving."

"Thank you." Dusting her hands, Livy said, "Shall we?"

They continued on. Livy tried not to be distracted by the spectacle around them, but it was difficult when there were fire-eaters swallowing flames, monkeys dancing jigs, and acrobats performing tricks on horseback. Passing by a throng of drunken masked men, the girls had to dodge groping hands.

Fi swatted the men away like flies. "Now, fellows, I be workin'—"

"I'll pay your wages, dove." A cad leered at her. "Why don't you and I get acquainted in one of the alcoves off the walk?"

"Not tonight, dearie," Fiona said firmly.

*Not ever,* Livy thought with a shudder.

The proposition made her think of Hadleigh: he would have an apoplectic fit if he knew what she was up to. Since he had laid out his expectations for marriage yesterday, she'd been torn between yearning and confusion. She knew she wanted him, yet his rules went against the grain of who she was. While she understood his possessiveness—she felt the same way about him—his desire for obedience was an obstacle. She could not give up her independence any more than she could give up the man she loved.

*You have until tomorrow night to figure something out,* she counseled herself. *For now, concentrate on the mission.*

They were almost at the banqueting hall, a long building with two levels of supper boxes, arched windows framing the diners enjoying their half-crown supper.

Glory drew to a halt. "Over there, by the wine stall," she whispered.

Livy shifted her gaze to the bustling stall some fifteen yards away. A queue of guests waited to sample what the stall's sign boasted was "Cremorne's World-Famous Sherry." She saw Longmere immediately. Accompanied by his four cronies, he cut a dashing figure in an oxblood-red jacket. As she watched, an urchin approached the group. If she hadn't been vigilant, she would have missed the boy slipping something—a piece of paper—to Mr. Thorne before vanishing into the crowd.

Thorne scanned the note, whispering something to his companions.

"I need to improve my lip-reading," Glory said under her breath. "I cannot tell what he's saying other than something about a *fountain*."

"They're moving," Fi replied. "We must follow."

The three wound their way through the crowd, using the sea of people as their cover while they followed the men. They ended up on the arterial walk that traversed the gardens north and south. Stalls selling food and trinkets lined the graveled path, and a glowing fountain splashed up ahead.

Smaller paths branched off from the main route, and as Livy glanced at the openings to those dark veins, a shiver chased over her skin. Cremorne was infamous for its labyrinthine "lovers walks," used by trysting couples and those seeking paid pleasure.

As they neared the fountain, the throng thinned, and it was harder to tail the targets discreetly. The men paused at the fountain, and Livy pulled her friends behind an unoccupied stall.

"We should split up to surveil Longmere," she whispered. "We're too easy to spot as a group."

Fi nodded. "We'll meet up at the banqueting hall as planned."

As Livy was about to reply, she felt a familiar tingling sensation. She peered around the corner of the stall...and her heart banged against her breastbone at the sight of the tall, masked figure who'd emerged by the fountain.

She whipped back around. "*Zounds.* Hadleigh's here."

"Hadleigh?" Glory's brow puckered. "Are you sure—"

"It's him by the fountain. Dash it, he always sees through my disguises," Livy said in a panic.

She was lucky to have muddled her way through an explanation about the Black Lion; there was no *way* Hadleigh would accept her presence here tonight. If he found out, he would end things between them. Every fiber of her being resisted the possibility.

*I cannot lose him,* she thought desperately.

"Leave Longmere to Glory and me," Fi said. "Focus your energies on evading the duke."

Livy nodded. "You will take care?"

"Of course," Glory said.

Livy leaned in, her friends doing the same.

"*Sisters first will see us through,*" they whispered together.

One by one, Glory and Fiona returned to the main walk, blending with the passersby as they headed after Longmere. Counting to ten, Livy left her hiding place, going in the opposite direction. She did not dare to look back at the fountain and tried to keep her pace brisk without raising suspicion. As she melted into the stream of people, a feather of warning brushed her nape.

She paused at a flower stall, pretending to examine the offerings as she covertly glanced behind her. Her gaze collided with Hadleigh's. Through the eyeholes in his ebony mask, recognition flashed like lightning, jolting her into action. She half-walked, half-ran, trying to put distance between them. She passed a theatre, and luckily a show must have just ended for the audience flooded the walk. Livy took refuge in the swarm. Spotting a wooded offshoot up ahead, she let the crowd carry her there and then ducked into the opening.

She dashed down the narrow path, moonlight filtering through the ancient trees. Thumping filled her ears; she didn't know if it was footsteps chasing her or the cadence of her own panic. She ran into the twisting maze toward a source of light. Rounding a corner, she halted: bathed in a lantern's glow, a couple was rutting against a hedge. The woman's exposed breasts jiggled in her unlaced bodice, her skirts bunched at her waist. A man stood between her legs, his trousers down, and he was pumping his member in and out of her.

They both paused to stare at Livy. The man's assessing glance made Livy's skin crawl.

"Care to join us, dove?" He withdrew from his partner, brandishing his glistening member with a leer. "Plenty to go around."

Cheeks aflame, Livy ran on, the couple's laughter ringing behind her. The deeper she delved into the maze, the more distant the sounds of the pleasure garden became. The creaking and swaying of the ancient forest created its own music, and she found herself running to the primal beat. A strange exhilaration filled her: she would escape and find a way out of this catastrophe...

She skidded to a stop. Her path had turned into a nook bordered by tall hedges. There was a stone bench...and no exit. *Dash it, a dead end.* Turning to leave, she gasped as a large, cloaked figure emerged, blocking her way out. She took a step back as Hadleigh advanced toward her; he'd removed his mask, moonlight casting his features in icy silver.

"I-I can explain," she stammered.

He stalked her, his voice a low growl. "No more lies, Olivia."

*Uh-oh. He never calls me Olivia unless he's furious. I'm in for it now.*

Her spine hit the hedges. He planted his hands on either side of her head. He leaned his face into hers, so close that she could see the flames raging in his eyes.

In a lethally soft voice, he said, "What in blazes are you up to?"

As Ben stared into the face of the woman he thought he knew, a dark undertow threatened to suck him under. It wasn't the first time he'd been betrayed, not by a long shot, but the impact of Livy's lies sent him reeling. With Arabella, he'd come to expect duplicity and prepared himself for it.

But for Livy to deceive him? Pain tore through his chest. Like a trapped animal, he wanted to sever the part of him that kept him ensnared. To claw out the aching organ that left him open and vulnerable.

*This is what happens when you concede control to a female. They run roughshod over you.*

Livy wetted her lips. "If I tell you the truth, you must promise you won't be angry."

Was she *insane*?

"You play behind my back and think I won't be angry?" he snarled.

"Play behind your back..." She blinked.

In the moonlight, her eyes were luminescent pools, and their apparent innocence, paired with her harlot's attire, enraged him more.

"Why else would you be at the pleasure gardens by yourself? Dressed like a light-skirt?" He drove a fist into the shrubbery, the sharp jab of twigs a welcome distraction from the pain of betrayal. "I *knew* you were lying to me about why you could not meet tonight."

"I'm not here to...to consort with men," she protested. "You must believe me."

*You must believe me.* God, how many times had he heard those very words from Arabella? Each time, he had given in and taken her back. Because he was weak and did not guide his wife with a firm hand. Because he would rather challenge men to duels than face the fact that the woman he loved cared for no one but herself.

He could not change the past. But he would be damned if he travelled down this path again.

"I told you I will accept nothing but honesty from any future wife of mine," he said bitterly. "I will escort you home. After that, what you do no longer concerns me."

"Please, Hadleigh, let me tell you the truth—"

"I don't give a damn what you have to say, Olivia. Thinking we could be lovers was a mistake from the start, and I'm putting an end to it," he bit out. "I will not be with a woman whom I cannot trust."

He turned to go. She grabbed his arm, her expression stricken.

"This is about the Earl of Longmere," she blurted.

He froze. "You are having an affair with Longmere?"

*"No."* She looked so appalled that he knew she told the truth. "He is Pippa's husband, for heaven's sake."

"Then how the devil are you involved with him?" When she didn't reply, he caught her chin. Forced her gaze to his. "Do not try my patience any further this eve."

"I'm involved because of Pippa. She's in low spirits, and you know she is never that way."

Having socialized with the countess, Ben knew she was possessed of a sunny disposition.

"And how does this pertain to you?" he asked, frowning.

"Well, she, um, told me that she was concerned about Longmere. He hasn't been himself, apparently. He's been moody, not sleeping well, staying out until all hours at his painting studio...he's a painter, you'll recall." When Ben gave a curt nod, she went on, "Pippa even suspects that he might be unfaithful. I could not stand to see her in such distress...so I offered to help her. To find out what he is up to."

Ben stared at her. A thousand responses flew through his mind.

He settled for, "Tell me you are joking."

"It is no jest." She had the audacity to raise her chin. "I consider my friend's happiness a serious matter. If I can do something to help, why wouldn't I?"

Pressure built in Ben's head. He opened his mouth...and closed it. As far-fetched as her story seemed, it was also exactly the sort of damned foolish thing Livy would do. She was loyal to a fault, would do anything for the people she loved...and the recognition punctured his bubble of rage.

This was *Livy*. Not Arabella. Livy was a maddening, mischief-making minx...but she was no cheater. Relief flooded him with almost painful intensity.

"You believe me, don't you?" Livy searched his face with

anxious eyes. "I swear to you, I would never betray you in that way, Hadleigh. I couldn't. I love you."

Already shaken by the force of his relief, he was staggered by her profession.

"Livy—"

"I didn't want to lie about tonight." Her beseeching look melted away his fury. "I just didn't think you would understand my desire to help Pippa."

"I understand your motivation; it is the way you are going about helping your friend that alarms me." Another realization struck him. "Were you at the Black Lion because of Longmere as well?"

"Yes," she said in a small voice.

"Why didn't you tell me?"

"I didn't think you would approve."

"I absolutely do *not* approve." He gave her a severe look. "Putting your life and reputation at risk is unacceptable, no matter the reason."

Her bottom lip trembled. "But I have to help Pippa—"

"That is no excuse," he stated. "As for Longmere, leave him to me. I have business with him."

Business that had once again been delayed because of Livy. By Jove, the chit was a handful. The kind of woman who would age a man before his bloody time.

"What sort of business?" she asked.

"It's irrelevant at present," he said shortly.

Her expression tentative, she said, "Are you still angry?"

He gave her the truth. "Yes."

"Do you still want to...to court me?"

Her vulnerability constricted his chest. She was so young. Pure of heart and intention, even when her actions were reckless in the extreme.

"You said I needed time to think, but I know what I want: you.

Always you." Her voice broke a little. "Please, Hadleigh, won't you give me another chance?"

Staring into her pleading eyes, he *felt* the beauty of who she was: it shone through her tawdry disguise and hit him straight in his gut...and in his prick. His jealousy had faded, but now his blood was pumping with a different sort of need. Whether it was right or wrong, he wanted Livy. Wanted to cherish and protect her as much as he wanted to own her surrender. For some reason, Fate had seen fit to give him his precious little queen, and he could deny destiny's gift no longer.

The instant he made the decision, a boulder lifted from his shoulders. A sense of rightness settled inside him. Concurrently, anticipation heated his loins. His girl needed a firm hand...and it would be his pleasure to give her what she needed.

"Don't lie to me again," he said.

"I won't." Livy chewed on her bottom lip. "Will you still court me then?"

"No," he said firmly.

Her eyes glimmered. "Please, I swear—"

"We are beyond courtship, Livy." He cupped her cheek, trailing his thumb along her delicate cheekbone, swiping away the single tear that had fallen. "Our bond has changed over time, and my mistake was trying to convince myself that I still see you as a little girl when it is clear that you are a woman now. A woman who knows her mind and who wants to be my lover and my duchess. Who is willing to follow my rules and guidance. Am I correct?"

For a heartbeat, she just stared at him.

Then she breathed, "Yes. Oh, *yes.*"

"When we are together like this, you may address me as Ben." He tested her. "Or *sir.*"

Her quiver of excitement electrified the space between them and sent a stiffening jolt to his cock. God help him, she *was* aroused by dark games. The things he could teach her...

"Yes, sir," she whispered.

"Now you have been a naughty minx not once but twice," he said in a deliberately cool tone. "Taking risks and lying to me."

Her expression instantly grew contrite. "I am sorry—"

"And you will make amends." Taking her hand, he led her over to the stone bench. He sat upon it and patted his thigh. "Put your-self over my knee for your punishment."

# Nineteen

Shaking with anticipation, Livy lowered herself onto Ben's lap, her torso pressing against the hard rack of his thighs. She could hardly believe this was happening. For a terrifying moment, she'd thought she had lost him forever, but somehow he had decided to give her another chance.

Guilt gnawed at her; she hadn't told him the entire truth. Yet how could she, when she knew that he would forbid her from being an Angel? When she'd given her vow of secrecy to Charlie? Livy could not choose between her love for Ben and her independence.

*I'll find a way to make this work.*

She shivered, thinking of the consequences if she failed.

"You are certain you wish to play this game, little one?"

She twisted her head to look at Ben. Seeing the concerned dent between his brows, she realized that he'd misread the cause of her shiver. He thought she was afraid of what they were about to do when, in reality, she was afraid that he *wouldn't* want to make love to her.

"Yes, sir," she said in a rush.

She didn't know why calling him "sir" put her into a lather.

The wicked glint in his eyes told her he felt the same way. She'd always enjoyed playing with him, and this felt like a new, exciting, and very adult game.

"Then pull up your skirts for me."

At his commanding tone, something in her went as pliant as wax held over a flame. With trembling hands, she reached back, tugging the flimsy material to her waist. Beneath the short acrobat's skirt, she wore no petticoat, just stockings and a pair of drawers. Her breath whooshed from her lungs as he palmed each cheek of her linen-covered bottom in turn and squeezed. His proprietary touch made desire bloom inside her.

"Given your many trespasses, I think you need a bare-bottom spanking."

*Heavens.* A heady blend of excitement and embarrassment enveloped her as he drew down her drawers, leaving them to hang by her ankles. Imagining what he was seeing, how she must appear to him, caused heat to spread over every inch of her skin.

"Ready to count out your punishment, little one?"

She turned her head once more. He'd never looked more handsome or more serious. And in his question, she heard what he was asking. *Are you certain you want this?*

"Yes, sir," she said breathlessly.

He brought his hand down, the loud smack echoing through the leafy alcove. She gasped in shock at the burning sensation on her left cheek.

She blinked at him. "That hurt."

"Did you think it would not?" he inquired. "Count, Livy."

"One," she blurted and dropped her head.

He swatted her other cheek.

"T-two," she said.

Her cheek pressed against his trousered leg, she scarcely heard the next slap over her thundering heart. Who knew that being spanked could be so...titillating? The heat in her bottom set off a chain of reactions in her body. Her skin felt itchy with need, her nipples throbbing with engorged heat. In the secret cove between her thighs, she'd grown distinctly damp, and sudden anxiety besieged her.

*Am I supposed to be this...this wet? Is it normal? Will he notice and find it disgusting...?*

*Smack.* The firmness of his palm jolted her out of her thoughts.

"You forgot to count," he said.

Botheration, she'd lost track. "Um, four?"

"Incorrect." For some reason, his reprimand aroused her further. "Am I boring you?"

"N-no, sir," she stammered.

"Then look at me." When she did, he said, "Tell me what is distracting you."

Her face burned worse than her bottom. "It's, um, nothing..."

"I will be the judge of that." He spanked her again, then rubbed the spot in a way that made her squirm in his lap. "You are not to hide anything from me, Livy. Ever."

*If he only knew all that I'm hiding...*

She bit her lip, not wanting to be distracted. Ben had asked her what had diverted her in this moment, and she could give him the truth.

Gathering her courage, she said, "It has come to my attention that I've become rather...damp. In, um, an indelicate place."

A devilish smile lit his eyes.

"Have you now?" he said. "I shall be the judge of that."

Her breath hitched as his touch trailed down the crease of her bottom. His fingers dipped lower, and she gasped when they touched her most intimate place.

"Hmm, you *are* wet, you little minx." The satisfaction in his voice caused more viscous heat to trickle from her. "But there is nothing indelicate about this part of you. This is your pussy, and it's supposed to weep pretty tears when we are together."

Her cheeks flamed at the naughty word, made naughtier by the way he was stroking her as if she were a prized pet. As a girl who liked to take charge, she didn't understand why being over Ben's lap, exposed to his gaze and powerless to his experienced touch, aroused her to such a shocking degree...but it did.

He delved lower, finding an exquisitely sensitive place that pushed a moan from her throat.

"What a sweet little bud this is," he said. "This is called your pearl. Have you discovered its pleasures?"

As bold as she was, she couldn't answer him. She couldn't.

He smacked her bottom hard. "Tell me, Livy."

"Yes," she admitted, her face and entire being on fire.

"Good girl." The knowing rasp in his voice scraped over her nerve endings, heightening her sensitivity to his words and touch. "You deserve a reward for your honesty."

He began to stroke her, and she moaned, letting her head fall by his leg again. She could hear how wet she was, the slick sounds his fingers made as they rubbed her pearl and pussy. His mastery of her body, the fact that he obviously knew more about it than she did, fed her wanton surrender. She gave herself up to the sensations—to Ben, who knew how to give her such pleasure.

For him alone did she wish to be a good girl.

Then she felt him probe deeper, touching her where she'd never been touched before.

"What a nice, tight cunny you have." His words caused that part of her to clench. "I can feel it sucking on my finger, wanting me inside yet afraid at the same time. Relax, little love, I won't hurt you. Will it help if I frig your pearl like this...?"

His delicious depravity drove her toward a frenzied peak. She squeezed her eyes shut as the pressure inside her built and built. She needed more, even as it was too much. The stimulation of her pearl, the filling thrust of his finger pushed her right to the edge...

He took his hand away, and she moaned in frustration.

"Look at me, Livy," he said.

Panting, needing, she twisted her neck to meet his gaze.

"Who does your pleasure belong to?" he asked.

"You, sir," she said with tremulous longing.

"Will you look for it elsewhere? Seek diversions without my permission?" His eyes bored into her. "Will you keep secrets from me?"

*Surely, he only means secrets of a carnal nature, and I would never betray him that way.*

She shook her head.

He touched her drenched folds with a lightness that frustrated rather than relieved. She quivered as his fingertip neared her needy bud...and groaned when he skipped over it.

"I want the words, Livy. Will you lie or keep secrets from me?"

"No," she gasped.

"Good." He stroked her pearl in a hard, circling motion. Satisfaction burned in his gaze, the sapphire flames searing her soul, incinerating her will and returning it as fiery pleasure. "Then come for me. Spend all over my hand like a good girl."

The wickedness of his demand and touch catapulted her into bliss. She cried out as she crested on ecstasy, his caresses keeping her soaring. Each time she thought it was over, he unleashed another gust of pleasure that kept her afloat.

When Livy returned to earth, she was utterly spent and as limp as a rag doll. Ben set her clothing to rights and sat her beside him on the bench, keeping an arm around her. She gazed contentedly at the man of her dreams, who was even more potent in reality. In the play of shadow and moonlight, his chiseled features had an austere cast that made him seem like a stranger...and it excited her.

*Finally*, he was showing her the part of him he'd held back. He was treating her not like a little girl, his pseudo-sister, but like a woman. The lover she wanted to be...and which, she realized, she wasn't quite yet.

She peered down at the huge bulge straining the front of his trousers.

"Is there, um, anything I can do?" She moistened her lips. "For you?"

He smiled then. That slow, beautiful smile she had always loved.

"You have done quite enough, little queen," he said.

"But you didn't...you know," she said shyly. "Enjoy yourself."

"Oh, but I did," he replied.

His gaze holding hers, he brought his hand to his mouth. He licked the tips of his index and middle fingers. When she realized those fingers had coaxed her to bliss, her inner muscles trembled.

"Delectable," he murmured. "Next time, I am going to sample from the source."

Even as her brain steamed up at the possibilities his words conjured, she said anxiously, "Will there be a next time?"

He studied her with unwavering intensity. "Do you want there to be?"

"More than anything," she said fervently. "All I have ever wanted is to be with you, Ben."

The possessiveness that darkened his eyes sent a thrill up her spine.

"Your wish is my command," he said softly.

*He wants me, he wants me!* her inner voice sang. And if the teensy part of her not given over to joy fretted over the promise she'd made to not keep any secrets, she told herself she would deal with it later. The details of their relationship could be ironed out; for now, it was enough—*everything*—that he wanted to be with her.

Giddy with happiness, she teased, "I rather thought *you* were the one in command."

His lips twitched. "Then stop being cheeky and give me your mouth."

Smiling, she tipped her lips up and welcomed his claim.

*Finally.*

A while later, Livy snuggled up against Ben in his carriage. He was taking her back to Charlie's. Luckily, before they'd departed Cremorne, Livy had spotted Charlie by the banqueting hall. She'd given her mentor, whose impeccable male disguise fooled even Hadleigh, a discreet signal that all was well. The other's nod confirmed the same was true on her end.

Reassured that her friends were well, Livy was able to enjoy the present interlude. To bask in the joy of being with the man she loved. Ben had tucked her against his side, his arm around her, his knuckles softly stroking her cheek. She'd never felt safer or more content.

"Did you enjoy yourself?" he murmured.

"With all my heart." She gave him a mischievous look. "And other less mentionable parts."

He tweaked a lock of her hair. She'd dispensed with her wig, leaving her own locks loose and free.

"To think I was afraid of corrupting you," he said dryly.

"You may put that fear to rest. I love being with you, Ben." She angled her head up to meet his gaze. "And not just in the way we were together tonight. Since I was twelve years old, I have always gravitated to you, always wanted to be in your presence. We could be playing cards or chatting or doing nothing at all: I just want to be with you. I will always want that."

"I feel the same way." The note of wonder in his voice squeezed her heart. "I don't pretend to understand why or how my feelings for you changed, but I accept that they have. Accept that I want you more than I've wanted anything."

"I'm yours," she said happily.

He was silent long enough for her to worry.

"Ben?" she prompted.

"For years, I was an opium user."

His jarring words made her sit up and face him. "Pardon?"

"You should know this part of my past." His expression was bleak, but he met her gaze readily. "I had an opium habit. It started before you first met me and lasted until two years ago."

As her shock wore off, pieces fell into place. She remembered his pallor and bloodshot eyes, his painful gauntness. The times he'd seemed listless and ill.

"Have you...do you...?" She didn't know how to ask.

"Not for two years and never again," he said resolutely. "I don't touch spirits either. Opium is in my past, but I felt it was only fair that you know. In case it...it changed anything."

His raw honesty humbled her.

"Nothing could change how I feel about you," she said softly.

He let out a breath that she hadn't realized he'd been holding. "Good."

*Can I trust you to feel the same way? If I told you my secret, would you still...*

She drew her brows together, realizing that he hadn't spoken of love yet. But they had covered a lot of ground this eve, and the fact that he accepted his desire for her was enough for now. She did not doubt his care for her and was certain he would get to love eventually.

"Why the serious expression?" Ben asked.

"Oh, nothing. I was just thinking."

"About?"

She gave the first excuse that came to mind. "Pippa."

She regretted her choice when Ben lowered his brows.

"You must desist in your efforts to help her. I mean it, Livy," he said with emphasis. "The situation is dangerous: you do not know what Longmere is involved in."

An obvious fact struck Livy, one she couldn't believe she'd overlooked.

"But you do?" She stared at him. "Is that why you were at the Black Lion Inn and Cremorne Gardens? Were you following Longmere? For what purpose?"

He studied her before replying. "I have reason to believe he may be involved in the distribution of a deadly drug. It is similar to opium but far more lethal. Several lives have been lost to this substance just in the past few weeks."

She blinked. "And how do you know this?"

"It is a long story, and we're at Lady Fayne's."

She hadn't realized that the carriage had stopped. "Fine. You can tell me before we speak to Longmere together."

"There is no way in hell I'm taking you—"

"I can help. Please trust me. I know Longmere better than you do." Taking a risk, she said, "At the Black Lion, I heard him say that he wanted out of some scheme he and his cronies are embroiled in."

Ben's mouth formed a grim line. "What else did you hear?"

"I will tell you...if you bring me with you to interrogate Longmere."

He narrowed his gaze. "Are you attempting to coerce me?"

"I'm trying to negotiate with you," she countered. "Please, Ben, you know how much Pippa means to me. I *must* help her. Besides, I won't be in any danger if you are there. I know the address of Longmere's studio, where Pippa says he spends most of his time. You and I could go together tomorrow."

After a moment, Ben muttered, "Was I under the delusion that I was captain of this ship?"

"Every captain needs a first mate." She gave him her most winning smile. "If we are contemplating a future together, we should know how we deal with one another in everyday life."

"We're talking about interrogating a man on his involvement in a drug enterprise. Not choosing a china pattern."

"Nonetheless, we would be working together. And that is what I want from marriage," she said in a heartfelt rush. "I know you want my obedience, and I will try my best to be guided by you. But I also want us to be trusted friends, the way we have always been. I want us to share everything: our darkest fears, brightest hopes, and grandest passions."

He opened his mouth...then closed it. She saw the conflict and yearning on his handsome features. It heartened her that he, too, wanted the kind of closeness she described even though he had to reconcile it with his protective nature.

"Devil take it." He looked thoroughly disgruntled. "Fine, you may come—"

"Thank you!"

"*If* you do as I say before, during, and after the meeting."

"Where you lead, I follow," she said promptly.

With an exaggerated sigh, he directed his gaze at the ceiling. "God help me."

# TWENTY

The following afternoon, Ben picked Livy up from Lady Fayne's. The little vixen had told Lady Fayne that Ben was taking her for a drive through Hyde Park in his phaeton, an activity that did not require the presence of a chaperone. Ben did not know whether to find Livy's ingenuity impressive or worrisome. Likewise, he was ambivalent about his decision to bring her along on his visit to Longmere.

Last night, he'd been persuaded by her sincere appeal. Loyalty was one of Livy's most endearing traits, and he understood her desire to help her friend...and to be a part of his life. The intimacy she'd described had stirred a tingling recognition, a whisper of a forgotten dream. He'd never had that before: a lover who was also a friend. A woman who wanted to share everything with him and whom he could trust with his deepest secrets.

Perched next to him as he handled the reins of the two chestnuts, Livy was as pretty as a picture in her mint-green frock embroidered with yellow rosebuds. Her bonnet had a spray of fresh yellow roses and was secured by green ribbons, which fluttered against her smooth cheek. Encased in delicate kid, her small hands were primly folded in her lap.

He was enchanted by the contrast between her demure exterior and her wantonness under his command, and he wanted a taste of the latter.

"Does it hurt to sit?" he asked.

Livy's blush set off a satisfied hum in his blood. "Not really."

"Perhaps I ought to spank you harder next time," he said thoughtfully.

She slid a glance at him, an impish sparkle in her eyes.

"But why?" she asked coyly. "I was a good girl for you, wasn't I?"

Christ, she was a quick study. He'd always enjoyed their banter, and flirtation made it even more delightful.

"You were," he allowed. "But you were also naughty, spending on my lap in a public garden."

Her cheeks turned even rosier. "I, um, thought you liked that?"

"I did. It makes me hard just thinking about it."

Her gaze fell to his burgeoned groin, and his balls tautened when she wetted her lips. She was an adorable, natural wanton, and her needs perfectly matched his own. How did he get so bloody lucky?

"I offered to, um, help. With your condition," she said in a breathy voice.

"You would like to serve me, would you?"

"I would love it, sir."

The earnestness of her reply sent more blood rushing to his cock. He nearly groaned at the filthy image that sprang into his mind: Livy on her knees in front of him, staring sweetly up into his eyes as he pushed his prick between her pretty pink lips...

He took a composing breath. "You will have a chance soon enough."

"How soon?"

At her unmaidenly impatience, he had to stifle a laugh.

"You will have to wait to find out, little brat," he said. "Until then, let us talk of other matters. The present topic isn't helping my concentration, and I don't want to drive us off the road."

Her reply was a lighthearted giggle. Bemused, he shook his head. How could his little queen be so sweet and seductive at the same time?

The fun moments made it easier to address the darker topics Ben had promised to tell Livy about. He spent the remainder of the ride sharing about his recovery from opium, including his work with Master Chen. He told her about the night watch, the discovery of the lethal drug, and the clues that had led to Longmere and his cronies.

At the conclusion of his tale, Livy said softly, "You have always been a hero in my eyes, and now I admire you even more. It took great strength to free yourself from opium's clutches. And you are doing the right and noble thing in trying to stop the spread of this dangerous substance."

He had to look away, fighting back an embarrassing surge of heat behind his eyes. Hell, she had a way of undoing him. Even as a little girl, she'd touched his heart in a way no one else had. As a woman, she would own him completely...and the realization was both alarming and heady. He couldn't fail her the way he had his sister and his dead wife. Couldn't lose her when she meant more to him than anyone.

"Thank you." His voice felt scratchy in his throat. "That means more than you can know."

"It means everything to me that you were willing to share your past," she replied. "Now I understand the importance of our mission. We must discover who is behind this scourge and stop them."

The determined angle of her chin renewed his fears. He cursed his weakness in bringing her today. He ought to start this relationship the way he meant it to go on: with him in charge and her doing as she was told.

"This isn't *our* mission." He levelled a reprimanding stare at her. "I will not have you endangering yourself for any reason, Livy. If something happened to you, I could not bear it. Perhaps I made a mistake in allowing you to accompany me today."

"No, you didn't," she said quickly. "I promise I will not interfere."

He did not trust her innocent expression. Yet it was too late to regret his decision, for they had arrived at their destination: a row of terraced brick houses in Fitzrovia, a fashionable area for artistic types. Longmere's studio was the corner property. The large windows on all three floors were sparkling, free of the coal dust that clung to the glass panes of the neighboring addresses. As a painter, Longmere presumably needed good light.

Handing Livy down, Ben led the way to the front door. "Let me do the talking."

"You are in charge," Livy said cheerily.

He was doomed. Sighing, he rang the bell. After several minutes passed, he did it again.

"Do you think no one is here?" Livy asked.

He felt a quiver of amusement as she balanced on tiptoe, trying to see through the window at the top of the door. She looked like a girl trying to peep at the treats in a sweets shop.

"I'll try again," he said.

When moments passed with no response, his foreboding grew.

"According to Pippa, Longmere practically lives at his studio. It is odd that he is not answering." Livy's wide eyes reflected his own misgivings.

He reached for the door handle...and it turned in his palm.

"Go back to the carriage, Livy," he said tersely.

"But I—"

He took out a pistol. "Now."

With obvious reluctance, she complied. He entered Longmere's studio and didn't like the stillness that greeted him. He cocked his weapon, crossing the antechamber to the nearest room. The door to the front parlor was cracked, and he pushed it open.

The curtains were drawn; in the dimness, easels and paintings lurked like exotic beasts. Seeing no movement, Ben crossed to the windows and parted the drapes. Light flooded in, illuminating the jungle-green walls, the splashes of color on canvas...the pair of gleaming boots sticking out from behind a divan.

Heart hammering, Ben went over. It was Longmere. The earl's eyes were open, his hair a dark halo against the carpet. As Ben crouched to check for a pulse he knew would not be there, his gaze caught on the bottle tucked in the dead man's hand. He read the familiar label.

*Laudanum.*

Footsteps made him jerk upright, and he turned to see Livy dashing into the room.

"I couldn't wait..." Her gaze fell on Longmere. "*Zounds.* Is he...?"

"Dead," Ben said grimly. "Of a laudanum overdose, it appears."

# TWENTY-ONE

1845, FALL

*Livy is 16; Ben is 28*

*Dear Hadleigh,*

*It has been three months since I saw you last, and I hope you have been getting my letters. The ones I have been sending you twice a month. Mama says—and Papa agrees—that I must not pester you while you are in mourning, but I hope you find my correspondence a comfort and not a bother.*

*I wish I had more entertaining tales with which to regale you but, alas, you must content yourself with my schoolmiss adventures. Things have improved considerably at Mrs. Southbridge's Finishing School now that Glory and Fiona are here with me. Sally Sackville is still up to her tricks—next time I will tell you what she did to poor Miss Tomlinson, a new pupil—and she even tried to give me, Fi, and Glory a mean-spirited moniker: the Willflowers.*

*Unfortunately for Sally, my friends and I like the name and have decided to keep it.*

*I hope you are sleeping and eating better and that the country air is improving your constitution. If you wish to reply, I will be at our London address until October. After that, we will return to Scotland. We will be hosting our usual Christmas and Hogmanay celebrations at Strathmore Castle, and you are invited, of course, but by no means obligated to attend (although I do hope you will).*

*Your ever faithful,*
  *Livy*

## 1846 EARLY SPRING

*Dear Hadleigh,*

*We missed you at Hogmanay, and I hope the Yuletide season brought you some cheer. Wherever you were, I hope you were not alone. I still have not received a reply from you, but I did see Aunt Beatrice, who said she paid you a brief visit. She seemed concerned about you, as any sister rightly should be. Yet when I suggested that I might visit you, she said something about leading a horse to water. In her example, I believe you are the horse, and I am not to try to force you to do anything.*

*Thus, I shall continue to wait for your return. Patience, as you know, is not one of my virtues, but for your sake I will strive for self-improvement. Mama read the last sentence over my shoulder and started laughing... I do not see what she finds so amusing.*

*Your ever faithful,*
  *Livy*

## 1846, SUMMER

*Dear Hadleigh,*

*Thank you ever so much for the lovely birthday gift!*

*Even before I read the accompanying note, I knew it was from you. Who else would understand my fascination with spiders and send me such a marvelous book on the subject? The engravings are wonderful and delightfully lifelike. I could not resist showing it off to my friends at school. Of course, Sally Sackville had to butt in to comment on my "peculiar interests"...so I showed her the drawing of the Theraposa blondi (the Goliath bird-eating tarantula).*

*Her resulting case of the vapors made your present worth its weight in gold.*

*Now that I am seventeen, preparations are underway for my debut. Soon I will be presented at Court, and I have been practicing my curtsy for the Queen. Suitors have also begun to call, which is more a testament to Papa's title and my dowry than any personal attractions I can lay claim to.*

*In this regard, I am sad to report that I haven't changed much since you saw me last. Mama says I am a late bloomer, but I fear I might not bloom at all. I take comfort in knowing that, while I might not be the prettiest blossom, I am at least a hardy Willflower.*

*Your ever faithful,*
   *Livy*

*P.S. My family and I visited Aunt Bea's country estate last month, and I took my brothers swimming in the pond. Remember the swimming lesson you gave me there? As a tribute to your teachings,*

*I dunked Chris and Will quite thoroughly. You would have been proud.*

## 1846, WINTER

*Dear Hadleigh,*

*This will be the last letter I write. I fear your ongoing silence is a reply in and of itself, and the last thing I wish is to be a nuisance to you. Please know that I will continue to think of you and pray for your happiness and health. Whenever you are ready, I will be here.*

*Your ever faithful,*
*Livy*

## 1847, SPRING

*My Dearest Livy,*

*I beg your pardon for my silence and thank you for your many letters. Even though I did not reply, I read each of them, often more than once. They were beacons in the darkness and gave me hope during what has been a long and rather unexpected journey. I am pleased to report that I am now recovered and plan to return to Society next month. It is my fondest wish that your face will be among the first that I see, little friend.*

*Please convey my regards to your family.*

*Your servant,*
*Hadleigh*

# TWENTY-TWO

The day after Longmere's death, Livy sat with Pippa in the latter's drawing room. Glory, Fi, and Charlie were there as well. Pippa's parents, Mr. and Mrs. Hunt, had left a few minutes ago to tend to funeral arrangements for their son-in-law.

Before they departed, Mrs. Hunt had drawn Livy aside in the hallway.

"Keep an eye on Pippa, will you?" she whispered, bright concern in her blue eyes. "She did not sleep a wink last night. She is not taking Longmere's death well."

"Can you blame our daughter?" Her husband, Gavin Hunt, did not whisper. A tall, powerfully built man with a scar on his right cheek, Mr. Hunt said derisively, "The bastard didn't even have the decency to exit in a proper manner."

"Now, darling, you mustn't speak ill of the dead," Mrs. Hunt began.

"I spoke ill of him when he was alive," Mr. Hunt reminded her.

"Well, you are consistent, I grant you that."

At his wife's exasperated tone, Mr. Hunt's lips twitched. He put a large, proprietary hand on her waist. "I'm constant, Percy, which is more than I can say for that penniless, pompous fop. What Pippa saw in him, I'll never understand."

"As a painter herself, Pippa was drawn to his artistic sensibilities," Mrs. Hunt explained.

"I was a cutthroat." Mr. Hunt snorted. "Did you see me wanting to marry a lady cutthroat?"

Mrs. Hunt's gaze flitted upward. "Come along, dear. We have a meeting with the florist."

She dragged her husband off.

Now Livy shared a settee with Pippa, and her heart ached to see her friend's waxen countenance. It was as if Pippa's inner lamp had been doused: her blue eyes had lost their sparkle, and her hair was dull and lifeless, pulled back in a severe knot. The frock she wore had been hastily dyed for the occasion, the heavy black deepening the shadows beneath her reddened eyes.

For several minutes now, Pippa had been staring off into space.

Worried, Livy asked, "Could I pour you some tea, Pippa?"

"No. Thank you." Pippa's reply was monotone.

"Perhaps there is something else you would like?"

"Actually, there is." Pippa's gaze sharpened and circled the room. "Now that Mama and Papa are gone, I want the truth: was my husband's death an accident?"

The last two days had been an exercise in delicate maneuvering. After discovering Longmere in his studio, Livy had convinced Ben to let her break the news to Pippa. She, accompanied by Charlie, had had the painful task of informing Pippa of her husband's death. Given that Livy had found Longmere's body, Charlie had had to reveal the true purpose of the Society of Angels and the Willflowers' involvement.

Pippa, in an obvious state of shock over her loss, had absently agreed not to disclose the true purpose of Charlie's charity to anyone...including Ben. Charlie remained adamant that Livy keep her vow of secrecy, and Livy wasn't certain the time was right to tell Ben anyway. Despite the deep roots of their relationship, their romance had just sprouted, the feelings tender and new. She didn't want to risk damaging Ben's budding acceptance of her as his lover.

*I will tell him when the time is right,* she promised herself.

According to the note she'd received from Ben, he planned to pay his respects to Pippa today. Apparently, he had news to share. Before the arrival of the police, he and his friend Master Chen had done a search of Longmere's study. Livy was burning to know if the two had discovered any clues to the earl's death. For now, however, she concentrated on supporting Pippa as best she could.

"Do you have reason to believe that Longmere's death was not an accident?" Livy asked with care.

"The police inspector who came by this morning stated that Longmere died from an overdose of laudanum. That makes *no sense,*" Pippa said feverishly. "My husband despised the stuff. It made him feel ill, and he never touched it, even when he had the most horrid toothache. When I tried to tell the inspector about this, he brushed me off, told me I was being hysterical and needed bed rest."

Ben had guessed that the police might not be much help. Apparently, he'd been correct.

"Since you found Longmere, Livy," Pippa said, swallowing, "I want to know what *you* saw."

Uncertain how much to tell Pippa, Livy looked to Charlie for help.

"I want to hear the truth from you, Livy. Not Lady Fayne." Pippa glowered at Charlie, who remained composed, her hands folded in the lap of her dove-grey dress. "If I had known that she was involving the three of you girls in this mess, I would never have accepted her offer of assistance."

"It is not Charlie's fault," Livy protested. "We *wanted* to help."

"It was our choice," Fiona agreed.

"And we still want to help, if you'll let us," Glory chimed in.

"You are *girls*," Pippa burst out. "What can you possibly do?"

"Anything they want to." Charlie's manner was confident. "I have been training the Angels for weeks, and I have never seen anyone—male or female—learn the skills of investigation so quickly."

Pippa frowned. "What skills?"

"We know how to observe subjects and glean information discreetly," Livy said.

"We are also versed in physical combat, weaponry, and disguises," Fi added.

Pippa's forehead creased. "And your parents approve of this?"

"They might." Livy cleared her throat. "If they knew about it."

"That is *precisely* my point," Pippa argued. "Lady Fayne has no right to involve you in danger and deception—"

"*I* wanted to do this." Livy willed her friend to understand. "Sometimes one must go against the wishes of others to pursue one's true purpose and desires."

Pippa's lashes trembled.

Realizing that she might have inadvertently poured salt on her friend's wounds, Livy took Pippa's hands and said contritely, "If you let us help, we will do our best to find out what happened to your husband."

Looking torn, Pippa said, "Then you *do* think that it wasn't an accident?"

Livy nodded.

Pippa released a shuddering breath. "Tell me everything."

Livy gave a summary of the facts, including the conversation she'd overheard at the Black Lion and Longmere's appearance at Cremorne Gardens. While Livy had been detained by Ben that night, Glory and Fiona had tried to track Longmere, but he had seemed to sense that he was being followed, giving them the slip. Livy also shared that Longmere and his cronies had likely been involved in a deadly drug ring headed by a mysterious Chinese partner, and Longmere had wanted out of the enterprise.

Pippa sat with her gaze trained on her lap, where her fingers twisted a lace-edged handkerchief. Livy feared that she'd been too candid, given Pippa's delicate state of mind. Then Pippa raised her eyes, and the blue orbs were as hard as ice.

"How do you intend to find my husband's killer?" she demanded.

Livy gave the floor to Charlie, who replied in business-like tones.

"There are several paths we could take," Charlie said. "First, with your permission, I would like to search Longmere's personal effects for possible clues."

Pippa gave a tight-lipped nod.

"Next, we will determine our strategy with regard to Edgecombe, Stamford, Thorne, and Bollinger. I would wager that at least one of them knows something about the earl's death. Indeed, the killer could be amongst them. However, I do not believe they will be truthful under interrogation."

"We could continue spying on them. Who knows, they may even lead us to this supposed Chinese partner." Glory wrinkled her nose. "The business smells like the Billingsgate Fish Market, if you ask me."

Pippa bit her lip. "That sounds dangerous. If something happened to you girls—"

"We can take care of ourselves," Fi reassured her. "Come watch us train, and you'll see."

"Other than Edgecombe and his group," Charlie said, "did your husband have any other people in his life, family or friends, who he might have confided in?"

"He had *me*." Pippa's poise cracked. "If only I had insisted that he tell me what was going on. If only I hadn't been afraid of being a nuisance—"

"You cannot blame yourself," Charlie said firmly. "It was Longmere's decision and his alone to participate in this scheme and to keep secrets from you, his wife. The only thing that is within your power now is to see that his murderer is brought to justice."

Pippa nodded, taking a composing breath. "He was painting a lot...near the end. He'd recently been selected to exhibit at the Royal Academy, and he spent hours in his studio perfecting his entry. You could talk to the housekeeper, Mrs. Ingerson; the day you found Longmere was her day off. I am sure Mrs. Ingerson could provide you with a list of visitors to the studio. Longmere also used a number of models in his work. His favorite was Alicia Hoskins, a lovely woman."

Pippa was interrupted by the butler, who announced the arrival of the Duke of Hadleigh. As the butler went to fetch Ben, Livy turned anxiously to her friend. "You will remember not to say anything about the Society of Angels to Hadleigh?"

"Yes." Pippa frowned. "What is going on between you and him? You never said why the two of you were together when you found Longmere."

"It's, um, a long story," Livy said. "I'll explain later, but I appreciate your discretion."

"As I appreciate yours." Pippa addressed them as a group. "Whatever you discover about Longmere, I must ask that you do your best to keep it confidential. I do not wish to give the *ton*—or my parents—any more reasons to dishonor his memory."

Ben had not been looking forward to visiting the Countess of Longmere. Not because he found her as anything but amiable, but because of the news he had to deliver. Examining her husband's body, Chen had found specks of blood in the eyes, purple splotches on the face and neck, and foaming in the airways, all of which pointed to asphyxiation, rather than a laudanum overdose, as the cause of death. The laudanum pooled at the back of Longmere's throat suggested that it had been poured in after he'd died.

Ben hadn't known how Lady Longmere would react to such grotesque news, but she appeared calm. Livy was of obvious comfort to her friend, holding the lady's hand. Ben was grateful that Livy had already delivered the unpleasant news of Longmere's involvement in the drug business. Having discovered no clues in Longmere's studio, Ben now had to delicately ask for the widow's permission to search her dead husband's study.

"Why don't you rest, Pippa? I'll show His Grace the way," Livy offered.

Thus, he found himself with Livy in Longmere's study. Lady Fayne had left a while earlier due to a megrim, taking the other Willflowers with her, and he had promised to take Livy home. Even though their purpose was grim, he relished having time alone with her.

His little queen looked regal and diminutive in her little coronet, with looped side braids brushing her cheeks. She appraised the cluttered study with a keen gaze. The walls were covered in oil paintings, the furnishings showing signs of wear. Longmere's desk sat in a corner; it was heaped with papers, charcoals, and assorted painting implements.

"Shall we split up the task?" Livy asked.

He debated keeping her out of the endeavor. With her loyal nature, however, Livy would want to help her friend...and she was not one to sit idly by. He supposed that no harm could come of her looking through the study with him.

"I'll take the desk," he said. "Why don't you look through the rest of the room?"

She beamed at him as if he'd given her the moon and stars, and they went to work. The companionable silence tucked around them like a cozy, familiar blanket. It had always been this way with her: their togetherness had no need for words. They were in separate parts of the room, yet her presence lightened the burden of his task. As he sorted through the mess of the desk, he looked up now and again, his mouth twitching at the sight of his pretty miss, searching the room as methodically as a burglar.

He found nothing of interest until he opened the bottom drawer. He pulled out stacks of bills, many of the amounts large, all of them marked unpaid. Longmere's financial situation was no secret: he came from a distinguished line of impoverished aristocrats. Many said that the earl had married for money, yet it seemed —at least on the part of Lady Longmere—that the marriage had been a love match.

Finishing up with the desk, Ben went to Livy, who was standing in front of a wall, staring up at a row of paintings.

"Did you find anything?" she asked.

"Evidence of Longmere's debt," he replied. "What about you?"

"Nothing yet." Pursing her lips, she pointed at the paintings. "Do you notice anything odd?"

He regarded the three works. Framed in gilt, each one depicted a fruit bowl from various angles. "They appear unexceptional," he said truthfully.

"The one at the end is jutting out a bit, isn't it?"

Looking closer, he was amazed at her eye for detail. "You're right."

He reached up and grabbed hold of the heavy frame. Surprised when it didn't budge, he examined the painting closer. It wasn't just hung on the wall...it was affixed to it. Why? He ran his fingers over the ornate gold border, encountering a switch. He pressed it, and the panel that had been concealed by the painting swung open like a door.

"Zounds," Livy breathed. "What's inside?"

He reached in and pulled out the contents: a leather-bound volume.

He flipped through the handwritten pages.

"It's Longmere's journal," Livy said excitedly.

Side by side, they skimmed the passages. The earliest ones

detailed Longmere's despondency over his artistic ambitions. His hopes of becoming financially solvent through his painting had been met with failure after failure. Ben paused at an entry that proved to be a turning point:

> Two nights ago, as I stumbled out of a Whitechapel tavern, drunk on despair, a stranger came to me. A Chinese man with a long braid and beard, his face hidden behind a mask. Shrouded in fog and mystical secrets, he wore the robes of his ancient civilization. He offered me salvation...and I took it. The Devil's Bliss has all the pleasures of the poppy's tears and none of the pains. It is as if I've been looking through a filthy window all this time and never knew it.
>
> Now the panes are clear, and I see the world in a rapturous new light. Last night, I fell into a trance, painting until I must have lost consciousness. When I awoke, I saw before me a canvas at last deserving of my name. My talent and genius are finally revealed...

Memories flooded Ben: he saw himself in the soaring euphoric prose...and was not surprised by what soon followed.

> My muse has become my nemesis. Inspiration has become anguish, which can only be held at bay by taking more. Like Midas, I regret my foolish choice. I am held captive, will never be able to free myself from the bargain I made with the Devil.

Longmere's last entry, written mere days before his demise, turned Ben's insides to ice.

> I have not seen the Devil since that first fateful night. Sometimes I wonder if he is a figment of my darkest imagination: the Chinese warlord, the brilliant alchemist, the spy with eyes and ears every-where. His minions lure my friends and me in with promises of

*riches and happiness. The Devil knows everything, sees everything, is everything.*

*If he knows what I am thinking, then he knows that I suspect the truth: the Devil's Bliss can bring ecstasy...and it can kill. While this poison is in my blood, I cannot have it upon my conscience as well. I will be a weakling no longer. I must purge myself—and the world—of this toxin. I must stand strong and confront the felonious Master Fong once and for all.*

Eyes huge, Livy said, "Do you think Longmere confronted this Master Fong and was killed for his efforts?"

"That is a likely hypothesis," Ben said grimly. "Which makes it all the more important to find this murderous villain and put a stop to the Devil's Bliss."

# TWENTY-THREE

The following evening, the Willflowers attended a soiree hosted by Lady Newberry. Glory's parents had offered to chaperone Livy, and Charlie had taken them up on the offer. Livy knew her mentor planned to spend the evening making inquiries into the mysterious Master Fong.

Ben was on a similar mission, and Livy wished with all her heart that they could join efforts. When she had brought up the notion, however, Charlie had opposed it.

"*Give a man an inch, and he will take over the entire case. The Angels do not require male assistance,*" Charlie had said with cool finality. "*You are an adult, Livy, and I will not diminish your independence by telling you what to do in your personal affairs. Do not, however, forget the oath you took when you joined.*"

Livy's insides knotted. How could she possibly forget? At times, it seemed all she could think about was the secret she was keeping from Ben.

"Do try to enjoy yourself, Livy." Cheeks glowing from a recent whirl around the dance floor, Fiona murmured, "There is nothing we can do to help Pippa at the moment, and an evening's distraction from the dark business might do us all good."

"The magic show should start soon," Glory added. "The papers have been raving about the magician's tricks, especially the one with the interlocking rings."

The touring Chinese illusionist was all the rage in London. Passing through the drawing room earlier, Livy had seen the stage where he was set to perform, the banner above it reading, "Behold the Secrets of the Orient." There was nothing like exoticism to draw a crowd.

"If you ask me, our hostess was a bit heavy-handed with the decoration," Fi said dryly.

The ballroom showcased a mishmash of Orientalism. Strings of paper lanterns rustled over pots of tall, leafy bamboo. A stuffed tiger prowled over a Kashmir carpet, its expression disturbingly hungry. *Objets d'art* inspired by *The Arabian Nights,* including Aladdin's golden lamp, were sprinkled throughout the room. Upon the walls hung tasseled silk scrolls of "calligraphy"; Glory had derisively noted that the Chinese characters weren't real characters at all but made-up symbols.

The lack of authenticity did not seem to bother the guests, many of whom wore elaborate costumes, embroidered chrysanthemums and cranes in abundance. The scents of sandalwood, jasmine, and amber came from the guests' perfumes as well as the censers releasing fragrant smoke into the air.

Livy cast a look at Glory's parents, who were standing a few feet away. Since they appeared engrossed in their conversation, she said in an undertone, "It is not just the case I'm thinking about; it's Hadleigh."

"I thought things were progressing well and he was to stop by tonight," Fi said.

"Yes, but I feel terrible that I haven't told him about the Angels."

"*We will not betray our Society's aims,*" Glory quoted.

"Even if it weren't for the oath, I don't know how to tell Hadleigh that I want to be an investigator. As you know, he is overprotective when it comes to my well-being." Livy gnawed on her lip. "And he wants an obedient wife."

Fi snorted. "Then why does he want to marry you?"

"I am not going to look a gift horse in the mouth," Livy rejoined. "All that matters is that he *does*, and I am not going to give him reason to change his mind."

"If you show Hadleigh how competent you are by helping him track down the villain, then perhaps he won't be as overprotective," Glory suggested.

Livy brightened. "Good point. He did seem impressed when I found Longmere's journal."

"Then keep badgering him to let you help. You didn't win Most Determined Debutante for nothing," Fi teased.

A gong interrupted their conversation. Lady Newberry announced that the magic show was about to begin in the drawing room. As they followed Glory's parents and the wave of guests headed toward the performance, Livy saw a pair lingering behind some potted bamboo at the other end of the ballroom. Her pulse raced when she recognized the pale hair and angelic features of the Honorable Simon Thorne. Thorne was with a voluptuous brunette, whose full red lips and cat-like eyes jolted Livy with an unpleasant memory: it was Cherise Foxton, the lady who'd consorted with Hadleigh in the stables.

Lady Foxton and Thorne appeared to be deep in conversation. The former was tearful, wiping at her eyes with a handkerchief. Thorne bent toward her, murmuring something in her ear. As Livy watched, Lady Foxton nodded, then discreetly exited through the curtained doors at the back of the ballroom. Casting a look around, Thorne waited a minute then followed.

Livy's intuition told her something was going on. Tapping on the shoulder of Glory, who was ahead of her, she leaned forward and whispered, "Thorne is here, and I want to see what he is up to. Will you cover for me?"

"Should I come too?" Glory whispered back.

"Just keep your parents occupied. I'll be back soon."

Livy subtly maneuvered herself out of the throng and headed in the direction where Lady Foxton and Thorne had gone. Exiting through the curtains, she found herself on a balcony overlooking the garden below. Planting her gloved hands on the balustrade, she scanned the darkness for signs of the pair but saw no one in the hedge-lined rectangle.

*Drat. Where did they go?*

A tingling sensation hit her nape the instant before a deep voice inquired, "Looking for someone?"

She spun around to see Ben enter the balcony. The light seeping through the curtains limned his long, lean frame. He'd eschewed exotic costuming, opting for timeless black and white. Her heart sighed; he cut such a dashing figure in evening dress.

She hurried over. "You came. I was waiting for you."

"Were you?" He quirked a brow. "Out here alone and unchaperoned?"

She decided to test the waters by telling him the truth.

Lowering her voice, she said, "I saw Simon Thorne. He was having what appeared to be an intense conversation with, um, Lady Foxton. She was crying, and they left the ballroom. My intuition told me to follow them out here, but I don't see anyone in the garden."

She searched Ben's features to see if the mention of his ex-lover had any impact. His expression was hard, and she saw no signs of interest, thank heavens. Cursing under his breath, he went to the balustrade, surveilling the darkness below. Obviously coming to the same conclusion that she had, he took her hand, pulling her into a secluded corner of the balcony, out of view of the garden. He pressed her against the windows, the curtains inside preventing them from being seen from the ballroom. She shivered as the exposed skin of her back touched the cool glass, but more because of the way he leaned into her, caging her with his delicious strength.

"What did I say about you endangering yourself?" he said in a stern tone.

"That I'm, um, not supposed to go looking for trouble?" For an instant, she dropped her gaze to his mouth, the strict line causing a flutter of her intimate muscles. "But this wasn't dangerous. Nothing is going to happen to me at a ball—"

"Leave the business to me, Livy. I mean it."

"But I want to help you. I was useful in Pippa's study, wasn't I?" she wheedled.

"You'll help me by staying safe." He cupped her cheek, and she was captivated by his touch. By the burning blue of his eyes. "I shouldn't even be here tonight, shouldn't be near you."

"Why?" Anxiety flared. "You haven't changed your mind about me—"

"You are mine." His firm reply calmed her. "But there has been a new development, and I need privacy to tell you about it. Will you be able to get away tomorrow night?"

"Charlie will be out of town, visiting a sick friend," she extemporized. "I could meet you whenever you want."

"I will fetch you at seven," he said. "Behind the house?"

She nodded.

"Until tomorrow," he murmured.

He bent his head, and her entire being quivered at the hot demand of his kiss. His lips were hard and commanding, his tongue sweeping into her mouth. She sucked eagerly on his offering, and he growled against her lips, thrusting in deeper. A needy pulse started at her core, spreading to the taut tips of her breasts and the aching place between her thighs.

He broke the kiss all too soon.

"Are you wet for me?" he rasped in her ear.

His question made her wetter.

She nodded bashfully.

"Is your little pearl throbbing? Does it want to be stroked?"

When he circled his thumb on her bottom lip, she felt his touch on the place in question.

"Yes," she sighed.

"Well, you're not to touch it tonight."

She blinked at him. Heat scalded her cheeks when she realized that she couldn't protest his unfair decree without admitting to her furtive bedtime activities. Activities, she thought with squirmy embarrassment, that had started because of him and the feelings he roused in her. Seeing him with Lady Foxton had awakened Livy's body to a need that had to be assuaged, and she had discovered a temporary and altogether wicked solution.

His slow, knowing smile made her blush even harder. "Christ, you're a naughty chit. Refrain this eve, and I shall make it worth your while tomorrow."

She overcame her embarrassment enough to say, "Promise?"

"Promise. Now go back inside, before I debauch you on this balcony."

"I wouldn't mind—"

"Go, Livy."

Reluctantly, she turned to leave, pausing at the door to say, "Sweet dreams, Ben."

His smile reached his eyes. "If you visit them, they certainly will be."

Livy floated back to the drawing room in time to see the ending of the magic show. From her vantage point at the back of the packed drawing room, she saw Glory go up and exchange a few words with the handsome magician, who at first looked surprised and then threw back his long braid and laughed.

Livy waited for Glory and the rest of the group to join her.

"Long wait in the retiring room, Livy dear?" the beautiful, russet-haired Duchess of Ranelagh and Somerville asked. "I hope you caught some of the show."

"I was watching from the back of the room, Your Grace," Livy said.

"I'll never understand that trick," Glory's papa muttered. "How in the devil did the fellow manage to link and unlink *solid* metal rings?"

"I asked him," Glory said. "In his native tongue."

"What did he say, dear?" her mama asked.

"He winked and said, '*That is the art of the illusion, young miss: to give the audience what they want to see.*'"

Livy was waiting at the back of Lady Fayne's house when Ben's carriage pulled up the next evening. He handed her up, asking her if she had any trouble getting by the servants. Since she'd pranced out, waving farewell to Mrs. Peabody and the cook, she could truthfully say no. Hawker *had* muttered, "Duke or no duke, that fellow o' yours better treat you well, Lady Olivia, or 'e'll be answering to me," but Livy knew he only had her interests at heart. Over the weeks, the Angels had discovered that the brawny butler was like a gently boiled egg: hard on the outside and mushy soft at his center.

Sitting beside her, Ben said, "How beautiful you are, Livy."

Seeing the masculine appreciation in his eyes, she was glad she'd taken special care in choosing the rose-colored taffeta embellished with ruffles and lace. She'd also worn her hair in a different, more sensual style: her dark tresses were combed smooth and secured at her nape, thick curls hanging over one shoulder. Her only accessories were the fresh peony in her hair and the golden crown necklace Ben had given her.

"Thank you," she said softly. "You look very fine yourself."

He always did. Tonight, his frock coat matched his eyes, his silver-grey waistcoat and charcoal trousers fitted superbly to his virile form. A diamond stick pin winked in the folds of his cravat. The lamplight kissed the chiseled contours of his face, the lines of experience adding to his masculine beauty.

He cocked his head. "Where has my little queen gone?"

She knitted her brows, not understanding. "I am right here."

"But you are such a polite young lady. You are not arguing with or pestering me."

"I don't always argue," she said primly. "And things are different now that we are lovers."

At the word "lovers," his eyes smoldered, and he took her in his arms. His passionate kiss robbed her of her senses. When he lifted his head, she was clutching his lapels, panting.

"Would you like to know where we are going?" he asked.

*What I would really like is more kisses.*

"Yes," she managed.

"We are making a quick stop to meet with a friend. After that, I am taking you to supper."

"What friend?" She was instantly intrigued. "Where are we going for supper?"

He smiled, kissing her on the nose. "There's my little queen."

Yesterday, Ben had met with Chen, showing him Longmere's journal and telling him about the plan that had taken shape in Ben's head. The stratagem would require that Ben stay away from Livy for a time—to protect her from the perilous world he would be entering. He knew he couldn't absent himself from her life without an explanation and, as much as he wanted to shield her from the dark business, he knew her. She would not accept the separation without a rationale, and who knew what measures she might resort to in order to discover the truth?

She might inadvertently compromise her own safety and Ben's. In the long run, it was safer for him to tell her about his scheme. To be upfront about his undertaking and his expectations for her during that time.

That had led to his decision to introduce her to Chen this eve.

While Ben was on his mission, the healer could act as the go-between if Livy needed to get a hold of Ben. Ben also trusted Chen to protect Livy if he, himself, was unable to get to her. Finally, it felt right to Ben that the two most important people in his life should meet.

When he introduced the healer to Livy, her eyes shone with genuine pleasure.

"It is an honor, sir," she said sincerely. "Hadleigh has told me what you've done for him, and I could not be more grateful."

The healer was generally stoic and formal, yet his brown eyes gleamed as he said, "Hadleigh has mentioned you as well, Lady Olivia. And now I see why you have been a distraction to him during his meditation practice."

Turning to Ben, she said with girlish glee, "You find me distracting?"

Ben rolled his eyes while Chen, the bastard, stifled a laugh.

The healer gave a brief tour of his clinic, beginning with the meditation room. Livy poked around the Spartan space, lowering herself gracefully onto one of the sitting cushions.

"How does sitting still help anything?" she asked.

Amusement flickered in Chen's gaze. "Have you tried it, my lady?"

"Not willingly." A sheepish smile tucked into her cheeks. "I have always preferred action to inaction."

"Sometimes non-doing is the most powerful action of all," Chen replied.

At Livy's perplexed look, Ben felt his lips quirk. He helped her to her feet.

"Don't mind Chen," he said. "He is full of mind-boggling notions."

Chen lifted his shoulders. "What is mind-boggling to some is obvious to others."

Livy chuckled. "I see what you mean."

They moved on to the courtyard, which was brightly lit by

lanterns and filled with disciples in training. Some were practicing fighting moves on wooden dummies, others lifting buckets of water fastened to a wooden yoke to build their strength. Students in one corner were throwing small daggers at a cross-section of a tree stump to see who could get closest to the white circle painted in the center.

"Did Hadleigh undergo this training, Mr. Chen?" Livy said, wide-eyed.

"His Grace was an apt pupil." Chen nodded at the men practicing with the daggers. They bowed and moved aside, and Chen picked up one of the small blades, handing it to Livy. "Would you care to try?"

Knowing how sharp the little knife was, Ben frowned. "Are you certain—"

"I would love to!" Livy snatched the weapon from Chen.

"Keep your eyes on the target, my lady," Chen instructed. "Before you throw, picture the dagger in your mind: see it hitting the white circle."

Livy's clear gaze focused on the tree stump. Her delicate gloved fingers held the hilt at a ninety-degree angle next to her ear, and she let the dagger fly with a snap of her wrist. Ben blinked as the blade pierced the center of the board with a decisive *thunk*.

"Impressive, my lady." Chen raised his brows. "Have you done this before?"

Livy shot Ben a quick glance, then shrugged modestly. "Beginner's luck."

They continued on to Chen's study. Tea was waiting on the round table, and the three of them took seats. Livy sipped the fragrant amber beverage.

"This is delicious," she said. "What kind of tea is this, Mr. Chen?"

"Chrysanthemum, my lady. It is noted for its beautifying properties," the healer replied. "Of course, you have no need for those."

As Livy blushed, Ben arched his brows at his friend's heretofore hidden gallantry. He decided to address the business at hand. The sooner he got this unpleasantness over with, the sooner he and Livy could enjoy a private night together.

"There is a reason I brought you here today," he said to Livy. "Chen and I conferred yesterday about the best way to capture Fong."

"Do you know of Fong, Master Chen?" she asked, wide-eyed.

Chen shook his head. "The Chinese community here is not large, based in Limehouse and consisting mostly of men involved in the sea trade. Yet I have never heard of this Fong character, and I do not see how he would be able to conduct his operations without drawing attention."

"Perhaps Fong doesn't live in London," Livy mused. "Longmere described Fong as a warlord, chemist, and spy. Perhaps he only passes through now and again...like a ghostly ship in the night."

"Hmm." Chen looked unconvinced. "I am inclined to think that Longmere's description is grossly exaggerated. Nonetheless, I have sent word to my contacts in Limehouse to be on the lookout for Fong. Longmere's journal does provide us with other useful information. We now know that the drug is known as 'Devil's Bliss,' and it seems Longmere and his friends were distributing it until he realized the drug could be lethal and grew a conscience."

"The night before his death, he was at Cremorne Gardens with his cronies." Livy's thick lashes fanned upward. "I saw a boy slip a note to Thorne, and then the group headed off into the gardens. Do you think Longmere managed to find Fong that night?"

Ben gave her a reprimanding look. "Since I had my hands full with you, I cannot answer that question, can I?"

She blushed, her pearly teeth sinking into her plump bottom lip. The naughty, rather unrepentant sparkle in her eyes revealed that she was thinking about their steamy rendezvous at the gardens. His own loins heated at the memory. By Jove, he wanted to make love to her again...and he would, once he settled the present matter.

"My lady has a good hypothesis," Chen said, stroking his chin. "Perhaps that night Longmere followed the boy to Fong's lair. Longmere confronted Fong, wanting out of the operation, threatening to expose Fong and the drug's lethal properties."

"Opium is not illegal, but murder is," Livy said. "Fong could be facing imprisonment or worse if he were caught. Not to mention the financial losses he would incur. At the Black Lion, Stamford mentioned that one shipment alone netted a thousand pounds in profit for each of them. Fong, being the mastermind, must receive an even larger share."

"Excellent reasoning, my lady." Respect glinted in Chen's gaze. "Thus, Fong was motivated to permanently silence Longmere. He suffocated the earl, returned the body to the studio, and planted the laudanum to make it look like an accidental death. That also explains why there were no signs of struggle in the studio."

"So how do we find Fong?" Livy asked. "Do we monitor Longmere's cronies, waiting for Fong to contact them?"

"That is one approach," Ben said. "Given the close call with Longmere, however, Fong is likely now on alert. He may lie low for a time. Which is why I've come up with an alternative plan."

Livy tilted her head. "What is it?"

He paused, his instincts warring. A part of him wanted to protect her from the filth of his past, which had bled into the present. Another part trusted her to handle the truth. She had accepted everything he'd shared thus far, and he craved her sweetness, the absolution that only her love could give.

Squaring his shoulders, he said, "In my younger days, I was friends with Edgecombe, Bollinger, and Thorne. We were known as the Four Horsemen due to our wild rakehell ways. I stopped associating with the scoundrels years ago, but my plan is to infiltrate the group. To become a Horseman once again so that I may track down Fong and eradicate the Devil's Bliss."

# TWENTY-FOUR

It was nine o'clock by the time Ben led Livy into his suite. Having her in his private sanctuary, looking so petite and innocent in her rosy frock, brought his fantasies to vivid life. As she took in the forest-green walls and mahogany furnishings with avid curiosity, she could be Little Red Riding Hood stumbling into the dark woods. He didn't know if he was the huntsman or the wolf: he wanted to both protect and ravish her.

"It is strange how many times I have been in your home but never in here," she mused.

He came up behind her, helping to remove her pelisse and stealing a whiff of her mouth-watering scent: peach blossoms, subtle soap, and Livy.

"A gentleman's bedchamber was no place for a little girl," he murmured.

"I am no longer a little girl." She gave him an adorably smug look. "Now, I am your lover."

Hearing her say the word "lover" sent a sizzle through his blood. It didn't help that she was currently peering at his massive tester bed with unmaidenly interest. He flashed to an image of her lying on that mattress, naked and moaning as he ate her pussy, and his groin burgeoned with heat.

*Keep a rein on yourself. Tonight may be the last time you see her for a while. Make the occasion special for her.*

At the very least, he could feed her before he pounced on her.

He led the way to his sitting room, where he'd instructed his staff to set up an intimate supper that he could serve himself. They'd followed his instructions to a tee. Hothouse roses bloomed on every surface, beeswax candles bathing the room in a warm glow. A small table stood cozily by the fire, covered with crisp linen and gleaming silver and china. A tiered cart filled with silver-domed dishes sat by the table, as did a bucket of iced champagne.

Ben held out one of the velvet-covered chairs for Livy. "I hope you don't mind having supper at home. I thought privacy would be best."

"This is beautiful, Ben." She gazed around the room in wonder. "All these years, and I never guessed you were a romantic."

"You did not know me as a lover," he said huskily. "Would you like champagne?"

She looked at him. "Are you partaking?"

Only she would think to ask. Would care enough to do so.

He shook his head. "But don't let that stop you."

"I don't need champagne." She smiled at him. "I feel giddy already."

The truth was he felt a bit giddy himself. Like a lad going courting for the first time, filled with anxious hope and desire. Given his advanced years and experience, it was rather embarrassing.

Ben cleared his throat and reached for the dishes at the top of the cart. "As we are fending for ourselves this eve, allow me to serve you."

He placed the *hors d'oeuvre* in front of her, grilled oysters wrapped in bacon and drizzled with a creamy caper sauce. Taking a plate for himself, he joined her at the table.

"I am famished." She dug in, her eyes closing briefly in bliss. "This is delicious."

Ben had always enjoyed watching Livy eat. Unlike Arabella, who'd constantly been on some slimming plan or another, Livy ate the way she did most things in life: with gusto and unaffected joy. As she slid a bacon-wrapped morsel between her lips, making a little sound of pleasure, he felt a primal tug low in his belly. *Christ, the passion in her...*

"Tell me more about the Horsemen," she said between bites. "How did you meet them?"

Her question punctured his lustful musings. At Chen's, she had greeted his plan to infiltrate Edgecombe's group with remarkable equanimity. She had, of course, voiced her concerns about his safety, and he had tried his best to allay them while pointing out the merits of his strategy. His prior connections to the group gave him a unique opportunity to discover what those bastards were up to currently. All he had to do was bluff his way back into the fold and follow the trail to Fong.

Livy had pleaded for him to let her assist, but he'd stood firm.

*"The best way you can help is by giving me peace of mind,"* he'd told her. *"I can better concentrate on convincing Edgecombe and the others to reveal their secrets if I know you are safe and out of harm's way."*

She'd sighed. *"Will you always be this overprotective?"*

*"Of you? Always."* He'd meant it. *"I will always try to keep you safe...even from me."*

*"I do not need to be protected,"* she'd protested. *"Least of all from you."*

Her present question, however, reminded him that he hadn't told her everything about his degenerate past. As he looked into the limpid pools of her eyes, shame crept over him. Their difference in age was magnified by their difference in experience: her heart and soul were untainted by life whereas his were stained by so many sins, big and small.

Yet he'd promised himself that he would not lie to her; he owed
her the truth so that she could decide whether he was worthy of
her love. Buying himself time, he served the soup course before
answering.

"After my actions led to Griggs's suicide, I numbed myself with
vice to avoid the infamy of what I had done," he said in hollow
tones. "That was when I associated with Edgecombe, Thorne, and
Bollinger. We caroused day and night. I drank, smoked opium,
gambled, and engaged in fisticuffs and duels." He inhaled. "I
changed bedpartners almost as frequently as I did my cravats."

Livy's spoon slipped from her fingers, clattering against her
soup bowl. In her pleated brow, he saw the calculations she was
making in her head. She knew he'd wed when he was eighteen, and
the inevitable conclusion she'd arrived at molded her expression
into lines of aching uncertainty.

"Weren't you married at the time?" she asked.

"Yes," he said flatly. "Adultery is among my many sins."

Livy stared at him, her heart clenching. She didn't know why his
admission shocked her, after everything else he had shared about
his past. Perhaps because in her mind he was a loyal man...indeed,
his loyalty to his sister had played a part in his misguided and tragic
attempt to punish Griggs, the man who had hurt Aunt Bea.

To hear Ben say that he had broken his marriage vows,
however, sent Livy reeling. As a McLeod and a Kent, she valued
loyalty above all, and she could not reconcile her steadfast friend
and protector of seven years with the man who was now confessing
to breaking his sacred vows. After finding him drunk and miserable that Christmas when she was fifteen, she'd known that his
marriage wasn't perfect. There was also what he'd said recently
about Arabella's habit of goading him into jealousy. Yet nothing
justified infidelity.

For the first time, Livy felt a twinge of doubt about Ben. Could she be with a man who might be untrue to his promises? She stared at him, unable to hide her dismay.

"I deserve your judgement, little one," he said with grim acceptance. "I have no defense for how I conducted myself. At the same time, you should know that Arabella and I had an understanding."

Livy knitted her brows. "What kind of an understanding?"

"An understanding wherein we were both allowed to seek pleasure outside of the marriage bed," he said. "As long as we were careful and discreet."

"I don't understand." Bewildered, Livy flashed back to his duchess's funeral. His grief and despair then and afterward. "I thought you loved Arabella."

"I did." His lips twisted, his pupils expanding and edging out the blue. "As you know, I was eighteen when I married. Arabella was the only woman I had been with. A couple of years into our marriage, she told me that only the bourgeois lived in each other's pockets and suggested that we experiment with a more...sophisticated lifestyle. Such arrangements are not uncommon in the *ton*."

"I do not care about the *ton*," Livy said hotly. "I would not want to be with anyone but my husband, nor for him to be with anyone else. That would be a betrayal, and it would *hurt*."

"You are right, little queen, on all counts." Ben's tone was gruff, his shoulders hunching. "The novelty of the forbidden soon wore off...at least for me. Being with other women felt wrong."

"As it should have," Livy said with emphasis.

"When I tried to change our agreement, Arabella refused. She said I was trying to spoil her fun, that it was up to me to *make* her want to be faithful. I became jealous and possessive, fighting duels over her, but it was not enough to make her stop." He stared at his untouched soup. "*I* was never enough for her."

"Oh, Ben." His self-doubt squeezed Livy's heart. "You are enough for any woman."

"Even for you?" He slid her a glance, and the tormented

yearning in his eyes seared through her. "I swear I would be a faithful husband. I would never betray you, Livy, or lie to you. I do not wish to discuss the specifics of my marriage any more than necessary, but I will say that Arabella enjoyed manipulation, and I cannot abide it. That is why I have insisted upon honesty and obedience in our relationship," he said. "That is why I am laying my cards on the table now, so that you know what kind of man you would be taking on."

Livy thought of the secrets she was keeping, and a shiver passed through her. Surely her actions weren't comparable to Arabella's. She wasn't trying to manipulate Ben. She just wanted to do what she loved while being with the man she loved. How she *wished* she could tell him everything. Yet she knew he wouldn't understand and, even worse, would try to stop her.

He'd been furious upon discovering her presence at both the Black Lion and Cremorne Gardens. He'd stated in no uncertain terms that putting her life and reputation at risk was unacceptable, for any reason. Thinking of how he'd nearly broken things off with her at the pleasure gardens cinched her throat. Even now, facing a foe like Fong, he refused to let her get involved.

*I cannot lose him,* she thought desperately. *But I cannot let go of my purpose either.*

"I have disgusted you."

Ben's stark words joggled her. Realizing that he'd misinterpreted her silence for rejection, she reached across the table to touch his hand.

"Nothing you have said has changed my mind about our future," she said.

"Do you mean that?" His fingers gripped hers, and the hope on his face was heart-wrenching to witness. It was the look of a desert traveler who spots an oasis but fears it might be a mirage. "After everything I have done?"

She crossed over to him, and he rose immediately. He towered over her, the need in his eyes a vulnerable contrast to the sharp slash of his cheekbones, the honed muscularity of his form. Although he was older than her and far more experienced, she realized that she had something to teach him.

"I love you, Ben," she said softly. "No matter what and for as long as we both shall live. That is what love is all about."

"Livy." His serrated voice scored her insides with a blend of beauty and pain. "I know I don't deserve you, but I cannot let you go."

"Then don't." She took his granite-hard jaw in her hands. "And I won't let you go either."

She felt a tremor go through him. Then he snatched her into his arms, slamming his mouth onto hers with fierce possession.

# TWENTY-FIVE

Kissing Livy drove Ben mad with desire on a normal day. Following her unconditional acceptance of his flaws, the taste and feel of her made him feel like a starved beast. Her plush mouth was bliss against his own, and he knew there was more to savor. He licked her seam, and her instant parting of her lips injected steel into his cock. He drove his tongue inside, laying claim to her honeyed cove, her moan setting off a howl of need inside him.

The urge to back her into a wall, toss up her skirts, and sheath himself inside her tight pussy nearly overwhelmed him, as if he were a greenling randy for his first wench. He wasn't that inexperienced boy any longer, however—hadn't been for over a decade. When it came to his sexual history, he had plenty of regrets; the one thing he was glad for was that experience had taught him self-control.

Before Livy, he'd enjoyed dominance. With Livy, he *craved* it. Her surrender wasn't just a game for an evening or a whim to indulge: it was an act of love and trust. When she melted for him, her sweetness filled the cracks of his parched soul. His spirited little queen submitted to him and him alone...and this made him harder than a steel pike.

He lifted her into his arms. She felt like thistledown, her soft smallness arousing him. Clutching his shoulders, she stared at him with lust-glazed eyes as he carried her into his bedchamber. He set her down by the foot of the bed. Turning her so that she faced the bedpost, he wrapped her fingers around the dark pole.

Standing behind her, he said in her ear, "Hold on for balance while I undress you."

"Yes, Ben," she said breathily.

"I like hearing you say my name." He swept her long curls off her nape, planting a kiss there, relishing her shiver of response. "Tell me, were you a good girl for me last night?"

"Yes, sir."

Hearing her embarrassment, he smiled to himself. He had no problem with her indulging in a bit of self-play; indeed, he planned to watch her doing it someday. Yet he also knew that keeping his naughty miss on edge would deepen the pleasure, for both of them.

"Then you shall have a reward, as promised," he said.

He started working on the pearl buttons along the back of her gown, stirred by their delicate tenacity and the enchanting, precise moment when they popped free of their silken loops. He wanted Livy to come undone for him. Wanted it as badly as he wanted to tenderly put her together again afterward. The possessiveness he felt for her was matched only by his protectiveness. He alone would play with his wanton miss, and he would never, ever allow her to get hurt.

Even tonight, he would not do anything irrevocable. He would not take her maidenhead until his ring was upon her finger. She was so damned precious, and he would not dishonor her trust in him. And knowing that he was about to embark on a perilous mission, that it might be weeks before he held her in his arms again, he was determined to make tonight one that they would dream about when they were apart.

Livy's gown whispered to the ground, and his blood heated at the sight of her in her unmentionables. They were crisply modest, white linen edged with the finest lace. He expertly released her petticoats and started loosening her corset strings.

"I like undressing you," he murmured.

She twisted her head, raising her brows at him. "You are remarkably practiced at it."

"Enough sauce from you, little brat." He tugged on the strings for her impudence, just enough to make her breathless, the way he liked her. "You need someone older and more experienced to keep you in hand. You would run roughshod over some namby-pamby chap like Sheffield."

"Beg pardon." She gave him a coquettish look. "Who is Sheffield again?"

"Now you're learning," he said with approval. "Turn around and arms up, sweeting."

She did as he asked, and he pulled her chemise over her head. His lungs strained as he saw her bare for the first time. He'd never seen anything half as erotic as Livy, bashful and blushing all over. Her exquisite breasts heaved, her thighs squeezing together above the shell-pink stockings he decided then and there to leave on. And between her legs was the prettiest little pussy he'd ever beheld.

When she tried to cross her arms over her breasts, he stopped her. Maneuvering her back against the bedpost, he placed her hands above her head, curving her fingers around the grooved wood.

"Stay like that," he told her.

"This is rather immodest." Roses bloomed in her cheeks, but she didn't move.

"When you are with me, you have no need for modesty." He tipped her chin up, looking into her beautifully discomfited eyes. "I want nothing between us, not even clothing. And you have nothing to hide." His voice thickened as he swept his gaze over her nubile form. "By Jove, you are a goddess, and I mean to worship at your temple."

He kissed her again. Plundered her mouth until she was panting, squirming against the bedpost. He winnowed out pleasure from her sensitive spots, flicking her earlobe with his tongue, sampling the silken column of her neck. He palmed her breasts, appreciating their rounded heft. She gasped as he thumbed the stiffened pink tips.

"Do you like it when I pet your tits, love?" he inquired.

"Yes," she moaned.

"Would you like me to kiss them?" He chuckled at her expression: a bit surprised, mostly intrigued. "I think you would."

Bending his head, he dropped a kiss on the slope of her right breast. Her flesh was firm and supple and carried her intoxicating scent. He licked his way around the smooth mound, circling his way to her areola. He blew against the straining peak, and she trembled like a leaf.

"Offer yourself to me. No, keep your hands on the bedpost," he murmured. "Arch your back and present your breast to my mouth."

Although Livy had never swooned in her life, she thought there might be a chance of it now. She adored Ben's imperious manner, which made her feel demure and daring at the same time. She wanted to do anything he asked of her. To worship him, this beautiful, complex man whose strength and vulnerability made him god-like in her eyes. The desire to please him was as urgent as the need to take her next breath.

Her gaze on his, she arched her back, thrusting her breast toward his lips. When she couldn't quite get the burgeoned tip to his mouth, she stood on tiptoe, holding onto the bedpost for balance. The weeks of training with Charlie paid off in an unexpected way; although her muscles trembled under the strain of the pose, she was strong and flexible, managing to touch her nipple to his waiting lips.

He rewarded her with a proprietary kiss on the sensitive bud, the brief swirl of his tongue threatening her ability to maintain her posture. Her knees wobbled as he placed a gentle kiss on the other nipple.

"Such a good girl. You may relax." The warmth in his gaze washed through her, and she sagged against the pole. "Since you asked for my kiss so nicely, you shall have it."

Then his mouth was on her breast, and pleasure consumed her. Who knew that it would feel this good to be suckled here? He did things with his tongue that forced whimpers from her throat. When he drew on her nipple, she felt a corresponding tug in her pussy, a gush of honeyed heat between her thighs. He switched to her other breast, going back and forth until she was writhing against the wood.

She was so lost in the sensations that it took her a moment to realize that his kisses were migrating downward, his tongue tracing over her ribs. Her hips bucked when he drew a circle around her navel. He kept going, his lips traversing her quivering abdomen and then...

Going down on one knee, he planted his hands on the insides of her thighs, pushing them apart. Her breathing grew fitful as he studied her sex. He was examining a part of her that she, herself, hadn't really looked at. Yet there he was, scrutinizing her as if she were on the block at Tattersalls, and she didn't know why it aroused her. When he parted her with his thumbs, she felt faint with mortification and need.

"How pretty you are." His gaze consumed her. Then he leaned forward, and she cried out at the hot swipe of his tongue along her private cleft. "And even sweeter than I remembered. I am going to want more of this pussy, most definitely. Slide your leg over my shoulder."

Helpless to his command, she did as he bade, resting her knee on his broad shoulder. The flexing bulge of his deltoid muscle pushed against the back of her knee, the rough silk of his hair brushing her inner thighs. His breath gusted warmly against her quivering pussy. She squirmed against the wooden pole when he inhaled deeply, his eyelids growing heavy.

"You remind me of a peach," he rasped. "Juicy and ripe."

He licked her again, this time long and slow. Pleasure obliterated her thoughts as he feasted on her as if she were a delectable morsel. Gripping her bottom, he kept her spread for his masterful devouring. Swirls and flicks, hard sucks and forceful thrusts of his tongue took her to her peak. When he laved her pearl with rough, demanding strokes, she shattered. Ecstasy melted her bones, and she would have collapsed had he not been supporting her, holding her steady, his mouth tenderly coaxing out every blissful spasm.

He rose then, towering over her like some god of carnality. When he dragged the back of his hand over his mouth, it came away wet with her excesses. His eyes on hers, he stripped off his frock coat. The fact that he was still dressed while she was naked and panting from her climax sent an illicit thrill through her...as did the prominent ridge at the front of his trousers.

"You may let go of the bedpost," he said.

She hadn't realized that she was still holding on. Even in the depths of passion, she had followed his sensual command. It pleased her, and she could tell it pleased him too when she let go of the wood, stretching her arms this way and that. He ran his hands along her shoulders, and she moaned as he expertly massaged out the knots.

"Are you sore, sweeting?" he murmured.

"Quite the opposite," she assured him. "I feel rather limber."

His lips twitched. "Then on your knees, little queen."

She complied with unladylike haste. Then again, she didn't have to be a lady with Ben, and the freedom was exhilarating.

From her position at his feet, she watched him undress and felt like she had the best box in the theatre. She greedily took in his flexing shoulders and the delineated blocks of his chest. Dark hair was sprinkled over his taut skin, a trail bisecting the stacked muscles of his torso. He was a man in his prime, and she could hardly believe that he was all hers. When his long fingers went to the waistband of his trousers, her pulse kicked up a notch.

Was he going to show her his manhood...finally? She'd only had a glimpse of it that time she'd spied on him in the stables. Having felt the thick ridge pressed up against her, she was dying to see it. The other example she'd seen—brandished at her by that fellow at Cremorne Gardens—hadn't been all that inspiring.

Her breath held as Ben lowered the flap; a column of flesh fell forward with weighty momentum. She swallowed. *Goodness.*

Removing the rest of his clothes, he gripped the huge rod. Her heart thudding, she watched the slow pump of his fist along the thick and veiny shaft. She noticed the supple movement of his skin and the way it pulled back to reveal a purplish dome. At the base, his male sac hung heavily between his corded thighs.

His raw masculinity melted her insides like wax. Despite her recent climax, viscous need trickled from her core. Her fingers twitched against her thighs.

"Do you like what you see, sweeting?"

The arrogant jut of his chin told her he knew the answer, but she gave it to him anyway.

"Yes," she breathed.

His eyes gleamed down at her. "Yes, what?"

"Yes, sir." Just saying the word made her feel awash.

"Very good. Since you are such a well-behaved miss, I am going to let you frig my cock. Put your fingers around me, like this."

He took her hand, wrapping her fingers around the thick stalk. He was steel beneath velvet, the contrasting textures intriguing beyond measure. He put his hand over hers, tightening the pressure of her grip, teaching her how to caress him. Her fingers didn't reach all the way around, so she intuitively added her other hand, and he gave a low, appreciative growl.

"You are doing so well, frigging my cock." His approval was almost as arousing as holding him, hot and turgid between her palms. "Tell me, what does it feel like?"

"You're so big and hard." After a heartbeat, she confessed, "And I feel like a wicked girl for liking it so much."

He shuddered, a droplet seeping from his tip.

"Look what you've done," he said in a husky voice. "You've made me spill a little seed. A quick study, aren't you, love?"

She looked at him from beneath her lashes, her best try at modesty. "So I've been told."

"Cheeky, too." His stern glance scattered goose pimples over her skin, and he took his cock from her. The slow, thoughtful pumping of his fist made her pussy flutter. "I believe you require another lesson. Put your hands on my thighs."

Her palms moist against the hard, hair-dusted muscle, she looked adoringly up at him.

"You are going to learn to suck my cock," he said. "And there are some things to keep in mind."

She eyed his member, swaying like a giant branch.

*Hmm, like...not choking?*

Aloud, she asked, "Such as?"

"Keep your jaw loose. Breathe through your nose since your mouth will be in use. And mind your teeth—that is important." He raised his brows. "Do you think you can manage all that?"

Was there anything she loved better than a challenge?

At her confident nod, he smiled faintly. Then he brought his cock to her mouth.

"Open," he said.

She parted her lips, and the proud heat of him slid inside. Even though she was well aware of his size, the feel of him inside her mouth was rather astonishing. His girth stretched her lips, his length an advancing incursion. Her eyes widened at how much more of him there was to accommodate. He wasn't even halfway in yet...

"Stop thinking so much, sweeting." He cupped her cheek, his sapphire eyes holding hers. "Trust me to guide you. I won't hurt you. Ever."

She knew that, of course. Knew that Ben would take care of her, as he had always done. Remembering that, she relaxed and surrendered into his keeping. His eyes glinted with pleasure as he slid in deeper, his big hand cupping the back of her head. Soon he was thrusting steadily, overwhelming her senses with his maleness. His torso rippled, his features harsh with arousal as he took his pleasure in her.

Eager to serve him, she experimented with her tongue as he plunged between her lips. His groan urged her on, and when she licked the underside of his crown, his thighs turned to steel beneath her palms. His fingers digging into her scalp, he thrust harder, deeper, her pussy fluttering with each pass. All of a sudden, he nudged a place deeper than he'd gone before, and her throat clenched in reflex.

"*Devil and damn.*" With a groan, he withdrew. "Are you all right?"

"Yes. Don't stop," she gasped.

In a smooth motion, he lifted her so that she lay on his bed, her legs dangling off the side. He nudged her thighs apart, standing between them, and she moaned as he fingered her pussy. Her hands twisted the coverlet as he screwed a thick digit into her, the slick sounds bringing a hot flush to her cheeks.

"You're drenched," he said through harsh breaths. "You liked sucking my prick, didn't you?"

She arched her hips for more of his touch. "Yes, sir."

"You want more of it, don't you? In here. In this needy little cunny."

He added another finger, his palm slapping her wet folds.

"Yes, Ben," she moaned. "Oh, yes."

"Maybe one day you'll be ready for it."

She raised her head, narrowing her eyes at his devilish smile. "I'm ready for it *now*."

"Not tonight, love." He chuckled darkly. "Now stop complaining and come on my fingers like a good girl."

Before she could argue, he curled his fingers, touching some magical place deep inside, setting off quakes of bliss. As she trembled in the aftermath, he stood between her legs, pumping his massive erection. He was all power and discipline, all delicious male. She was beginning to understand her own power as well, which was complementary to his and no less potent. He brought her so much pleasure...and she wanted to give him the same.

She got onto her knees. Even though she was on the bed, he was still taller, looking down at her with hooded eyes, a sensual curve to his lips.

"Will you please spend for me, sir?" she asked prettily.

Hunger leapt like a flame in his eyes. "You would like to see that, would you?"

"Yes, please," she said, as demure as any debutante.

*Those lessons at old Southbridge's have finally come in handy.*

"Such a polite young miss," he said, jaw clenched. "All right, then."

His biceps flexed, his fist gliding faster and faster along that thick truncheon of flesh. She wouldn't have dared to stroke him with such ferocity and felt breathless as she watched him, nearing his finish like a stallion at the Derby. His skin gleamed with a sheen of sweat, the shifting musculature beneath a sight to behold.

"You wanted it, Livy," he gritted out. "Here is my seed."

He aimed his cock at her breasts, and she gasped as the hot, milky streams lashed her skin. Groaning, he shot his seed copiously, covering her with his essence, the earthy scent curling her toes against the mattress. A droplet trickled down the slope of her breast, and she caught it with her fingertip. She swirled it over her nipple, shivering at the slippery, erotic feel. At the primal rightness of being marked by him.

"Bloody hell." His chest heaving, Ben took her face between his palms, dropping his forehead against hers. "You have no idea what you do to me."

She smiled tremulously. "I think it might be similar to what you do to me."

"I am never letting you go," he said fiercely.

"That is just as well. Because I am never letting you go either."

They arrived at Charlie's before dawn.

"We're at Lady Fayne's, love," Ben murmured.

Cuddled up against him, Livy did not want to leave. Their night together had been magical. After making love, they'd both been famished. Ben had carted in the remaining supper, and they'd eaten naked in bed. They'd fed each other, Ben smiling at her voracious appetite. When sauce had dribbled down her chin, he'd licked it off.

Afterward, he'd lain atop her, courting her with slow, stirring kisses. Pinned by his sinewy weight, his hardness rocking against her mound, she'd found ecstasy twice, and the second time, he'd joined her with a ragged sigh, his pleasure a warm flood over her belly.

Having shared such precious intimacy with him, she feared the separation ahead.

"I don't want to leave you." She looked imploringly at her beloved. "There must be some way I can help—"

"We have been through this." He cupped her jaw, his touch gentle yet firm. "I cannot concentrate on this dark business unless I know you are safe. I need to know that you will not be running around London, in disguise or otherwise. You will help me by doing as you are told."

The unyielding set of his features told her that further argument was futile. She swallowed, unable to bear the idea that she might prove to be a harmful distraction.

"You may depend upon me," she whispered.

He studied her, then nodded. "My plan may take weeks to come to fruition. During that time, we will not be able to meet. I do not want those scoundrels to know what you mean to me, for it could put you and my mission at risk."

"I won't see you at all?" she asked in dismay. "I'll come to you at night. I'll be careful—"

"No." His tone had never held more authority. "If our relationship is discovered, the bastards could use you against me. You must stay away. Give me your word, Livy."

Reluctantly, she did so.

"There is another thing." He exhaled. "During this time, you may hear gossip about me. Rumors about my conduct. I give you my word that I will be true to you, and I ask for your trust."

"I trust you," she said.

"There's my brave little queen." He tipped her chin up and kissed her with a tenderness that made her heart soar. "When this is over, we will move forward with our future together. You will wait for me?"

"I would wait forever," she vowed. "I love you, Ben. Be careful and come back to me swiftly."

# TWENTY-SIX

*1843, COUNTRY ESTATE OF BEATRICE AND WICKHAM MURRAY*

*Livy is 13; Ben is 25*

"I have changed my mind." Standing on a large rock looking down into the stream, Livy shook her little head, her plaits whirling. "I am not going in."

"But it is hot out, and the water is refreshing." It was getting damned cold, actually. Ben had been standing in the chest-deep water for ten minutes, trying to coax the girl in. "And you are wearing your swimming outfit."

"I don't care," Livy said stubbornly. "I will go change."

"Hadleigh, why don't you just leave the chit be?"

He turned his head in the direction of Arabella's sulky tones. His wife was standing by the side of the stream, several yards away from the rock. She was wearing an immaculate white gown that was better suited to a drawing room than a riverside picnic. Even from a distance, he could see the twin lines of annoyance between her brows. Arabella had not wanted to come to his sister's house party, which she considered too "rusticated."

Even though he thought it was rather obvious—at least to anyone who cared a whit about him—he had explained to her how important it was for him to make amends to Beatrice. His sister was the only kin he had left, and after what he had done, an invitation from her was nothing short of a miracle. He had thought that Arabella, too, might want to mend fences with Bea, who'd once been her bosom chum. Yet Arabella had remained dead set against attending, and in the end, he'd had to set his foot down.

His duchess had been pouting since they arrived three days ago. She'd been cold and rude to the other guests, which didn't help his goal of becoming something other than *persona non grata* in his sister's life. Frustration built in him, a gnawing ache in his chest that never seemed to go away. He had a sudden urge for the opium that he knew Arabella had brought with her, even though he'd instructed her not to. He and his wife had developed too many bad habits, and he wanted to steer their marriage onto a healthier path.

Telling Livy that he would be right back, he strode through the water toward Arabella.

In a low voice, he said, "I am trying to get Olivia into the water because her parents say she hasn't gone in since the accident, and she used to swim like a fish. If she doesn't give it a go now, she might have a fear of water for the rest of her life."

"Why do you care?" Arabella asked coldly.

With her raven curls and emerald eyes, his duchess was a stunning beauty. Yet more and more, he saw the ugliness beneath, and it made him weary. He loved her, yes, but after seven years of marriage, he concluded that he did not like her very much.

Nonetheless, he did not want to give up on the closest relationship he had left. They were stuck with one another for the duration. And he was determined for them to make a go of it.

Thus, he controlled his temper and said, "I care because she is young, and her future should not be shaped by fear. And what if she falls into water again? For her own safety, she should learn to swim."

"That is utter claptrap," Arabella retorted. "You only care because you like playing the part of her hero. You like that the girl looks at you like some dewy-eyed mooncalf!"

He shot a look over at Livy, afraid that she'd overheard. Luckily, she was peering up at a vee of flying geese and didn't seem to be paying attention to his row with his wife.

"Are you mad?" he said in disgust. "For God's sake, she is thirteen and like a younger sister to me."

"Maybe if you hadn't alienated your *actual* sister, you wouldn't be so pathetically desperate for more family."

Incredulity slammed into him, loosening his grip on his temper.

"I would give my soul to undo my sins," he said with vibrating anger, "but I will not be lectured by you. I think you and I both know that, of the two of us, I am not the only one who has wronged my sister."

Arabella blanched. He'd never brought up her shameful abandonment of Bea after Bea's injury. The two had been the best of friends until Bea's scar had ruined her popularity. Years ago, Bea had tried to tell him that Arabella had, indeed, been behind some of the cruel monikers aimed at Bea, but he had refused to listen. Refused to believe that the woman he loved could be so heartless.

He'd nearly lost his sister because of his stupidity. Paid for it in the years of estrangement between them. Now that Beatrice had given him a second chance, he'd sworn to himself that he would do his best by her...and so would his wife.

"You will be on your best behavior for the duration of this visit," he clipped out. "No more sulking, no more complaints."

"I am not a servant, and I will not take orders from you." Arabella's face was now red with fury. "You and your sister think you are so much better than me just because my father's wealth came from trade!"

The accusation was ludicrous. His sister was the least snobby person he knew. Her closest friend was a tinker's daughter, for God's sake, and she treated her tenants like they were her family. He, himself, hadn't given a thought to Arabella's background when he'd proposed to her. Yet Arabella had a way of twisting things in her mind, and he knew from past experience that he could not sway her from her beliefs. He hated his feeling of help-lessness. The impulse to find oblivion, even temporarily, rose within him.

Just then, voices sounded, a group emerging from the woods next to the stream. Ben's jaw tightened as he recognized his rake-hells-in-arms Edgecombe, Thorne, and Bollinger. In the past, he'd done plenty of carousing as part of the Horsemen, but of late he was trying to distance himself. A fresh start for him and Arabella included getting away from corruptive influences.

The scoundrels weren't getting his message. Or they found it amusing to confound his efforts to turn his life around. Although the Horsemen weren't on his sister's guest list, they must have found out about her party and come to make trouble.

"I say, is that the Hadleighs?" Edgecombe came over, bowing to Arabella. "What a coincidence."

Like hell it was.

"What are you doing here?" Ben's words were filtered through his teeth.

"We were just in the n-neighborhood." Thorne kissed Arabel-la's hand, and she giggled.

"The better question is, what are you doing in the water, old boy?" Bollinger eyed the creek with a shudder. "It looks positively frigid."

"Cold water is good for the constitution," Ben said curtly.

"But you've left your pretty wife high and dry." Edgecombe winked at Arabella. "And that is a crime."

"Indeed, sirs, this day has been a dreadful bore," she said with a pout.

"We are headed to town, my lady, to see a travelling troupe perform." Bollinger made a leg. "Perhaps you would care to join?"

"I forbid you to go," Ben told her in a low voice.

Shooting him a triumphant look, Arabella declared to the group, "That sounds like the perfect antidote to rustication."

Edgecombe gave her his arm, and she headed off with the group. Ben could not chase after her without looking like a fool. As the party disappeared from sight, he punched the water in frustration. Bloody hell, why could nothing go right? Why couldn't he control the simplest damn thing?

He felt as powerless to stop the wreckage of his life as he had been to save Griggs's daughter. Disaster was approaching like an oncoming train. No matter how he tried to stave it off, he was destined to fail. To feel again her fingers letting go of his, to hear the whoosh of air as she'd fallen, dark triumph glittering in her eyes...

"Hadleigh?" a girlish voice called.

*Devil take it.* He'd forgotten about Livy.

He made his way back to her, the water swirling in agitated waves around him. She was still standing on the rock, and she looked down at him with child-like curiosity.

"Why did Her Grace leave? Is everything all right?"

"Everything's fine," he said curtly. "We should return to the house."

"No...I want to swim."

"You don't have to." He dragged a wet hand through his hair. He knew it wasn't fair of him to be impatient with her, a mere girl, but his mood was ruined. "You're scared, and it's not my place to push you—"

Before he could finish, she took a running start off the boulder, landing with a loud splash several yards away in the deepest part of the swimming hole. Panic thudded in his chest when she did not surface, and he rushed toward the frothing spot where she'd hit the water...

Her head popped up, hair plastered over her eyes.

"Hadleigh," she gasped.

"Right here, I've got you." He caught her against his chest, where his heart was still hammering. With his other hand, he brushed the wet hair from her eyes. "Bloody hell, you could have given me some warning."

She grinned at him. "I knew you would be there to catch me...*if* I needed it."

The knot in his chest loosened a little, and he couldn't help but smile.

"Are you saying you don't need my help?" he asked.

When she nodded, he let her go. She began treading water like she'd been born doing it.

"I just remembered," she said with an infectious smile, "that I am an *excellent* swimmer."

"In that case." Reaching out, he placed his palm on the top of her head and dunked her.

She broke the surface seconds later, sputtering. A playful yet unholy gleam lit her eyes.

"You," she said cheerfully, "are going to pay for that."

After spending the afternoon splashing around with Livy, Ben returned to his bedchamber to get ready for supper. His valet helped him to bathe and dress, and when there was no more delaying the inevitable, he went and knocked on the door of the adjoining chamber. While he was still simmering over his and Arabella's latest row, he didn't want it to color the rest of the evening. The other guests were bound to notice the Siberian state of affairs between them, and the last thing he wished was to cause an unpleasant scene at his sister's party.

Luckily, he knew how to appease his wife. He'd brought along several pieces of jewelry, including the diamond bracelet he had in his pocket, precisely for this purpose. While he did not like to resort to bribes, he'd become a pragmatist where his duchess was concerned.

The door opened to reveal Arabella's maid.

"Your Grace," she said with a curtsy.

"Where is my wife?" he asked.

"She has not returned, Your Grace."

His anger, already smoldering, burst into flame. "*Bloody hell,* supper is in fifteen minutes."

"I-I am sorry, Your Grace."

Seeing the fear in the maid's eyes, he dismissed her with a curt wave. He stalked through Arabella's chamber, trying to calm his temper, his thoughts whirling like a dervish.

*Where in the devil is she? Is she still gallivanting with the Horsemen? What will the other guests say—is she determined to humiliate me and lay waste to our marriage?*

A roar left him, and he swept his arm across her dressing table, sending the pieces of her vanity flying onto the floor. Her cloying perfume assailed his nostrils as he gripped the edges of the table, trying to regain his control. He looked in the mirror and hated what he saw: a worthless bastard capable of nothing but destruction.

*Why does everything I touch turn to shite?*

Anguish roiled in him as he took stock of his handiwork, smashed up bottles and broken bits everywhere. Then something caught his eye: Arabella's vinaigrette. Going over, he picked up the globe-shaped locket. The body was constructed of pure gold mesh to diffuse the perfume it was designed to hold within. Exquisite enamelwork in the shape of peacock feathers adorned the sphere, diamonds glittering among the swirls of cobalt and turquoise.

A pretty piece, for which he'd probably paid a bloody fortune.

Bringing the vinaigrette to his nose, he smelled nothing. He released the latch, and the two halves split open, revealing a small pouch. He dumped the contents into his palm: opium.

He'd known Arabella would not go without it.

Despair and dark craving overcame him.

*And tonight, damn my own eyes, neither will I.*

# TWENTY-SEVEN

*PRESENT DAY*

Entering the exclusive club, Ben headed for the private chamber where he knew he would find his former cronies. The establishment was the premier domain of scoundrels and rakehells, and he hadn't set foot inside for years. He saw the lifted eyebrows as he strode through the opulent surroundings toward the room at the back.

Several acquaintances called out greetings.

"The prodigal son returns," one said drunkenly. "Good to have you back, old boy."

Misery always loved company. Ben gave a terse nod and continued to his destination. He didn't bother knocking, opening the door with the key he had never returned. The men in the four wing chairs swung their heads in his direction: Thorne, Bollinger, Edgecombe, and Stamford.

*Perfect. All the bastards are here.*

"Your Grace." Edgecombe rose, concealing his initial surprise with a smirk. His brows rose toward his pomaded auburn hair. "To what do we owe the honor?"

Ben closed the door behind him. Faced the men who were all standing now.

"I want in," he stated.

"M-membership in our group is by invitation only, old boy," Thorne said. "And you forfeited your right to be h-here when you abandoned the Horsemen years ago."

Ben fought the distaste that rose like bile in his throat. Thorne hadn't changed a whit. With his artfully mussed blond curls and brooding gaze, he had a Byronic magnetism that drew females to him like moths to a flame. It didn't matter that he was famed for his cruelty and inconstancy, discarding his lovers like last season's fashions.

"I concur with my brother." Bollinger stood next to Thorne, striking a belligerent pose. "You are not welcome back."

Back in the day, Bollinger had been the follower in the pack, content to take the others' orders and leftover scraps. Apparently not much had changed. The brown-haired viscount retained his boyish looks, although he'd gone softer in the middle and the line of his chin.

"Your position has been taken," Stamford said.

Although Stamford had been recruited after Ben's time, Ben was acquainted with the other, who'd been a year behind him at Eton. Back then, Stamford had been a runty, sniveling sort, his bony nose shoved up the arse of the popular boys.

Ben sauntered toward the refreshment-laden table close to the men. Aware of the gazes fixed upon him, he took his time selecting a ripe berry. He made a show of eating it slowly.

"I am not *asking* to be reinstated, gentlemen," he said. "I am telling you that I want Longmere's cut in your venture."

The men exchanged startled glances, with the exception of Edgecombe. The earl was too clever to betray his reaction.

"I'm afraid I don't know what you mean," Edgecombe drawled.

"Perhaps this will clarify matters."

Ben withdrew the red snuffbox he'd found clutched in Pete's lifeless hand. As he placed it on the table, the enamel gleamed like blood, a reminder of what was at stake.

*I have failed at so many things. I will not fail in this,* Ben silently vowed.

"Longmere told me about the Devil's Bliss and your supplier," he said coolly. "Mr. Fong, is it?"

In that instant, it was as if the air had been sucked out of the room. Fear burgeoned in its place. Radiated from the Horsemen's paling faces and dilated eyes.

*These bastards are terrified of their so-called partner,* Ben mused.

"For G-God's sake, do not say his name aloud." Thorne darted his gaze around the room as if he feared the Chinese man might emerge from the shadows. "He has eyes and ears everywhere."

"Then he will hear me when I say that I want Longmere's place in the enterprise," Ben said.

"You're bluffing." Edgecombe's eyes slitted. "Why would Longmere tell you anything? As far as I know, he and you were acquaintances at best."

"The sod owed me money." Ben had prepared his story, the lies rolling smoothly off his tongue. "That was why I was the one to discover his dead body. I'd gone to his studio to collect the two thousand pounds I'd lent him and instead found him with his toes cocked up. Longmere could never hold his drink...nor his laudanum, it seems."

He added the quip to appeal to the cold-blooded bastards. His instincts proved correct when Edgecombe's mouth edged into a smirk.

"Longmere's constitution was rather delicate." The earl studied Ben with a calculating expression. "Unlike yours. You had the heartiest appetite for sin amongst us...that is, before you succumbed to abstinence. Rumor has it that when you parted ways with us, you also gave up your vices."

"I made a mistake. After Arabella's passing, I wasn't thinking clearly."

"The duchess's passing would befuddle any man," Edgecombe said grudgingly. "She was exceptional."

"God rest her soul," Thorne murmured.

Not to be left out, Bollinger blustered, "She was a fine lady. Splendid hostess."

For once, Ben did not doubt the bastards' sincerity. When it had suited her purposes, Arabella could be vivacious and charming, and she had enjoyed entertaining the Horsemen, flirting with them to rile Ben up. She'd hung on Edgecombe's every word, stroking the bastard's vanity. With Thorne, she'd discussed poetry and exchanged innuendos. She'd even indulged Bollinger, taking part in his amateur theatre evenings.

Whereas these memories would have once sucked Ben into a tar pit of bitterness and anger, he now felt only twinges of regret over his failed marriage. He credited his improved state of mind to Livy. He hadn't wanted to let her go this morning. The way she'd clung to him in the carriage had conveyed that the feeling was mutual. And if he'd been too stupid to realize that, then her words had left no doubt.

*I love you, Ben. Be careful and come back to me swiftly.*

He had wanted to give her the words burning in his heart. But he didn't. Not because he didn't love her—because God knew he did—but because when he offered her his love, he wanted it to be worthy of her.

He was a man who'd done too much damage. Even though Livy accepted his sins, he yearned to go to her with a clean slate. While he did not know if absolution was possible, he did know that Fate had put him in the present situation for a reason: he had the power to stop the Devil's Bliss from taking more lives. This was his shot at redemption, and for Livy, for their future together, he had to see this plan through.

"I will admit the loss of Arabella clouded my judgement." Ben kept his manner nonchalant. "I thought I needed a change, some-thing different. Since the grief has passed, I see that what I truly need is more stimulation, not less." He twisted his lips into a deri-sive smile. "Life is too short as it is, and I have no wish to be bored to death."

A pause. Edgecombe gave a bark of laughter, the others joining in.

Edgecombe waved him to a chair. "Have a seat, Hadleigh."

"But that's my chair," Stamford whined.

"Find yourself another. We have a guest," Edgecombe said sharply.

Ben did not miss Stamford's fulminating glance, nor Edge-combe's emphasis on the word *guest*. He knew he had other hurdles to pass before he would be allowed back into the group and given access to the secrets that would bring down their opera-tion once and for all.

Knowing the dog-eat-dog nature of the men in the room, he took Stamford's chair with deliberate arrogance. "It is good to be sitting amongst old friends. Especially ones so enterprising."

Edgecombe handed him a whisky, which he had no choice but to take.

"To old friends," the earl said silkily.

Ben raised his glass and took a sip, his first taste of spirits in nearly two years. The seductive burn clenched his gut. Yet he had to play the part of the rakehell to win the group's trust.

He took another sip. "As Longmere's replacement, I believe I have much to offer."

"First of all, we haven't agreed upon anything." Bollinger moistened his lips. "Secondly, what could you have to offer?"

"I am a duke. My title affords me many connections," he said. "All of which may be used to promote the circulation of the Devil's Bliss."

"We all know you're as rich as Croesus," Thorne said suspiciously. "Why d-do you want a part of this h-hypothetical venture?"

"A man can never be too rich. Money, however, accounts for only part of my interest."

Stamford's close-set eyes were skeptical. He'd dragged a wooden chair to the circle. It looked uncomfortable, the seat putting him at a lower level than the rest of the men.

"Why else would you want to poke your nose in our business?" he said in nasally syllables.

"Because, dear fellow, I *can*." Ben gave him a condescending smile. "This is before your time with the Horsemen, but the other gentlemen know that I am a man who enjoys diversions with an element of danger. Nothing works better for *ennui* than the forbidden."

"You always were the w-wildest of us," Thorne admitted reluctantly.

Edgecombe's mouth formed a sly curve. "You and your duchess."

Ignoring the bait, Ben said, "Arabella was always one for an unusual adventure. She would have found the Devil's Bliss delightful, no doubt."

"You cannot just barge in and claim a share of something that isn't yours," Stamford burst out.

"Can't I?" Ben crossed an ankle over his knee, his posture relaxed and gaze challenging. "Longmere told me that men have died because of your goods." He took a calculated risk. "Baron Winford and John Hagan, for instance."

A heavy silence fell.

"There is no proof that their deaths had anything to do with our product," Edgecombe said defensively. "Countless people have taken the Devil's Bliss with no harmful effects."

"Our clients have reported nothing but the purest pleasure." Bollinger crossed his arms over his chest, his jowls reddening above his cravat. "To accuse us of harming anyone is slanderous—"

"No need to get up in the boughs, old boys. As far as I am concerned, no risk, no pleasure, and anyone who partakes of Devil's Bliss is making their own choice." Ben paused, just long enough for the others to let their guards down. "However, the authorities might have a differing viewpoint of your enterprise. And they would undoubtedly frown upon your connection with a Chinese mastermind whose product is killing Englishmen."

"Are you b-blackmailing us, Hadleigh?" Thorne's tone was icy.

"On the contrary. I do not betray my friends. Which is why you would rather have me on your side than against it."

In the wake of his threat, the crackle of the fire seemed to grow louder. Ben kept his expression neutral. *Take the bait, you bastards...*

"In that case." Edgecombe raised his glass, his tone sardonic. "Allow me to be the first to welcome you back, old *friend*."

# Twenty-Eight

Since parting from Ben a week ago, Livy had been consumed by thoughts of him. She worried about his welfare and the progress he was making with his villainous former cronies. He had succeeded in getting back into their fold; stories were emerging in drawing rooms across London about Hadleigh's reunion with the Horsemen.

While attending a luncheon with Fiona and Glory, Livy had overheard two ladies gossiping loudly about a certain duke who'd fallen back into his old ways. Tittering, they'd sipped tea and savored the tidbits about tavern brawls, drunken wagers, and visits to houses of ill repute. Livy's hands had fisted around her silverware, her stomach too knotted for her to eat.

Although Ben had warned her about the possibility of gossip, she hadn't realized how painful it would be to hear such dreadful tales told about him. To witness Society's glee at the Duke of Hadleigh's apparent relapse into degeneracy. Knowing his true reasons yet being unable to defend him frustrated her to no end. She'd wanted to tell the clucking hens to shut their beaks and mind their own business.

How she yearned to see Ben. Yet she could not: he had made it

abundantly clear that contacting him during his covert undertaking could compromise her safety and his own. In the case of an
emergency, she could relay a message through Mr. Chen, who had
ways of getting in touch with Ben.

Even if Livy couldn't be with Ben, she was determined to help
him. She and the other Angels had spent the week conducting
their own investigation into Longmere's killer. They'd spoken with
the earl's housekeeper, Mrs. Ingerson. The good lady had provided
a list of models who had posed for her employer in recent weeks.
When Fiona had delicately inquired if the deceased had seemed
friendly with any of the women, Mrs. Ingerson had denied it.

*"The master, God rest his soul, had eyes only for his wife,"* she'd
said.

For what it was worth, Livy was relieved at Longmere's
apparent fidelity. Since the funeral, Pippa had spiraled deeper into
grief, and the last thing Livy wanted was to add to her friend's
burdens. She, Fiona, and Glory had interviewed various models,
who'd all confirmed that Longmere's behavior had grown increas-
ingly agitated leading up to his demise but had little new information to share.

At present, the Angels were en route to visit Miss Alicia
Hoskins, one of Longmere's favorite muses who'd just returned
from the countryside where she'd been tending to a sick relative.
The carriage ride gave the trio a chance to chat. Glory and Fi
shared the opposite bench, their pastel skirts overlapping like
petals.

"Any news from Hadleigh?" Fiona asked.

"No." Livy sighed. "I do miss him so."

"You will be reunited soon." Framed by the pleated green silk
lining of her bonnet, Glory's face was sympathetic. "He has
managed to infiltrate his former group. Once he finds Fong, there
will be nothing stopping you from your happily ever after."

In front of her closest friends, Livy couldn't hide her worries
any longer.

"Hadleigh and I still have a rather large barrier to surmount," she said in a rush.

Fi's blue eyes were keen. "The fact that you haven't told him about the Society of Angels, you mean?"

Livy nodded, recalling her last night with Ben. After their second round of lovemaking, he'd cuddled her in bed. With her cheek pressed against his hard chest, her body warm and relaxed, she'd never felt more content. She'd almost drifted off when his deep voice lured her back.

*"I cannot wait until the day I make you mine,"* he'd said.

Giddy with joy, she'd looked into his intent sapphire eyes. *"I love you so much, Ben. Marriage will be the grandest adventure for us."*

He'd rolled atop her, his weight braced on his arms. His grave expression had caused an uncertain flutter in her belly.

*"Marriage isn't just about love. As an adventure, it comes with perils,"* he'd said. *"I have been married so I know the pitfalls. A relationship can go astray if two people are not on the same page."*

Guilt had tensed every filament of her being, the truth burning in her throat.

*"I will not repeat my mistakes,"* he'd continued. *"As I've said, I mean to be the master of my own house, and I need to know that you will follow my guidance and not just in bed. I expect your loyalty, honesty, and obedience, even during my absence."*

Recalling his solemn gaze and the inflexible set of his jaw, Livy swallowed.

"The longer I put off telling him the truth, the harder it gets," she blurted. "But Charlie still hasn't budged on the secrecy oath. And even if she gave me permission, I am afraid of telling Hadleigh since he would force me to quit the Society."

"Are you certain he would do that?" Glory knitted her brows. "What if you explained to him how much you love being an investigator?"

"You *have* seen Hadleigh with Livy, haven't you, dear?" Fiona's tone was wry. "Even when he wasn't courting her, he was like an overprotective older brother. I can only imagine what he is like now that he intends to make her his duchess. He will forbid her from taking risks, ergo she can bid adieu to our group."

Frowning, Glory said, "That sounds dreadfully high-handed."

"Hadleigh isn't high-handed most of the time." Thinking of his lovemaking, Livy felt her cheeks heat. "At least, not in a way that I mind. But when it comes to my personal safety, Fi is right. He is determined to protect me."

"I would not want my future husband to dictate what I do," Glory declared.

"In that case, you would do well to avoid matrimony," Fi said with a snort. "All men are dictatorial to some degree. Even our fathers, who are the most doting of husbands."

"You have a point." Glory wrinkled her nose. "Well, if my future husband were to try to tell me what to do, I'll simply do what Mama does."

Fi lifted her brows. "And what is that?"

"Whatever she pleases," Glory said.

They laughed because all their mothers took that approach.

Smiling, Fi said, "Livy is taking a page out of that particular book."

"But I fear that strategy will only get me so far." Livy chewed on her lip. "Eventually Hadleigh will find out, and he will be displeased." *To say the least.* "I feel so guilty lying to him, especially since he despises dishonesty because of his past, which is, well, complicated. I cannot share the specifics, but he has his reasons for being overprotective."

"Can you share any details?" Fi asked. "We promise not to tell."

"*Pinky* promise," Glory said.

Livy usually held back little from her bosom friends, yet circumstances had changed. Now she owed her loyalty to Ben as well, and she knew he would not appreciate her bandying his affairs about. She settled for a compromise, sharing the bare minimum needed to get her friends' advice.

"You know, obviously, about Aunt Bea's scar. But there is more behind that story and the man who caused it," she said slowly. "Suffice it to say, Hadleigh was a hot-headed young man at the time, and his reaction to his sister's injury led to consequences for which he feels guilt, even to this day. His family fell apart, and he and Aunt Bea were even estranged for a time."

"I have noticed the two of them are rather stiff in each other's company," Glory said.

"They don't tease or pester one another," Fi concurred. "How strange is that?"

Since the girls all had brothers, they knew that was highly unusual.

"Beyond Aunt Bea, Hadleigh's marriage also had...problems," Livy said.

Which was putting it lightly. Thinking of Ben's "understanding" with Arabella made Livy feel ill. Now that he was hers, she would never countenance him being with another woman. Luckily, he was as insistent as she was upon fidelity.

"Poor chap," Glory said softly. "He's had a rough go of it, hasn't he?"

"He has." Livy felt a sharp pang. "I would do anything to make it all better for him."

"If anyone can, it is you," Fiona said. "You have loved him forever."

"And love heals all wounds," Glory added.

Ben's words echoed in Livy's head: *Marriage isn't just about love.*

The statement had made Livy feel young and naïve. And, admittedly, a bit out of her depth. She'd never thought of their age difference as a problem, but she was realizing how much more he knew of the world. This was her first romantic relationship, and love was far more complicated than she'd anticipated. Instead of weaving the beautiful web of her dreams, she was getting the threads terribly tangled.

*If at first you don't succeed, try and try again,* she thought with an inner sigh.

Not knowing what else to do, she focused on her goal with single-minded resolve.

"My best course of action remains to prove my skills to Hadleigh," she said. "I will warm him to the idea of my being an investigator little by little, so it doesn't come as a shock when I finally tell him."

"Like tempering milk when making custard," Glory said.

It was lovely to have friends who understood.

"And let's not forget that I've already made progress," Livy said with growing optimism. "Hadleigh took me to Longmere's, we searched the earl's study together, and he introduced me to his friend Mr. Chen."

"Those are positive signs," Fiona agreed.

"If I can help track down Fong, then I will demonstrate my competence once and for all," Livy concluded. "Hadleigh is a reasonable man. Once he sees that I'm perfectly safe working as an Angel, and I apologize for keeping him in the dark, I'm certain he'll support my dreams."

Her friends looked at her...and grinned.

"Then let's solve this case, shall we?" Glory said.

"Thank you for seeing us, Miss Hoskins," Livy said politely.

"Call me CeCe, luv." The stunning blonde woman curled up on the threadbare chaise dabbed her eyes with a handkerchief. "All my friends do, and any friend o' Edwin's is a friend o' mine."

At the intimate use of Longmere's name, Livy exchanged uneasy glances with her friends, who occupied the mismatched chairs next to hers. They were in the shabby parlor of Miss Alicia

Hoskins's cramped flat. The model was gorgeous, with wavy hair, heavy-lidded turquoise eyes, and a curvaceous figure barely contained by her flimsy pink robe.

Sensing an opening, Livy took it. "That is the reason we are here today. We know that you were one of his favorite models."

"I sat for him just a week before 'is passing," CeCe said with a sniffle.

"Did you notice anything out of the ordinary about his behavior then?"

"Why does that matter now?"

"It might be related to his death," Glory said.

CeCe's long lashes fanned rapidly. "I thought that Edwin's death was an accident. An excess o' laudanum, the papers said."

"We are investigating all the possibilities," Livy said. "At the request of his widow."

"Oh, the countess is such a dear thing; 'ow she must be griev-ing. I do want to 'elp if I can." Twin lines forming between her brows, CeCe said, "Come to think o' it, there was something unusual that 'appened before one o' my sittings. Edwin was 'aving an argument with someone. A woman."

Livy's pulse sped up. "Do you know her name? Can you describe her appearance?"

CeCe shook her head. "I didn't see 'er. I'd arrived early and was waiting for Edwin to let me in, it being the 'ousekeeper's day off. I 'eard raised voices coming from the front parlor. I couldn't make out most o' what they were saying, but the woman sounded like a blue blood..." The model mimicked in aristocratic tones, "*After all I've done for you, this is how you repay me.* That part I 'eard. By the time Edwin came to the door, she was gone. I asked 'im about it, but 'e brushed me off. Said it wasn't important."

*Who was the mysterious woman?* Livy wondered. *What was the quarrel about?*

A sudden intuition gripped her as she recalled Cherise Foxton at the ball with Simon Thorne. Was Lady Foxton involved with the

Horsemen? Could her tears have been related to Longmere? Could she be the mysterious aristocratic woman CeCe had overheard?

"There's something else." CeCe gnawed on her lip. "A few days before that, I was supposed to pose for Edwin, and when I arrived 'e was in a feverish state. 'E'd been up all night, working on a painting and, by the looks o' it, drinking as well. 'E was ranting and raving about being *'useless'* and a *'weakling.'* Said the painting meant nothing if 'e lacked the fortitude to get to the *'heart o' the matter,'* as 'e put it. Then 'e shoved the canvas at me and told me to throw it in the rubbish bin.

"At the time, I didn't think much o' 'is outburst—artists are a temperamental lot, and Edwin was always bemoaning this or that. But the piece wasn't so bad, so instead o' tossing it out, I kept it. I thought Edwin might want to work on it again someday."

The hairs tingled on Livy's nape. "Do you still have the painting?"

The model nodded. "I'll fetch it." She rushed out of the parlor, her slippers flapping against the floor and robe fluttering against her calves.

"In his diary, Longmere called himself a weakling for not standing up to Fong," Livy said with barely suppressed excitement. "I wonder if this painting has something to do with the villain."

"*I* wonder why Pippa wasn't worried about her husband being alone with the spectacular Miss Hoskins for hours on end," Fiona murmured.

"Pippa is just as beautiful," Livy pointed out.

"Nonetheless, one should never be too trusting," Fi said sagely. "Especially when it comes to men."

Glory snorted. "I think Charlie is rubbing off on you."

Just then, another woman entered the parlor. In contrast to CeCe's voluptuous sensuality, the newcomer was thin, dark-haired, and angular, and most surprisingly of all, dressed in male attire. She held a tray with a chipped teapot and a plate of biscuits.

"Morning, ladies," the woman said in a friendly manner. "Thought I might offer you a spot o' tea seeing as CeCe most likely forgot."

Accepting a cracked cup, Livy smiled at her. "How kind of you, Miss..."

"You can call me Marg." The woman winked at her. "All the pretty ladies do."

Livy blinked in confusion, wondering if she'd imagined the innuendo.

CeCe returned, huffing, her arms stretched around a painting covered in an oilcloth.

"Are you teasing the poor girl?" she asked Marg.

"Just 'aving a bit o' fun." Marg gave her a playful grin. "Let me 'elp you with that, luv."

Marg took the canvas, propping it on the chaise. CeCe tugged off the cloth.

Livy studied the painting. She hadn't known what to expect, but it wasn't this: a bland riverside scene done in muted strokes of beige, blue, and grey. A small, nondescript two-story building occupied the center of the canvas. It was perched on the banks of a river, an empty field to the right of it. To the left was a dock where several small boats floated, including one with the figurehead of a mermaid.

"Did Longmere say anything about the significance of this piece, CeCe?" Livy asked.

"Just what I told you: that he'd failed to get to the 'eart o' the matter." The model tilted her head. "But the painting isn't so bad, is it?"

"Looks like a scene from the Thames." Marg stroked her chin, studying the piece. "If I 'ad to wager, I'd put my money on Shadwell, Limehouse, or thereabouts."

*Limehouse is one of the places Fong might be hiding,* Livy thought. *Could this painting be a clue to the mastermind's whereabouts?*

"May we take this piece with us, CeCe?" she asked. "It may help us discover what happened to Longmere. We will return it to you afterward."

"Keep it." CeCe shuddered, Marg wrapping a comforting arm around her shoulders. "If the painting 'as something to do with poor Edwin's death, then I want nothing to do with it."

# TWENTY-NINE

The next morning, Livy was practicing with her pistol when she received a summons from Charlie. She promptly headed for her mentor's study, which was a feminine version of the typical male retreat. The wood furnishings were sculpted in flowing elegant lines, the walls papered in raspberry silk. Dressed in a yellow gown, Charlie was seated at her desk, which was carved with exotic birds and flowers. Sunlight glinted off her reading spectacles as she sorted through a pile of correspondence.

"Hello, dear." Setting down her spectacles, Charlie said, "Have a seat, will you? I apologize for interrupting your training, but I have some news to share."

Livy plopped into the chair facing the desk. "Have you already identified the location in Longmere's painting?" she asked eagerly.

"Not yet," Charlie replied. "Although no one knows the Thames better than the mudlarks, even they will need time to locate the scene. Buildings such as those in the painting are plentiful around the river."

The mudlarks were urchins who scavenged the Thames for a living. Charlie knew their leader, known as the Prince of Larks, who apparently dealt not only in the sales of scavenged goods but of information. The mudlarks had eyes and ears everywhere, especially in the territories by the water, and Charlie had decided to hire them to scout out the location in Longmere's painting.

"What is your news then?" Livy asked.

"It concerns Hadleigh."

Livy sat up straighter. "Tell me."

"As you know, while you Angels have been interviewing Longmere's models, Mrs. Peabody, Hawker, and I have divided our time monitoring Edgecombe and his group," Charlie said. "I've been surveilling Bollinger for the past few days. Having ascertained that his habit is to take afternoon tea at Mivart's, I secured a position as a serving maid there, and yesterday he had a guest. Lady Cherise Foxton."

A frisson shot through Livy. She'd told Charlie about seeing Foxton with Thorne at Lady Newberry's ball and her hunch that the widow might have been the lady quarreling with Longmere.

"Lady Foxton is popping up everywhere," Livy muttered.

"Indeed." Charlie paused. "Are you aware of her, ahem, history with Hadleigh?"

That they had *not* discussed.

"I am," Livy said, her insides churning. "As I understand, it was a short-lived affair."

"That is my understanding as well," Charlie said briskly. "Lady Foxton runs with a fast crowd and has a reputation for being a sensation seeker. The fortune her late husband left her provides her with freedom, and she has an uncanny ability to avoid scandal whilst participating in it with, shall we say, remarkable enthusiasm."

"What was Lady Foxton doing with Viscount Bollinger?" Livy asked.

"From what I could gather, it was a business transaction cloaked as a social one. Bollinger promised Foxton 'a devilish good time' this evening. She, in return, slipped him a purse filled with banknotes."

Livy chewed on her lip. "She is one of the group's clients?"

"I believe so. They will be meeting tonight at the Hellfire Club, an exclusive establishment catering to debauchery. Foxton was particularly keen when Bollinger mentioned that the newest member of the Horsemen would be in attendance."

Invisible hands yanked on Livy's corset strings. Struggling to breathe, she said, "Hadleigh is going to be there?"

Charlie inclined her head.

"Then I have to be there as well," Livy burst out.

"I thought you might feel that way." Crossing to Livy, Charlie leaned against the desk's edge, her daffodil-colored skirts spilling over the panel of flora and fauna. "The Horsemen will be distributing the Devil's Bliss to their clientele at the Hellfire Club, which could yield critical information about their operation. But I must be frank: because of your personal stake in the situation, I have reservations about taking you."

"You can trust me," Livy said at once. "I haven't let you down yet."

"No, you have not. You have been a loyal Angel." Charlie's look was measuring. "All right, then. No matter what you see tonight—and I warn you, the club is known for its depravity—you must stay disguised. You cannot give yourself away, especially to Hadleigh. It will be a test of your strength and commitment to the case."

"I will not fail," Livy said.

Charlie gave an approving nod. "I've been impressed by your discretion with Hadleigh."

"I *want* to tell him the truth," Livy admitted. "Vow of secrecy aside, however, I am afraid that he will not understand."

"You have made the right choice, my dear. He would undoubtedly try to put an end to your work." Her mentor's tone was blunt.

"In fact, by carrying on with our society's mission, you are helping him, even though he does not know it."

Livy hadn't thought of it in that way before. Ironically, in keeping the truth from Ben, she *was* better able to aid and protect him. The sooner the Angels could help wrap up the case with Fong, the sooner Ben could stop playing this dangerous game. Then he and she could be together at last.

She cocked her head. "What time do we leave tonight?"

Livy was no wilting violet, yet as she wandered through the Hellfire Club, the debauchery on display gave her a buffle-headed feeling. A few minutes ago, she and Charlie had arrived at the club —inconspicuously housed in a Mayfair mansion at the end of a tree-lined cul-de-sac—and the guards at the door had asked for a secret password. After Charlie provided it, she and Livy were led through a dark passageway into the raucous Bacchanal.

Like many of the other guests, Livy and Charlie were masked and heavily disguised. Livy's hair was hidden beneath a wig of cascading red curls, and she wore a low-cut black lace gown that had seemed scandalous when she was getting ready, but now appeared prudish compared to those around her. A blonde clad in nothing but swirls of paint sauntered past, her dimpled buttocks jiggling.

"Stay close to me," Charlie murmured.

Livy nodded, scurrying after her mentor when a shirtless man in tight black leather breeches winked at her and ran his tongue slowly over his lips.

The Hellfire Club had several floors, and Livy and Charlie made their way through each, looking for Ben and his group. Each floor showcased a different theme of depravity. Livy's cheeks burned behind her mask as she passed glass cubicles where guests were tupping in front of a cheering audience. The astonishing variations made her blink. In one coupling, a man sat upon a chair with a brunette astride him, her back to his chest. His large hands fondled her breasts as she impaled herself on his erect member, moaning loudly.

Swallowing, Livy moved on, her gaze locking upon a darkly erotic *tableau vivant*. Upon a stage, men and women dressed as satyrs and nymphs held as still as a painting while in the midst of sexual acts, their expressions frozen in unmistakable ecstasy. That look of bliss was shared by a man on a nearby dais who, shockingly, was naked and held in a pillory. A woman in a red leather corset and black stockings applied a birch to his backside as he yowled in delight.

Circling through the stories of the building, Livy grew numb to shock. The top floor, however, proved that her nerves could still be jolted. She followed Charlie into a chamber decorated like a feverishly imagined seraglio. Plaster arches framed murals of a Turkish courtyard on a starry night. The ceiling was festooned with swathes of gauzy jewel-colored fabric, the bright, sensual colors echoed on the carpets below. And upon those rugs...

Men and women were engaged in a lascivious free-for-all. Bodies were connected to one another—sometimes to *more* than one person—in an undulating chain. Guttural sounds filled the air, and the smells of sex, perfume, and a strange, sweet smoke were everywhere. Livy's bosom surged on rapid breaths, her cheeks throbbing against her mask. She didn't know what to make of her reaction: a mix of shock, repulsion...and titillation?

Yearning for Ben pierced her. She missed him so, and witnessing all this carnality was oddly adding to her physical ache. Her brain conjured up an image of Ben taking her the way a man was taking a brunette on a nearby rug: with his hands holding her hair like reins, his hips pounding her bottom in disciplined thrusts...

"I see them." Charlie's low tones focused Livy on the mission. "By the palms."

Livy directed her gaze at the row of potted plants that separated the seraglio from the seating area just beyond. Through the barrier of fronds, she spotted their targets, her heart banging into her ribs at the sight of Ben. In shirtsleeves and a black mask, he sat on a low divan...*with Cherise Foxton cozied up next to him.* Lady Foxton wore a skimpy crimson robe edged with black lace and, it was obvious, nothing beneath. Her mask did not hide her expression, like that of a cat with a dish of cream.

Livy's hands curled when the bloody woman ran a finger along Ben's jaw.

*Get your dashed claws off him,* Livy's inner voice yelled. *He's mine.*

Ben didn't reciprocate Lady Foxton's flirtation, but he did not stop the odious woman's advances. Instead, he seemed intent upon talking to her while she flirted and laughed in an intoxicated manner. Suddenly, she surged to her feet, teetering; she might have fallen had Ben not risen and put steadying hands on her waist.

Livy gnashed her teeth as Lady Foxton took the opportunity to mold herself against Ben, pushing her nearly exposed breasts against his chest. When he set her aside, she grabbed his hand, leading him out of the seating area toward a corridor just beyond. As they departed, Edgecombe, Thorne, and Bollinger gave hoots of approval.

*The bastards,* Livy fumed.

"I have to go after Ben," she muttered.

"Have a care, and make sure he does not see you," Charlie whispered. "I will stay here and monitor the others."

With a nod, Livy took off after Ben and Lady Foxton, reaching the corridor just as the two entered a room at the far end, the door closing behind them. Jealousy pounded in Livy's chest. While she trusted Ben, she did *not* trust Lady Foxton.

*How can I spy on them when they are locked in that room?* she thought desperately.

"First time, my sweet?" a voice drawled.

Livy started at the man who'd materialized next to her. He was in his thirties, wiry and slim, his eyes the same shade as his bronze mask. Wanting to get rid of him, she gave a dismissive nod.

"You like to watch, I presume?" He smirked at her. "Well, I shall let you in on a little secret: the best performances are the ones given by unwitting actors. Such as in those rooms." He gestured at the corridor.

Livy's heart thudded. "You mean...there is a way to see inside those rooms?"

"Your wish is my command." The stranger bowed. "Follow me, my sweet."

# THIRTY

Alone in the room of a pleasure house with a woman he'd once swived, Ben was confronted by his sordid past. In truth, he felt disgusted with himself. Not long ago, he would have thought nothing of fucking Cherise at this orgy. Of playing their mutually agreed upon games. Yet even then he'd known that he was just going through the motions. There'd been no care or connection between him and Cherise. They'd merely used each other to spend.

Afterward, he'd felt even more alone. The feeling of emptiness would spread like a cancer. And he'd known with a stark certainty that happiness would forever elude him.

Being with Livy had shown him a different possibility. A desire that connected his body, mind, and heart. That didn't deplete his soul but enriched it and made him feel...whole. Although he hadn't made love to Livy yet, at least not all the way, her sweet, wanton passion aroused him more than anything at this Bacchanal, no matter how depraved, ever could. Because what she gave to him wasn't a veneer. A show.

It was *real* and so bloody generous and sweet.

God, he missed his little queen.

Yet he'd forced himself to stay focused on the mission. He'd more or less blackmailed himself back into the Horsemen's fold, and while his aggressive maneuvering might have garnered the men's respect in the short-term, he knew they would push back eventually. It was the nature of these men. They had a pack mentality: the strongest survived, and the weak were left to perish.

The image of Longmere's unmoving body flashed in Ben's head. It was a perilous game he was playing, and he couldn't afford any missteps. He had not yet earned the group's trust: they remained tight-lipped about their operations, including how and when the Devil's Bliss was delivered, saying that he would learn more when he was ready.

As for Fong, the Horsemen seemed to fear and revere their partner in equal measure...even though they'd never met him. Only Longmere had seen Fong in the flesh and only the one time. Fong communicated via his henchmen, who reinforced the power of their venerable master. The Horsemen ascribed mystical qualities to Fong, as if he were some all-knowing deity.

Bollinger had confided that he'd once "miscounted" the payments he'd received from clients. The day after he'd submitted the money to Fong, he'd found a bill and a dead rat on his desk. The amount due was precisely what he'd held back...and the bill had been written in the rat's blood. Bollinger had never miscalculated again.

*Did the Horsemen suspect that Fong had killed Longmere?* Ben wondered. *Did they fear that they would meet the same end if they tried to abandon their deadly enterprise?* Whatever the case, their greed, sensation seeking, and idolatry of the forbidden kept them ensnared.

To gain the bastards' trust, Ben had gambled, drank, and raised hell with them all week. Returning to his old habits, even under pretense, had brought a sickening feeling of shame. His strategy had borne fruit, however. Deep in his cups one eve, Thorne had revealed that Cherise was one of the group's earliest and most prized clients. Introduced to the drug by Longmere, she'd apparently spent a small fortune on the Devil's Bliss and couldn't get enough of it.

*"For her, the drug works like an aphrodisiac,"* Thorne had said drunkenly. *"Turns her into a bitch in h-heat. Wore m-me out the last time. On our next outing, she is your problem."*

Ben found the metaphor as distasteful as his present situation. Yet given Cherise's entanglement with the group, she might have useful information about the operation.

"Finally, we are alone," Cherise purred. "Why don't you join me, lover?"

She lounged on the bed that took up most of the room, her bare legs sticking out from her clinging scarlet robe. Her heavy perfume, the black and gold damask walls, and large looking glass affixed to the ceiling created an oppressive atmosphere.

Instead of going to the bed, Ben went to the chaise longue that faced it. He sat, draping his arm along the chaise's back, his pose arrogant and casual. Despite Cherise's pout at having her invitation declined, lust gleamed in her eyes. Ben understood her personality: the more something was withheld from her, the more she wanted it. When he'd ended things after their brief affair, she'd tried to cling on, merely because he did not want her.

"Why don't we chat first?" he said.

When he'd arrived, she'd already partaken of the Devil's Bliss. Luckily, she showed no adverse effects, only signs of approaching oblivion. Her eyelids were beginning to droop over her dilated gaze, and he guessed she would pass out soon. Until then, he would ward off her advances while questioning her.

"If I wanted to chat, I would have gone to some insipid ball." Her gaze narrowed, suggesting that she was not as far gone as he'd hoped. "I'm randy, and I want to fuck."

"You cannot always have what you want, Cherise." He flicked a speck from his trousers. "Not with me, at any rate. You would do well to remember that."

"I do remember," she said sultrily. "I remember *everything* about our time together."

He gave a cool nod. "Longmere was too easy on you. That will not be the case with me."

"I want you to be *hard* on me, lover. Very hard. But I would hate for you to be jealous." Her shiver said otherwise. "Longmere, God rest his soul, was never my lover."

"Then how did he come to introduce you to the Devil's Bliss?"

"We met through art." Holding Ben's gaze, she sat up and untied her robe. The material slithered off her, and, naked, she sprawled back onto the mattress in a come-hither pose. "I saw one of Longmere's paintings: a portrait of a beautiful woman that far surpassed his other work. When I asked him about his progress, he credited it to a devilish new muse he'd found, and I couldn't resist. You know I am game to try anything once."

Cherise coyly touched herself. No doubt she thought it was an alluring show. As long as she kept her hands to herself and answered his questions, Ben didn't give a damn what she did.

Then, with a stab of unease, he thought of Livy. While he couldn't give a farthing about Cherise's performance, would Livy consider this a betrayal? His chest tightening, he wondered how he could explain to his little innocent that Cherise's antics meant nothing and left him entirely unmoved. He might as well have been watching grass grow.

Self-disgust roiled in his gut. If he hadn't been such a degenerate in the past, he wouldn't be where he was now. He was a sinful bastard, and Livy deserved better.

*There's nothing you can do about it now,* he told himself grimly. *Extract the information and get the hell out.*

"Come join me, sir," Cherise said in a throaty voice.

Her use of *sir* made him recoil. During sexual play, he only wanted to hear Livy address him that way. Only wanted to play with her and her alone.

"You are doing fine on your own," he said dismissively. "Carry on."

His disinterest perversely egged Cherise on. She lay on her back, staring at her own image in the looking glass above the bed. Her ploy to seduce him gave way to an easier path to satisfaction. For her, it was only about her own needs anyway. She touched herself with practiced ease, with a look of intoxicated pleasure that he judged was evidence of the drug taking full effect.

He pressed on. "Did Longmere tell you how he found this miraculous muse?"

"He said it was a gift. From a mysterious stranger." Cherise was breathing heavily, transfixed by her own image. "A masked Chinese man who'd stopped him in the street one night and gave him a sample. Not ordinary opium, mind. This was a taste of the true secrets of the Orient, mystical and rare, available only to the select few who dared to take it."

*And those who could afford it,* Ben thought wryly. Fong certainly knew how to set the stage for his product. He understood his audience: jaded aristocrats had a fascination with anything exotic and scarce and would pay a premium for it.

"What else did Longmere say about this man?" Ben asked.

Cherise moaned, her hand working furiously between her legs.

"Concentrate," Ben said impatiently. "How did Longmere get the Devil's Bliss?"

"It was part of the excitement, the thrill." Her eyes squeezed shut as she chased her finish. "The Devil could send more of his treasure at any time."

"Where did Longmere receive shipments?"

She shrieked as she found her release. A few moments later, her head lolled in Ben's direction. She was glassy-eyed, her expression vacuous, the muscles of her face slack from her climax and the drug. A good thing, because he'd prefer that she didn't remember their conversation.

He tried again. "How often did Longmere supply you with the drug?"

"Bastard wouldn't give me more." Her voice was slurred. "Fought with him the last time I saw him. I begged, offered more money, but the ungrateful wretch refused. Even after all I'd done for him, putting in a good word with friends at the Royal Academy, getting his bloody painting accepted into the exhibition..."

"Did Longmere say why he wouldn't sell you more of the drug?"

"Said it was too dangerous. Said that the Devil had floated in on a Siren's song, luring him to an inescapable death, but I could still break free..."

Her eyelids drooped, and she began to snore.

Livy eased back from the peephole. She felt shaky and feverish. She *hated* that Ben was in the same room as Cherise Foxton as the latter pleasured herself; at the same time, Livy could tell that his only goal was to get information. Even though she could only hear snippets of the conversation, Ben's disinterest in Cherise's performance was obvious. And Livy now knew that Cherise had been the woman arguing with Longmere and the cause of the disagreement.

Nonetheless, she felt a prick of satisfaction when Cherise began to snore. Loudly.

*I hope she drools too,* Livy thought darkly.

"How was your show?" a male voice asked.

Livy had been so absorbed with Ben that she'd forgotten the stranger who'd led her into this hidden passageway behind the rooms. He'd kept his distance, standing a few feet away and peering through a squint into another room, where the occupants were clearly still at it, their moans and groans leaking into the passageway.

The stranger had seemed harmless enough, but now the wall sconces revealed a menacing glint in his eyes. Before Livy could move, he backed her against the wall, his hands pinning her shoulders.

"Get off me," she hissed.

He smirked. "Didn't I tell you this is the price of admission?"

He ground himself against her. She felt his member poking against her... *Ew.*

"I said *no.*" She shoved at his shoulders. "Get away from me."

"Not until I get what I want."

Enough was enough. Livy jerked her knee upward. Her attacker doubled over, emitting a howl of pain.

"You bitch," he groaned.

She stomped on his foot for good measure. "Remember this the next time a lady says *no.*"

His curses followed her as she exited the passageway. She saw doors open along the corridor, Ben emerging from one of them.

*Zounds.* She kept her face averted, walking away from him, panic buzzing through her. *Did he hear me in the passageway? See me just now?*

She didn't dare look back. She moved as quickly as she could without drawing attention, pushing through the crowded seraglio toward the stairs. Her nape tingled; dash it, she could *feel* Ben giving chase. As soon as she made it to the stairwell and out of his sight, she broke into a run, racing down the steps. She made it to the first floor—and a hand closed around her arm.

Her heart shot into her throat, but it was Charlie. *Thank God.*

"This way," her mentor said.

Charlie led her to an open panel in the wall: a servant's passage. The two hastened into the tunnel, closing the door behind them. Charlie spoke as they raced along.

"This will take you to the exit at the back. Hawker's waiting one block east. Once you get back to the house, dispose of your disguise and go to bed. *At once.*"

"Why the rush?"

"Because Hadleigh saw you and will no doubt pay you a visit."

Livy didn't know if her shiver was one of fear or anticipation. "What should I do?"

"Keep the truth from him however you can." Charlie shoved open a door, pushing Livy out into the foggy night. In the holes of her mask, Charlie's grey eyes shone with urgency. "I've picked up critical information tonight, and I must stay to learn more. Your assignment is now to protect the secrecy of our mission: the safety of the man you love depends upon it. Now *go*."

# THIRTY-ONE

Propelled by grim determination, Ben scaled the tree in Lady Fayne's garden. As Livy had once described, one of its sturdy branches conveniently extended toward a second-floor window, which had to be her bedchamber. At the windowsill, he reached for the double glass panels; he'd been prepared to break in if need be, but the panels opened smoothly.

*The damned chit didn't even bother to lock her windows on the way out,* he thought with simmering rage.

Climbing through the window, he landed in the room, which was faintly lit by a fire in the hearth. He was certain the chamber was unoccupied, for he had no doubt that he'd spotted Livy at the Hellfire Club tonight. In disguise *again*, in a place more disreputable than the Black Lion Inn and Cremorne Gardens combined. After she'd given him the slip, he'd made an excuse to the Horsemen and headed straight over to Lady Fayne's.

If Livy had snuck off to go to the club, then she would need to hail a hackney to get back, not the easiest thing on a busy Saturday night in Mayfair. He reckoned she wouldn't be home for another half hour. When she arrived, he would confront her. He would not let her get away with lying to him...with risking her goddamned neck. Not to mention her virtue.

He couldn't allow himself to imagine what Livy had been exposed to on her little jaunt through an orgy. If he did, he might plow his fist through the nearest wall.

*What was she thinking?* he raged. *Did she follow me, think it was some kind of lark? Bloody hell, she gave me her word...and I will not be lied to. Even by her.*

He strode toward her bed in the far corner. He would wait for her there, he thought with dark satisfaction. She would sneak back in, thinking she'd pulled the wool over his eyes. She'd prance toward her bed and then...

He would catch her red-bloody-handed. There would be no more lies or excuses. Deep in his gut, he'd always suspected that there was something she wasn't telling him. Yet he'd let his feelings —his *love*, why not call a spade a spade—sway him. He hadn't wanted to confront his worst fears: that she was deceiving and manipulating him.

God, he thought with a stab of anguish, it was his marriage all over again.

Approaching the canopy bed, he made out a lump beneath the covers. Pillows no doubt, the oldest damned trick in the book. He stalked over...and froze.

Livy lay there, asleep. Her lashes were dark fans against her cheeks, and an ivory counterpane was pulled up to her neck. She looked like a slumbering angel.

*She's been here the entire time?* he thought numbly. *I imagined seeing her...she wasn't at the club? She didn't lie to me?*

Disbelief warring with hope, he reached for the coverlet. As he pulled it down, he dreaded that he would expose a trollop's black gown. What he found was a chaste white night rail.

Remorse pumped through him. Along with shattering relief.

*Bloody hell, I'm an idiot. This is Livy, not Arabella. She would not betray me.*

At that moment, Livy opened her eyes. She blinked, as if surfacing from a dream. She stared up at him...and a dazzling smile of welcome lit her eyes. "Ben?"

"Yes," he said hoarsely.

She sat up. "What are you doing here?"

One look at Ben's face as he struggled to answer her, and Livy could tell that he hadn't expected her to be here. That he now felt guilty for suspecting her of being at the club. Of course, that made *her* feel guilty for her charade. Yet Charlie had said that Ben's safety depended upon Livy's concealment of the truth...and Livy would do anything to protect the man she loved.

Livy pushed aside the confusing tangle of thoughts. She would sort things out later. The truly important thing was that Ben was *here*, and they were together after what had felt like an eternity of separation.

"Whatever the reason, I'm glad you came. I've missed you so much, Ben," she said with heartfelt sincerity.

"Ah, bloody hell." He framed her jaw with his hands. He was shaking a little, his eyes bruised with shadows, his hair disheveled waves around his face. "Livy, I...I..." He squeezed his eyes shut, as if struggling with himself; when he opened them, need glittered in the blue depths. "It's been hell without you. *God,* I've missed you."

He bent his head, and she tipped hers up, their lips meeting in a tender kiss. The taste of him, being in his arms...nothing had ever felt this right—this essential. In a blink, the desperate tensions of the night transformed into another kind of need. He must have felt that way too, for when she parted her lips, he delved in, a feral sound rising from his throat.

They fell onto the bed, melded by their fiery kiss. She threaded her fingers through his rough-silk hair and pressed herself against his hard length, her tongue dancing with his. She tasted a trace of whisky, and while it was not unpleasant, it was strange because the Ben she knew abstained from spirits. It reminded her of his night at the club: the scene with Cherise Foxton came rushing back, billowing the flames of possessiveness. The need to reestablish her claim collided with desire, and it was a combustible combination.

Livy rolled atop Ben, and he let her, the dim light showing the glint of surprise in his gaze. She attacked him with feverish passion. He groaned when she peppered his bristly jaw with kisses and suckled his earlobe, flicking it with her tongue. Tearing off his cravat, she nuzzled the strong, warm column of his throat. His spicy male musk maddened her with wanting. She wanted more of him, but his clothes were in the way.

When she fumbled clumsily with the buttons of his waistcoat, he gave a husky laugh.

"Eager wench, aren't you?" His eyes smiled up at her.

"I want you," she whispered. "So badly."

He tucked a tress behind her ear. "I burn for you, my love. But we mustn't go too far. Lady Fayne—"

"She is out and will not be home for hours." This was no lie. "We have all the privacy we need. Please, Ben, I *need* you."

Her plea seemed to snap his restraint...and his willingness to let her be in control. He lifted her off him and rose from the bed, stripping off his coat.

"Take off your nightgown," he ordered.

Her eyes on his, she undid the pearl buttons along the front placket until she could pull the garment over her head. Kneeling on the mattress, bare as the day she was born, she felt pride at the proprietary lust in her lover's eyes. Her own gaze was equally possessive as she watched him undress. He was the essence of virility, long lines of sculpted muscle and taut hair-dusted skin. When he shed his trousers, a hot, viscous tremor passed through her core. His cock was huge, a thick and heavy truncheon between his thighs.

"See something you want, little one?" he inquired.

She loved the hint of arrogance in his tone. "I want all of you."

"Then come here, greedy chit." He crooked a finger at her.

She crawled to the edge of the bed, and he swept her against him. At the contact of skin against skin, they both exhaled as if they'd been holding their breaths, waiting for this moment. For this return to perfection, the way they were meant to be together. Body to body and heart to heart. He sank his fingers into her hair, holding her steady as he kissed her. First with tenderness and then with a ferocity that sent pulses of heat through her blood.

She was wet for him, wet with the need to pleasure him.

Ben, being Ben, seemed to understand what she wanted. What she craved. He broke the kiss, and with his big hands curled against her scalp, directed her lips down his body. Swoony with excitement, she worshipped his maleness, kissing the rigid planes of his chest, licking the flat discs of his nipples. Grunting with pleasure, he guided her downward, her tongue tracing the grooves on his taut torso.

The heady male scent of him deepened as she arrived at his manhood. It stood fiercely erect, the dusky tip bobbing with anticipation. Her mouth watered, yet he held her slightly away from him.

"Give me your eyes, sweeting," he said.

She looked up at him, and the controlled burn in his eyes stole her breath. Desire carved his features in hard, unyielding lines. He looked like a vengeful god, and she wanted to feel his passionate wrath. To feel everything he chose to bestow upon her.

"Why is it that in bed you are obedient," he murmured, "and outside of it you're a naughty minx?"

She thought about it. "Actually, I'm quite naughty in bed as well. It's just that here you instruct me on how to be wicked."

"A corruptive influence, am I?" The sensual curve of his mouth chased quivers up her spine. "I think it is time for you to have another lesson."

"Yes, please."

His lips twitched. "Lie on your back, love. With your head at the edge of the bed."

She hastened to do as he instructed. From that angle, his cock looked massive in the clasp of his fist, the plump sac below dangling close to her lips. Close enough for her...to kiss.

At the wanton notion, her nipples throbbed, wetness trickling from her center.

"I want to feel your mouth on me here." He looked down at her. His eyes held a dark yet playful challenge as he positioned his stones even closer to her face. "Is that too wicked for you?"

She answered by pressing her lips to the bulging underside. Ben's hitched breath told her he liked that. Emboldened, she licked, swirling her tongue against the velvety curve, wanting to give him as much pleasure as she possibly could. Wanting to do everything, feel everything with him.

With her Ben. Her love.

"Bloody hell, that's sweet," he said in guttural tones. "Lick me, love. Just like that."

He was jerking on his shaft as she lapped at his balls and mouthed him gently. When she experimented with suction, he bit out an oath. In the next instant, he was on the bed next to her. He parted her thighs, his head swooping down. The hot, hungry swipe of his tongue made her cry out. He licked her intimate seam, from her pearl to a place so dark and secret that she trembled with forbidden longing.

Awash with need, she was desperate to share the pleasure with him. She reached for his cock, and to her surprise, he shifted one leg so that his knees braced her head. The position was outrageous...and unbearably exciting. Grasping his big shaft, she brought the dripping crown to her lips. She took him in as deep as she could. He responded by parting her folds, stabbing his tongue into her pussy while he strummed her needy bud.

She mewled as he turned her into an instrument of desire. Feeling his masterful strokes while his thickness filled her mouth and throat brought her over the edge. Her spine bowed, and her release cascaded over her in bright, sparkling waves.

Wrenching free of Livy's generous kiss, Ben reversed direction, lying beside her so that he could watch her face as she came. He knew with absolute certainty that, in all his life, he would never see anything as beautiful as Livy in her climax. The pleasure-daze in her eyes, the flush that spread across her cheeks like a sunrise across the sky...

God, she was incomparable. His fantasy of lust, love, and all the shades of longing in between. Entranced, he stroked her hair and fingered her pussy.

"You are so bloody beautiful," he murmured.

"So are you, Ben."

She gazed at him as if he were everything she wanted to see. His chest tight and hot, his cock throbbing, he took her mouth in a deep kiss. To his delight and astonishment, her thighs tightened around his hand, a fresh gush of dew dampening his palm. She was ready for more, and he was the luckiest bastard alive.

He rolled on top of her, positioning his turgid prick against her silken mound. He rubbed against her valley, groaning as her wet lips kissed his shaft. She arched into his thrusts, and their bodies moved in perfect, natural synchrony.

She got wetter and wetter. The slick slide and erotic sounds of her juicy slit turned him inside out with pleasure. Nothing had ever felt this good, and he wasn't even inside her. He ground his steel-hard base against her pearl, rolling his balls over her swollen folds, bliss sizzling at the base of his spine. Her knees found the notches of his hips. Whimpering, she rubbed her virgin cunny against his thrusting cock, and it was too much, not bloody enough...

"Ben, I need you." The plea in her eyes mesmerized him. "I want you to come inside me."

He fought to hold onto his control. "We should wait—"

She canted her hips, and his cockhead suddenly lodged against her entrance. Her wet, pulsing flesh sucked at his sensitive tip. Sweat beaded upon his brow. His muscles bulged with the effort to hold back. To keep from taking what he wanted more than anything.

"I want to be yours. Irrevocably and forever," she whispered. "Please, sir."

*Holy hell.* It was over.

He claimed her with a firm thrust. He pushed past her jolt of resistance, wanting to make her pain as fleeting as possible. An instant later, a welcoming flood of honey bathed his cock. It eased his way into her untried pussy, her snug heat squeezing the breath from his lungs. And the truth from his heart.

"You are mine," he said raggedly. "I love you, Livy. Always and forever."

She trembled, the sheen in her eyes undoing his control. He bent his head and kissed her as he began to move his hips. Their joining felt as elemental and inevitable as the changing seasons. He'd finally claimed his Livy, who as a girl had tended to his spirit and as a woman owned him heart, body, and soul. He couldn't get enough of her, and she lifted her hips to take him deeper. Each plunge felt like absolution, each withdrawal a burning reason to go back.

His restraint decimated, he began to pound into her. Her breathy cries urged him on. Leaning down, he captured her plump nipples between his lips, sucking fiercely as he rammed his way home. Flutters started in her pussy, the contractions milking his cock. She was coming around him, the pleasure almost too much to resist. With his last ounce of willpower, he pulled out and fisted his prick. Two jerks and his climax hit him with the force of an oncoming carriage. Biting back a shout, he shot his seed in luxurious bursts, marking her belly with his pleasure.

Panting, he hung over her. Her love-stunned eyes reflected everything he was feeling. A universe of emotion that no words could convey.

She reached up, sweeping his hair from his damp brow.

"Now *that* was worth waiting for," she said tremulously.

"There is no going back. I've claimed you now." He took her jaw in his hand, daring her, or anyone, to deny it. To try to take away the most precious gift he'd ever been given. "You're all mine."

A spark of mischief danced in her eyes. The corners of her lips tipped up.

"I will let you in on a secret." She bent her finger, and he leaned closer to catch her whisper. "I've always been yours...and now you're mine too."

# THIRTY-TWO

*1847, SUMMER*

*Livy is 18; Ben is 30*

Ben found Livy in the orangery. She sat at the table where they'd spent many pleasurable hours playing games together and appeared absorbed by the wooden tiles she was pushing around. Anagrams were one of her favorite amusements, and he should know. She'd trounced him often enough.

"I thought I might find you here," he said.

She spun in her chair to face him. "Hadleigh! Goodness, you startled me."

The truth was, he was a bit startled too...by the changes that had taken place in his little queen. Spending more than a year in seclusion, hitting rock bottom before finally wrestling free of opium's grip, he had returned to society a changed man. A better man, he hoped.

During that time, Livy had undergone a metamorphosis as well.

She'd shed the cocoon of childhood, hovering somewhere between adolescence and womanhood. Her figure still had a girlish topography, yet her features had blossomed into vivid prettiness. Those exceptional eyes of hers, which regarded the world with that uniquely innocent-yet-wise manner, now seemed more mature. Seeing the changes in her and sensing more to come, he felt an acute pang of loss.

The seasons were changing, and soon she would enter another stage of her life. One where she would meet some lucky young fellow and fall in love. She would become a wife and a mama, her life filled with all the good things a girl like her deserved. For his part, Ben would dance with her at her wedding, see her on special occasions, and perhaps someday dangle her children upon his knee.

But she would never be his little friend again. The one who'd kept him company through the years, who'd written him the letters that had kept him afloat during his darkest times. She would belong to someone else and, slowly but surely, he would take her away from Ben. She would depart from Ben's life...like everyone he had cared about.

He felt old, stricken by unaccountable grief.

He cleared his throat before speaking. "You disappeared at your own ball."

"I am surprised you noticed," she said. "You were busy dancing all night."

He drew his brows together at the odd edge to her tone. If it had been any other female, he would have thought she sounded jealous. But this was Livy, which meant he must have misheard.

"Alas, since your dance card was full, I had to make do with substitutes," he said.

After a moment, she wrinkled her nose. "Does that flummery work with ladies?"

The strange tension dissipated. He hid a smile. "Usually. But they are not as clever as you."

"As Mama likes to say, *clever is as clever does*," she muttered. "Which makes me singularly stupid at times."

"Why do you say that? Having trouble with an anagram?"

He went over to her, glancing down at the table just as her hands went to cover the letters. It was too late, however. The hairs on his nape stirred at what he saw spelled out:

FALLING IN LOVE.

Her cheeks rosy, she said, "I was playing around. It's just a stupid game."

*Who in blazes is she thinking about?* Ben wondered.

She'd been surrounded by a herd of young bucks this evening, but no one of note. No one that Ben would deem worthy of her. The idea of Livy throwing herself away on some lordling or frivolous fop roused his protective instincts.

"Take it from me: love is not a game," he said firmly. "And should never be treated as such."

She stared at him, chewing on her bottom lip. He burned to know what she was thinking about. Hopefully not some undeserving bastard.

She sighed. "I don't think I'm ready for love quite yet."

For some reason, he felt like a prisoner who'd been issued a stay of execution.

He strove for a lighter tone. "You aren't missing much anyway. May I?"

She moved aside so that he could fiddle with the letters, rearranging them. When he was done, she laughed in her old, carefree way, and he smiled at her, savoring the moment...and his rather clever reordering of the letters in FALLING IN LOVE:

FILLING A NOVEL.

## PRESENT DAY

Livy woke from a deep sleep. As the vestiges of a marvelous dream fell away, she saw a dark shape at the foot of her bed, limned by the rosy glow of the hearth. The night returned to her in a flash of pure joy. It hadn't been a dream.

Ben was here, and he'd made love to her. Made her his. Afterward, he'd cuddled her, and she'd drifted off to his whispers of love.

It was still dark out, and she felt a frisson of unease at his posture, which conveyed that he was deep in thought. In her experience, nighttime rumination was rarely a good thing. She pushed aside the blankets, moving over to him. He turned, the stark set of his features softening. When he held out an arm to her, she got under it, snuggling into his warmth. He'd thrown on his shirt without buttoning it, and she savored the contact with his rippling muscles.

She could hardly believe that this magnificent male was *hers*. She felt giddy and a wee bit smug. But mostly, she was grateful to Fate for giving her what she'd always longed for: her soul mate.

He slanted her a look. "How are you feeling?"

"I feel wonderful."

At her prompt reply, his lips twitched. "You are not sore?"

She ran her mind over the part in question. "Perhaps a little. But in a good way...like after vigorous exercise."

"I hope I wasn't too vigorous." Grooves formed around his mouth, and the shadows in his eyes confirmed that she had been right about his somber mood. "It was your first time, Livy, and I should have been gentler."

"I loved every moment of being with you," she said with emphasis. "If you were any gentler, I would have complained."

"Well, we couldn't have that." Despite his light reply, his demeanor remained serious.

Hesitantly, she asked, "You don't regret making love to me...do you?"

If he did, she couldn't bear it. Her bubble of giddiness burst, and she suddenly felt young and unsure. At the time, giving her virginity to the man she loved had felt right...but now the enormity of what had transpired washed over her in an unsettling wave.

"God, no." He curled a finger beneath her chin, making her meet his gaze. "Livy, being with you...I cannot tell you how special it is. How special *you* are to me. If I regret anything, it is that I did not treat you with the respect you deserve. What happened between us should have taken place on our wedding night, not after I'd spent the night..."

He drew his brows together, and she finally understood. Relief filled her that he didn't regret making love to her; he felt guilty about the Hellfire Club. She wished she could tell him that she knew about Cherise Foxton and understood why he'd done what he'd done, but she had to talk to Charlie first.

*If I have to keep up the pretense to protect the man I love, I will,* she vowed.

"Did you have a bad night?" she ventured.

He gave a tight nod. "It was bloody awful. It reminded me of who I used to be, and I...I am ashamed of that man. He is not good enough for you."

"You are not that man any longer. You've changed," she argued. "And it doesn't matter anyway because I love the man that you've always been when you're with me. I love your strength, your good heart, the way you protect me and order me around."

Wonder glittered in his gaze.

Clearing his throat, he said, "Like being ordered around, do you?"

"Only when we're making love," she clarified. "In bed, I do not mind being the novice. In life, however, I want us to be partners."

"You are not the only novice, you know."

She tilted her head.

"It is true that I have more experience in bedroom matters than you. But when it comes to love, *real* love, the kind that owns and completes you, that perseveres and never fails..." He tucked a tress behind her ear, his knuckles brushing tenderly against her cheek. "It turns out that I am a novice too."

# THIRTY-THREE

Later that afternoon, Livy convened with Charlie and the other Angels in the study. Charlie was sitting at her desk, the Angels clustered in the chairs on the other side. They were discussing the information Charlie's surveillance had yielded last night.

"Stamford may be the weakest link," Charlie said. "He was not at the club last eve, and Edgecombe, Thorne, and Bollinger seem to think he has developed cold feet. They whispered amongst themselves that one of Stamford's clients, a rising opera singer, died a few days ago."

"Because of the Devil's Bliss?" Livy asked with a shudder.

Charlie nodded. "Edgecombe, Thorne, and Bollinger did not admit it, of course. Greed is the North Star of their moral compass, and they've convinced themselves that it is not the drug that is the killer, but some 'unfortunate predisposition' possessed by their dead clients."

"They are blaming the victims?" Glory said in appalled tones.

"Rather convenient for them," Fiona remarked. "Should we approach Stamford?"

"We could, but he will likely not tell us much." Charlie looked at Livy.

Before leaving this morning, Ben had given Livy a brief summary of what he'd learned, and she shared it now with the group.

"When I, um, was with Hadleigh last night," Livy said, fighting back a blush, "he told me that the Horsemen are afraid of Fong and treat him like some all-knowing deity. Longmere's death served as a warning, and I doubt Stamford would dare to betray Fong."

Fi tilted her head. "Was Hadleigh able to discover how the supply of Devil's Bliss is delivered to the group?"

"There hasn't been a delivery since he's been back in the fold." Livy chewed on her lip, her worry for Ben surfacing. "He says he has not yet won the men's trust. They are tolerating him because he knows too much, but they are keeping their secrets."

A knock interrupted them. It was Hawker.

Charlie tilted her head. "Yes, what is it?"

"A guest has arrived, my lady." The butler's gaze shifted to Livy. "Mrs. Beatrice Murray."

"I hope the others will not think me rude for requesting a moment alone with you," Aunt Bea said.

"My friends are not easily offended," Livy assured her. "Why don't you tell me what is on your mind, Aunt Bea?"

She could tell something was bothering her aunt-in-name-only. Aunt Bea shared Ben's exceptional looks, hers being a fair and feminine version. She was tall, willowy, and elegantly attired in a mauve carriage dress that was a perfect foil for her white-gold hair and lavender eyes that, at present, were shadowed with concern. Her smile had an edge of tautness, as did the delicate pink scar that curved over her right cheek.

"You were always perceptive, even as a little girl," Aunt Bea said ruefully. "I shan't shilly-shally: I am concerned about my brother and hope you can help."

Perhaps Livy oughtn't have been surprised but, like Ben, Aunt Bea was private by nature. What could bring her to ask for help... and from Livy, no less?

*Does she know about me and Ben?* Livy thought with a frisson of worry.

She and Ben had planned to keep their relationship under wraps until Fong was captured. Even then, Ben was concerned about how others might react...in particular, her papa. Livy had reassured him that her family adored him and, even if they were surprised at first, they would come around. She hadn't considered how Ben's family—namely Aunt Bea—might take to the news.

She was very fond of Aunt Bea and hoped the other would support the match. It would take some getting used to, but she thought it would be lovely to have Aunt Bea as a sister-in-law.

Thus, Livy asked with care, "How can I help?"

"I know you and Hadleigh share a special bond. Ever since that time he came to your aid." Aunt Bea's smile was wistful. "He told me once that rescuing you was the one good deed he'd done in his life."

Livy had to defend him. "Hadleigh is a good man with a brave and noble heart."

"That is why he likes you so much. You are more of a loyal sister to him than I ever was," Aunt Bea said somberly. "I have not supported my younger brother as I ought to have."

Livy felt her cheeks burn. Of course, she couldn't tell Aunt Bea that her feelings for Ben were far from sisterly. At the same time, she heard the regret in Bea's voice and recalled what Ben had said about the distance between him and his sister. How he'd caused it by his foolish and reckless pursuit of vengeance on Bea's behalf.

"Hadleigh does not blame you," Livy said, wanting to help

heal the breach. "On the contrary, he holds himself responsible for the estrangement."

Aunt Bea looked startled. "He has spoken to you about our relationship?"

*Botheration.* Livy wanted to kick herself for giving too much away.

"Um, not exactly. But I know Hadleigh, and he is a man of honor who tends to take responsibility for things," she said awkwardly.

Bea studied her with lavender eyes that were a little too perceptive.

"You understand him well," Bea said at length, "and that is the reason why I came to you. When I arrived in town yesterday, I saw Mrs. Garrity. Out of concern, she told me the recent gossip about Hadleigh. Even if she hadn't told me, I would have seen it: it is in all the scandal rags."

"You cannot believe everything you read and hear," Livy said quickly.

How she wished she could tell Aunt Bea the truth behind Ben's behavior. But doing so would compromise his mission. And she knew for a fact that he would not want his sister involved in that dangerous business.

"I saw Hadleigh with my own eyes when I paid a call upon him this morning," Aunt Bea said flatly. "He looked like he hadn't slept all night. And there were signs that he...he has reverted to some of his old behaviors. You are too young to understand, Livy, but while my brother has good intentions, his actions have not always reflected that."

Livy could hardly tell Aunt Bea that Ben looked tired because he'd been up most of the night making love to her. As for the other "signs," Ben had admitted that he had been drinking with the Horsemen. Thus far, he'd avoided taking opium and the Devil's Bliss; he felt he couldn't convince his old cronies that he'd reverted to a life of sin if he was a teetotaler as well.

Livy knew the week had taken a toll on Ben, stirring up the demons from his past. His voice echoed in her head: *It reminded me of who I used to be, and I am ashamed of that man. He is not good enough for you.* She prayed that his undertaking would be over soon so that they could have a fresh start. She wanted to take care of him and lavish him with love.

She also needed to tell him the truth and beg his forgiveness for her deception.

"Did you tell Hadleigh your concerns when you visited?" Livy asked.

A frown marred Bea's brow. "I asked him what was going on, but he would not talk to me. To be honest, I am not surprised. He and I have been dancing around each other these years past, and we Wodehouses have never been good at discussing our feelings. Nor showing them, in truth." She reached into her reticule, taking out a handkerchief and dabbing her eyes. "For a long time, I believed that my brother was a destructive force, and I cut him out of my life. Then I met Mr. Murray, and he convinced me that Hadleigh had changed and was deserving of another chance.

"I allowed Hadleigh back into my life, but I always kept my distance. I was afraid to be hurt again," Bea said, her voice hitching. "In spite of the bad blood between us, he is my kin, and I...I do care about him."

Livy's heart hurt for Aunt Bea...and for Ben, too. She vowed that, once the business with Fong was over, she would do whatever she could to help them mend fences.

As her mama oft said, *"Where there is love, there is a way."*

"He loves you too, Aunt Bea," Livy said. "And while he might not seem himself of late, I am certain there is a good reason. You can trust him not to repeat the mistakes of his past."

"Even if I trusted him, I cannot trust the band of rakehells who have drawn him back into their fold." Bea's lips formed a hyphen of disapproval. "Edgecombe, Thorne, and Bollinger were a bad influence years ago; from what I gather, they are even worse now.

My brother's loyalty has always been his greatest strength and weakness. If it hadn't been for Arabella's influence..." She shook her head. "I will not speak ill of the dead. But I will say that in recent months, I have seen Hadleigh show the promise of the man he could be. If those scoundrels compromise his progress, draw him into their depraved world again, I vow I will give them a piece of my mind."

With gnawing unease, Livy observed the determined angle of Aunt Bea's chin. It took one to know one, which was how she knew Bea was as strong-willed as they came. And the last thing Ben needed right now was for his sister to get involved.

"You won't interfere, will you?" Livy said desperately. "I do not think that is what Ben needs right now."

Aunt Bea's eyebrows shot up. "Ben?"

*Botheration again.*

"Hadleigh, I mean." Livy's face flamed. "Since he is, after all, a grown man, I think it is best to trust his judgement."

A pause. "Is there something you are not telling me, Livy?"

*That Ben is infiltrating a drug enterprise? That I'm protecting him while participating in a secret investigative agency? That you and I may soon be related?*

Livy shook her head lamely.

"Well, I hope you are right about trusting Hadleigh." Aunt Bea heaved out a breath, her eyes worried. "Because my brother has a history of being his own worst enemy."

# THIRTY-FOUR

After Aunt Bea's departure, Livy acted on her instincts and scribbled a brief note to Ben. Knowing discretion was paramount, she kept the message as brief and free of particulars as possible.

*Your sister paid me a visit. She is concerned and may try to help, even though I tried to dissuade her. I thought you should know.*

Instead of signing her name, Livy drew a little crown. She hoped that Ben would receive it before he headed off for a planned night of revelry at Bollinger's.

Shortly after Livy sent the note, a mudlark arrived. The girl, who didn't look a day over thirteen, introduced herself as "Fair Molly." She had a dirt-smudged cap crammed over her profusion of curly hair, and her amber eyes sparkled with intelligence as she relayed the message from the leader of her group.

"We found the scene in the picture. The Prince o' Larks says I'm to take you lot there personally." Her little chest puffed up with pride. "Since I'm the leader o' the team wot found the spot."

"We are much obliged to you, Fair Molly," Charlie said.

The sun was dipping into the horizon by the time they arrived in Limehouse. Here the squat brick buildings were crammed jowl to jowl, homes and businesses piled atop one another on the narrow streets. The dockside community was home to residents from all over the world, and they passed groups of Chinese, Lascar, and Spanish sailors talking in their native tongues.

They arrived on a street on the banks of the Thames. Fair Molly pointed out the carriage window at a building; even though Longmere had painted it from the opposite side of the river, Livy recognized the structure, as well as the open field next to it. From the front, the small, shuttered edifice looked like it might have been a shop at some point, with a living area on the second floor.

"A job well done," Charlie said warmly. "Thank you, Fair Molly."

Fair Molly shrugged. "It were the old ropemaking field next to it wot pinpointed the location. Otherwise, it'd be like finding a needle in the 'aystack." She opened the door, jumping down. Turning, she said, "I almost forgot. The Prince says to tell you this job is gratis."

Charlie frowned. "That is kind, but I am not in the habit of accepting favors."

"'E said you'd say that. 'E didn't become the 'ead o' the mudlarks from being stupid." Fair Molly's smile reflected her pride in her leader. "The Prince says it ain't a favor if you're doing somefing for 'im in return."

"And what am I expected to do for your prince, precisely?"

"You're to bring the villain wot killed that toff Longmere to justice."

Livy cocked her head. "The Prince has a connection to Longmere?"

"Ain't my place to question my leader's connections. I just be passing along the message. Good day, ladies." Fair Molly dipped her knees and disappeared in a blink.

"That was odd," Fi said.

"Undoubtedly. But let us concentrate on the task at hand." Charlie's gaze homed in on the building. "We'll make our move when the sun sets. Until then, we'll monitor the building."

Shadows bled through the sky and onto the street. No light leaked from the shuttered windows of the house, and Livy hadn't seen anyone enter or exit. Charlie led the way from the carriage, the darkness and their disguises as male dock workers allowing them to blend in.

They circled around to the back of the building, where the property abutted the Thames. The rickety dock shown in the painting was presently empty. Charlie and the Angels scaled the fence at the back of the building, landing softly in a small courtyard.

No light shone from the back windows. They found the door locked.

"Allow me," Fi said, taking out her lock picks.

Within moments, they entered. The air inside had a stale, fishy smell. Charlie lit some candles she'd brought, eerie shadows chasing over the cracked walls.

"Let's split up," she said. "Glory and I will take this floor, Livy and Fiona the one above."

Livy and Fi headed up the creaking stairs. The plan of the top floor was like the bottom: three rooms separated by a hallway. The front room held a few worn furnishings. While Fi poked around in the middle room, Livy went to the one at the back. As she held up her candle, the light illuminated a head of black hair.

Heart seizing, she yanked out her pistol; the figure did not move. She inched forward...and realized that she was looking at a dressmaker's form. A wig of long black hair tied in a Chinese-style single braid sat upon a blank wooden head. Below, the form wore a long tunic over matching trousers.

Fiona came up behind her. "Heavens. Is that...?"

"I think we've found Fong," Livy said grimly.

She shone her light over the desk next to the dummy: the

surface was covered in pots of face paint and brushes. As Charlie and Glory came into the bedchamber, Livy pinched a strip of hair between finger and thumb, holding up a straggly black beard.

"Master Fong is a fake," she said. "Someone is pretending to be the Chinese mastermind."

"Who?" Glory asked, her eyes wide.

"I have four likely suspects in mind," Charlie said in a hard tone.

"That makes perfect, diabolic sense." Fi opened the cupboard, revealing more garments cut in the Chinese style. "One of the Horsemen is supplying the drug, but he is protecting himself by using a false persona."

"Then if the lethal effect of the drug is uncovered, he can deny having knowledge of it." Livy picked up the theory. "He will claim that he was an unwitting dupe like everyone else. The upstanding Englishman can blame everything on the evil foreigner...who, of course, will never be found."

"A stratagem as brilliant as it is despicable. One that society is primed to believe, given its prejudices," Glory said darkly. "Now, who of the four is responsible for this heinous crime?"

As the others rifled through the room, Livy tried the drawer beneath the desk. When it didn't open, she crouched and picked the lock. Inside were assorted papers. She pulled out the loose sheet on top and read the scrawled lines.

> A favorite of pirating swaps,
> And mannered grocers,
> I am the cause of a nightdress furor.
> To find me, head on yonder towards snails
> And swim with the fish beating gills.

"Did you find something?" Glory asked.

Livy frowned. "It appears to be an odd bit of verse. A riddle, perhaps?"

She continued searching through the drawer. She found a note. Unfolding it, she scanned the lavish feminine hand.

*My darling,*

*I count the days, hours, and minutes until I can see you again.*

*Every moment while I am trapped in this country prison with Hadleigh as my warden is torture. How I loathe my husband. He seeks to stifle my soul with his bourgeois ways. He cannot hold a candle to your manly sophistication, my darling. How I miss you!*

*I dream of the day we can run away together. Until then, the life you put inside me gives me hope for our future. Come for me soon, my love, or I shall expire from wanting you.*

*Your loving,*
*A.*

The words sunk in, chilling Livy's blood. "I have to warn Hadleigh."

"About what?" Charlie asked alertly.

Livy dashed toward the door. "I think whoever is masquerading as Fong had an affair with Hadleigh's wife...and may thus have a personal vendetta against Hadleigh!"

The spotted billiard ball dropped into a pocket. Across the baize-covered table, Thorne's smile was smug as he straightened after taking his shot. "Sorry, old b-boy. I win again."

Ben knew the bastard wasn't sorry in the least. Which was why he'd been deliberately letting the other win at billiards all night, with substantial wagers made on the outcome. Men in good spirits were easier to tap for information.

"Where is Stamford tonight?" Ben asked casually as he retrieved the balls.

"He sent a m-message saying he has a head cold or something of the sort. Namby-pamby fellow." Thorne gave a derisive shrug. "Stamford never managed to fill your shoes. I'll confess that I wasn't certain at first about your return, Hadleigh, but now I can say that it is g-good to have you back. Cheers, old boy."

Thorne held up his whisky in a toast.

Ben had no choice but to reach for his own glass. "Cheers."

It was only his second serving of alcohol thus far; he'd managed to appear like he was drinking more than he actually was. The more the other men indulged, the less they would notice his minimal participation in the various forms of depravity Bollinger had made available to his guests this eve. As Ben set up another billiards game, his vision briefly wavered.

His period of abstinence had affected his ability to hold his drink. Luckily, the wave of dizziness passed, and his mind cleared once more. He couldn't help but see the irony of it: abandoning his vices had made him more susceptible to their effects. In trying to become a better man, he'd made his present mission more difficult.

The memory of Bea's visit flashed in his head. His chest knotted as he recalled the doubt in his sister's eyes, the resignation and anger. Even if he had been able to tell her that his recent behavior was just a ploy, would she have believed him? He'd broken her trust too many times. Caused her pain for which he could never make amends. He'd deserved her parting shot.

*"It was my fault for thinking better of you, Hadleigh,"* she'd said bitterly. *"A leopard never changes its spots."*

Perhaps there was no escaping his past. Perhaps redemption was a mere illusion.

Yet for Livy, his love and duchess-to-be, he had to try to wipe his slate clean.

Edgecombe sauntered in. "Still at the billiards, fellows?"

The earl had lost his cravat, his shirt unbuttoned at the throat. His face bore traces of rouge from the two French prostitutes he'd taken upstairs.

"Bed sport isn't a m-man's only choice of entertainment," Thorne said.

"While the two of you play with your own balls, I prefer," Edgecombe drawled, "to delegate the task."

The risqué quip drew appreciative guffaws, and Ben found himself laughing along.

Rising from the divan where he'd been nursing a bottle of brandy, Bollinger stumbled over.

"Speaking of tasks, I've been thinking." His words were slurred. "I should take Hadleigh with me on my errand tomorrow night."

Seeing the significant looks exchanged, Ben felt a surge of euphoria.

*At last, news of Fong. My plan is coming to fruition.*

Giddy with success, he strove to keep his wits about him.

"Have you heard from Fong?" he asked. "Is a shipment arriving?"

"Yes. And the fellows and I think you're ready to help," Bollinger said.

"You have to earn your keep along with the rest of us, Your Grace," Edgecombe said with a smirk. "If you want Longmere's cut, then you'll be taking over his position on the route."

"There's a route?" Ben asked.

"It's all very hush-hush." Thorne's gaze glittered with illicit thrill. "We had to solve a r-riddle to figure out where to pick up the Devil's Bliss."

"You'll see for yourself tomorrow night," Edgecombe said.

He gave Ben a slap on the back. Ben pitched forward, catching himself against the billiards table, his vision swimming. He felt as if he'd suddenly plunged underwater, the voices and faces around him growing blurry and indistinct. At the same time, he was oddly content to float there, listening to the ebb and flow.

"You all right?" someone asked.

"Old boy has lost his touch..."

Laughter...were they laughing at him? He frowned, trying to think.

*Not supposed to look weak. Have to stay strong—about to bring down Fong at last...*

"Just need some air," he managed.

He staggered from the billiards room. In the hallway, the walls seemed to curve around him, and he found himself laughing at the absurdity of the situation. Of him being foxed from two drams of whisky. He couldn't remember spirits making him feel this way before. So free of care, the world bathed in a rosy glow. It was almost like how he felt when he was with Livy...

*...or when I had that first hit of opium.*

The realization jolted him. Gave him enough presence of mind to lurch over to the lavatory. Inside, he went to the looking glass, gripping the edges of the water basin.

Darkened pupils. Flushed cheeks. The rush of euphoria.

*Holy hell...I've been drugged.*

At that moment, his legs gave out, and he was sucked into a terrifying quicksand of exultant torpor. The harder he tried to fight it, the more ensnared he became. Time floated, he floated, suspended in a fuzzy kaleidoscope of color and shapes. Something slapped his cheek. His awareness sharpened on an object in front of his face.

A glittering pendulum of gold mesh swung from a chain. The peacock feathers swirling around the globe stirred a distant memory. Behind it, a masked face blurred in and out of his vision, accompanied by a muffled voice.

"Do you remember this vinaigrette? I gave its twin to Arabella. You left her no choice but to seek the freedom within when you locked her up. It was your fault that she took the drug during her pregnancy and died...

"Do you like your first taste of the Devil's Bliss? You always thought you were better than the rest of us, but now you'll see who truly holds the power. By the by, Arabella's babe was mine. And now you shall pay for taking them both away..."

The voice grew distant, and Ben couldn't fight the darkness any longer. As he succumbed to the airless depths, his last thought was of Livy.

*Forgive me, little queen. I love you...*

# THIRTY-FIVE

"Where do you think they are headed?" Livy said, peering ahead anxiously.

She was on the driver's perch with Hawker, who kept his good eye trained on the unmarked carriage several lengths ahead.

"'Ard to tell," he said. "We'll keep on 'em."

While Charlie had stayed at the villain's lair to look for the cache of Devil's Bliss—without which they had no evidence—she had sent Hawker along with the Angels to find Ben. The group had arrived at Bollinger's townhouse in time to see two burly footmen load Ben into a carriage and take off at a rapid clip. Even from a distance, Ben had looked unstable, as if he was heavily foxed...or drugged. Any fleeting hope Livy had that the servants were merely delivering Ben to his residence vanished when the vehicle continued south past Piccadilly, turning east at St. James's Park.

Now Hawker was following the other carriage through the streets sandwiched between the Strand and the Thames. Several conveyances separated them, and the view was obscured by the thick layer of fog rising off the river. Angling to keep an eye on Ben's carriage, Livy tapped her foot in a restless rhythm.

*Where are they taking Ben?* she thought frantically. *What is their plan?*

"Bleeding 'ell," Hawker bit out.

He swerved to avoid a produce wagon that had emerged from a side street and straight into their path. Livy grabbed onto the side of the perch, holding on for dear life as the carriage tilted, skidding on the edge of its wheels. The horses neighed in fright, but Hawker managed to keep the carriage upright through the hail of cabbages and carrots. They came to a juddering stop.

"Everyone all right?" Hawker barked.

From the cabin, Glory and Fi called out, "We're fine!"

Heart pounding, Livy strained to see ahead. "We've lost the other carriage. We have to find it!"

Hawker picked up the reins, and they sped off. Livy's stomach sank as she saw no sign of the vehicle carrying Hadleigh. It could have gone down any of the small dark lanes branching off the arterial route.

Glory poked her head out of the carriage window. She'd taken off her cap and wig, her hair streaming in the wind. "Do you see the carriage?"

"No," Livy said desperately. "If they mean to do Ben harm, where would they take him?"

Fi's head appeared next to Glory's. "If he's drunk, they could dump him into the river. Make it look like he fell in and drowned."

A likely ploy. Where would the villains go to do the heinous deed, to make it appear like an accident instead of foul play? Livy's mind raced through the closest places...

"*Waterloo Bridge!*" she and her friends exclaimed as one.

Hawker reacted by pulling a sharp right. The bridge was mere blocks away, infamous in recent years for a spate of accidental deaths and suicides taking place there. Indeed, Waterloo Bridge had been immortalized in "The Bridge of Sighs," a poem about a woman's tragic taking of her own life. They arrived at the granite bridge, the lamps on its span illuminating a smattering of vehicles and people crossing on foot.

"How would the villains toss Ben in without anyone seeing?" Livy muttered.

"I see them. The embankment, to the right of the bridge," Hawker said.

He drove them toward the spot where the other carriage was parked. Livy made out two figures in the swirling mist. They were standing on the edge of the embankment. They hoisted something between them and heaved it into the river.

Seeing and hearing the heavy splash, Livy felt terror flood her being.

The sound of their approach tipped off the scoundrels.

"'Urry, let's get out of 'ere!" The figures dove into their carriage, the vehicle speeding off.

By the time Hawker brought the carriage to a halt seconds later, Livy had stripped off her jacket and shoes. She ran toward the river, her gaze trained on the dark waves where she'd seen Ben go under. She heard the others shouting at her, but there was no time to spare. Scrambling up the embankment, she dove in.

She fought the cold currents, slicing her arms through the water. It was dark, and she could hardly see, but she guessed she had to be close to where Ben had landed. Taking a breath, she dove under. She waved her arms out blindly, hoping against hope to find him. When her air ran out, she surfaced, gasping for breath. Then she went under again. And again.

With each successive dive, her fear and panic grew.

*Where are you, my love? Help me find you. Don't let go.*

The chill numbed her limbs. She fought off fatigue, staring over the dark mirror of the river with burning eyes. At that moment, a light from a passing barge swept over the water's surface, and she saw something bobbing in the water some fifty yards away, the current pushing it through the third arch of the bridge.

*Ben.*

She cut through the water with determined strokes. She pushed herself past cold, past exhaustion, past fear. Her mind and body were united in a single purpose: *get to Ben.*

She reached him, turning him over. His eyes were closed.

"Ben!" Frantically, she checked for the pulse at the side of his neck. His skin was horrifyingly icy. When she felt the faint leap beneath her fingertips, relief poured through her. Then she looked for the shore; the fog had thickened, and all she could see was water.

*I will get us to safety. Hold on, my love.*

With one arm hooked around Ben, Livy used the other to paddle. It was a struggle: she had to keep Ben's face above the waves, and her energy was sapping. She felt heavier and heavier, the chill burning into her bones. Her strokes slowed, the fog pressing down upon her, watery chains dragging on her arms and legs...

"Livy! Hold on, we're almost there!"

Livy blinked, disoriented. Glory's voice—*where was it coming from?* An instant later, the prow of a lighter cut through the thick mist, Hawker rowing, and Fi and Glory leaning over the side. The Angels hauled Ben and Livy into the boat.

"Ben, wake up." Livy knelt at Ben's side, shaking him. She asked fretfully, "Why isn't he responding?"

"Reckon he drank too much o' the Thames." Kneeling on the other side, Hawker placed his large palms on Ben's chest, pressing down in quick succession.

Water spewed from Ben's mouth, and he began to cough.

*"Ben."* Heat trickled down Livy's cheeks.

"He'll live," Hawker announced, stripping off his jacket and bundling it around Ben. "But we need to get the two of you somewhere warm straightaway."

An awful pounding awakened Ben. It came from inside his head, a hammer whacking against his skull. Pain and nausea surged in an overwhelming tide. Rolling over, he retched.

"There now, my darling. Get it out. You'll feel better."

"Livy?" he croaked.

Through his stinging eyes, he saw that it *was* her. She was sitting by his side, her hair hanging loose over her shoulders. She was clad in a tunic and set of trousers that looked too big on her. He was lying on a bed in a Spartan room that was familiar...*Chen's clinic?*

"What am I...how did I get here?" Ben asked in confusion.

"You nearly drowned last night in the Thames. We brought you here so that Mr. Chen could tend to you," she said gently. "You've been unconscious for several hours."

Memories returned in flashes. The party. Playing billiards with Thorne. Drinking the whisky...whisky that had been laced with the Devil's Bliss. He remembered the rush, his inability to fight off the drug, that hopeless, euphoric weakness he'd sworn never to feel again.

Now he felt the drug withdrawing from his system, bringing with it that despicable low. The cancerous emptiness for which the cure was more poison. Soon weakness would take over, make him chase relief from the craving, even as he hated himself more. His stomach roiled, and he was sick again, this time into a bucket that Livy hastily shoved toward him.

When he was finished, he took the towel she handed to him. His face burned with humiliation as she used another to wipe up the mess he'd made on the floor. He felt like shite, his head pounding like the devil. He didn't want her to see him like this. Didn't want to be near her in his present state. A state to which he'd vowed never to return...and yet here he was again.

*A leopard never changes its spots.*

"Do you know who did this to you?"

It took Ben a moment to focus on Livy's question. To his ever-lasting shame, he realized that he didn't know who the villain was. He'd been too far gone, soaring so high on the Devil's Bliss that he couldn't be sure who had been speaking to him. Or if he'd imagined it all.

*Arabella and my babe are dead because of you...and now you will pay the price...*

He saw the vinaigrette swinging like a pendulum. The glittering of peacock feathers. Felt himself moving in darkness, rough hands shoving him into a carriage.

*Make it look like a suicide.*

Had any of that happened...or had he been hallucinating? It wouldn't be the first time that a drug twisted his mind, mixed reality with fantasy, and this Devil's Bliss had been ten times more potent than opium.

Realizing that Livy was watching him, waiting for an answer, he said gruffly, "I think I was drugged, but I do not know who did it." Even as he cursed his own ineptitude, a thought occurred to him. "How did you find me?"

Livy bit her lip. Strangely, she remained silent.

"Livy?" he prodded.

She drew a breath, as if she'd come to some internal decision. "We were following a lead that brought us to the lair of Master Fong. It turns out Fong is a façade: there is no Chinese master-mind. We believe the villain is one of your ex-cronies...and he was having an affair with your wife. I'm sorry, Ben." She paused, then went on, "We found a letter that Arabella wrote to him. She, um, wanted to run away with him, and she...she intimated that the child she was carrying was his. Knowing that whoever was posing as Fong might have an axe to grind with you, we came to warn you. At Bollinger's, we saw you being loaded into a carriage by brutes, and we followed you to Waterloo Bridge. They threw you into the water—to make it look like a suicide or accident, most likely—and

I went in after you. Luckily, I found you, and we brought you here to Mr. Chen."

As Ben tried to comprehend the astonishing summary, questions proliferated like weeds.

"By *we*, who are you referring to?" he asked in confusion.

She took another breath. "The Society of Angels."

"Lady Fayne's charity?" His brain felt thick and overgrown, slowing his ability to take in the information. "I...I don't understand."

"It is not a charity. At least, not in the traditional sense." She averted her gaze, fiddling nervously with the folds of her tunic. "We do help people but not through the usual benevolent means. Our approach is, um, more investigative in nature. Charlie has been training us to...to do detection work."

Suddenly, he understood. The suspicions he'd had...the gut feeling that Livy was hiding something from him. He'd convinced himself that the problem lay with *him*: that his past with Arabella had made him distrustful. Now the truth blazed, igniting a scorching rage.

"You have been lying to me this entire time?" he bit out.

Livy's silence was damning.

"The Black Lion Inn, Cremorne Gardens...bloody hell, *the Hellfire Club.*" He pinned her with a stare, daring her to lie to him. "You were there, weren't you? Spying on me?"

She gave a small nod. He didn't know why that pushed him over the edge, but it did. The guilt he'd harbored, the shame...and she'd seen him at his goddamned worst. When he shoved aside the blankets, surging from the bed, she jumped up with a startled gasp. A wave of dizziness overcame him, and he had to steady himself against a wall.

"Be careful, my love. You've only just recovered—"

"I am not your love," he snarled. "If you loved me, you would not have lied to me for the entire length of our relationship."

She looked as if he'd struck her, her eyes wide in her pale face.

"Of course I love you. It is *because* I love you that I had to hide the truth. I knew you wouldn't understand my desire to be an investigator because you're always trying to protect me. I didn't want to give you up...but I couldn't give up my work either. And when I joined the Angels, I took an oath of secrecy.

"Ultimately, though, it was fear that paralyzed me. Every time I thought about telling you, I panicked. I was afraid you would end things between us." She gripped her hands in front of her, her gaze pleading. "I kept putting it off, telling myself I would wait for the right moment. I know it was cowardly of me, and I am sorry. So sorry. Please try to understand..."

"I understand perfectly," he said acidly.

Bitterness welled inside him. It was his marriage all over again. Only this time, the betrayal cut deeper, for his love was deeper. The shock of learning that Arabella had been carrying another man's child—that she had died from taking a drug during her pregnancy—paled in comparison to that of discovering that his Livy, whom he'd believed to be his soul mate, was just another deceptive bitch. How could he be such a damned fool *again*? How had he let himself believe that a man like him was worthy of happiness?

Fury hardened his heart and his tone. "You've been playing me for a dupe this entire time, and it is my own fault for letting you do it."

"I didn't want to lie to you, but I was scared to tell the truth," Livy whispered. "Please forgive me."

Tears were trickling down her cheeks, and he hated that his first instinct was to wipe them away. To soothe and protect his little queen...who was obviously capable of taking care of herself. Who had no qualms about doing whatever the hell she wanted.

"I could forgive you most things but not this," he said flatly.

She took a step toward him, her hands outstretched. "You cannot mean that..."

"Do you remember what I said to you after I took you to my

bed?" The memory of that night, once a cherished gift, now felt like a blade jammed between his shoulder blades. "What I told you I expected from marriage?"

Rivulets ran down her cheeks. "You said you expected my loyalty, honesty, and obedience. But while I may have deceived you about my work, I *never* lied to you about my feelings. My love is true and real—"

"I don't want to hear another word about your love," he clipped out. "I am done with it."

"D-done?" she asked, her voice cracking.

"I would be done with you, too, if it were not for my honor. I took your virginity, and I will pay the price for it." Resentment frothed to the surface, covering the agonizing undertow. "We will be married, Olivia, and when you are my wife, there will be no more of this investigating nonsense. This time around, I *will* be the master of my own house, and you will do as you are told—even if I have to keep you under lock and key."

Her eyes were wide, her features frozen in shock.

*Good,* he thought with vicious satisfaction. *Let her see that I mean business. Let her know that I will not be played for a fool again.*

"Charlie was right," she said in a whisper. "I just didn't want to believe her."

What rubbish was Livy spouting now? Ben's temples were throbbing, and a queasy feeling rocked his gut, as if he might disgrace himself again. It hurt to think, to feel...he wanted her gone. He didn't need a witness to his pathetic misery.

"What was Lady Fayne right about?" he said curtly.

Livy raised her gaze, and the resignation in her eyes cut him to the quick.

"She said the cost of love would be my freedom. I didn't believe her. I defended you, told her you were different from other men, that you understood me." Her voice trembled. "I told her you would not make me choose between my love for you and my calling, yet here you are, issuing me an ultimatum."

His hackles rose. She had the gall to accuse *him* of being unreasonable when she'd been deceiving him for the duration of their affair?

"Stop twisting things around," he said through gritted teeth. "I'm not giving you an ultimatum; I am telling you the way things are going to be. When you are my wife, you will do as I goddamned say. Those are the terms."

"If those are the terms," she said with vibrating emotion, "then I will not marry you."

Her words plowed into him like a fist. Not *once* had Livy wavered in her desire to be with him. Since the outset, she had been steadfast in her so-called love for him, in her certainty that they were meant to be together. *Of course, she had been lying the whole time*, he thought savagely, *so who knew if her feelings were genuine?*

Now that he'd uncovered her web of deception and was trying to set things right, to sort through the rubble she'd made of their relationship, she was trying to force his hand yet again. Unluckily for her, his marriage to Arabella had made him an expert in dealing with this kind of manipulation, and he wasn't about to back down.

"That is, of course, your choice," he said coldly. "If you turn down my offer, I will not ask again. I mean it, Olivia."

Her eyes glimmered with pain, but her chin didn't waver from its obstinate angle.

"You saved my life once," she said, her voice choppy, "and I vowed to myself that I would return the favor. After last night, I have paid my debt."

"You never owed me anything," he snapped.

She gave a tight nod. "Good-bye, then."

He curled his hands as she exited the room, leaving him alone.

The way he'd always been.

Walking away from Ben was the hardest thing Livy had ever done.

It was not her habit to retreat from anything. To give up. Yet now even she had to admit defeat.

She managed to keep her composure until the carriage came round. She had to look away from the sympathy glinting in Hawker's exposed eye for fear that she would break down. When he handed her up into the carriage, she saw that Charlie had come.

She sat stiffly beside her mentor.

Charlie studied her with calm grey eyes. "How did it go when you told him the truth?"

The irony didn't escape Livy. After finally getting the other's permission to tell Ben about the Society, the truth no longer mattered. The years with him flipped like pages through Livy's mind: their friendship that had transformed into passion, their affection that had deepened into love. She'd been convinced that there would be a storybook ending for them, yet the pages of their future were...empty.

*If you turn down my offer, I will not ask again.*

"It's over," Livy said numbly. "You were right. I told Hadleigh, and he...he..."

The pain and grief came in a rush. Suddenly, she was sobbing.

"Oh, my dear. I am sorry," Charlie said.

Charlie put an arm around her, and Livy wept for everything that had been and would never be. For herself and Ben. For the discovery that, no matter how hard one strived, some dreams could not be spun, nor some battles won.

# THIRTY-SIX

After Livy's departure, Ben was ill again, his body purging the remnants of the drug. He didn't know which was more ragged: his emotions or his physical state.

Livy had broken things off with him. Left him.

After everything they'd shared, she was gone.

He sat at the table, his head in his hands. He speared his fingers through his hair, the small pain a welcome distraction from the aching hollow inside him. He felt...gutted.

*How could Livy deceive me?* His fury had slowly faded and in its place was something far worse. A feeling he was more than familiar with, but one he'd never thought to see in Livy's eyes: resignation. The death of hope.

A knock sounded, and he dragged himself over to open the door.

It was Chen, looking crisp and dapper in a blue suit.

"I thought you could use a bath," he said.

Servants carrying a tub and buckets of steaming water followed the healer into the room. After they set everything up behind a bathing screen, Ben gave himself a much-needed wash. It felt good, scrubbing away the accumulated grime. He felt nearly human again when he emerged, washed and dressed in a new set of clothes.

Chen waved him over to the table and felt his pulse.

"Better," Chen said with a nod. "I still feel disturbance in the flow of your *qi*, however. You are blocked in some way, my friend."

"I feel like shite," Ben said grimly.

"After being drugged and nearly drowning, it is to be expected."

Ben's chest tightened. "Not only because of that."

"Ah." Chen poured tea into cups, his movements precise. "I saw Lady Olivia when she left. She did not appear herself."

"How did she appear?" Ben couldn't help but ask.

"I do not claim to be an expert when it comes to the emotional state of young ladies, but if I had to guess..." The healer sampled his tea. "Heartbroken."

The reply twisted a knife in Ben's gut. He hated the idea of Livy hurting...which frustrated him even more. After all, she was the cause of her own pain, not to mention his.

"It is her own bloody fault. She *lied* to me, Chen," he said bitterly. "After my marriage, you know how I value honesty. Livy promised to be truthful and obedient, and she's been neither. She's been keeping secrets from me this entire time."

"I hope I do not regret asking." Chen sighed. "What sort of secrets?"

As Ben told his friend about the Society of Angels and Livy's shenanigans, his righteous indignation grew. How *dare* she take such risks, put herself in danger? Did she have no bloody sense at all? Obviously, he'd had *no choice* but to put his foot down.

"Can you *believe* Livy was doing all of that and behind my damned back?" he concluded.

Chen's mouth gave an odd twitch. "It does explain her proficiency with daggers."

"That is not amusing," Ben said, scowling.

"Not at all."

Ben clenched his jaw. "And she had the *nerve* to accuse me of limiting her freedom. She is a gently bred young lady—a duke's daughter, for God's sake! She knows full well her behavior is beyond the pale. Was I supposed to just stand there and allow my future bride to run around pell-mell, courting disaster at every turn?"

"To be fair, Lady Olivia seems quite capable of taking care of herself." Chen cleared his throat. "And, if anything, she prevented a disaster last night. She saved your life, and from what she told me of her group's undertaking, they have discovered some critical facts concerning the true identity of the villain behind the Devil's Bliss. 'Master Fong' was a subterfuge." The healer paused, muttering, "Why am I not surprised that it is an Englishman spreading the opium?"

"You are taking *her* side?" Ben asked in disbelief.

"I do not see sides in this situation. Merely perspectives."

God save him from Chen's philosophizing.

"From my *perspective* then, Livy betrayed my trust," Ben said savagely. "I told her from the start that I would not tolerate a relationship built on lies. Indeed, that was why I hesitated to start things with her; in my gut, I *knew* she was not a biddable sort, yet I let her convince me otherwise. Which makes me the biggest fool alive."

"Perhaps. Or perhaps your gut knows something that your brain does not," Chen said.

"Hell's teeth, stop talking in riddles."

"Love *is* a riddle, but I shall do my best to lay it out clearly. I believe that you fell in love with Lady Olivia not in spite of who she is but *because* of it. You have known her from the time she was twelve years old; I have known her for less than a fortnight. If I am not surprised that she is a spirited and independent female, how can you be?"

Flummoxed, Ben thought it over. "I suppose...well, I am not surprised, exactly. Even so, she should not have lied to me."

"Why do you think she did?"

Ben's first instinct was to say that Livy wanted to twist him around her little finger and manipulate him...but the explanation struck him as false. He'd known her too long and that had never been her character. He forced himself to dig deeper, past his anger and the bitterness of betrayal. Why would Livy lie to him?

He realized with a flash that she, herself, had given him the answer.

*I didn't want to lie to you, but I was scared to tell the truth.*

Why would *Livy* be scared? She was bold and fearless, the most determined female he'd ever met. Understanding prickled through him like sensation returning to a limb that had fallen asleep.

"Because she loves me," he said hoarsely. "And I made her obedience a requirement of being with me. I made her think that she...she could not be herself."

Remorse throbbed in his chest. How could he have been so unfair? If he truly thought about it, he adored her spirit and independent ways. Yet he'd been afraid too, he recognized. Of repeating his past. Of losing someone he loved, the way he'd lost his sister, his parents...and even his wife.

But his relationship with Livy was different from those others. He knew in his bones that Livy's loyalty to him was steadfast. While she had lied to him, she had done so for entirely different reasons than Arabella had. His wife had twisted the truth to manipulate him.

Livy had done so because she'd wanted to be herself *and* to be with him.

And he wanted that too. More than anything.

"I have been a fool," he said, stunned.

"Love makes fools of us all. I would not be too hard on yourself, my friend. While Lady Olivia's youth and inexperience may have led her to make some wrong choices, your experience and history also blinded you to certain truths."

"Livy is nothing like Arabella. She is loving and loyal..." He trailed off as a sudden premonition slammed into him. He surged to his feet. "*Holy hell,* I have to find her."

"Why the urgency?" Chen asked, frowning.

Panic propelled him toward the door. "Knowing Livy, she may have walked away from me, but she won't stop trying to find my attacker!"

Accompanied by Chen, Ben arrived at Lady Fayne's less than an hour later. He rang the bell, and an eternity seemed to pass before the door opened, revealing the butler.

The mountain of a man glared at Ben, his unpatched eye glinting with hostility. "What do you want?"

"I'm here to see Lady Olivia," Ben said.

"She is not at home."

Fear clawed at Ben. "Where is she?"

"She nearly drowned saving your useless 'ide. Bravest and stupidest thing I ever saw," the butler growled, his fists planted on his hips. "And 'ow do you thank the lass? You made 'er *cry*. This is me being polite, Your Grace, when I say *sod off*."

Ben's chest clenched, as did his fists. "I'll see for myself if she's here. Stand aside."

"No bleeding way—"

"Hawker, let him in."

At the sound of Livy's voice, relief crashed over Ben. The butler grudgingly moved aside, and Ben strode into the antechamber...stopping at the sight of Livy. Standing a few feet away, she wore a simple blue frock, her hair in its usual braided loops. Her eyes were a bit puffy, her arms crossed beneath her bosom, and she was the most beautiful sight he'd ever seen.

"You are all right," he said hoarsely.

Her expression was guarded. "Why wouldn't I be?"

"I feared that you might..." He scrambled to find the right words. "Do something impetuous."

She tilted her head. "Like what?"

"I thought you might go after the villain...put yourself in danger."

"As *if* I would do something stupid like run pell-mell into danger." She sounded exasperated and so much like his little queen that he wanted to fall at her feet and beg her forgiveness. "I am a trained professional, not some ninny. When I go after the bastard, I will do it properly. With a plan and a team behind me."

*God*, he adored her.

He took a step closer. "Before you prove how alarmingly resourceful you are, may I ask a favor?"

She shook her head. "I am not giving up this case—"

"That's not what I want." He took another step, drawing in a breath. "What I want is to tell you how sorry I am. To beg your forgiveness...and ask for another chance."

# THIRTY-SEVEN

L ivy wondered if she was dreaming.

After crying all the way home in the carriage, she'd fallen into an exhausted sleep. When she'd awakened mid-afternoon, she'd felt hollowed out, as if a piece of herself had gone missing. Glory and Fiona had arrived, trying to cheer her up. Their presence and the work they had to do managed to distract her a bit. They'd just started laying out the plan for catching Ben's would-be killer...and now Ben was here.

Hope warred with fear. As much as Livy loved Ben, he'd dealt her a blow. His rejection had shattered her naïve optimism; she saw now that there wasn't an easy solution to their problems. What if love wasn't enough to bridge their differences?

"You asked for three favors, not one," she said tentatively.

"I am asking for a lot, I know." The fierce longing in Ben's eyes made her breath catch. "I vow I will make it worth your while if you let me."

He was within reach now, and yet the distance between them seemed so vast.

"How?" She laced her fingers together, afraid that she might reach for him otherwise. "I realize now that I pretended to be someone I am not. And while that was unfair to you, it was to me as well. It was wrong of me to lie, and I won't do it again. But I don't see how we can be together when I am not the woman you want."

"You *are* what I want," he declared. "You and only you, Livy. When you told me about your society, I reacted badly. It's no excuse but being drugged and finding out about Arabella's infidelity...I wasn't in the right frame of mind. I took it out on you, and for that I am sorrier than I can say."

His explanation made sense. Livy didn't know why she hadn't considered his state of mind at the time. Probably because she'd been so wrapped up in her own hurt.

"You had every right to be angry." Her throat cinched. "I lied to you...like Arabella did."

"You are nothing like her. The situations are different. Night and day," he insisted. "Arabella had affairs after we had agreed to recommit ourselves to our marriage. And she told me the babe she was carrying was mine when it wasn't. You, on the other hand, just wanted to be who you are. Hell, you tried to show me in so many ways, but I refused to see it. I insisted on smothering you with my asinine expectations because...because I was afraid, you see."

"Afraid of what?" she whispered.

"Of losing you. It sounds stupid, I know." He rubbed the back of his neck, his brows drawn. "I realize now that everyone I've cared about has...left. Sometimes because I've deserved it, other times because of circumstances beyond my control. But you, Livy, you've been my constant for the last seven years. You were always there for me, and I loved you even before I fell in love with you. The idea of not having you in my life..."

His throat bobbed above his cravat. "I could take anything but that. And I reacted by holding onto you too tightly. In trying to protect you, I ended up pushing you away. I lost the one person who I love more than anything."

Hearing the anguish in his voice, she couldn't stand it any

longer. She closed the last bit of distance between them, and he closed his arms fiercely around her. His heart thundered against her cheek, and being held by him, inhaling his familiar scent, she felt the world right itself again.

"You haven't lost me," she said. "I am right here."

"Promise me you always will be." He drew back, cupping her face with a reverence that made her eyes sting. "Although I cannot promise to be less protective, I *will* listen to you and support your desires. When we disagree, I will do my best to compromise."

Hesitantly, she asked, "What about my investigative work?"

"I will learn to live with it." His words were a solemn vow. "As long as you're mine, I can deal with anything."

"I'm yours," she said instantly. "Oh, Ben, I've missed you so much!"

His eyes flared with passion...and a hint of laughter. "Although I can't deny that I missed you like the devil, sweeting, the truth is we were only apart for a few hours."

"It felt like ages, didn't it? Let us never fight again," she said with feeling.

"The thing about fighting," he murmured, tipping up her chin, "is that there's the making up that follows..."

Then he was kissing her with a hungry passion that made her heart sing. She kissed him back just as eagerly, losing herself in the spell of their love.

"Ahem."

The sound of Charlie's voice jolted Livy. Blushing, she tried to disentangle herself from Ben, but he kept her firmly tucked against his side. Together, they faced Charlie. Mr. Chen was standing there too, his austerity compromised by the smile he was obviously trying to hide.

"Lady Fayne. Chen." Ben spoke with ducal poise. "You may be the first to offer your felicitations. Lady Olivia and I are to be married."

Charlie looked at Livy. "My dear, you are certain that this is what you want?"

"Yes," Livy said happily. "Hadleigh says he will support my work as an Angel!"

Charlie arched her brows at Ben.

"Whatever my future duchess wishes," he said simply. "If it is within my power to make her happy, then consider it done."

*Hooray!* Livy's eyes rounded as she considered the possibilities.

Catching her look, Ben shook his head ruefully...then winked.

Sighing, Charlie said, "Then you might as well begin as you mean to go on. Come to the drawing room; we still have a villain to catch."

The group gathered around a coffee table. Ben and Livy shared a settee, the Willflowers to Livy's right, Charlie across, and Chen to Ben's left. As refreshments were passed around, Ben gave an accounting of what he could remember of the night before. Unfortunately, his memories were hazy.

"I wish I knew which of the bastards drugged me," he said in frustration. "But the drug distorted my senses, and he was wearing a mask. I recall him dangling Arabella's vinaigrette in front of me, telling me that she had died from taking the contents within. He implied that he was exacting revenge on me for her death...and that of his babe, which she was apparently carrying."

Livy laced her fingers with his. He squeezed her hand, delicate yet strong. While he would always bear regret for his past mistakes, he realized that those memories could no longer hurt him. Because he had Livy by his side, sharing her light with him, the brightness of their love chasing all shadows away.

"Those facts align with the letter we found in the villain's hideaway in Limehouse." With obvious care, Livy asked, "Of the

Horsemen, have you any idea whom the duchess might have, um, had a preference for?"

Ben shook his head. "She was friendly with all of them. Her lover could have been Edgecombe, Thorne, or Bollinger."

"At least that rules out Stamford," Livy said.

There was a discreet knock; it was the butler.

"Yes, Hawker?" Lady Fayne said.

"I've received word from Mrs. Peabody," Hawker said. "She was monitoring the three suspects at a club, but they caught wind of her. Gave her the slip."

Lady Fayne frowned. "That is unfortunate. Those scoundrels are undoubtedly up to no good."

A sudden memory surfaced in Ben's brain.

"Bollinger said he had a shipment to pick up tonight," he said tersely. "That he meant to take me with him to do the job."

"Did he say where?" Livy asked.

"Edgecombe implied that there was a regular route, and I was supposedly going to take over Longmere's delivery. *Devil take it.*" Ben drove his fist into his palm. "If only I had had the presence of mind to question the bastards further. We might have been able to intercept a delivery this very eve—and perhaps catch the black-guard behind all of this."

"Let's not give up hope," Livy said. "As Mama likes to say, there is more than one way to cook an egg. We are dealing with a puzzle, and my intuition tells me we have most of the pieces."

Her face was set in determined lines that, in spite of the situation, Ben found adorable. She had always been clever, and he saw now how well her abilities suited investigative work. His bride-to-be had always marched to the beat of her own drum...and he was proud of her independent spirit. Proud of *her*.

"We have yet to thoroughly examine the clues we found in the villain's hideout," she went on. "If we put our heads together, perhaps we will come up with answers."

"How did you manage to find the hideout?" Ben wanted to know.

"Longmere's painting," Fiona answered, waving to a small landscape on an easel behind her. "One of his models had it in her possession. Our hypothesis is that Longmere somehow tracked the villain, or the villain's henchmen, to the lair. He wanted out of the enterprise but lacked the courage to take the final step. Then one night, he did confront the so-called Fong...and paid for it with his life."

Ben crossed over to look at the painting, Chen doing the same.

Livy followed behind them, pointing out the building at the painting's center. "While we found some clues there—including the Duchess of Hadleigh's letter and an odd poem—we did not find the supply of Devil's Bliss."

Ben stared at the painting. Cherise's voice floated from the recesses of his mind.

*He said that the Devil had floated in on a Siren's song, luring him to an inescapable death, but I could still break free...*

The answer struck Ben.

"Could the drug be kept on a boat? According to Lady Foxton, Longmere said that the Devil had floated in on a Siren's song..." Ben tapped his finger against the boat next to the building, which had a figurehead of a mermaid. "And that, I believe, is a Siren."

"That would explain why we didn't find evidence of the drug in the house." Livy's eyes lit with excitement. "When we were there last night, the dock was empty."

"The question, then, is how do we find the boat?" Lady Fayne mused. "That sort of figurehead is exceedingly common."

"We could keep following the Horsemen," Glory suggested. "The villain will eventually slip up."

"We could also confront Stamford," Fiona said. "He is the weakest link in the chain. If we were to tell him that Longmere was killed—and Hadleigh nearly so—by a member of his own group masquerading as Fong, he might tell us everything he knows. Two men out of five targeted for murder: even Stamford will recognize that those are not good odds."

"Do you think Stamford knows who the real villain is?" Chen queried.

"Probably not," Lady Fayne said thoughtfully. "The scoundrel has hidden his tracks well. If Stamford tells us his delivery point, however, we could stage an ambush."

From Chen's expression, Ben could tell his friend was impressed with the Society of Angels. As was he. These ladies were uncommonly shrewd.

Suddenly, Ben remembered something else from last night.

"This might be unimportant," he said slowly. "But Thorne did mention that the Horsemen had solved some kind of riddle to figure out where to pick up the Devil's Bliss."

"Five men." Livy blinked. "Five delivery points. And five *lines.*"

She rushed back to the coffee table, snatching up a piece of paper. Standing behind her, Ben read over her shoulder. It appeared to be a nonsensical verse:

> A favorite of pirating swaps,
> And mannered grocers,
> I am the cause of a nightdress furor.
> To find me, head on yonder towards snails
> And swim with the fish beating gills.

"Where did you get this?" Ben asked.

"The villain's desk. Hold it, will you?" Livy shoved the paper at him. "I'll be right back!"

Watching her dash from the room, Ben felt his lips quirk. Some things never changed. Inside his beloved's alluringly adult body still beat the heart of his bold little queen...and he hoped that she never lost that exuberance of spirit. Hoped that she would pass it onto any children they might be blessed to have together.

The notion of siring offspring had once filled him with ambivalence. He hadn't known if he had anything worth passing on...had begun to think it would be better for the title to be passed down his sister's line. The idea of having babes with Livy, however, led to heady elation. Their children would be as bright and beautiful as their mama, and what fun he and Livy would have raising —and making—them.

Livy was back in moments, breathless and clutching a small velvet bag. She plopped into one of the chairs and emptied the satchel onto the coffee table; her anagram tiles spilled out. She lined up the letters, spelling out MANNERED GROCERS.

Having been crushed by Livy during their games, Ben was used to the nimble speed of her fingers as she rearranged the letters. The result made his breath catch nonetheless:

CREMORNE GARDENS.

"That one I saw straight away since I knew Cremorne Gardens was one of the delivery points." She was already working on the next words, PIRATING SWAPS. "I believe each line contains a location."

She triumphantly revealed the next site: WAPPING OLD STAIRS.

Torn between amusement at her smug expression and pride at her intellect, Ben chucked her under the chin. "Should I offer to help...or will I be in the way?"

Her grin was impish. "Your *moral* support is appreciated."

Within minutes, she had unscrambled the anagrams into five locations: Wapping Old Stairs, Cremorne Gardens, Hungerford Stairs, Old Swan Stairs, and Billingsgate.

"The delivery tonight is likely to be at one of these places. But which one?" Livy mused.

"We could split up, monitor all of them." Lady Fayne looked at

Chen. "If Mr. Chen could offer assistance, we may have enough numbers."

Chen inclined his head. "It would be my pleasure, my lady. My team and I could take two of the locations."

"Why don't you monitor Wapping Old Stairs and Cremorne Gardens?" Lady Fayne said. "The Angels and Hadleigh can take Hungerford, Hawker and Mrs. Peabody the Old Swan, and I will call in some of my associates to help me patrol Billingsgate. How does that sound to everyone?"

Ben leaned over to whisper in Livy's ear. "Be honest, love. How do your fighting abilities compare to your riddle-solving skills?"

She gave him a demure look. "They're better."

He'd figured.

Grinning, he said to the group, "I say that sounds like a plan."

# THIRTY-EIGHT

Dusk was falling as Livy and her group arrived at the Hungerford Stairs. The steps led from a wharf on the Thames up to a large market that spanned three sections all the way to the Strand. The market was constructed in an elegant Italianate design; from the colonnaded galleries, one could purchase all manner of foodstuffs, from fish to produce to freshly butchered meats.

At this hour, the market and wharf were at a lull, the quiet period between the closing of the shops and the arrival of the next day's goods. As Livy patrolled the shore with Ben, the two of them dressed as a working-class couple, she observed nothing out of the ordinary. The wharf was dotted with empty crates and barrels, and boats were departing for the day. A pair of mudlarks scavenged along the water in search of overlooked treasures. At a sagging blacking factory to the right of the pier, weary-faced workers were filing out, their empty lunch pails clanking.

Waves lapped against the shore. Seabirds cried, mourning the setting sun.

To Livy, it felt like the quiet before the storm.

"No sign of Bollinger or our villain," she said under her breath.

"Patience, little one." Ben lit a lamp, his gaze on the short pier that reached out into the Thames. "It has only turned dark. If this is the place for the exchange, we will see them soon. There is no way we will miss them...not with the Angels on the watch."

She glanced at the top of the stairs where Glory and Fi, posed as flower girls at a lamplit barrow, stood at the ready. Glory gave a discreet thumbs-up, the signal that all was clear.

Livy tilted her head at Ben. "You seem to be taking this remarkably well."

"Taking what?"

"The fact that I'm involved in danger and intrigue."

"As the proverb goes, better to bend than break." His eyes turned serious. "At any rate, I've realized that your obedience was never what I truly wanted. What I desire is your love, the kind that never fails or falters. Everything else is immaterial."

"You have my heart," she vowed. "Forever and longer."

His gaze smoldered. "I look forward to a lifetime of adventures with you, little queen. Especially in bed." His wickedness heated her cheeks. "That is the one place where I think you do not mind being biddable, hmm?"

She looked at him from beneath her lashes. "I do not mind at all...sir."

"Christ, you little minx." His voice was edged with laughter and arousal. "Do not tempt me when we have a mission to accomplish."

A fog came in, swirling over the dark water as they continued their surveillance. Their diligence was rewarded an hour later when a carriage pulled up near the top of the stairs, close to Glory and Fi's barrow. A cloaked figure emerged, accompanied by a manservant bearing a lamp.

"Bollinger," Livy whispered.

Dousing his lamp, Ben pulled her behind a stack of crates at the edge of the wharf. "Let's keep out of sight until we see what he's up to."

Bollinger and his servant descended the steps at a rapid clip. They went to the end of the pier, scanning the water. Through the heavy veil of mist, Livy glimpsed the viscount pacing. A few minutes later, a gleaming mermaid cut through the fog. The figurehead was followed by the rest of the boat, a sleek vessel that came to a stop in front of Bollinger. Two men vaulted from the deck and moored the boat. They tipped their caps at Bollinger as he boarded, his footman behind him. The pair disappeared into the boat's cabin.

Twisting her head, Livy saw Fiona and Glory heading down the steps. They'd detached their skirts, moving with unhindered stealth in the trousers they'd worn beneath. Unhooking her own skirts and silently thanking Mrs. Q for her innovative designs, Livy was ready to join her friends.

"Time to go in," she said.

Ben leaned in and kissed her hard. "Let us finish this once and for all."

They met with the other Angels, the fog giving them cover. Glory and Fiona went in first, taking the brutes on the dock by surprise. One of the men got off a shout of warning before Glory downed him with a swift kick to the gut. Footsteps and voices rumbled from the ship, two more brutes emerging.

Livy took on one of them, Ben the other. She dodged a punch, going in low and landing one of her own in her foe's midsection. He straightened and flashed a rotted smile.

"That all you got?" he taunted. "You 'it like a girl."

Glory sailed through the air, her foot planting in his chest, sending him sprawling.

"We certainly do," Glory spat, then turned to Livy. "Fi and I will manage things here. You and Hadleigh go capture the villain."

Livy saw that Ben had felled his opponent, and the two of them vaulted onto the boat. They saw Bollinger on the deck: he was gripping a large valise, as was his manservant behind him. They were blocking the way to the cabin.

"H-Hadleigh?" Bollinger's features froze with shock. "What are you doing here?"

"Putting an end to the Devil's Bliss," Ben said flatly. "The drug has led to the death of multiple men, and you could be next if you don't leave those bags and get off the boat."

Bollinger's throat bobbed. "Surely you don't mean to cross Master Fong," he said hoarsely. "I just saw him, and he'll kill us all—"

"Get out of our way," Livy snapped. "Or we will make you."

To show him she meant business, she took out her pistol.

Bollinger paled, gesturing at his footman. "Leave the bags. We're getting out of here."

As the two scurried off, Livy followed Ben to the cabin. The ship was eerily quiet, her heart thundering as they took the creaky steps down to the main berth. Reaching the door, Ben cocked his pistol, and she did the same. He pushed open the door, his firearm held at the ready...

No one was inside. The room had a bunk in one corner, cupboards along two walls, and a large table at its center. A pyramid of red snuffboxes sat on the table's surface. Going over to the cupboards, Ben opened them, revealing an apothecary shop's worth of powders and liquids upon the shelves.

"The makings of the Devil's Bliss," Livy breathed. "But where is our villain?"

She gazed over at the bed, at the black wig and costume laid atop it.

*I just saw him, and he'll kill us all...*

She and Ben looked at each other.

*"Bollinger,"* they said.

They raced back up to the deck in time to see Bollinger and his man running down the pier.

"Angels!" Livy shouted. "Stop Bollinger! He's Fong!"

She heard the affirmatives of her partners as she and Ben sprang onto the wharf. Fiona took aim and fired. Her shot whizzed past Bollinger's shoulder, forcing him to swerve away from the steps. As Fi reloaded, Glory got off a shot, keeping Bollinger away from the steps. With his servant at his heels, he headed toward the nearest building...the blacking factory. He shot at the door, kicked it open, and the pair disappeared inside.

Moments later, the Angels and Ben arrived at the factory entrance.

"Glory and Fi, secure the perimeter," Livy said. "Don't let them escape."

"Right-o." Glory reloaded her pistol and put out her free hand.

Fi put her hand on top, Livy following suit.

*"Sisters first will see us through!"*

Livy parted from her friends and followed Ben into the building. Wall sconces cast a dim glow over the large square room, the air pungent with the smell of boot polish. The building was four stories high, a rickety stairwell winding upward at the center of the room. Floorboards squealed overhead, dust sprinkling from the ceiling. As Livy stepped cautiously forward, something scurried over her foot.

*Rats. Ew.*

"Stay behind me," Ben said in a low voice. "I hear them on the floor above."

She and Ben crept to the stairwell. He held his pistol out as he mounted the steps, and she did the same. She caught a movement on the next floor. "Watch out!"

At her warning, Ben dove forward. The bullet hit the banister where he had been seconds earlier, sending splinters of wood flying.

"Thanks," he muttered.

He sprinted up the steps, with her at his heels. They chased Bollinger and his brute all the way up to the top floor. At the landing, the servant flew at Ben, tackling Ben to the ground. Livy spotted Bollinger a few feet away, his pistol aimed at the fighting men. She shot first, Bollinger letting out a cry as her bullet drove the pistol from his hand. His weapon skidded through the wide gap between the railing's spindles and plunged over the edge, the loud thump echoing from four stories below.

Livy sprinted over to face Bollinger. "Give up. We have you surrounded."

"I don't think so." He drew out a knife, his boyish features as menacing as the glinting edge. "I have no problem getting through you...by any means necessary."

He attacked, his blade coming at her in a lethal arc. She dodged and spun, slamming her elbow into his ribs. He howled with pain but came at her again. This time she went low, kicking out and knocking him off his feet. He landed on his back, his blade skittering from his grasp.

She kicked the weapon aside and came toward him, fists raised.

Moaning, he said, "Bloody hell, I give up..."

"You should have done so in the first place," she said.

She glanced over at Ben, making sure he didn't need her help, and that was her mistake. Bollinger leapt up with startling speed, plowing into her with vicious force. She hurtled backward through the air. Her spine hit the railing, and a loud crack filled her ears. Suddenly, she was falling into space. She reached out wildly, her fingers somehow grabbing onto the edge of the floor. She held on desperately, dangling four stories above the ground, unable to pull herself up.

She was afraid to move, to even cry for help.

"Hold on, Livy. I'm coming!"

Ben's voice reached her like a lifeline. Reminded her of everything that she had to fight for. She concentrated on following his command, battling gravity's powerful pull with everything she had left. She heard shouts and thumps and didn't know if seconds or hours passed as she clung on. As her fingers began to slip, Ben was there. He grabbed her wrists and hauled her to safety, dragging her away from the edge.

"You're safe." His arms closed around her like a vise. "I've got you."

She clung to him, drawing deep breaths until her tremors subsided.

When she was sufficiently recovered, she peered around his shoulder. The servant lay unconscious on the ground. And Bollinger...he was lying on his back as well. His eyes were open, his blade protruding from his chest.

"He grabbed his knife and tried to kill me. We fought. I won," Ben said flatly.

"Are you all right?" she whispered.

He stared at her. "You were dangling four stories above the ground, and you're asking *me* if I am all right?"

She gave him a shaky smile. "Thank you for saving me. Again."

"I had no choice." He tucked a loose tendril behind her ear. "Since you told me there was no longer a debt between us, I had to find a new way to bind you to me."

"Wouldn't marriage vows suffice just as well?" she said with a muffled laugh.

"With you, they will." The teasing light left his eyes, replaced by heart-fluttering intensity. "I love you, Livy, and I'm ready to start our happily ever after."

"I want that more than anything," she whispered.

As their lips met in a tender kiss that heralded new beginnings, the voices of Angels—Fiona and Glory, that was—floated through the building.

# Thirty-Nine

Three days later, Ben was getting ready to call upon Livy and the Strathavens, who'd returned from Scotland, when Beatrice arrived unexpectedly. He received his sister in the drawing room. Dressed in a gown that matched her eyes, she was as beautiful and remote as always. As they drank tea in painful silence, he racked his brain for some way to break the tension.

He had been planning to call upon her. He'd put it off because he hadn't known what he would say. He'd feared that the visit would play out the way it always did...the way it was doing so now.

He said awkwardly, "How are Murray and the children?"

"They are fine." She took a breath. "But I didn't come for chitchat. The truth is...I am here to apologize."

Ben assumed that she'd been reading the papers. Since Bollinger's death, the police had started conducting an investigation based on the testimony and evidence that Ben had provided. They'd brought Stamford in for questioning, and he had sung like a bird. His account corroborated the theory of events Ben and the Angels had cobbled together.

Masquerading as Fong, Bollinger had contacted Longmere, the

most impressionable of the group. Longmere had recruited the others, who were all desperate for money...and for the thrill of the forbidden. Bollinger had read his cronies like a book, using the guise of a "mystical Chinaman" and clandestine games to further entice the Horsemen into doing his bidding. Stamford recalled the group's excitement over the arrival of the riddle with the delivery places; Bollinger had been the one to solve it when the others failed to do so.

After learning that two of his clients—Baron Winford and John Hagan—had died because of the drug, Longmere had begun to panic. He'd told the group he wanted out and was found dead shortly after.

Before his death, Longmere had shared his suspicions with Stamford: he thought all was not what it seemed with the mysterious Fong. The drug supplier knew too much about the group...as if he were an insider. After Longmere's demise and the death of one of his own clients, Stamford got cold feet and tried to distance himself from the group. He claimed that he had no idea that the Devil's Bliss was lethal and that he would have never gotten involved if he'd known.

The papers speculated that Stamford, Thorne, and Edgecombe might be tried for conspiracy to commit murder. Whatever happened legally, the men were socially ruined. The papers also reported on Ben's role in the case; apparently, a source within the Metropolitan Police had labelled his efforts as heroic. Ben avoided the limelight as much as possible, especially since he couldn't share it with the truly deserving heroines. Lady Fayne had asked him to keep her group out of it; to protect the reputation of Livy and the other Angels, he'd agreed.

To his sister, Ben said, "I understand why you thought what you did. Given my past, your assumption was not unfair."

"It *was* unfair of me to judge you by your past actions," Beatrice insisted. "I should have forgiven you long ago, Hadleigh."

"What I did was unforgivable," he said quietly.

He had come to accept his past. He'd also realized that, while he would always regret his mistakes, he did not have to carry their burden into his future. He had atoned as much as he could. He could make the choice to not let his history define his future.

"What happened was a tragedy not only for me, but for our family. Everything fell apart for us Wodehouses—including you—and I was too wrapped up in my own pain to see that." Shaking her head, Bea said, "You were a young man, Hadleigh, and although your quest for vengeance was wrong, I think I understand some of your motivation. You felt you had failed me; by seeking revenge on Griggs, you thought you were protecting my honor."

Ben swallowed. "What I did was still beyond the pale."

"I don't disagree. But the fact that you acted out of love makes a difference. And I know this because I have recently wronged you, for much the same reason." Bea looked at him with troubled eyes. "I spoke with Livy yesterday."

"You did?" he said warily.

He and Livy hadn't yet made their relationship public. In fact, that was his purpose in calling upon Strathaven today: he intended to ask for Livy's hand. He hoped that his friend would approve the match...and not demand to meet him at dawn.

"You needn't look so surprised," his sister said with a hint of wryness. "It is obvious that the two of you have, ahem, a special bond. I knew she would answer my questions in a way you would not. And she did. She revealed that during your mission to uncover this drug enterprise, you were drugged. That you'd nearly died." Bea gripped her hands together in her lap. "And I believe I am the cause of that."

Ben angled his head. "I don't follow."

"The last time we spoke, I did not express my concern in the best way." Bea bit her lip. "But I *was* worried about you...and so I did what I thought was right at the time. I went to Bollinger."

Ben stilled. "For what purpose?"

"Of your former cronies, he seemed like the most harmless one. I appealed to him to release you from the group. I told him that you had worked hard to give up your bad habits and that I was afraid of what a relapse might lead to." Her throat worked. "I told him that I...I didn't want to find you someday floating in the Thames."

*So that is where Bollinger got the idea to get rid of me in that fashion.*

Aloud, Ben said, "It is not your fault, Bea. Put it out of your head."

"I cannot." Her eyes glimmered. "In trying to protect you, I inadvertently compromised your brave undertaking and caused you great harm..."

He crossed over, sitting beside her on the settee. He took her hands in his.

"You were trying to help," he said. "I am fortunate indeed to have an older sister who cares enough to do so."

"I *do* care, Ben." She gave him a squeeze. "I always have, and I do not know why it took me this long to tell you."

"We Wodehouses are not the most expressive lot."

They smiled at each other, the healing power of forgiveness needing no other words.

After the moment passed, Bea said, "May I offer a word of advice?"

"I would welcome it," he said sincerely.

"Since Livy was a little girl, she has always seen the best in you. She still does." Bea gave him a sisterly look. "A woman like that does not come along often."

"I know." He was damned grateful for the gift he'd been given. "I have an appointment with Strathaven shortly. Although I wouldn't blame him for turning down my suit; Livy deserves a better man."

"Nonsense." To his surprise, Bea reached over and straightened his lapels. The way she had when they were children. Her expression open and warm, she said, "You are a good man, little brother. Now go win the hand of the woman you love."

"Livy, dearest, if you don't stop pacing, you'll wear a trench in the rug," Mama chided.

"What could be taking them so long?" Livy asked. "They've been in the study for half an hour."

"They are probably coming to terms."

"Or blows," Livy muttered.

Mama patted the cushion beside her. "Come sit by me, dear."

When Livy acquiesced, her mother looked her in the eyes.

"*Where there is love, there is a way*. That was one of your grandpapa's favorite sayings," Mama said softly. "Trust me, dear girl. Everything will be well."

A moment later, Papa strode into the drawing room. Ben was behind him, lingering in the doorway. Papa looked first at Livy, then at Mama.

"You were right, Emma." He sounded slightly stunned.

"Really, darling, one would think you would be used to it by now," Mama said.

Livy went up to her father. "Papa...do Hadleigh and I have your blessing?"

"Is this truly what you want, poppet?" Papa's face had never looked more serious. In a low voice, he said, "While Hadleigh is a fine chap, he is older than you—"

"I want to marry him," Livy said with absolute conviction.

Her father exhaled slowly. "While I may have doubts, the one thing I have never questioned is that you are a girl who knows her own mind. And you have clearly decided on Hadleigh. You have my blessing, Livy. For what it is worth."

"Oh, thank you, Papa! That means everything to me!"

She threw herself into her father's arms, and he held her tightly.

"Be happy, poppet," he murmured. "That is all I want for you."

"I will be," she promised. "As happy as you and Mama are."

Releasing her, he cleared his throat.

"I believe I'm ready for tea." He held his arm out to Mama. "Didn't you say something special was on the menu, pet?"

"I made your favorite Scotch pie. I had a feeling you would need it." Mama leaned up to kiss his jaw. "Well done, darling. You handled that magnificently."

"Because of you." Papa tucked her hand in the crook of his arm, saying in an undertone, "Thank God you prepared me. I might have had a fit of apoplexy otherwise."

"We'll be in the orangery," Mama said cheerfully to Hadleigh as they passed by. "You and Livy may join us when you are ready."

Her parents exited the room, their heads bent together.

Ben strode over to her, looking bemused.

"How did everything go?" Livy asked.

"It went better than I anticipated. Not only did your papa not call me out, but he also offered me some advice."

"And that was?"

"A happy wife makes for a happy life."

"That is exceedingly good counsel," Livy said brightly.

"In that case..."

Ben went down on one knee. His eyes the warm blue of a summer night, he took out a box and opened the lid. Livy's vision blurred at the sight of the ring: it was shaped like a delicate golden spider, its body a huge, faceted diamond.

It was a ring that only Ben would give her. A symbol of their love, which had changed over time, yet remained steadfast in its essence. A love between two souls meant to be together.

"My darling, determined Livy, who never gave up on me...will you be my wife?"

"Yes," she said through her clogged throat. "Yes, please."

He rose, slipping the ring onto her finger. It was a perfect fit.

"I love you." The words left them both simultaneously.

They laughed. Then they kissed, touched by the wonder of two solitudes joined as one.

# FORTY

Ben carried his bride over the threshold, kicking the door shut behind him.

"You're mine," he said with infinite satisfaction.

Livy smiled at him. "At long last."

He couldn't agree more. Although their six-week engagement was one of the shorter ones on record, it nevertheless felt like an eternity since he'd had Livy all to himself. The Strathavens had loosened the rules, allowing him a few private moments with his fiancée; this had resulted in several steamy interludes, including one at an arachnid exhibition. As sweet as those times had been, Ben had yearned for more than furtive snippets of time with his beloved.

Now he had his wish. Livy was his duchess. *His.*

Wonder expanded his chest...and his cock.

He set Livy down by his bed, marveling at her beauty. When she'd walked down the aisle of majestic St. Paul's toward him, his breath had stuttered. She'd been a queen in her frothy white gown embellished with lace, her hair a shining coronet studded with pearls. She'd kept her jewelry simple: the crown he'd given her nestled in the hollow of her throat, the delicate spider ring upon her finger. She gazed up at him now as she had then, with adoration in her verdant eyes, reinforcing that he was the luckiest bastard alive.

And also the randiest.

Throughout the wedding luncheon hosted by her parents, Livy had flirted with him, teasing him with sultry looks and naughty caresses under the table. Now the minx was going to pay for her tricks. He took her soft, pink mouth in a demanding kiss. She wound her arms around his neck, pressing herself against him. Her enthusiasm was all the lovelier for its underpinning of feminine need.

Knowing the cause, he hid a private smile.

He murmured against her lips, "Have you been a good girl for me?"

"Yes." Blushing, she added, "All week, like you instructed."

The pout in her voice made him harder.

"Patience makes passion sweeter." He drew a finger down the column of her neck, feeling her silken shiver in his balls. "And there's no need to rush. We have all night."

"I am not going to last all night," she protested.

At the reversed text, he had to laugh. His bride knitted her brows, looking adorably confused. With her confident ways, he sometimes forgot how innocent she still was. It would be his pleasure to corrupt and cherish her for the rest of their lives.

"That is not something *you* need to worry about, sweeting," he said. "Women don't have to last. As we've proven on numerous occasions, you can find pleasure again and again. Whereas men need a recovery period in between rounds."

She slid an ingenuous glance at the bulge in his trousers. "Even you?"

"Keep looking at me like that, and we shall soon find out."

"Promise, sir?" She fluttered her lashes at him.

His duchess was becoming an accomplished tease. Since she

only flirted with him, he didn't mind. The sizzling sexual under-tones made their banter even more fun.

"Turn around and hold onto the bedpost while I undress you, brat," he said.

He didn't miss the way she trembled at his strict command. She obediently wrapped her fingers around the dark post, reminding him of their other encounter in his bedchamber, one he'd spent many long nights fantasizing about. Now she was here, and he would never have to sleep without her again. The notion fired his heart and his loins.

He let her hair down first, relishing the luxuriant glide of her long locks between his fingers. Then he undressed her slowly, unwrapping her like the precious gift she was. He removed all her layers, except for her white silk stockings and dainty, blue ribbon garters. He liked the way they showed off his bride's shapely legs and drew the eye to her pretty arse.

He slapped one of the creamy curves, enjoying the firm bounce of her flesh and her breathy gasp.

She twisted her head to look at him. "What was that for?"

The twinkling mischief in her eyes told him she knew exactly why she was being spanked.

"For making me hard during our reception." He swatted her other cheek. "Did you think you could tease me, touch my cock in public without consequences?"

"No one saw," she argued. "After all, I did it under the table."

Her impudence earned her another smack. This time a needy moan escaped her. He spanked her again, knowing that the heat of her pinkening flesh was adding to her burn elsewhere. Goddamn, he could see the wetness smeared between her thighs; her pussy must be drenched.

His erection tested the limits of his trousers, but he was having too much fun to stop their little game.

"I had to stand to give the toast," he said sternly. "If it hadn't been for the breathing techniques I learned from Chen, I would have given our guests quite the show. Is that what you wanted? For the world to see how much your husband desires you?"

At the word "husband," Livy gave him a dreamy smile. "Would it be bad if I said yes?"

Christ, she was a handful. And she was all his.

"Honesty is never bad, sweeting. I think you know that."

He bent and kissed her nape. Her back arched as he planted kisses down the ladder of her spine, stopping at the crevice between her buttocks. He took her rosy cheeks in his hands, massaging them but not touching her where she wanted it most.

Clutching the post, she whimpered, "Please, Ben."

"You know you have to ask for what you want, love. And ask nicely."

"Please, sir...won't you touch my pussy?"

He rewarded her sweet request. She shivered when his fingertip circled her pleated rosebud before moving down to her slit. As he'd suspected, she was plump and juicy. A part of him wanted to make her wait: to extend her submission, which was doubly sweet since it happened only in the bedchamber and only for him.

Another part of him couldn't resist the need in his wife's pleading eyes. When Livy looked at him like that, he would take down the moon and stars for her, give her anything she asked. Seeing that all she wanted was for him to make her come, one of his favorite pastimes, he could not deny her.

And, as he'd said, she didn't suffer any limits in this arena. This would be the first of many releases for his duchess on their wedding night. It would be his husbandly pleasure to see to that.

"You may rub this wet little pussy against my hand," he instructed.

Sighing, she rocked against him eagerly. While he diddled her, he used his other hand to play with her nipples. She was sensitive here, and he knew the exact moment to give those pretty pink tips a hard pinch. She cried out, clenching her thighs around his hand, bathing him in a gush of honey that made his mouth water.

He picked her up, tossing her onto his bed. When his haste made her bounce upon the mattress, she giggled. Those giggles melted into moans as he spread her thighs and dove in for a taste. Holy hell, she was delicious.

"Oh, heavens." She wove her fingers into his hair, gasping, *"Ben."*

He was too busy eating her cunny to respond. He savored her with long, swirling licks. As he teased her pearl with his tongue, he slid his middle finger into her sheath. The snug clasp made him shudder. He hadn't put his prick inside her since the first time, and she felt even tighter than he remembered. He added another finger to the first, pumping into her while he feasted.

Whimpering, she came again, her rippling culmination testing his self-control. As she lay with her rounded breasts heaving, he stripped off his clothes. He grasped his bobbing erection, so aroused that even his own touch caused a drop of seed to leak from his tip.

Frigging his cock slowly, he bent a finger at his duchess.

"Come here," he commanded.

She came to the edge of the bed, and he adored the hunger in her eyes. She'd spent twice already, yet she was ready for more.

"I'm going to put my cock in you soon," he said. "Before I do, I want you to make it wet for me. With your mouth."

"With pleasure, sir," she said with a flirty grin.

If only she were this biddable in everyday life.

"On your stomach, then."

She obeyed, putting her mouth on level with his cock.

He brought the seeping crown to her lips. "Open for me."

She did, and he pushed inside. *Devil and damn.*

The moist heat of her mouth swept fire up his spine. During their engagement, they'd practiced this skill; Livy had become somewhat of an expert. Fisting the satiny streamers of her hair, he watched his thick shaft disappear between her lips, stretching that delicate entryway. Undeterred by his size, she took him into her deepest recesses, her throat muscles squeezing a groan from him. As he withdrew, she swirled her tongue along a knee-weakening groove. Chest heaving, he pulled out before he unmanned himself.

She peered up at him through her lashes. "Are you wet enough, sir?"

In answer, he rolled her onto her back and crawled atop her. Parting her sleek thighs, he notched himself to her opening and drove home. They both sighed at the moment of joining. For Ben, the incredible pleasure of being inside his wife was enhanced by something he'd only felt with her: a sense of rightness. From the moment he'd saved her life, she had saved his. And destiny had only strengthened their unique bond by forging it in the hottest fires of love.

"I love you, Livy," he said hoarsely. "Until my last breath and beyond."

"I love you, Ben," she whispered back. "Always and forever."

Gazing into his beloved's eyes, he began to move in a rhythm that was ageless yet full of discovery. With Livy, everything was new and special. Urged on by her panting cries, he plowed her faster, deeper, his control unraveling. His stones smacked her dewy folds as he hilted himself in her snug sheath, over and again, needing to own her as fully as she owned him.

When Livy went over the edge again, he went with her. Pressure shot up his shaft, pleasure exploding from him in endless bursts. Groaning, he emptied himself into his wife's generous keeping, and she took it all, giving him pure bliss in return.

He collapsed beside her, gathering her close. Lying skin to skin with Livy, their hearts beating in unison, he knew he'd found his absolution. She had given him peace...given him everything. And what did he have to give her in return?

He gazed into her eyes. "Livy, is there anything you would like?"

She smiled. "You already gave me a wedding present. The wedding trip to Italy, remember?"

He couldn't wait to travel with her. To have adventures with his duchess. Which meant the present was for him as much as for her.

"I would like to give you another gift," he insisted. "Something just for you."

"You've supported my work with the Angels. What is that, if not a gift?"

With Charlie's blessing, he had assisted the Angels on a few missions. He had enjoyed working with Livy and felt proud of her prowess.

"Supporting your calling isn't a gift," he said dismissively. "That is just common sense."

"You are the best of husbands." She beamed at him. "Come to think of it, there *is* something I would like."

"Name it, and it's yours."

"It's not a thing. More like a certain, um, variation I've been curious about..."

Blushing, she whispered her wish into his ear.

They each made further discoveries that eve. Livy learned that she did indeed like the position in question and moaned her approval into the pillow...twice. For his part, Ben found that when he was with his new duchess, recovery periods were, in fact, unnecessary.

A fortnight later, Livy and the other Angels accompanied Pippa to the opening night of the Royal Academy exhibition. Although she was in mourning, Pippa had been adamant that she wanted to see Longmere's entry in the show, and Livy wanted to support her friend. Ben had escorted the group and now stood at a distance, examining a landscape.

Livy knew he wasn't particularly interested in the art. He was giving her and her friends space to talk, and she adored his thoughtfulness. Adored everything about her new husband, in truth.

Pippa led the way over to the painting. "Here it is."

Longmere's piece had been hung at eye level, a place of honor on the crowded wall, yet it would have stood out even in an obscure position. Frankly, Livy was astonished by the painting: its quality surpassed that of his others by leaps and bounds. The glowing oils portrayed a woman, modeled after CeCe, staring out a window. The mix of sensuality and sadness in the lady's eyes captivated the viewer. One wondered what she was thinking as she looked into the beyond.

"How lovely," Fiona breathed.

Other visitors stopped to gaze at the painting, their murmurs appreciative.

"It is a fitting memorial to the earl," Glory said sincerely.

"Longmere would have been pleased," Pippa said in quiet tones. "All he wanted was recognition for his work. That is the irony of life, I suppose: now that he has his greatest desire, he cannot enjoy it."

Privately, Livy thought that Longmere had been a bigger fool than she realized if his wife had not been his greatest desire.

She touched Pippa's dark sleeve. "How are you faring, dear?"

"Some days are better than others." Pippa's blue eyes darkened with grief...and some other emotion that Livy couldn't quite name. "I will get through this."

"I know you will," Livy said. "Perhaps some distraction will help?"

"Charlie said the same thing," Pippa replied.

Livy lifted her brows. "You have been talking to Charlie?"

"Yes, and she proposed a rather intriguing diversion." The spark that lit Pippa's eyes banished some of the shadows. "I may just take her up on it."

# Epilogue

*A few months later*

As Livy surfaced from sleep, she drowsily reached for Ben. Instead of her husband, she found a folded note on his side of the bed; it was labelled "A Riddle for Livy." Yawning, she sat up and read it.

> For My Queen,
> Who last night sat so prettily upon my throne,
> I have written this my first, and likely last, poem.
> Come find me where our love first took root...
> It's cold out so wear your boots.

"That riddle is too easy," she murmured.

Then, smiling from ear to ear, she tossed aside the covers and rang for her maid.

Soon she was dashing through the snow toward the pond. The sun was bright, casting diamonds across the fluffy white landscape.

She knew she was on the right track when she spotted Ben's large footprints. She followed his trail to a Scots pine by the side of the pond.

Looking up, she saw something dangling from the lowest branch.

Mistletoe. Tied safely *away* from the water.

A smile curved her lips as strong arms circled her waist.

"I have you just where I want you, Your Grace," Ben murmured in her ear.

She turned around in his arms, gazing happily up at her handsome duke. Since their marriage, contentment had erased the weary lines from his face. He looked younger; free of shadows, his eyes were the sultry blue of a summer night.

"There is no other place I want to be," she said simply. "Happy Hogmanay, Ben."

Love and desire smoldered in his gaze. He claimed her lips in a kiss that curled her toes in her boots. When they parted, she was gasping, her breath crystalline puffs in the air.

"We should go back inside and celebrate properly," he said.

She gave him a demure look. "By properly, I take it you mean in an *improper* fashion?"

"Insatiable minx." His slow smile quickened her pulse. "When have I ever failed to debauch you thoroughly?"

The answer to that was *never*. Just last night, he'd made her ride his cock and spend so many times that she'd collapsed atop his hard chest, boneless with bliss. He'd finished his own ride by ramming into her from beneath, his hands squeezing her bottom, his hoarse words of devotion warming her inside and out.

She was living her dreams. And there were still more to come.

"Before we go inside," she said, "I wanted to give you your new year's present."

He traced her mouth with a gloved finger, his eyes heavy-lidded. "I believe you did that last night, love."

"I do *that* all the time—"

"Praise God."

"But this is something I've never done before." Feeling unaccountably nervous, she said in a rush, "I am increasing."

He stared at her. "You...*we* are having a babe?"

"Late next summer. Are you pleased?" she blurted.

"Christ, Livy." He cradled her face in his palms. He was shaking, and the sheen in his eyes brought joyful heat to her own. "You've given me everything I've ever wanted and still you find a way to give me more."

Her smile was a bit watery. "I believe in keeping my promises. And I made one to you here years ago, remember?"

"You pledged me your allegiance." His eyes filled with wonder. "I didn't realize that you would give me your love as well."

"You may have noticed that I am not one for half-measures."

He laughed, and she did too when he picked her up and whirled her in an exuberant circle.

Setting her gently on her feet, he said fervently, "Don't ever stop being you, Livy. My little queen, who rules me heart, body, and soul."

They kissed, celebrating the resilient bond of their past, the enduring love of their present, and the shining promise of all the days ahead.

# AUTHOR'S NOTE

There's an adage about writing what you know. The seeds of this story were planted by two loves of my childhood: an American TV show featuring female investigators and a Hong Kong Cantonese martial arts epic. Both showcased clever, badass women who could fight, solve mysteries, and battle injustice. Add in my love of historical romance, and my series concept was born.

In *Olivia and the Masked Duke*, I used the word "Orientalism" to refer to a ballroom decorated in a style felt to be representative of the nations and peoples of "the Orient," including Asia, the Middle East, and North Africa. The use of "Orientalism" in that sense has been around since 1769[1]. There is also a more modern meaning to the word, popularized by Edward Saïd's seminal book, *Orientalism* (1978)[2].

Saïd's conceptualization of "Orientalism" as a Western (European) social construct that systematically perpetuates stereotypes and myths about the East as "the Other" for multiple reasons —including cultural, financial, and political gain—was a theme that felt timely to explore. Of note, *Olivia and the Masked Duke* takes place between the two Opium Wars[3]. The first war started when China attempted to ban Britain from illegally importing opium into China in exchange for coveted Chinese goods, a practice that resulted in widespread social and economic harm for the Chinese. The second war resulted from Britain and France's imperialistic agendas to gain more economical, territorial, and legal control in the East.

During the Victorian era, Orientalist tropes and ideas were pervasive in literature and the arts[4]. Examples can be found in the works of many popular writers of the era, including Charles Dickens, Wilkie Collins, and the Brontë sisters. In doing background research for my hero, I read Thomas De Quincey's *Confessions of an English Opium-Eater* (1821), an autobiographical account of the author's addiction to laudanum. De Quincey's portrayal of the East as dangerous and threatening to the Western way of life is especially notable in his characterization of the "ferocious looking" Malay. In part, De Quincey's fear and fascination with his feverish imagining of "the Other" inspired my idea for the villain of this story.

# Notes

## Author's Note

1. Etymology Online.
2. Saïd, E., 1978. *Orientalism*. 1st ed. New York City: Pantheon Books.
3. Pletcher, Kenneth. "Opium Wars." Encyclopaedia Britannica. February 05, 2020. https://www.britannica.com/topic/Opium-Wars
4. Kennedy, Valerie. "Orientalism in the Victorian Era." Oxford Research Encyclopedia of Literature. August 22, 2017. Oxford University Press. <https://oxfordre.com/literature/view/10.1093/acrefore/9780190201098.001.0001/acrefore-9780190201098-e-226>

# Acknowledgments

First and foremost, thank you to my fans! You are the best readers in the world. Your support and cheerleading of my characters put a smile on my face and motivate me to hit the keyboard every day.

Thank you to my editor Ronnie Nelson for her tireless brilliance. And to my cover artist Erin Dameron-Hill for making my books beautiful. Thanks also to Period Images for their wonderful photo shoot.

To my writing besties: our video chats and texts have kept my muse busy and spirit lifted, and I can't wait until we can retreat in person again.

Last but not least, to my soul mate, whose solitude is the perfect match for mine. Love you forever.

# ABOUT THE AUTHOR

*USA Today* & International Bestselling Author Grace Callaway writes hot and heart-melting historical romance filled with mystery and adventure. Her debut novel was a Romance Writers of America® Golden Heart® Finalist and a #1 National Regency Bestseller, and her subsequent novels have topped national and international bestselling lists. She is the winner of the Daphne du Maurier Award for Excellence in Mystery and Suspense, the Maggie Award for Excellence in Historical Romance, the Golden Leaf, and the Passionate Plume Award. She holds a doctorate in clinical psychology from the University of Michigan and lives with her family in a valley close to the ocean. When she's not writing, she enjoys dancing, dining in hole-in-the-wall restaurants, and going on adapted adventures with her special son.

Keep up with Grace's latest news!

Newsletter: gracecallaway.com/newsletter

facebook.com/GraceCallawayBooks

bookbub.com/authors/grace-callaway

instagram.com/gracecallawaybooks

amazon.com/author/gracecallaway

Printed in Great Britain
by Amazon

27110571R00207